Summer on the Cold War Planet

A NOVEL

PAULA CLOSSON BUCK

Fomite
Burlington, VT

ISBN-13: 978-1-942515-11-1
Library of Congress Control Number: 2015939542

Fomite
58 Peru Street
Burlington, VT 05401
www.fomitepress.com

for Conrad and Jim

PART I

1

IT MIGHT HAVE BEEN aphids or low humidity that made the
buds drop before the lilies ever had a chance to flower. It might
have been a gas leak or contamination by paint. Maybe what
Lyddie thought were aphids were thrips. Or mites. Lyddie turned
off the misting apparatus and walked through the greenhouse, more
witness than caretaker. She stopped to examine the South African be-
gonias—their leaves burnt, stems rotted at the base. Too much water?
Not enough light? She wondered if she were capable of taking
care of anything. The wild herbal quarter looked as though it had
undergone an experiment on the effects of sequential disasters—
natural and human-inflicted. Some of the plants appeared to have
suffered overwatering; some to have been pruned without mercy, as
if by leaf-cutter ants. Others had grown leggy and acute freeloading
on sunlight. A few that had flourished under her benign neglect
threatened the others with encroachment.

Lyddie left the greenhouse and went in by the back door of
the house, up the back stairway and into the bedroom. Digging

deep into the closet, she pulled out a few hangers and their contents, none of which seemed right for the art opening she was
supposed to speak at in less than thirty minutes. The only thing
even halfway suitable was the black dress. The opening featured
the work of six young German artists, and young Germans
wore black—for everything. They would not be present, but she
would allude to their sense of style.

The dress still had its tags dangling from the underarm. She
had bought it as a way of making real to herself the likelihood
that Phelps wasn't coming back. She had not meant to wear it
until they'd found him and there could be a funeral. Nearly three
months she'd been waiting. She walked to the full-length mirror,
turned sideways and examined her profile: still mostly flat. In
the bathroom, she scrubbed at the dirt under her nails. It wasn't
for her lack of trying that so many of the plants had died. At
first, she'd spent countless hours reading and watering, trimming,
pleading with them. It seemed the least she could do for Phelps.
She didn't want to hire someone to do what he had left her to do,
though they had both thought he'd be gone just two weeks. Lately,
however, the plants' distress seemed an indication that Lyddie was
nearing the end of her ability to cope. She took the dress from its
hanger and slipped it over her head. She struggled with the zip-
per, wondering, when it was halfway up—at the very point Phelps
would have assisted—if she had given up hope.

Black heels in hand, Lyddie crossed the yard to the white Olds
98 parked on the gravel pad behind the house. She slid onto the
vinyl seat and eased the car into the alleyway. At dusk, against the
leafy outlines of the trees, starlings gathered. Streetlights flickered
on, tentative but insistent. Everything was poised for obscurity yet
utterly clear. Lyddie felt as though she were behind the wheel of
an ark. The fuel needle dipped below empty and when she pulled
up to the pumps at the mini-mart on Elmwood, hundreds of tiny

white moths descended from the bank of lights overhead onto the windshield of the car. They were everywhere, their white bodies crushed against the grills of other cars and flitting at the cashier's window like something that should last seven days or seven years. Were the moths a curse? (Seven more months of grief deferred?) Or was her life just a rest stop for them on some kind of migration? What Lyddie did know was that the passenger seat remained an obstinate blank, and she felt oddly relieved to have chosen the black dress. A couple of months longer and she wouldn't be able to wear it anyhow.

The months since Phelps had disappeared seemed an eternity. And the time she'd spent in Berlin—another lifetime. But that had been just four years. Four years before, Phelps had convinced her that Axel was something of a madman. Now, all over again, she had begun to doubt it. Even looking at Axel's paintings had been dangerous for her.

She pulled out of the gas station, a remnant of the moth plague smeared onto her windshield by the wipers so that she could barely see out. In the relatively happy years with Phelps, her desire for Axel had tightened into a sadness she carried like a stone in her pocket. But lately, in Phelps's absence, she'd found herself pulling it out and feeling its edges, some worn smooth with time, others still rough. Axel had told her once that he liked her "presence." She often had the feeling that she was not really present in her own life, which seemed somehow pointless now that Phelps was gone from it. It was hard for her to focus on anything in the moment. The exhibition, including paintings by both Axel and their friend Lothar, had been proposed long before Phelps's disappearance by a donor who knew of Lyddie's Berlin connections. Back then, Lyddie had felt confident enough in her relationship with Phelps to re-establish communication with Lothar and, through him, with Axel. She had hoped that the show would help her confirm the rules of their reacquaintance. They were artists worthy of recognition. She was a curatorial fellow. But the telephone conversations with Lothar and the hours she'd spent with slides and canvasses of his and Axel's work now felt like the event horizon of the black hole that was the past. Into which she was falling. She squirted fluid onto the window and managed to clear only a small arc through which she could see what lay directly in front of her.

When she arrived at the Albright-Knox, voices drifted out from the special exhibits gallery. She entered the gaunt light of the gallery space, which she herself had designed using a corolla of projectile fluorescent tubes like the ones she had seen in public buildings in East Berlin. Men and women milled around, sipping wine, communicating by a nod, a word spoken quietly, the raising of an eyebrow. Immediately, Lyddie's neck felt itchy and close inside the dress. She pulled at the neckline and a white moth flew out. And then the scene blurred and dilated, as if she were still behind the windshield of the car with its film of moth dust and guts, or further back, in a station of the U-Bahn surrounded by anxiety followed by cottonwood. And Axel was there, acting a little insane and unpredictable. Wanting the truth about something. But here was the donor who had made the show possible, and Ray, Phelps's brother, standing in front of one of Lothar's paintings. Lyddie avoided Ray's eyes because she was late and maybe rumpled. Ray wore a charcoal gray suit with a pink shirt, and the women who had come out for the affair had chosen springy greens and bold multi-colored prints. Lyddie looked not like a devotee of the German sensibility but like a self-styled widow. Someone was talking about repression and censorship and the art from the East that never materialized or found its audience. About Cold War politics and Reagan's negotiations with Gorbachev to reduce the nuclear arsenal. Ray mentioned the artists: Lothar Weber. Uta Krohn. Axel Herzog. Lyddie herself rose to the lectern and spoke of the negative spaces in the work of the East German defectors.

Moving across the gallery, she drew the attention of the audience to Axel's monochromatic painting of the gutted cathedral, where Trabis and Black Marias gleamed under a utility light like great black beetles. The Communists, she explained, weren't big on religion. They were the extreme of functionality, of utility. Beauty was something to be deleted as thoroughly as possible, though in this case, the high, vaulted ceiling could not help itself. It reminded one of a ribcage, did they see that? It was like an illustration of the artist's condition. There was a part of him, it seemed, made for lofty things, for longing and maneuvers of the spirit; but that space had to coexist with—was often appropriated by—the monkey wrenches and oil cans of daily life, particularly under Communism. She had loved that painting from the first time she had seen it. She leaned in to examine the small figure that stood in the weirdly degenerate landscape of the painting. Was it Axel? A self-portrait? Why had she not looked closely before? And what would he have been doing in the cathedral? Perhaps they had all misjudged him. *You remind me of a time when I might have believed in something.* He had said that to her once.

The crowd began to murmur and she realized she had not been speaking aloud. Lyddie felt an impulse surface the way a pathogen in the blood makes itself known suddenly as dryness in the throat, and you know you will be sick for weeks. Then there was a question from the curious woman with a gallery in Chelsea: What were Axel Herzog's attitudes toward the West?" She asked it innocently enough.

His collarbone in moonlight. His hands up her skirt. Where had the time gone? Was it the black dress that released so much of this in her?

Before Lyddie knew what was happening, Ray had her by the elbow and was shepherding her away from the reception and down the hall to the empty boardroom. "What is happening to you?" he said.

"It isn't graceful, whatever it is," Lyddie said.

"And why the dress? They don't kill botanists, Lyddie. Botanists are like journalists. They have diplomatic immunity."

"If he's alive, then where is he? He would be here. He would let us know. How long do you think your need can keep him alive?" Lyddie said, looking away.

"My need?" he said. "You may not think you need him, Lyddie, but what about the baby?"

There was, in fact, a baby to think of. And that made everything harder.

LYDDIE HAD THOUGHT PHELPS KNEW about making things survive. At night, he had read catalogues and planned, months in advance, what he would grow in the greenhouse. He had planted and watered, monitored temperature, humidity and light. Phelps had created a world of his work and he had assumed Lyddie into it—the part of it that centered on the little house they owned together. She had even agreed to have a child, though she had not felt ready. After she'd given in to him verbally, for two or three months she had hidden the little console of pills under the mattress and continued to take them.

And now, just four years into their marriage, he was gone. It was spring, 1989. In spite of advisories from the Department of State, Phelps had at last convinced pharmaceutical research at Dow Chemical to send him to Kurdistan. The Iraqis' genocidal Anfal campaign against the Kurds had officially ended. Phelps was in touch with Kurds who had taken refuge in the mountains, away from their villages and from the prohibited

areas. Kurdish culture, along with its unique heritage of medicinal herbs, Phelps said, was in jeopardy. There might not be
another time. He was investigating the potential in a family of
indigenous plants unique to the region, harvested from the wild
and used to treat prostate cancer. He hoped to determine a way
in which the plants might be cultivated and adapted to modern
pharmaceuticals. That's how he had explained it to Lyddie. He
left her with instructions for the greenhouse. He took with him
logbooks and maps and bilingual dictionaries. He expanded his
basic Kurdish vocabulary as a gesture of good will. He took his
Konika with zoom lenses and a tripod, took film, drawing pen-
cils, and a list of contacts he had worked months—years, really—at cultivating. It had never occurred to him that he would
need a bulletproof vest.

Because, in fact, the Iraqis had not given up on eliminating
the Kurds. Nor, apparently, were they checking IDs when they
obliterated villages with thousands of inhabitants in one of the
prohibited areas where Phelps was rumored to have been visiting a traditional healer and gathering specimens. Bodies had
been disposed of in mass graves yet to be excavated because the
violence continued and the authorities claimed to know nothing
of the whereabouts of the disappeared.

Did it only seem to Lyddie that the last time she had been
with Phelps their lovemaking had been fierce, as if something
were opening up between them, a distance you might leap as a
boat pulled away from the dock, if you were quick enough, if
your instincts were good? Phelps's usually were. But afterward,
he had looked at her as if she were already growing small in the
distance, and though he touched her, out of sadness or kind-
ness, by the time the sensation reached her, it was like a note still
hanging from the mouth of a pigeon that had been shot down.

And was that trouble about Axel too?

The only time Axel had ever called them in the States, Phelps had answered the phone. He had sat in the kitchen, his long legs reaching halfway across the floor. "Who is this?" he said. "What could you possibly want?" Phelps was silent awhile, drawing long scuff marks on the linoleum with the heel of his boot. "And how, exactly, do you know this when nobody else does?" he said. Lyddie stood by, expectant, waiting for an indication from Phelps of what Axel was saying, but he waved her off and she went into the living room and plopped into the armchair, waiting.

"Yeah, well thanks," Phelps said, and he hung up.

"Thanks for what?" Lyddie said, following him out the back door into the yard and down the walk toward the shed.

"What you detected there was sarcasm," Phelps said.

Inside the shed, he began tying bundles of gladiolas to hang for winter. The smell of dirt and hemp in the dark shed and the rustle of the dry stalks when he gathered them were elements of a confidence in the future she'd often admired in him. He knew she was there and he didn't turn around.

"What did he say?" Lyddie insisted. "Was it about the show?"

"Why do you care so much?" he said, the irritation that had been directed at Axel seeping too easily into their own conversation.

"I'm the curator of this exhibition, remember?" In a quiet, reasonable voice, she asked, "Did you ever find out anything more about him? From Sabina, I mean. After that time at the border."

Phelps set down the bundle of gladiolas and turned to gaze at her. "The way you talk about him, it's as if all of that were yesterday."

"You think I can't handle whatever it was?" she said.

In the room of things that had died but would come back, Phelps returned his attention to the bundle of stalks, which his hands worked deftly with the twine. "Has it turned out for the best with us, or hasn't it?"

"Of course it has," she said. "That's not the point."

Phelps put down the clippers and walked over to where she stood. "What is the point, exactly?"

Lyddie's face alone would usually tell Phelps more than he wanted to know. It was a region with its own weather—storms in the brow, turbulence around the mouth. Her eyes reflected her mood the way the surface of a body of water reflected light and barometric pressure. And the dents that appeared in her chin, he had told her, were always the first sign of trouble, like dimples on a lake when a breeze picked up. He ran his fingers over them and shook his head in dismay.

Lyddie said, "It's just that you and Sabina knew things you didn't think I should know. And now it's happening again. At least with you it is."

"Take my word for it, Lyddie," Phelps said. "None of it mattered at all. I just really don't like to talk about people."

"Except with Sabina. And it mattered only enough to change the course of my life."

Lyddie was surprised and immediately sorry she had said this. Phelps's face darkened. He looked as if, for the first time in their life together, he had acknowledged in her the potential to conceive of a life without him. "OK," Lyddie said, backing up into the doorway. "I admit I'm jealous of your relationship with Sabina. It's just that I would like to be on equal footing, with you and with her. I don't need to be protected."

THREE MONTHS LATER, THE HEART of the child Phelps wanted was ticking inside her. Her grief kept blossoming in new ways, like some subterranean catastrophe waiting to happen rather than the aftermath of one that already had happened. Sometimes she wasn't even sure of the object of her grief. Was it Phelps himself? The life she wouldn't now have with him? Or was it made up of all she would never know because she had entrusted her life to him. Now her grief grew inside her against her will, her own body, it seemed, having turned on her. She had told no one but Ray about the pregnancy. Lyddie had no real friends in Tonawanda. Somehow she'd spent the friend-making part of her life away and she had come to feel like a foreigner among the people she knew. Her parents were gone. The closest thing to a sister she had ever known was Sabina, her housemate in Berlin. And still, their friendship was made of equal parts admiration and mistrust. ·

Leaving the gallery, Lyddie drove out away from home on Elmwood, then took a left on Delavan and followed it all the way to Genessee. The lights were all green, as happened when one was going precisely the designated speed. She passed the pharmaceutical headquarters of Dow where Phelps had worked. She passed the airport and the derelict parking lot of the Westinghouse plant. The deafening crescendo of a jet taking off directly overhead tore through her thoughts as she made her way home, half expecting to find Phelps there, working late in the greenhouse that stretched all the way to the alley. Just beyond lay the river, where now, in July, the water had diminished to a few dull ribbons, exposing grocery carts and tires like great eels sleeping on the bottom. Where Lyddie had lived with Phelps, the river was shallow, everything exposed. Most everything.

IN HER LIVING ROOM THAT NIGHT, Lyddie sat on the couch and turned on the eleven o'clock news. Kurdish refugees in boats were washing up in Greece. They appeared huddled on shore in some white village, the men in flat turbans and great mustaches, the women in headscarves. They were the ones who had fled Hussein's attacks. The survivors. She turned the TV back off. She couldn't endure another night envying refugees. The nightmares hadn't stopped: Phelps at the brink of a mass grave, where the Ba'athists will shoot him, thereby avoiding having to carry his body. Or worse: they riddle him with machine-gun fire and he won't go down. He is trying to give her instructions. The news said that after they exterminated the inhabitants, the bulldozers leveled the villages, closing over the gash that the existence of the Kurds had made in the so-called "perfect garden" of the Arabs. The Arabs stitched together the before and after so seamlessly that the atrocity had no face. Lyddie sat for a few minutes in the dark and then, as an antidote to despair, went upstairs to the hall closet and took out the pile of architecture books from her Berlin days.

She climbed into bed and studied a big volume called *The Bauhaus* the way Phelps had used to study his botany books and catalogues. The Bauhaus principles of design were sensible. Form wedded to function. Lyddie paged through the photographs of the boxy, white *Haus am Horn*; the mushroom-globed table lamps, stable and practical; the tubular steel and canvas chairs of Marcel Breuer, inspired by the handlebars of Breuer's bicycle; and the stern-faced portraits of Gropius and Klee.

She remembered the old mantra of beauty and utility—the quotidian hum to which she had fallen asleep in the old days: Phelps walks up the sidewalk from the greenhouse. He stamps his feet on the stoop before opening the screen door. The sidewalk serves as a bridge between Phelps in the opaque humidity of the greenhouse and Phelps with her in the smoky kitchen where she has burnt the rice. There are screens she brings down from the attic to let the outside in, storm windows to keep it out. There is beauty in the way Phelps stamps his boots on the stoop three times before he opens the back door. There is utility, too, in the sound, the dull thump, thump, thump—the thumps always in threes—before he enters the house with the winter air on his coat, or in summer the smell of fresh dirt clinging to his shoes—one shoe always cleaner than the other.

Lyddie put the books on the floor and tried to sleep. But when she closed her eyes, she saw the faces of the refugees again. Angular and dark, they carried coded information from a world where death was the obvious and likely ending to every story. She thought of the children who had been gassed, then pictured the fetus floating in the darkness of her womb. Though she had thought about having an abortion, she could not destroy the life she knew was there. Phelps would never forgive her. But then again, Phelps might never again forgive anyone for anything.

Phelps had taught Lyddie that if you avoided danger, it would avoid you. She had built her life with him on that fallacy. From all of his care and tending, what had she gained but a few years of stability swallowed up in grief? A botanist in a body bag, only not even.

Outside, the wind was like a dirge in the trees. Something kept banging. Lyddie crept from bed over to the open window and looked out. The streetlamp in the alleyway cast a stagey light over the yard, emptying it of darkness. The wind buffeted the aluminum door of the greenhouse. She had not latched it properly.

She left the house in her nightgown and followed the sidewalk out to the greenhouse, which she entered. The orchids and the fuchsias hung like tiny burnt-out lanterns under the bright moon. She froze, listening to a trickle of water, the sound of earthworms doing their million-year-old labor, building sleek, loose corridors in the soil. "Phelps?" she said, listening. She waited.

No answer.

She turned on the spigot. The hose stiffened in her hand at the surge of water. She felt Phelps's presence there, and in the dirt and the silences, in the vast repertoire of coded Latinate names. "Phelps, where are you?" she said, her voice swallowed up by the glass corridor and the thirst of plants. In the northeast corner, sitting on the ledge, were the little bottles with skull and crossbones, labled Dow Chemical, that Phelps had warned her not to touch. He used them for the lilies, to encourage mutations. He experimented with outcomes. In front of them, each lily was labeled on a stake with a name and a number. The one in closest to the bottles, failing to bloom in a shrug of shriveled buds, was the one he had named *Lydia Exotica*.

She felt rage rising in her chest. Two frightened sparrows flitted around the greenhouse. One of them banged against the glass two or three times, believing it had access to the sky. "You can't just leave and say nothing!" she shouted. "This baby—it was for you!" She picked up a plastic pot with a nameless plant that she had killed trying to guess its needs and dumped it upside down on the ground beside where she stood. She began to overturn, in a systematic fury, flats of leggy seedlings. She took strength from the dirt that piled up around her, as if she were raiding a grave. She tore at the great leaves of the banana plant and denuded the nutmeg saplings before uprooting them both and kicking over the containers that had held them. "Where are you?" she screamed. "Stop hiding from me, you coward! This is what all your care and tending has come to!" She ripped bulbs out of their contented sleep and vines from their aspiration to the light. She picked up a small clay pot, read the label—*cryptanthus*—and sent it sailing upward until she heard the shriek of glass breaking. Then she was still. Above the gaping arc in the glass, a thin veil of cloud drifted quickly over, moved by a high wind. She leaned against the wooden platform and watched the sky. A star streaked overhead. And then, oddly, another. Lyddie had only ever seen two or three shooting stars in her life, but as she sat in stillness beneath the broken glass, she saw eight or ten in the course of half an hour—each so rapid in transit that she wondered, until the next one slit the dark, if she were only imagining it. She knew then that she wanted to live as Phelps himself had in fact lived, not in the climate-controlled environment of the greenhouse or even the museum, not behind the wheel of the Olds 98 like an afflicted saint, but as if on a motorbike moving fast down a curved road at night, the head-light out, danger pulsing in her fingertips. Maybe it was a wish for her own destruction. She would not allow him to deprive her of it again.

2

THE FIRST TIME HER HOUSEMATE, Sabina, had taken Lyddie to the flat on Naunynstrasse in the neighborhood of Kreuzberg, in Berlin, Lothar had appeared at the door, looking serious and impenetrable—like a revolutionary in a Russian novel. He had ushered them into an immense room, most striking in that, except for a piano along the wall, it was thoroughly unfurnished. Sabina had introduced Lyddie in English since, at the beginning, Lyddie still labored at German. Light spilling through the tall windows from the central courtyard filled the room like a giant tumbler.

"You are a student. What study you?" Lothar asked Lyddie. His mouth was pretty, like a rosebud, his nose upturned. He smoked furiously.

"The Bauhaus," she said. "Art history."

Sabina had told her that Lothar had defected from the East in 1981, when he was twenty-one. He had written a letter to the Communist authorities, requesting permission to leave. He had written another, and another. Finally, following his arrest for an underground exhibition of his paintings and a year-long prison term at Hohenschönhausen, he'd been granted the permission he sought. Lyddie was thinking about these things but didn't think she should ask about them. Lothar, having exhausted either his courage or his curiosity, went to the kitchen and re-emerged with two bottles of Tannat. Because Sabina had recently returned from a few months in Rio, they drank Brazilian wine.

Sabina worked in her mother's cosmetic shop in West Berlin, but her friends were mostly artists and writers who had defected from the East. Sabina had told Lyddie that all of them lived on government subsidies. They benefitted from a massive effort to revitalize the city, which had lost many of its young people and much of its culture since the war.

Lyddie and Sabina followed Lothar into the other room. Books that had not yet found shelves lay in stacks around the periphery. A baroque, amber-globed fixture on a long cord squandered its light on the steely surface of a utility table. Sketches and exhibition posters had been tacked haphazardly to the wall above a futon, which displayed several changes of clothes.

A dark-haired man with deeply cut features sat on the futon among the cast-off trousers and shirts, reading. He did not look up when they entered the room.

"Which prefer you?" Lothar asked Lyddie. The two bottles of red wine, one in each hand, appeared identical. Lyddie indicated the one on the right. "Good choose," Lothar said with a smile that appeared and disappeared just as quickly, like a gift that had been stolen in order to be given. "But disfortunate. I am able only with the left hand." He poured her a glass from the other bottle then filled the remaining glasses, nearly to the brim, for himself and Sabina. Still feeling awkward and drinking her wine too fast, Lyddie picked up a book from the table and leafed through its pages, all in German. "Do you know the poems of Paul Celan?" Lothar asked. "When Sabina and I are meeting just, I send to her the words of a poem from Celan. Not a love poem, with flowers *und zo*. Not as you Americans give for the valentine." The mere idea of the wine seemed to have loosened him up considerably, and his boyishness made him entertaining as he began to tell the story of how Sabina had at first ignored his overtures. "You will see. We will translate," Lothar said.

"Lothar, you cannot!" Sabina cried.

"Help me," Lothar said, smiling. "Let me see…" He experienced another moment of shyness before launching confidently into the first line. "*Good to fly, also this vun.*" His accent was heavy but, seeing Lyddie's amusement, he looked pleased with his beginning. "It is difficult also in German," he assured her.

Sabina protested wildly. Heartened by her resistance, he continued. "*Is singing the…*ah…*first? ahead?*" He paused, this time less certain of himself. "*Ach!* Axel, help me!" he exclaimed, looking expectantly at the figure slumped on the futon, book in hand. "Axel is a painter, but a poet also. He knows English very good. He is reading Shakespeare from twelve years." Axel, bemused, looked up but offered no assistance. The small dark swatches below his eyes made his glance vulnerable, though the scrutiny of his gaze countered that impression. His hands were unusually big on the small volume he held. Its cover, like that of all German literary publications, was unillustrated, serious-looking. Lyddie couldn't stop looking at Axel's hands, creased with paint. His little fingers were bent inward at the distal joint, almost as if they had been broken.

Sabina buried her face in her hands.

"Help me, then!" Lothar exclaimed, intent still on the task at hand, searching for the words that had somehow absconded with his meaning. He paused to look at Lyddie. "My English is not so good as I wish. But this poem I am giving to Sabina when we are meeting just. She likes it because it is not romantic. Axel could translate it, but I…" Lothar's voice trailed off. Standing beside the table in his tall black boots, he looked like a commando turned troubadour. He continued. "*Is singing the front wheel*—"

Sabina was decidedly gloomy, as if she had just been run over by Lothar's singing front wheel. Lyddie was absorbed in the tension between them, a remnant bearing as little resemblance to love as the poem would to its original. She was torn between pleasure and pity. But at the same time, she was aware of Axel's presence in the corner of the room, the quiet refusal of his mouth set like a stain on the pale skin of his face. She sensed his disapproval, and felt suddenly responsible for the debacle he was witnessing.

"Please," she said. "Don't do this for my sake!"

"Who other shall we do it for?" said Lothar gaily.

At that moment, they heard the door open. "Ah, in time, just!" said Lothar. "Here is Phelps!"

"His English is terrible," Sabina said, still apologizing for Lothar. "Because he is from the East. And the poem is difficult—impossible to translate. *Sings the front wheel*—it is not equal."

A tall man with fine, straight hair and a friendly smile entered the room, carrying a large, freshly potted schefflera. Sabina, relieved by the interruption, went and kissed him, first on one side of the plant and then somewhere in the foliage on the other. Phelps introduced himself to Lyddie. "What's going on?" he said.

"We are translating a poem for our new friend," Lothar said. "You can help."

Phelps turned to Lyddie again. "You're from the States? What are you doing in Berlin?"

"I'm Lyddie," she said, since no one else thought to. "I'm studying art history at the Free University."

"Phelps is an explorer of plants," Lothar said.

Phelps set the plant on the table. "I'm on a post-doc in ethno-botany at Humboldt. I study medicinal plants in Kurdish Iraq."

Axel, who had been silently absorbed in his book, looked up and interjected, "So that the sponsor of your research can destroy them more efficiently?"

Phelps, brushing his hands off on his jeans, turned to Lothar, as if communicating directly with Axel were not possible. "What is he talking about?"

Lothar mediated reluctantly. "Dow Chemical, it was manu-facturing Agent Orange for use in Vietnam." It seemed he and Axel had had this discussion before.

Even so, Phelps's good humor remained intact. "If it makes you feel better, Axel, I didn't work there in the 60s. And now Dow is funding ethnobotany. Think of it as a kind of atonement."

Whether or not he agreed, Axel said nothing in response. Phelps said, "Let's hear the poem."

"So," said Lothar, with sudden resolve. "*Good to fly, also this vun. / Is singing the front wheel...* Let me see. I go to the next." As if for inspiration, he looked at Axel again but, seeing the other's in-disposition, redirected his gaze to the corner of the room, where a fly batted against the clean plaster of the ceiling. "*The dark...* something...it is part of an airplane?" He stopped to think, then quickly waved his hand, dismissing the lost word. "*The dark some-thing...makes around you his arms.*"

Sabina looked directly into Lothar's face. Her eyes glistened yellowish green, like bits of scrub gnawed down to the root, in-tent on survival. It was clear that in some ultimate way she had removed herself from him. Lyddie felt the presence of the "dark something" in the room, though she couldn't say exactly what it was or where it had come from.

"*Your vine*... what do you call this part with the blood? *Vine?*"

Phelps, unaware of the mounting tension between Lothar and Sabina, was happy to help. "*Vein*," he said.

"*Your vein*"—here Lothar stopped to slash dramatically at his wrist—"like so," he said. "*Wake up!*"

Axel looked up from his book. An angry clump of hair fell from a cowlick onto his forehead and sharpened his features. Lyddie was startled by the disparity between the suicidal airport scene she had just imagined and whatever mysterious quality of the original poem might have brought Sabina and Lothar together and now caused them such trauma. Was that supposed to be love? In spite of herself, she began, suddenly, to laugh because Lothar had translated his passion into such nonsense. Lothar shrugged, and Sabina's distress seemed only to heighten the absurdity and humor of the situation. But they had gone too far. Phelps watched with the others as Axel got up from the futon and left the room without a word. They heard the door of the apartment close.

"But this is not the end," said Lothar gaily. "There is more flying." He climbed onto his chair.

"Your flying is worse than your English," Sabina said.

PHELPS HAD KNOWN LOTHAR and Sabina for several months by the time Lyddie arrived, and he would join them late for drinks or visits to friends after his work at Humboldt. Lyddie drank the dark, bitter coffee they offered her. She smoked their Galoises, shared in their jibes about the Ossies who were crossing the border with less hardship than Lothar and his friends had. Their lives were weighty with the grudge they bore history, their politics as close at hand and well-used as kitchen knives.

For Lyddie, the hard edges of the others were softened by

Phelps, who was generous and good-hearted—summed up by Sabina in a sentence: "He's so… *human*." In Sabina's idiom, this was something of a criticism.

One day, leaving Lothar's place and walking with Sabina along a segment of the Wall nearby, Lyddie and Phelps asked their friend what it was like to live in a divided city. "You are both romantics," Sabina said, smiling. "You know what this Wall demonstrates?" She stopped and kicked it. "That is what. If you want to go from here to over there, you have to find another way. But who would want to?" She shrugged and began walking again. "No one will give you an invitation to this life, no matter that you live in Berlin or San Francisco or Taiwan. It is like a party you have to wreck." She said all of this without the slightest indication of real resentment. As if she were some kind of avant-garde Emily Post.

The Wall was, indeed, more ordinary looking than Lyddie had imagined. Spray-painted German anger or sarcasm collided with the happy-go-lucky dog pissing of foreign tourists: ANITA TI AMO. GINNY WAS HERE 1972. A few days before, Lyddie had climbed the observation deck at Brandenburg Gate with Phelps and looked out over the acres of barbed wire separating the two Berlins and guarded by the heavily armed soldiers in square towers. She had seen there a desolation against which someone like Sabina or Lothar or Axel might weigh the relative importance of every action or decision. But really, it did not belong to her or Phelps. They were among the leg-lifters. The piss-and-run crowd.

In response to Sabina's explanation of life, Phelps glanced skeptically at Lyddie. He considered for a moment, and then said, "*Crash*," correcting Sabina. "For parties, it's *crash*."

"So we're romantics," Lyddie said. "Is that why Axel dislikes us so?"

"Speaking of wrecking parties," Phelps said.

It was early spring, one of those days when the sky seemed drunk on sudden bursts of sunshine and big cumulus clouds blundered by overhead. Sabina walked close to the Wall, her path defined by it for the moment. "He and Lothar were friends in the East," she said, as if that answered Lyddie's question. "They have known them many years."

Phelps said with false gravity, "You and I, Lyddie, do not know what it is to grow up under the gaze of Stalin. We are the spoiled children of democracy."

"But is it true what Axel said about Dow Chemical?" Lyddie asked.

"Look," Phelps replied. "Axel feels the need to demonstrate that Americans are no purer in heart than the Germans they're here to keep in line. That's not why you and I are here, of course, but it's all the same to Axel. He thinks we think we're morally superior."

Sabina shrugged. "I don't know. I thought you would be, as Americans, more free. More from the counter-culture."

Phelps laughed. "Should we drop some acid? Have an orgy in the minefield?"

"Like Woodstock. It would be more interesting, I think," Sabina said. She walked half a block or so, apparently distracted by her own thoughts. Lyddie tried not to imagine the three of them sexually entangled. Let alone in a minefield. She wasn't sleeping with Phelps then, and she wondered if it was for her sake that he had brought sex into the conversation. He caught her eye and smiled as if to affirm the reasonable possibility of a two-way alliance in contrast to the more inclusive situation he had joked about. "You know the best thing that ever happened to me?" Sabina said, stopping and looking up for a moment at the clouds roiling across the sky. "I went late one night to buy cigarettes from a machine at the S-Bahn station at York Strasse. The one who filled the machine—he forgot to shut the door. I got one hundred and sixty packs of cigarettes and gave each of my friends the brand they liked best to smoke. It seemed that a great fist opened to me. But I don't expect it will happen ever again. Those things don't happen."

"So you took all the cigarettes?" Lyddie said, astonished.

Sabina merely sighed.

Phelps found Sabina amusing, though her cavalier attitude was in open conflict with his policies of care and tending. When Lothar was too nihilistic, Sabina too dismissive, Axel—on the rare occasion that Lyddie saw him—too thoroughly aloof, it was Phelps who helped Lyddie feel welcome and accepted. Phelps did not allow the others to obliterate his view of the world as a place where reason and good will would prevail.

Lyddie went to her classes, mostly at night. During the day she worked at the university or sometimes at the Amerika Haus library, which was small and redolent of the fifties. On days when she felt more ambitious, she visited the Bauhaus Archive in Schöneberg and pored over documents on beauty and utility— the designs and architectural models of men like Gropius, Klee, and Van der Rohe for meeting the needs of the working class. She studied exhibits devoted to the influences of light and scale, form and color on the human psyche. Her favorite was a drawing of museum-goers gazing at the famous Greek Hermes of Praxiteles. The statue hung upside-down from its pedestal to demonstrate the eye's literal message and the brain's learned ability to invert the image its rods and cones delivered. Lyddie found it strange that the body possessed a physical mechanism for distorting the world and a psychological mechanism for setting it right again.

But her mind worked deceptions of its own. Sometimes, when she entered a room, she expected to see Axel lurking in a corner, leaning against a wall, his slattern composition a study in beauty and, in place of utility, perhaps neglect.

The next time Lyddie saw Axel was in late May at Mariannenplatz for a protest against the World Bank and the International Monetary Fund. Phelps was in Kurdish Iraq for a week to collect plant samples and conduct anecdotal research. Lothar and Axel arrived at the square to find Lyddie sitting on the edge of the fountain beside Sabina, who peeled an orange absently as people pushed in around them. Lothar's sign said, in a black painted scrawl, CAPITALISM IS TERROR.

Men in green and orange Mohawks and women with closely shorn heads carried signs with simpler analyses: *Free Trade Blows* and *Heil World Bank*. A punk/grunge band named Cpt. Kirk warmed up on stage, testing the sound system, and a series of loud screeches from the amplifier strained the conversation.

Wearing pants that bunched up at the top of his black leather shoes and shirtsleeves that were significantly too short, Axel gave the general impression that he might be molting. This was exaggerated by the slickness of his dark hair, still wet, which he had combed back from his forehead using his fingers. He acknowledged Lyddie with a barely perceptible nod and was quiet while Sabina and Lothar argued. Sabina said the problem wasn't capitalism but the systematic erosion of human rights, and the gap between the rich and the poor, which both the Communists and the World Bank exploited happily. "You should have seen the way people lived in Rio," she said. "I used to lie in bed at night in that city of massive wealth, waiting for the poor to descend from the mountains and mob the rich."

Lyddie, Lothar and Axel all listened, expectant. The band, apparently satisfied with the shrieking of its microphones, had left the stage.

"But each morning, I awoke and drank my Brazilian coffee," Sabina said, holding the orange in one hand like a sun

before she broke it into sections. "And in the evening, I ate fi-
let—and there was no blood. Only what was on my own plate."
She smiled vaguely.

Lyddie didn't know whether her housemate's words implied relief or disappointment. "You were afraid?" Axel said,
entering the conversation for the first time. He was the only
one not holding a sign, and his hands hung empty at his sides.

Sabina looked at him directly now, curious that he had
broken his silence. "No," she answered. She offered him half
of the peeled orange, which he refused.

"Guilty?" he asked.

Surveying the faces around her, Sabina said to no one in
particular, "Only a little surprised that I was neither." She ate
a segment of the orange absently. Then, at Lothar's urging, she
stood up and they all pushed their way through the crowd to get
closer to the band.

Later, before the speeches had finished, a fight erupted between some Skinheads and a group of Christian Democrats, and
the sky grew ominous, so the police broke up the rally without
much trouble. Axel, Sabina and Lyddie hurried to Kottbusser
Tor with its frenzy of street vendors and Turkish immigrants
pulling in displays of tube socks and plastic toys and then into
the station without speaking. They boarded the train and rode
together in silence.

When Axel followed the two women out of the train into the
underground at Görlitzer Bahnhof, the air was still. The absence
left by the train's departure was almost palpable. Then, against
the smooth whine of the train's receding, an ominous groan
moved toward them through the underground from the direction
of the exit. As it swelled to cosmic proportion, people stopped in
their tracks. Lyddie saw her own fear and confusion echoed in the
faces around her. Axel, too, froze. All at once, with an astonishing

roar, a commotion of white, cottony debris swept into the vacuum the train had created underground. A few long seconds later, the rain began. People laughed in relief, fumbling with newspapers and umbrellas as they moved toward the exit to watch in wonder. The first drops that swept in spattered Sabina's arms. But in this moment of understanding, of the terror made manageable—just wind, rain, the white fluff of cottonwood—Axel was not relieved. The nebulous threat having triggered something in him, he took Sabina roughly by the arms and pushed her against the wall, looking into her face as if searching for something there. Lyddie, helpless, shouted Sabina's name.

"You lied to me," Axel said to Sabina, emphasizing each word. The rain pelted their sides, but he did not let her move. She shook one arm loose and smacked him in the chest.

"Lied about what? We've barely spoken!" she cried above the sound of the rain. The rain gushed down the steps and around their feet. Sabina tried to pull away from Axel, her body breaking the plane of shelter and dragging him into the field of the downpour.

"Your fantasies," he shouted. "They aren't revolutionary; they're apocalyptic. People streaming down the mountainsides with machetes."

"What do my fantasies matter to you?" The rain distorted Sabina's face.

"You are guilty and you are afraid," Axel said. He loosened his grip on her arms. Then he let go of her, collapsing against the wall of the station, and Lyddie called out again for Sabina to come away, but she didn't. Lyddie left them, the rain pelting their faces in the aftermath of an accusation that seemed to take more out of Axel than any confession could.

3

IN THE SIMPLE WAY THE YOUNG East German at the border touched Lyddie's face, tipping her chin this way and that as he scrutinized her features in relation to her passport, Lyddie felt she understood the meaning of Cold War. He returned her passport with a hint of a smirk and nodded her release. She emerged on the East Berlin side of Checkpoint Charlie. She had crossed over to see Lemke House, the last house designed by Mies van der Rohe, one-time director of the Bauhaus school.

Along the streets of the old city center, she was surprised at how recent the war seemed. Not far from the Stalinist neoclassical Russian Embassy and the baroque palaces along Unter den Linden lay the crumpled shells of buildings still looking freshly bombed. Lyddie ate a slow, late lunch in one of the official restaurants, which reminded her in its vast spareness of a VFW hall. Its sobriety was nearly undisturbed by the stage band's singing, in English, "Girls Just Want to Have Fun." The vegetarian pizza she chose from the menu was topped with a medley of pickled cauliflower, pickled

peppers, and pickled green beans. It seemed the general idea was
to demoralize you so thoroughly that you wouldn't have the heart
to go on and see the rest of East Berlin.

By the time Lyddie had finished with lunch, there wasn't
time to visit the Radio Tower or the Pergamon Museum before making her way out to the eastern suburb of Hohenschön,
where Lemke House stood on the shore of the Obersee. She
bought a few postcards and hurried to the train. On board, people looked as if they were in a fallout shelter: so many attitudes
and poses struck against the darkness. There was no beyond
on which to focus. A woman with a large face and a miniscule
mouth could not make her dog sit. She held a rawhide chew but
seemed unable to decide whether to use it as a potential reward
or as a way of quieting the dog immediately.

Lyddie knew from her research that Lemke House had at
one time been requisitioned by the Soviet Army as a garage and
storage space. What she didn't know was that it had subsequent-
ly been co-opted by the East German government. After a long
ride out on the train, she couldn't get any closer than the big
spiked gate at the front. She could see the low, L-shaped brick
facade of the house, but the terrace was hidden from view, as
were the banks of windows that were signature Mies, dishing
up the landscape in structured segments to make it part of the
architectural project. No sooner had Lyddie snapped a couple
of photographs than a guard walked out through the gate and
said, "Your camera, please?"

"No photos? I'm sorry," Lyddie said. "I didn't know," and
she put the camera into the canvas bag she was carrying.

"I may have it, please?" the guard said.

"The bag?" Lyddie said. "This is Lemke House, right?"

He extended his hand. "Only the camera please." Lyddie
gave it to him. He opened the film compartment swiftly, removed

the film, and handed the camera back. "It is the Ministry of State Security, and you violate its purpose."

At the border again, Lyddie was escorted to a seedy room, badly in need of paint, and interrogated for forty-five minutes. Was it because of her photography that the officials wanted to know about her friends and associates in West Berlin? She didn't mention Axel, but they brought up his name in association with Lothar's and then chastised her for not having mentioned him, though she admitted she knew him. He was apparently of far greater interest to the East German border police than Lothar was. What was the nature of her acquaintance with him? Of her research? Did she have her papers from the university? What was her own political affiliation? Had she ever been involved in anti-Communist activities? How did she explain the fact that she, an American, spent so much of her time among former East Germans? What did they do when she was in their midst? How much time had she spent in Axel's company? How intimate were they? Had he ever asked her for a favor? When the border official asked this last question, he smiled knowingly.

Though Lyddie convinced him that she was an ordinary student of architecture and had never been asked to do a favor of any sort for Axel, she was shaken. Why would the East Germans concern themselves with her? Had she stumbled into a spy ring? Was that what they suspected—that Axel might be using her, an innocent American, to get information for the West German government?

Lyddie didn't mention the incident to Sabina. Even if she could get past her embarrassment over having been so careless with the camera, she had no idea what had happened between Sabina and Axel after she had left them in the rain three weeks before. She considered confiding in Lothar, but Lothar was too close to Axel—his best friend, as far as Lyddie could tell. She feared that she had drawn unwanted attention to them all, and she felt humiliated by what she'd experienced at the hands of the East German official. In the end, Phelps was the only person she felt she could talk to. But before she had finished telling him what had happened, he said, "Lyddie, Axel is someone you really don't want to be involved with."

"I'm not *involved* with him," she argued. "But I can't lie and say that I don't know him at all."

"You don't," Phelps said. "Trust me."

"And you do know him?" Lyddie said.

"Sabina knows things. And I know Sabina."

"And since when do you trust her judgement?" Lyddie said. Even Axel had accused Sabina of lying to them all. Lyddie had witnessed that.

It was about a month later, toward the end of June, when Lyddie ran into Axel in the stacks at the Amerika Haus library near closing time. Searching for a book on Gropius, she saw him watching her through a gap in the wall of books. She felt her face flush. "What are you looking for?" he said in a voice just barely audible from the other side. The disembodied question struck her as oddly metaphysical. She came back around the end of the aisle to face him.

She indicated the stack of books on the floor between the two aisles—on top, a large volume titled *Bauhaus: the American Years*. "I think the library is closing soon," she said. "Do you know what time it is?"

"No," he said, unapologetic. "Here in Berlin. What are you looking for?"

Perhaps because of the inquisition at the border, it seemed to her that he was more suspicious than curious. And what he'd said to Sabina the day he had pinned her to the wall of the U-Bahn—*You are guilty and you are afraid*—haunted Lyddie. It seemed to have come from nowhere, and still, Axel had alluded to something in Sabina that made Lyddie, too, uneasy. Lyddie had spent the weeks since then unsure whether it was Sabina she mistrusted, or Axel, or both. "I'm studying," she said.

As if reading her mind, Axel continued. "I was right about your friend?"

"Sabina?" Lyddie said.

"I think that I am right," he said, more sad than triumphant. His high forehead made the rest of his face seem weary.

"I know her almost as little as you do," Lyddie said, moving back out of his line of vision.

"Guilty and afraid," Axel said, stepping around the stack of books and into the aisle where she stood. "You, on the other hand, are, I think, innocent and afraid." He looked at her as if to read her face.

This was a very German thing, it seemed: to see her as innocent because she wasn't as jaded as the rest of them. Sabina often implied the same kind of criticism. Phelps, on the other hand, saw and admired her innocence. "Afraid of what?" she said.

"Hmm," he said, studying her face.

"I ate dirt and dog hair as a child. I stepped on the head of a cat once. What do you suppose that means?" She tucked her hair behind her ear and turned back to the shelves, running her finger attentively along the call numbers on the spines of the books.

As if aware that she was about to dismiss him altogether, he said, "I think you are not at all like Sabina. You are not like any of us."

When he looked at her, now from the side, she felt that however she had seen herself before, she may have been mistaken. "Why?" she said.

"I think you believe in absolutes. Right and Wrong. Bad and Good."

"What do you believe in?" Lyddie said, turning to him again and giving up on the illusion that she could still think straight enough to navigate the Dewey Decimal System.

He exhaled audibly through tightened lips. "Not much, I suppose. But I find this sweet about you."

"What you mean is that you think I'm naïve."

"I think you're sincere. And law-abiding."

Lyddie's thoughts returned to the hassle at the border and Phelps's warnings.

"However," Axel said, "you have broken the rules of the American library." There was a note of humor in his voice, and she saw that his eyes had a way of smiling without the cooperation of his mouth. He indicated, with a nod, the package of crackers she'd been eating despite the sign at the entrance to the library forbidding food and drink. The cellophane wrapper remained in her hand.

There was an announcement about closing, and she fumbled to gather the large stack of books she'd collected. "We'd better go," Lyddie urged, but Axel, passive, didn't move.

They stood still for a moment before the lights went out, and for reasons Lyddie would consider at length in years to come, she did not run for the exit. The dark settled in around them and she let it. Instead of calling out for the librarian she whispered to Axel, "He's forgotten we're here." Having included herself in a "we" with Axel intensified her feeling of panic.

Axel stood and put a forefinger across her lips to silence her. She did not reach up and remove his hand from her mouth. Both of them tensed at the touch, listening in the direction of the entrance. Then they heard the click of the lock and Axel's body slackened. He stepped backward toward the stack opposite them. "Have you always wanted to do this?" he said, his intensity dissolving to wonder.

"This?" Lyddie said, not sure what it was that they were doing. "To stay all night in the library."

At worst, she thought they might be under surveillance. At the very best, she felt as if she were waiting for some Higher Librarian to tally a lifetime of policy infractions—lost and water-damaged books, unpaid fines that continued to accrue, crackers in the stacks, and now this man after hours, who had, quite possibly, been stalking her.

"What did you think it would be like?" he said, assuming her sympathy.

"Not this," she said, still dismayed at her own lack of resolve. "Then what?"

It was quiet and dark. There was only the hum of the drinking fountain, the tiny green light of the elevator glowing like a distant planet. "I don't know," Lyddie said. "I don't know you." Echoing Phelps's wisdom, Lyddie remembered suddenly that she had agreed to meet him in front of Amerika Haus at closing time. Was he pacing outside? Or had he given up on her and left?

"I thought it would be like sleeping in the mind of God," Axel said, sinking to the floor.

"Do you think it's locked from the outside?"

"No. Look. We've much reading to do!" he said.

"There's no light."

Then I'll tell you a story," he said, as if in a stroke of aptness mixed with good intention. "Sit down." While he thought for a minute, Lyddie sank down beside him, at first relieved that he wasn't a sex maniac, and then wondering if it might be worse to be locked inside the library with a religious zealot. "This story my grandfather told me, long ago. There was once a monk," he began. But he stalled there, distracted.

"There was once a monk who…" Lyddie prompted.

"Lived in the desert of Egypt. In the fourth century after

Christ," he continued. "An ascetic. He built his existence on that which he denied himself. Because he believed in that discipline." As if suddenly weary, Axel ran all ten fingers back along his scalp, lifting his hair and combing it away from his forehead. The English he adopted for the sake of his story was formal, his voice deep and even, and when he spoke, it was as if he spoke the world into being. "For months," he said, "this monk would survive on a few crusts of bread and little more."

Her watching him as she listened seemed to make it hard for him to remember where the story was going. He stared at the little pile of crumbs she'd left on top of the big Bauhaus books and began organizing them with his hand, as if they would have a mnemonic effect. "Ah, so!" he said. "After many years the monk grew sick, and hearing of this, Macarios, one of the most respected of the ascetic brotherhood, went to visit him. And when he asked did the monk want anything to eat, the brother replied, 'Yes, I want some honeycakes.' Then Macarios set out for Alexandria, which was ninety kilometers distant, and brought back the cakes and gave them to the monk." Axel stopped again, his gaze settling on Lyddie's face.

"Just like that?" she said.

"That is the end."

She studied him for a moment. "Is it that you want something to eat?" she said.

"You see, none of them were supposed to have much to eat," Axel said.

"But why are you telling me that? Are you hungry?"

Suddenly, at her suggestion, he looked as though he might be famished. As if hunger were the entire point of the story. He looked so hungry he might die. "No," he said. "It's a story about humility."

"Who did you say told you the story?" she asked, standing and turning to the books behind her and trying to make out titles as the headlights of the cars on Hardenbergstrasse cycled past, sweeping the bookshelves in long, diminishing strokes.

"My grandfather."

"Do you see him often?" She looked back over her shoulder at him.

"No," he said. "I like these stories. They remind me of a time when..." His voice faded again and he stood up, moving toward the end of the shelves. She followed him.

"When...? " she repeated.

He turned to her. He looked the way she imagined the sick brother in the desert must have looked to Macarios—as though there were something he wanted very much and had denied himself for a very long time. "I might have believed in something," he said. They walked together to a wooden table in the middle of the room. He sat down on top of it and she stood near him.

"Why are we here?" she said, thinking again of Phelps and how he would worry. She was usually as good as her word. What was happening to her? She made a quick assessment of the windows, which were at ground level or just above.

"It's not that you are beautiful," Axel said, gazing back at her.

Lyddie waited, hoping the sting would subside and knowing that being hurt would only prove her shallow. Her insecurity was left over from the time before nature had, by some fluke in the finishing of her features, translated the displeasures of her face into the language of beauty's remote territories. In her early twenties, she had been taken by surprise. She understood now that the surprise itself had fed the beauty, the way hunger feeds hunger. Still, she had not lost the sense that the fruit she most wanted was either forbidden or out of reach, though her arms were lithe and long, the branches loaded.

"If you were only beautiful—"

"What is it then?" she said.

"It's your presence," he said. "When I look at you, there is no place else to go."

"Why would you need to go anywhere?"

He half smiled and shook his head.

"Axel," Lyddie said, feeling suddenly bold—or reckless, as if she had nothing to lose. "I'll tell you a story. There once was an American student who crossed over to East Berlin to see a house designed by an architect she admired. It turned out that what she was photographing had been converted into the Ministry of State Security. It wasn't enough that the guard destroyed all of her film. The officials interrogated her at the border and implied that she was involved with people who…might try to use her for some illicit purpose. I'm not so naïve as to believe that they care about you for no reason, Axel. You've told me a story, but still I know little about you."

Axel's face clouded. He laughed in a single, sarcastic exhalation. "I used to work in the State Library, in the East," he said. 'When I was there, working, I set the world right. I made things happen the way I wanted them to happen. They did not like that much."

"But you're here now. What do they want from you?"

Axel's demeanor was like that of an ascetic, pitted against some invisible force. "I don't know," he said. "It is possible that they are watching me still," he said. "They never understood my motives."

"Are you religious?" she said, thinking of the story he had told.

Axel grew thoughtful. A shaft of light from a passing car caught the white of his shirtsleeve, making it irresistible. Lyddie reached out and touched it—then, realizing what she had done, retracted her hand. He took her hand and drew it back to him. In the dark, the smell of his skin was tinged faintly with turpentine. She pulled herself up onto the table next to him.

"It is true that you stepped on the head of a cat?" Axel said.

Lyddie nodded.

"How did it happen?"

"The mother carried the litter from the garage to the front steps of the house."

Axel continued to study her with curiosity. "And you did, in fact, eat dirt?"

"Sand."

"Deliberately?"

"Whenever I got the chance."

"To punish yourself? To mortify the flesh? I think you are an ascetic."

"I liked the taste of it," Lyddie said, remembering. "The grit. I knew enough to be ashamed. It made my father angry, but he couldn't make me stop."

"Your father is living?" Axel said.

"No," she said. "He and my mother are both gone. Yours?"

"My father, he is dead," Axel said with little expression.

"Do you have a stepfather?"

"Also dead," he answered.

They sat for a long time in silence. Axel went and got two books and set them as pillows, and he and Lyddie lay back on the table, side by side, their hands folded on their middles. They drifted out for a while. When Lyddie awoke and sat up, the traffic outside had quieted. The moon was gone and she couldn't see Axel's face. But her eyes adjusted to the faint light of the exit sign. It felt very late. She could see the triangle of skin where his shirt had fallen open to reveal the smooth plateau formed by his collarbones. Axel, aware of her looking at him, awoke.

Lyddie said, "Tell me about your stepfather. Tell me another story."

Axel sat up and examined his big hands. He rolled a cigarette and lit it; then he stood and walked to the stacks again, where he used the wastebasket as an ashtray. This seemed to Lyddie not a good idea with so much paper, so many books on hand. But nothing seemed to catch. "When I was small," he said, "I often walked with him to the Jewish cemetery, which was full of dark trees."

"You're Jewish?" Lyddie asked.

"My mother's mother was Jewish, but my stepfather was not. So once he told me to get my coat; he said we were going out. 'To the cemetery?' I said. And he said, 'Not this time. This time, we will be in the company of the living.' I asked no more questions and we drove to the edge of the city."

Lyddie walked over to where he stood smoking and she leaned against the stacks, listening. "This was in the East? East Berlin?" she said.

Axel nodded. "We passed the highrises of the suburbs and then the fields of what seemed to me like a different country. At last the lights of the amusement park came into view. I rode the carousel and the Italian swings, and at dusk, I chose the Great Wheel. I sat beside my stepfather, and we rose out over the tiny families below, moving in bright rings around the dark center. But something was troubling me. Should I say something or no? At last, I found my courage. 'It isn't my birthday, Papa,' I told him.

"Why?" Lyddie asked.

"He had, in the past, forgotten when it *was* my birthday. Perhaps, I thought, he had also forgotten when it was not. 'We do not need a reason for an outing, do you agree?' my stepfather said to me. And I said to myself, 'This is happening for no reason I know. But that doesn't mean there isn't a reason.' When we returned to the ground, my stepfather pressed a D-Mark into my palm and pushed me toward the tent where the games of chance were played."

Even this story, Axel told as if it were a parable—its meaning not to be apprehended all at once. Each of his stories shed about as much light as a match, and made all of the dark around it worth wanting to know.

"And how did he die, your stepfather?" Lyddie asked. But she realized now that Axel was crying. She touched his shoulder tentatively, and he began to shake with sobs. He covered his face with his hands, and when she stepped toward him, he caved in over her shoulders, burying his sobs in her hair. She kissed his forehead and then his nose, tasting the salt of him. He lifted his head and, almost by accident, their mouths found one another. The clean edge of his teeth against her tongue was like the pungency of a rare fruit you must learn to like before you become obsessed with its texture, its flavor. A fruit eaten with salt. "What happened?" she said. "What did you come here for?" But his hand was exploring her thigh, moving up under her skirt. She buried her face in his neck. His fingers found the curves at the top of her legs. She unbuttoned his shirt and felt his biceps running smooth and long, flat on top like a burial mound.

Axel said, quietly, "Not this."

"What?" Lyddie said, taking her hand away.

"This is not what I came for."

She felt the palisade of bookbindings against her back when he pressed against her into the stacks. She had begun to undress him. But breathing hard, she pushed him to arm's length. "For what, then?" she said, holding him there. "Was it honeycakes you wanted?"

Axel seemed far away, as if he hadn't heard her.

"Tonight," he said, "we are in the mind of God. Tomorrow, we will be back out on the street." Lyddie started at a click over near the librarian's desk.

He stopped to listen. "The clock," he said.

Lyddie pulled him back to her and he grappled with the

buttons on her blouse while she unfastened his pants when a light came on searingly—blinding her, as if a car from Hardenbergstrasse had entered the library itself.

"Freeze! *Halt!*" a voice shouted. At the same time, two figures sprang onto the scene, one from behind the librarian's desk, the other over the four-foot-high display of new arrivals. Lyddie's pupils dilated as the light lowered slightly to admit the image of the first two cops, their pistols trained on her and Axel. She grabbed at the front of her blouse, but one MP shouted at her to stop. "Put your hands up over your head," he said in English, a second voice almost immediately shouting the same command in German.

Careful not to enunciate too clearly for fear she'd be shot, Lyddie pleaded, softly, "We got locked in." As they'd been locked in with telephone service and windows, her argument sounded distinctly lame. But not having elicited fire, she went on with what she knew, even before it left her mouth, would sound like the biggest lie of all. "We are innocent."

"You're both American?" the MP with the gun said.

"*I* am," she said.

"And you?" they asked Axel.

"I am living in exile," he said in German.

"You can leave," the MP said to Lyddie, indicating the door behind him. To Axel, he said in German, "You stay and talk to us."

Out on the sidewalk along Hardenbergstrasse, it was damp and breezy. Lyddie wanted to run and she wanted to stay and wait for Axel. She felt exposed—at once relieved and embarrassed that they had dismissed her on account of her being an American and a woman with her shirt hanging open. Taxis hurried past in the unfinished business of the night. She looked down at her blouse, the buttons of which she had misaligned with their holes on her way out of the building. Turning toward the hedge to put herself together, she was startled by movement in the dark on the ground near the shrubbery. She froze again, fearing that the place was surrounded by MPs. Then, as a tall, lanky figure approached her, she merely stared, incredulous.

"I saw you go into the library," Phelps said. "I was waiting for you to come out." His silky brown hair fell back down over his forehead immediately when he pushed it back.

"So you called the cops?" Lyddie said.

"I didn't, Lyddie," he said. "I thought about it, but I swear, I didn't."

"You've been here all night?" she said. The grass was wet with dew and she knew it must be near morning.

"I guess we all have," he said, bemused.

Phelps's dogged patience, which at times had endeared him to her, seemed at the moment almost absurd.

"Why didn't you come in when you saw me?"

"I saw Axel go in just after you. I knew the library closed at ten. I figured you were in a hurry to get something and would be back out soon."

The sky was showing crevasses of white in dense gray, and it was difficult to know which was cloud and which was sky. "You slept all night on the sidewalk?" Lyddie said.

Waiting all night would have been extreme, even for Phelps.

"On the grass. It's softer." He reached out and touched her arm. "Did he have you hostage?"

"You must have thought so, since you called the police," Lyddie said. "Though your reaction was a bit slow." Lyddie didn't know how the MPs would have been alerted had Phelps not called them. She didn't attempt to hide her dismay. Who knew what was happening to Axel inside the library? She didn't think he deserved the suspicion that he seemed to arouse. Though perhaps what they had done was illegal, it seemed to her, already, that she had been caught not in the act of trespassing in the building but in the act of making love to Axel. That was her trespass.

"I didn't, Lyddie, I swear," Phelps said. "Someone else must have. Maybe there is a night watchman."

Lyddie looked at him skeptically, though in the end she could hardly disbelieve him. The thing about Phelps was that, in those days, he was all there on the surface. He was the antithesis of mystery. And it was possible that someone had seen Axel's cigarette. Or smelled the smoke. "So why didn't you do something when you saw that I wasn't coming out?"

"On the off-chance that it was a consensual arrangement," he said a bit glumly.

Lyddie could only imagine how disheveled she looked. She still felt edgy with desire.

"Lyddie," he said, "I told you what I thought about Axel. People here are complicated. I'm no expert, it's true, but I've been here a good deal longer than you have and I think you're in over your head. Sabina agrees."

In spite of his being amused by Sabina's philosophies, Phelps was closer to her than Lyddie was, a fact that Lyddie couldn't help resenting. "What does Sabina know about me?"

"That you're fascinated with Axel."

"And what? He's a Communist? A psycho?"

"Lyddie," Phelps said, "Let's go somewhere and get a beer, like we were going to do. Or a coffee. You can't help Axel at the moment." The sky was growing lighter. With a look that betrayed a touch of jealousy, he added, "You stood me up. You owe me one."

That morning, Phelps sympathized as Lyddie told him how she felt—that each day in Berlin she entered more fully a world that had always before been sealed off in a big volume called

History. Some people were part of it. Axel and Lothar were. Sabina was. Even Phelps, with the ethnobotany that took him to Iraq and connected him with shamans. Others, like herself, had spent their lives riding bicycles around suburban cul-de-sacs and in the evening sat at TV trays trying to imagine what it would be like to figure in an epic feature rather than in the audience of one. Phelps agreed she would be a different person for the Berlin experience, but he said it was easy to mistake the excitement of what was foreign for the kind of reality one could render as a life. "Can you imagine any of these people growing old?" he asked her. "Axel—he'll be one of those strange, tormented souls you'd never want to see in the morning over a bowl of Shredded Wheat. You'd never know what he was thinking until he lashed out at you as if you were responsible for all of his life's disappointments. And believe me, he'll have a long list. Now that he and Lothar and the others are living in the West, all their political outrage is just a fashion, like dogs wearing rain boots. Sabina—I like her in many ways. She's a trip. But somebody who makes social statements by perpetrating luggage fraud in Rio and riding the U-Bahn without a ticket is almost sure to wake up one day to wonder if she's really gotten away with as much as she thought she had. The world, Lyddie, will not have taken notice."

Lyddie said, "I don't feel like I belong anywhere. I know what you're saying, Phelps. I do have romantic notions about lots of things. What sort of person do you think I wouldn't tire of seeing over Shredded Wheat? Maybe the Shredded Wheat is the problem."

"You have no idea how lovely you are," he said, shaking his head.

Lyddie couldn't hide her confusion.

"I think what you see in Axel is some romantic notion you

have about East Germans, but this way that you feel in Berlin is really about you. You want to see yourself in a new way. You need to be taught your own loveliness. And then you will continue to grow, but you need to grow in your native soil."

"Do I?" she said.

"Yes," he said. "You do. I can help you with that, Lyddie. If you'll let me."

Lyddie couldn't help but be moved by Phelps's revelation of affection for her and his desire to nurture her, like the dressinas and crotons that flourished under his care at the flat on Naunynstrasse. And it was true what Phelps had told her—that Axel was unpredictable. He could be cynical in the extreme. Nobody seemed to know him really. Lyddie was scaring herself with the recklessness she felt around him.

When she went back to the States and married Phelps, she thought of that life in Berlin as a sort of adolescent flirtation with nihilism. In Buffalo, on the basis of the unfinished Bauhaus research, she was given a fellowship at the Albright-Knox Art Gallery, where Phelps's brother, Ray, was director. The Bauhaus provided a model of order—cleanliness and rationality that acknowledged beauty as long as it could be useful, like a stainless steel percolator or a tubular chair. Phelps never asked her about what had happened with Axel in the library, and he never told her what, if anything, Sabina knew. Though Lyddie thought telling the truth was a virtue—all of it all of the time—Phelps said there was no point in resurrecting the past. He said sometimes you could spare another person what you were thinking or feeling at the moment. It was likely to change anyhow and had the potential to do harm that couldn't easily be undone. So they didn't talk about haphazard desires or resentments they believed they'd outgrow. They were honest. Just not exhaustively so. You had to take responsibility for shaping what you felt before you shared it. Lyddie tried to believe that.

But in the last few months, coming home from reviewing slides and poring over catalogue copy, and more recently from unpacking the paintings that arrived in crates from Berlin, Lyddie had felt exhilarated and restless. She had acknowledged, maybe for the first time, that she was more at home in the museum with absences—the absences those paintings conjured—than she had been in her own kitchen with the man she thought she loved.

She had tried hard to do what was required of her. She had cooked, though not without burning. She had driven the massive white ark of an oldsmobile, navigating carefully the avenues of Phelps's city. She had waited in that city of steel mills and dirty spring snow. Three months. What bothered her more, even, than the travesty of her having ended up alone and pregnant in that place was the confidence with which Phelps had closed the door to her past, as if only what was in their own backyard should matter to either of them anymore. Only the repeatable experiment of dailiness.

"You're so consistent, Phelps. I don't think you have…impulses," Lyddie remembered saying to him once. "You're the kind of person—"

He had interrupted. "What impulses do you have, Lyddie? Perhaps at least I can learn to count on those?"

That was the kind of person Phelps was. Or had been, until he'd disappeared.

4

MAROULA WAS THE ONLY VIRGIN Dimitri knew who would go with him to the cove in the early morning and crawl out onto the rocks below the whitewashed chapel while he observed from his station on the beach. She was his daughter and well past forty. Though he loved her as a father should, he would be the first to admit she wasn't much to look at. She had the bold Levantine nose of his mother, but her eyes receded behind it like two brown mice headed for the same massive piece of furniture from opposite sides of the room. He had studied them and had struggled with the question of how to render them. Maroula was so uninspiring that at times he wondered why he bothered with a model at all. The Virgin of the Last Resort. At least he could be relatively sure she was the real thing. But the older he got, the further the icons he painted strayed from idealized forms to—well, Maroulas. He'd gone from painting Maroula as Saint Anastasia, increasing the distance between the eyes, pulling in the lower lip, to painting Saint Anastasia as

Maroula. From Maroula as Saint Barbara to Saint Barbara as Maroula—holding, oddly enough, the traditionally beautiful head of the beheaded saint in her hand. Did he love his daughter, Maroula, more with time? The Virgin Mother less?

There was a story from the Desert Fathers of a monk who, in carrying his mother across a stream, had wrapped his hands in a piece of thick cloth in order not to feel her form and thus be reminded of the sumptuousness of other women. Maroula required no such delicacy in handling, even as he boosted her up onto the rocky little outcrop with a firm palm to the behind.

Though Dimitri had become a realist, he couldn't stop painting the icons or thinking of the stories from the Desert Fathers, the third- and fourth-century Greek mystics who lived as hermits in the Egyptian wilderness. He'd repeated them all his life since leaving his training in the monastery at fifteen. The stories weren't about God so much. Not anymore, not for him. They were all about the antics people performed to find God, the man with his hands wrapped in rags as he carried his mother a case in point. Or the one who drank only the water collected from sea sponges at night in the desert, cultivating a thirst he hoped would translate to spiritual desire. As time went on, Dimitri found himself experimenting with how far he could go before the icons he painted felt like desecrations.

One of Dimitri's favorite bits of wisdom from the Desert Fathers went like this: Abba Timothy said unto a certain brother, "How art thou?" The brother said unto him, "I destroy my days, O father." And the old man said, "My son, my days also are destroyed, and I give thanks."

Over time, however—and Dimitri had seen a lot of it pass— he had stopped giving thanks. His knees hurt and his hip worked like a grindstone. In Greece, people lived lives that were unnaturally long—it was painful to watch—and Dimitri was growing tired of his. The friends who remained seemed like contestants for Older Than God. At the café, he'd begun to teach Maroula how to handle things herself. Maroula was slow and not what you'd call friendly. She spoke little English, but she could take orders for meatballs and Greek salad and could count bottles at the end of the night and figure the bill now that they had a calculator, a gift from the Germans. His wife, Penelope, who had handled the cooking until a few years before, was no more. But there were younger women in the village who could cook and would be glad to have work. It just felt like it might be time for him to go.

When he was honest with himself, he knew he'd felt the pull for the past forty years. His mother, God rest her soul, had drowned when he was a boy. His son, who'd had so much promise, was dead in a motorcycle accident at the age of thirty-one. Now Dimitri felt just plain old. The previous morning, his birthday approaching, he'd made the awful discovery that for many years, he'd been mistaken about his own age—by a decade. He'd believed he was eighty-one, but in testing the new calculator, he had punched in the current year and subtracted the year of his birth and in vibrant green the number 90 had appeared. It was 1989. In August, his number would be up. Ninety! He had thought he knew how to do simple math and was still mentally acute, but this glaring sum brought his faculties into question.

Not to mention that the island was being taken over by tourists anyhow. First it was the Germans on their extended holidays. Now his café was becoming a regular Tower of Babel: Scandinavians who'd seen the island landscape in a movie, Brits extending their empire into holiday holdings. Thank God the Americans had stayed away! Let them have Naxos instead. He was Dimitri of the Last Resort. All used up and ready for an end. His mustache couldn't get any whiter, his beret any more drenched in sweat.

But finding time to die was another matter. There was always someone asking directions or wanting a Heineken or a photograph. It would be hard to give them the slip. He wanted to do what he needed to do without raising a ruckus. And when he was utterly honest with himself, he admitted he worried that his passing might be bad for business. These were the things he thought about sitting late one night in July on the terrace when the foreigners had gone to bed. "Maroula," he said. "Look up!" There were stars everywhere. Dimitri saw one shoot across the sky to the north. Maroula gazed upward but missed the next two or three that Dimitri pointed out. "It's the Perseids," he said. Maybe they were a sign. There were so many meteors that he didn't know how Maroula could miss them all. "Never mind," he said, relieving her of the failure to see. "It's finished, I think."

Call it grace if you are so inclined—what happened the next morning.

Dimitri parked the donkey in the shade of the only salt pine on the beach, tying it deftly. He called out to Maroula, who was testing the water with her sandals still on. She didn't know how to swim, and she rarely made it down to the sea from Hora, the village high up the mountain where they lived and kept the café. "Maroula, make up the palette like yesterday," he said. "Lots of Thalo and Prussian and the other blue. Cadmium and ochre over on the right. And don't get sand in it. Do you remember how it was yesterday?"

"Prussian on the right," she called, "but the words are all in German."

Dimitri held his breath for five seconds. "Blues on the left, Maroula; yellows on the right. I'll take care of the rest." The sun was climbing quickly, and Dimitri wanted an early morning sky. They'd told him down at the shop in the harbor where he sold the icons that people wanted more of the virgin saints, but also near water. It had come to that. Saints to order. On the rocks or straight up. So he was staging something he hoped might appeal. In yesterday's version, however, the result was very clearly Maroula. Candor but little reverence—as if the virgin were disappointed to find herself in that state. Now, he stood on the far side of the donkey, assembling the easel, thinking about how if what he painted didn't appeal it wouldn't much matter because he would soon be gone. Finished. Maroula sat on the rocks examining the colors inside the little tubes and squeezing them onto the palette. In his mind, Dimitri orchestrated a stumble in the course of which he might dash his brains out on a rock before toppling a short distance into the sea, thereby sparing Maroula the trouble of trying to haul him in for medical help. He didn't, however, want her to see his head bloodied. The trouble was that if he didn't hit his head, he'd be expected to climb back out of the water. He was old and arthritic in places but still strong. Hale, people said. Stronger than some of the younger men of the village, who played pinball rather than *tavli* and didn't know how to address a stubborn donkey or slaughter a goat. What's more, he knew how to swim. That's where his mind was when he heard Maroula exclaim, "Holy Mother of God!"

He put his hand to his forehead, wondering if he had inadvertently executed his plan. But he felt only the first sweat of the day. Setting the easel down in the sand, he hurried over to where she knelt on the rocks, peering into four feet of water. "Where's the palette?" he said.

She pointed to the sandy bottom, the undulation of the water doppling bright spots of paint. Dimitri took off his shirt and threw it onto the beach. He rolled his pants to the knee and waded out. The water was cool. He could not remember the last time he had entered the sea, though his son, Theo, had taught him to swim when Dimitri was in his middle age. Dimitri associated the sea with necessity. It was a source of food, or it was a background for Maroula, or it was a grave. He did not go to the sea for pleasure. Now, in July, the water was warm, its surface sleek and undisturbed. He hesitated. It was deeper than it looked. Giving up on keeping his pants dry, he took a few more steps. The water lapped at his privates and then at his waist. In the end, he tossed his beret onto the sand and submerged his body awkwardly. Like a turtle groping with appendages too short to reach bottom, he hovered, keeping his head just above the surface and peering down at the channels of white sand separating fields of Neptune grass. At last, he ducked under and retrieved the palette.

Upon returning to dry land, too wet and irritated now to paint at all, Dimitri looked another destroyed day in the face. He gazed up in dismay at the sky behind the mountain, still an early vacant gray touched with mauve. He bemoaned having passed up the opportunity to drown that had so neatly presented itself. Then, thinking these ruinous thoughts, he looked at the dripping palette in his hands while Maroula sulked on the rocks. The knobs of paint glistened, blue on the left, yellow on the right. He examined them, first with amazement (maybe his day wasn't destroyed) and then with curiosity. All thoughts of dying presently abated as he observed that the water beaded away from the paints. The oils and the water did not mix.

That was how Dimitri got the idea to go sub-marine.

It was as if his eye and his spirit had until then been misdirected ever so slightly, mistaking for their subject the human form in the foreground, when all along, the truer subject had been just behind it, and deeper.

There was a chance, of course, that if he went below, he might lose his religion altogether—what little was left of it. He might become an animist, believing that even sea grass had a soul. In any case, he found beauty in the backdrop. Dimitri gave thanks. Perhaps he wouldn't need the saints and the Virgin at all in these new paintings. He would need weights. A compressor and an air hose. And more than ever, he would need the help of Maroula. Faithful Maroula. Maroula Full of Grace.

5

BESIDE THE CANAL in Kreuzberg, the fronds of black willows hung in waves of heat like sea anemones. On her third day back in Berlin, Lyddie watched a group of one-legged women toss crusts of bread to the swans from their wheelchairs on the bank. The swans moved in fluidly, figuring the bony calculus of their necks into graceful curves as they glided to the crusts and devoured them, not acknowledging their patrons. Twenty-four vertebrae in the neck of the swan alone, Phelps had told her.

Not far from those great birds was the group of amputees parked in wheelchairs on the grassy bank. Each woman had one neatly stockinged leg, paralleled by an absence on the other side. Were they veterans of the war? Victims, merely? Everywhere in Berlin were these absences, these halvings.

The first two days, Lyddie had been lethargic and lonely. The place she'd subleased, in the upscale neighborhood around Charlottenburg Palace, was trim and contemporary in its furnishings, one wall dominated by black bookshelves. A brightly woven area rug staked out the living space, leaving wide margins of parquet flooring. At night, no curtains softened the black expanse of glass looking back at her, though during the day there was a lot of light.

Much to Ray's dismay, Lyddie had closed up the house in Buffalo—the house Phelps's parents had left to him—and had put the contents of the greenhouse in the care of a friend of Phelps, a professor of botany at the University of Buffalo. On their small savings, if she was careful, she could live until a month or two before the baby was due. Then she'd have to return to a life dominated by job applications and diapers.

Lyddie had pictured little beyond the time she would present herself at Sabina's door and be welcomed like a vision from the past. Welcomed with something that felt unconditional, as if by the sister she'd never had. She was no longer the naïve person she had been when Sabina first knew her. She would sit with Sabina in that divided city and tell her all the unorthodox things she had been thinking. You could not shock Sabina. Nothing frightened her.

But what if Sabina had moved on? What if all of them had? Things that had been unimaginable even a few months before were happening in East Germany. In early May, the Hungarians had opened a segment of the Iron Curtain and all summer long, East Germans pretending to go on holiday in Communist Hungary were escaping into Austria through that hole, often unimpeded by the border guards. Since Erich Honecker's illness in early July, the numbers had risen to nearly two hundred a day. East Germany was hemorrhaging its citizens. The Berliners Lyddie knew, with their ties to the East, might have been affected by these upheavals—or by any of the forces that rearranged lives.

So for two days after her arrival, Lyddie had ridden the U-Bahn aimlessly, afraid that her attempts to reconnect would be a failure and she would not then have any idea what to do. Lyddie had also not anticipated that the most present memories for her in Berlin would be those of Phelps—there in every scene she entered: drinking a beer at the counter of the tiny Indian restaurant near her flat, or showing her the boarded-up stops on the U-Bahn where the tracks still threaded swatches of the East to the West. Now she imagined that rather than the guard stationed there, it was Phelps looking out at her from the lit booth at Stadt Mitte, where the trains passed but no longer stopped. Phelps gone underground, inaccessible, watching her act against his will.

Finally, on the third day, Lyddie went to the flat where Sabina had lived in 1985. Someone there gave her an address in Kreuzberg, a neighborhood that was home to artists, punks, Turkish immigrants, and young bohemians. It was the neighborhood where Phelps had lived with Lothar. Leaving the swans, she walked along the canal, following the map to Forster Strasse, where she rang the buzzer at street level. The door clicked open and she climbed two flights of stairs. When Sabina saw her standing in the hallway, she shrieked with delight and amazement. She pulled Lyddie inside and kissed her on one cheek and then the other, seeming genuinely happy to see her. "I cannot believe it! Lydia!" she said in English. "My God! Can it be true?"

"You're more beautiful than ever!" Lyddie said in German. Four years had given Sabina a look of experience, of having grown into her sensuality. Her hair, blonder than before, fell loosely around her face, barely touching her shoulders. She wore a pair of black cloth Mary Janes with leggings and a skirt.

"Come!" Sabina said, "Lyddie, sit down." Having won the battle of the languages decisively, she went to the sink and ran water for tea. "We shall eat something together and you must tell me everything!" Lyddie relaxed into Sabina's welcome. The kitchen she entered was a study in ingenuity and open storage. Pan lids, coffee cups and mixers scaled the walls on pegs rigged as if by a convoy of veteran climbers. A system of pulleys made accessible the provisions floating overhead in baskets of wire mesh.

"The last time I saw you, I thought you never would return to *Ber*lin, Sabina said, emphasizing the first syllable of the city's name. Despite her best efforts, Lyddie had been unable to convince her that was not the way Americans pronounced it.

"It's strange to think that life has gone on here, the whole time I've been away," Lyddie said. "Do you still see Lothar? And your brother? Siegfried? How is Siegfried?" But before Sabina could answer, Lyddie spotted beside the entryway a pair of small red shoes. "Sabina, you have a child?" she said in disbelief.

"Ulla. She has three years and a half now," Sabina said. "It is a long time since we met us, you and I."

"Why, that's lovely!" Lyddie exclaimed, tears springing to her eyes.

"You are sentimental," Sabina said. "Still!"

"But it is wonderful, isn't it?" Lyddie insisted. She resisted looking at Sabina's hand for a ring. Sabina had always thought marriage a vestige of the 1950s.

"You'll meet her. She will come home soon. She goes to the American kindergarten. I want her to learn American English. And Phelps?" Sabina asked. "He is here with you? You are married with him still?" Lyddie hesitated. In a space beneath the counter next to the porcelain sink, a bite-sized washing machine accomplished its task in frothy, spasmodic surges, alternating with periods of hermetic rest.

"Oh, Sabina," Lyddie said. "It is not a happy story."

"Tell me," Sabina said.

So Lyddie told her what had happened—how the Kurdish villages had been leveled as part of Hussein's ethnic cleansing campaign and how she'd heard Phelps may have been there, over the border from Turkey. He'd been visiting a Kurdish medicine man when the men were rounded up and shot, the women and children taken off to camps, the village itself bulldozed that afternoon. No one had heard from him in months.

Sabina shook her head in disbelief. "You and Phelps," she said. I always thought you were very lucky. Meant for one another."

That seemed a pretty romantic notion for Sabina. Lyddie remembered the brutal love poem she and Lothar had shared, the one he had attempted to translate with its violent airport scene. Lyddie had loved Phelps, and her life with him had been more happy than not. But maybe every romance had its terrible awakening. And she had left not knowing if Phelps was dead or alive.

"I waited so long for some word of him," Lyddie said. "And then, Sabina, I don't know what happened. I just couldn't wait any more. I began to think about where my life had left off when Phelps came along, here in Berlin." Though Lyddie was judging herself even as she spoke, she hoped Sabina would not judge her. She knew Sabina could not be shocked. "I know there are women who wait decades for their men to return. Women who don't leave the house. Do you think I'm awful for being here?"

"It is what you did, Lyddie. It isn't awful." Sabina got up from the table, poured the hot water, and put the teapot on a silver tray. She laid out the teacups and cloth napkins on the table as she had so many times before. These rituals of hers were a way of stemming the chaos.

"I hope not," Lyddie said thoughtfully. "But meant for each other... If these things are intended, who is it that intends them?" Sabina laid a large hunk of chocolate on the table and began to cut an apple. "I've thought a lot about the idea of parallel lives," Lyddie said. "All of the possible existences for each of us. Is it possible to leap from one to another, as if they went on simultaneously, with or without you? This life here—I left it four years ago." Unsettled, Lyddie stood and walked into the hallway, looking at the cherubs Sabina had spray-painted gold that populated the high walls with nouveau Victorian grace. So strange a decor for someone as irreverent as Sabina. "And then, of course," Lyddie continued from beyond the kitchen, "if you believe we were meant for each other, you also have to believe Phelps was 'meant' to die. And that all of the children, too, who have been exterminated—there and here…"

"T'tis horrible," Sabina said, barely voicing the i as she contracted the words in the lilting, Irish-sounding way Lyddie remembered. Sabina poured tea for both of them. Then the door to the stairwell burst open and in ran little Ulla, whom Sabina's flat mate, Sylvie, had picked up at the Kindergarten on her way home from work. Sabina caught the little girl up and kissed her head. Ulla turned shyly to look at Lyddie. "*Kannst du 'hallo" sagen?*" Sabina said, putting the child down and pulling out a chair. She set a plate of apples, sprinkled with raw sugar, in front of Ulla.

Ulla said in German, "I want chocolate. I'm not tired."

"You must first eat your apples and then if you will promise to rest for a bit right after, without crying, you may have chocolate too," Sabina replied.

Lyddie admired the way Sabina arranged the universe of Ulla and the apples, setting into motion the laws that would govern it. There was something about her in her kitchen that inspired confidence, an ability Lyddie wondered if she herself would ever possess. How would she become the one with the answers? How would the child not see her uncertainty? Her ambivalence? Lyddie burst into tears. "What is it?" Sabina said. "Lyddie?"

Lyddie bit her lip to stifle her crying. She had made the decision to come to Berlin not out of desperation but out of the strength that had come over her that night in the greenhouse. Now it eluded her. "I'm going to be a mother," she said, stammering on the last word. "I didn't mean to announce it like this. Even Phelps didn't know," Lyddie said sadly. "Doesn't."

Sabina handed her a napkin. "How many months?" she said gently.

"Three and a half."

"And how long since Phelps is gone?"

"It is his child," Lyddie said.

"Do you want the child?" Rising and going to the sink with the cups, Sabina asked this question with utter openness to the possibility that Lyddie did not. She ran the water over a dishcloth.

"Phelps wanted it," Lyddie said, drying her eyes and looking intently at Sabina, who returned to the table.

"And you think you will betray Phelps or the memory of Phelps to make an abortion," Sabina said, wiping the table as efficiently as a waiter.

"I've seen too many photographs of dead babies in the last two months. As I waited for Phelps to be found, the baby kept growing. By the time I gave up on his coming home, it had eyelids and ears and a bony little bottom. Sabina, I feel completely betrayed by my body."

"By your body or by Phelps?" Sabina asked.

Lyddie looked steadily at Sabina, who had an instinct for the right questions. Which also felt, at the moment, like the wrong questions. "I don't know," Lyddie said. She was reminded that Sabina had been closer to Phelps than to her. "Maybe I can't talk this way right now," she said. Even if talking that way were what she had come for.

Ulla's apples lay untouched on the plate, but Sabina got the bar of milk chocolate out of the basket. She broke a large square off for Ulla; then she offered a piece to Lyddie and took one herself. Ulla got up and ran into the other room.

"You said she is three?" Lyddie asked.

"Nearly."

"And Lothar? Are you seeing him still?"

"Sometimes," Sabina said, ambiguously. "He will be shocked to hear about Phelps."

Is Lothar Ulla's father?" Lyddie asked.

Sabina hesitated, as if that were a question requiring deliberation. "For now, I suppose."

Lyddie's relief in speaking the truth to Sabina was already being eroded by discomfort as she recognized from the past this feeling that Sabina's stories ended just where they should begin.

BACK AT THE FLAT on Kaiser-Friedrich-Strasse, Lyddie looked at the clothes she had not yet removed from the suitcase in the bedroom. And the orange paisley duvet cover someone else had chosen. This room was not really her life and she was thankful for that. The box of books on the Bauhaus were mostly to make what she'd told Ray less of a lie—that she'd come to work on the unfinished thesis. Beauty and utility. Both concepts seemed foreign to her now. Nothing was so beautiful as the time before the incomprehensible present. When anything might have happened and the world was all possibility. Where was the utility in that?

Her meeting with Sabina had reminded her of the near miss their friendship had always been. Somehow she had imagined they would have outgrown their differences. She had forgotten how easy it was for Sabina to pull the curtain across her own experience just after she'd prompted you to expose your every weakness and uncertainty. It was true that Lyddie felt somewhat betrayed by Phelps, but that was for her to say. Not for Sabina to tell her. And *for now* Lothar was the father of Sabina's child? What did that mean? Sabina *supposed* Lothar was the father? Sabina was like the person who says "Hey, let's all take off our clothes and jump into freezing water on the count of three," and then you do it and shriek at the shock of it and look back and she's standing there dry and still at least mostly clothed, thinking what conformist fools you all are. The message? You're a free agent. Ultimately on your own. Lyddie remembered shopping with Sabina at Hennes and Mauritz and making the mistake of asking her opinion of a skirt or a scarf. Sabina's response was a shrug. "You're the one who has to dress it," she said.

But it was the matter of betrayal that gnawed at Lyddie. Phelp's disappearance had somehow made her come to doubt so many things about him. All his silences began to resemble Sabina's withholdings. Because if there were a few things she didn't and wouldn't know, how many more might there be? For instance: three-and-a-half years old. Sabina's child would have been conceived when Lyddie and Phelps were in Berlin. Lyddie wasn't aware that Sabina had been seeing anyone other than Lothar back then, though that relationship had been unstable, to say the least. Sabina's telling her that she and Phelps were "meant for each other" made her wonder, perversely, if there had ever been anything between Phelps and Sabina, who were so clearly not meant for each other. Lyddie had envied their closeness, at a time when she herself had had to work at being Sabina's friend. She'd found herself in the odd position of being the beneficiary of Sabina's multiple kindnesses but at the same time wondering if Sabina even really liked her. She'd found herself wanting the approval of a person she didn't fully admire. Phelps, on the other hand, had managed to be close to Sabina almost completely in spite of their mutual disapproval. Was it sex that made that possible? Or merely attraction? Was it enough that they were keepers of the same secrets? Lyddie always felt the two of them had decided how much to tell her about Axel.

A COUPLE OF DAYS AFTER Lyddie visited Sabina, the two women went, along with Ulla and Sabina's half-brother, Siegfried, to meet the others at the site of the old Görlitzer Bahnhof. Despite the fact that her own mother had made a living as a dancer in a strip joint, Sabina had an aristocrat's way of assembling the company of her friends and ex-lovers around her. This time, they brought with them poster board and spray cans to make signs for a demonstration against Coca Cola, which Sabina said had supported nearly every fascist regime it had encountered. It had supported Apartheid, and it had traveled with the Nazi troops, turning soft drink plants into Nazi Coke factories, kidnapping men and women to work in them. Sabina told her these things as she threw an old damask bedspread down on a patch of clover and laid out the stemware. No trains came to the station anymore and weeds trundled over the dirt. Ulla ran onto the spread in her dirty shoes and dug around in the picnic basket for the chocolate she knew she'd find there.

"*Nein, Ulla,*" said Siegfried. His voice was a high-pitched whine. He was nineteen and what Sabina called "simple."

"It's OK, Siegfried," Sabina said. "Here. We'll take her shoes off." Siegfried helped with the shoes and Ulla danced around on the spread before scampering off into the dirt in her socks. "*Nein!*" Siegfried cried. "Ulla!"

Sabina gave Siegfried a can of spray paint and sent him a few yards away to work on a sign.

Sauntering up to the group along with a friend Lyddie didn't know, Lothar flashed Lyddie one of his sheepish grins. Lyddie laughed. It was almost miraculously wonderful to see him again, this character from a place that had felt impossibly distant. Lothar embraced her. Afterward, as always, he looked mildly uncomfortable, his right arm hanging at an awkward angle from the elbow when he released her and stepped back. His face had lost none of its angelic quality, though he was thinner, not at all pudgy. Less a cherub than at twenty-five. He said, "How does it feel to be back in Berlin? How long is it? Three years? Or four, it must be. You will admire my excellent English. I have studied much since you were here." Lyddie told him what a success the exhibition had been in the States, said she was sorry he'd not been able to make it for the opening.

"*Hallo, Kristof,*" Sabina cried happily as Lothar's friend bent to kiss her on the cheek. "And Lothar," she added with equanimity. "Nice of you to come." Her tone forked deftly between the two men. The tension between Lothar and Sabina was more pronounced than when Lyddie had known them before, but almost comically familiar. Kristof stepped forward and offered his hand. "Pleasure to meet you, Lyddie," he said, his face relaxing into the deep lines around his mouth. Then he walked over toward Siegfried and set down an armload of one-by-twos and a staple gun.

Lothar settled at the outer edge of the blanket near Ulla in a way that suggested he had come to the gathering out of no love for Sabina, but rather for the child's sake. "Lyddie," he said in German, "I'm sorry to hear about Phelps."

"Hallo, Axel," Sabina called, as the latter approached, carrying a small boom box and fussing to secure its trailing cord.

Surprised to hear Axel's name, Lyddie said in the German that still came easily to her, "How is life for you, Lothar?" Out of the corner of her eye, she saw Sabina smiling at Axel, her full lips revealing the narrow channel and the naked bit of gum between her front teeth. Lyddie had the uncomfortable feeling that Sabina had just taken off the first bit of her clothing.

The percussive rattle of spray cans and the smell of paint drifted in and settled around them. Lyddie was not ready to see Axel, who had always been on the periphery; she had not expected that he would be included in the gathering. She got up and walked over to see Siegfried's sign. It said SCHEISSE. Shit.

In an old pair of flannel trousers and a discolored white shirt with a pointed collar, Lothar worked the dirt with a stick, listening idly to Sabina's two-edged small talk. No sooner had Axel sat down than he popped a tape into the player and the box broadcast what sounded to Lyddie like a discordant series of squawks and groans. "Hello," Lyddie said to Axel.

Against Axel's silence, and seeing Lyddie's expression, Lothar said, "It's Schoenberg. The fourth string quartet. It is— how do you say?—an acquired hunger."

Coolly and with authority, Axel pointed out, "He is using a structure with no tonal center, no reference to key."

"I've heard Schoenberg before," Lyddie said, "here in Berlin, at the Philharmonie. I went with you, Sabina. And Lothar, remember? Or maybe it was Phelps." Maybe it was Axel's lack of greeting that made his choice of music seem so passive aggressive. Or maybe Lyddie had just been away from Berlin too long to remember how things were.

"The music, it is highly expressive, though unpredictable," Axel said, letting his eyes come to rest on her face for a moment.

"'Tis interesting, don't you think?" Sabina said, putting down her spray can to run after Ulla, who had darted off in the direction of some strangers playing cricket.

Axel seemed to wait for Lyddie to answer. He didn't go on, so Lothar took over since Lyddie must have looked increasingly ill at ease. "The music is not sentimental. It has no melody. No plot."

Lyddie understood well enough. Whatever Schoenberg lacked, he was equipped for survival. The music was raw. It looked you in the face and stabbed you in the sternum without the swell of feeling that would be a kind of apology. Only the ravaged cawing of the violins. Axel seemed to think she might appreciate that. Maybe he had meant to demonstrate her ignorance about such things. To suggest she was some kind of emotional dwarf, existing in the fettered tonality of the plot she had chosen to live. But what had she expected from him? She had, after all, left him in the dark, never having explained her decision to return to the States with Phelps. Either way, he seemed like a different person than the one with whom she had spent the night at Amerika Haus. Was it her own unpredictability he had meant to suggest?

"It calls for crème brûleé," said Sabina in an open attempt to defuse the tensions around her. She opened the basket and laid several ramekins out on the blanket. Then, sitting on the spread, one leg tucked beneath her, she pulled out a small torch and began waving it over the tops to caramelize the sugar she'd sprinkled there. Lyddie looked at Lothar's face, studying the upturned nose, which was, indeed, the most like Ulla's of all the noses present. The wide, lax neck of Sabina's shirt flirted with the curve of her shoulder, and Lyddie noticed for the first time the scar tissue on her chest, like the skin that formed on scalded milk. Lothar scarcely looked at Sabina, though everything he said seemed in some subversive way to be addressed to her or against her. Maybe they were "friends" now, not lovers anymore. It wasn't easy to tell the difference.

The string quartet played on, its stabbing rhythms giving way to something more tentative and disquieting, something that plucked at any remaining confidence on Lyddie's part that she could ever know anything for sure. "I prefer

Beethoven," Kristof said. His smile, broadening into the outer reaches of his mouth, involved his eyes as well.

"Romantic," Lothar said, scornfully.

"Is anyone going to the *Spektak* at Wansee tonight?" Kristof asked. "There will be a light show on the water and the Philharmonic will play music from Sibelius.

"It has not interesting to me," Lothar said dismissively.

"I might like to go," Lyddie said.

"Maybe that's enough Schoenberg," Sabina said to Axel. Axel looked irritated, but he turned the tape player off.

They sat awhile, enjoying relief from both the music and the heat as the sun dropped and evening came on. Lothar and Kristof told about how they had worked as sappers, paid by the piece for locating and dismantling unexploded munitions in the very field where they were sitting. Lyddie found it strange that the war had been so long before but that the city was still recovering. She said so, and Kristof asked Lyddie if she had been to the East.

"Just once, a few years ago. I went to see Lemke house, designed by Mies Van der Rohe."

"Then you know that this is nothing in comparison. Parts of the East look like they were bombed last week. No one really cares, it seems. Or maybe it just suits the Eastern psyche to live among the ruins," Lothar said.

"Van der Rohe was a Nazi, wasn't he?" Kristof commented.

"That depends," Lyddie said, "on who you talk to."

Kristof said that the problem with trying to figure out anything that went on in Berlin as long ago as 1935 was that all the evidence left behind had been distorted by subsequent degradations.

"It's like interviewing the maggot on the life of the fly," Lothar said in German, smirking.

"Maggots. An attractive metaphor for who we are," Axel said, breaking his silence in English, as if to be certain Lyddie had the benefit of his sarcasm.

Lyddie replied, "I'm sure there are economic issues. But maybe the Eastern psyche prefers ruins to the new Brutalist architecture. Some of that stuff out near Marzahn is pretty incredibly awful."

"Axel, you know the Eastern psyche," Lothar said. What do you say?"

"The Eastern psyche doesn't need an American to analyze it."

It was quiet for a moment while all of them processed the insult.

"Do you say that in the spirit of Brutalism or only in the spirit of cruel commentary?" Kristof asked. In Phelps's absence, he was the kind one among them.

"Look," Lothar said. "Maybe, you know, because Phelps is lost and Lyddie is sad, you can treat just a bit more easy the Americans. Or Lyddie, at least."

Despite the Schoenberg, Lyddie hadn't been prepared for Axel's lashing out at her so directly. She felt cancelled by it, even though she was the one who had cancelled their intimacy. She felt suddenly that she wanted to defend Phelps against this assault. As if it were directed at him. Or maybe it hurt her less to think of it that way.

Axel poured himself some grappa and then turned and raised his glass, not toward Sabina or any of them, but away, into the setting sun, squinting to examine its contents in the light.

"I want some," cried Ulla, jumping up from Lothar's lap and reaching for the glass.

"Not for you, Ulla!" cried Siegfried.

"Look," said Axel, addressing the child. "We'll have our own Spectak. Ulla, hold it for me, very steady. And watch." He grabbed the little torch from the spread and, flicking it, waved a flame over the surface of the liqueur. Ulla, in her surprise and delight, shifted suddenly and a blue gauze of flame wrapped her hand. Too stunned to move again, she stood transfixed, while Lyddie and the others seemed to weigh, against the fact of Ulla's being, herself, on fire, the potential for the blanket and perhaps the entire field to go up in flames if she dropped the glass. Then Lothar leapt up and knocked the glass from Ulla's hand at the same time that she began to shriek. He smothered her hand in the damask spread while Axel trampled the flames that were springing up.

What happened next was hard for Lyddie to decipher, since everyone was shouting at everyone else in German over the awful noise of Ulla's pain. Axel's big hands hung help-less at his sides while Sabina shouted at him to do something. Lothar wanted Sabina to stop shouting. He spoke in a quiet, controlled voice, addressing first the child and then Sabina. Kristof groaned as he saw the blisters pucker on Ulla's hand. Lyddie rummaged through the picnic basket in a futile search for first aid. When she looked up, she saw Axel backing from the scene one slow step at a time. It was his expression that star-tled her: the intractable look of a man in a photograph some-one shows you—a friend or a brother, perhaps, who died in his late twenties. It was a look Axel often had. He stared directly into the face of the world without apology, as if he—maybe all of them—were beyond culpability, and beyond the capacity to intervene for the good. Seeing that look made Lyddie afraid of him again. She had no idea who he was, really, or what he had done. In the end, Axel disappeared, and Sabina, refusing Lothar's help, insisted on carrying Ulla back to the house her-self with the aid of Siegfried alone, who took along the basket of untouched crème brûlée.

6

SABINA BANDAGED THE BURNS on Ulla's hand and told her she was brave, like a performer in the circus. Lyddie wondered openly what Axel had been thinking, to give a child a glass of burning alcohol. But as he reviewed the events of that afternoon, Lothar couldn't see that Axel was really to blame. He had merely wanted Ulla to see the flame's magic. To give her the pleasure of holding it in her own hand. Lothar said, "Axel— whatever he does, he acts out of a place deep inside of him, and then he gets a shock about what happens on the outside because of what he did."

Lyddie observed, nonetheless, that she seemed to bring out the worst in Axel. Lothar argued that Axel was irritable not with Lyddie in particular but with everyone because so many Ossies had defected in the past few years, and now more were pouring out of the country and into West Germany through the hole in Hungary's fence. For reasons none of them fully understood, Axel had been forced into exile in the West by the

East German authorities soon after Lothar's arrest. Still, he had no desire to return.

Now, after eight years, Axel and Lothar still kept the company of artists and writers they'd known in the East who had also found a way out in the early eighties. But even before the Hungarian breach of the Iron Curtain, in the past year or two, the East Germans had loosened control over emigration. Axel wasn't the only one of the earlier wave who resented the presence of the new Ossies in West Berlin. Others like him thought they had left the East behind for good. Now it was following them. And even though the latest wave of those who had left through Hungary was unlikely to reach West Berlin, an island of the free world surrounded by East Germany, many found the surge unsettling.

Sabina said Lothar didn't understand Axel, though he had known him all those years. She said Axel's behavior had little to do with the immigrations. He had a persecution complex, because he was a Jew, on his mother's side. He thought everyone was persecuting him—even the Americans.

Lyddie told Sabina she supposed Axel had a right to be angry with her. She wasn't sure how much Sabina knew about the events leading up to her departure four years earlier, though she suspected Phelps had told her. Sabina said only, "Don't flatter yourself."

Lothar said it wasn't a complex when you'd actually been persecuted. Then he wanted to know what Lyddie meant. Why would Axel be angry?

Sabina said Axel had not been persecuted. His grandmother had.

Lyddie thought but refrained from saying that Phelps's being dead, or most likely so, should earn them both a reprieve from Axel's resentment.

She learned that though Axel's grandmother was dead, his

mother still lived in the East. Axel saw her once every year or two at a rest stop on the access highway between Berlin and West Germany. According to Lothar, Axel's mother had tried to persuade Axel to look for his grandfather, the father she never knew. She thought he might live in West Berlin. In a country whose recent history made digging into the past for anything a painful exercise, the whole business added to Axel's agitation.

Sabina was quiet when Lothar talked about the East. It was admittedly beyond her expertise.

"Did something bad happen to Axel in the East?" Lyddie said.

"Something bad?" Lothar said. "Did anything good ever happen in the East? Life for Axel was no worse than for the rest of us," he said. "But he always wanted to prove to himself that the system couldn't keep from him anything that he really needed. So he needed less and less. He'd go around with no socks in the winter. He'd sleep with the windows open, or close them when it was warm. Once his Trabi was in the repair in Prenzlauerberg for six or seven months, waiting for a donor clutch to materialize because, you know, Axel wouldn't give them anything to make it appear. He offered them poems and they laughed at him. That devastated Axel—that they could make him so powerless. Make what he did so worthless. If you had known him when we were nineteen, then you might understand him now, at least a little."

Maybe that was all Lyddie wanted. To understand Axel just a little. She didn't want to have to trust Phelps's judgment of him or Sabina's. Alone now, she wanted to learn to trust herself. And while she really disliked the reactionary Axel, she couldn't forget the boy Axel who worried that his father believed it was his birthday when it wasn't. The boy afraid to be given something for nothing. Or the man who told Fathers of the Desert stories about deprivation and desire.

Doubtful that she'd ever understand Axel, and not about to

excuse his callous behavior, Lyddie spent her days reading the notes she'd collected for her research on Gropius. She reviewed the three chapters she'd drafted during her time at the Free University four years before. Though earnest in their probing of Gropius's sensibility as it translated to his architecture, they felt oddly like juvenilia to her, as did her entire fascination with the Bauhaus. Thumbing through the unfinished thesis was something to do to make being alone not so tiresome and pathetic. Like smoking cigarettes, which she tried not to do more than once in a while on account of the pregnancy, though she liked the way the smoke abraded her lungs, helping her to get to the bottom of what was inside.

When she called Ray at home, there was no word on Phelps. The State Department was admitting now that it could be years before any remains could be exhumed from mass graves and identified in Iraq. The Iraqi officials were still denying that any such sites existed. Lyddie excavated them each night in her sleep.

LYDDIE GOT OUT OF THE cab and walked the wrong way in the dark, coming not to the gallery where Lothar and Axel's show was opening but to the end of Potsdamer Strasse, she encountered the Wall, and on it a sign scrawled in German that read STOP—FREEDOM ENDS HERE. Beyond the Wall, the light from the neutral zone semaphored up through a fine mist. There was little left of Potsdamer Platz, the frenetic center of Berlin at a time before the second World War when Einstein and Garbo might have shared a table at a café, or Gropius might have seen Schoenberg at the opening night of *The Threepenny Opera.* Lyddie lingered a moment, feeling oddly as though she might be willing to sacrifice some of her freedom to go beyond that point again—to stay awhile and see what the world looked

like from over there. Then she turned and walked the other
way a couple of blocks until she saw the lit sign for the gallery.
Axel and Lothar stood outside the open door, smoking intently.
Lothar looked like a terrorist, having no doubt tended to his own
hair that morning with his canvas-cutting knife. He was forever
trying to get one friend or another to cut his blonde curls. "Ah,
Lydia. You have come," he said. His mouth puckered outward
when he spoke.

"Are you avoiding your critics?" she asked, peering inside.

"We know we are for now, just, and after us will follow nothing so good for talking about," he said in English, his mouth
turned in a nervous smile.

"Brilliant," Lyddie said.

"Brecht," Axel said to Lyddie, and then to Lothar, "Another
awful translation. Why must you do it?"

So Axel did have a memory.

"And for Brecht," Axel added, "we, Lothar and I, are the nothing—'nothing so good for talking about'—since we came after."

When Lyddie stopped inside to pour herself some wine,
their watching at her back sent a millipede of sensation up
her spine. In front of her, five or six feet high, the first canvas
groped out of a dark, amorphous lower stratum into something of form and color, suggesting trees. As Lyddie's eyes
grew accustomed to the dimness of line, she saw in the subter-
fuge of the darker part the shapes of human bones ordered as
if catalogued beneath the ground. Like an illustration of the
dreams that had troubled her sleep. This was Axel's work—she
didn't have to see the placard to know. Nor did it seem strange
that he should tap into her psyche that way.

At last she turned to look back at the doorway, but Axel and
Lothar were gone.

In another of Axel's paintings, a woman wearing an apron

poured something into a great void, past tired images that dis-
integrated as one looked down. The saucers and cups and the
table sank into some dark mouth at the bottom of the canvas,
as if they were being swallowed. The woman pouring seemed
casually unafraid or unaware of the chasm to which her pouring connected her. Lyddie considered the somewhat oblivious
domestic pleasure she had taken in her life with Phelps. The silent dark of the painting was corrosive, like Axel's scorn, leaving
intact just enough of beauty to be elegiac.

Lothar's work, in the second room, was more abstract, using
bold color and geometric shapes mixed with playfully rendered
artifacts of contemporary life: a fish tank, a bicycle, a tire iron,
a tube of lipstick. Rather than trivializing those items, it made
them somewhat holy, as he often christened the shapes with pale
aureoles or even gold leaf.

The small gallery began to grow warm with the heat of bodies and breath. A group of East Germans Lyddie had not seen
before strolled past, laughing too loudly. Lyddie had learned
from Sabina that Ossies were easy to identify in their overzeal-
ous attempt at assimilation—the women in short skirts and vinyl
"fashion" boots that made them look like dancers in a club, the
relatively short men in off-brand blue jeans hemmed by hand.

Lyddie completed the circuit of the gallery and, feeling
somehow exposed, as if Axel were reading her, she wanted to
congratulate him and Lothar quickly and then go. She moved
toward the door, beside which the two men sat at a table talking.
Lyddie waited for an opening.

"So you are going to read?" Lothar was saying to Axel.

Axel took from the pocket of his coat one of his own books
and began to thumb through it in the brighter light over the
guest register; it fell open to a worn black-and-white photograph. He seemed surprised to find it there.

"Axel?" Lothar said.

"Take that, please," Axel said. He did not hand the photograph to Lothar but sat frozen, awaiting intervention. Lothar protested, but Axel's way of speaking without looking at him had a compelling effect. Lothar took the photograph from where it was cradled in the crease of the book.

"And… ?" he asked gently.

"Put it away," Axel said. He looked up from the page at Lothar.

Lothar took the photo and put it in his pocket. "Axel. Let's go have a smoke. I think you need one." They stepped outside and Lyddie followed, wishing there were more than one way out of the gallery. Axel scrutinized Lothar. "You have cut your hair like Beelzebub's brother," he said, shifting to English. "Has he not, Lyddie? What is your verdict?"

Snagged by what might be an invitation for her to join their conversation and what might be another barb suggesting what Axel perceived as her tendancy to judge, Lyddie hung in the doorway. Lothar, leaning against the railing, drew deeply on his cigarette and smirked. From inside came the sound of laughter and conversation. Axel nodded, indicating the new Ossies, who were refilling their wine glasses liberally. He said, "They arrive as if they are joining an artists' local. As if we'll all give them kisses and ateliers and rejoice that they have come over on just a complaint or two. We're supposed to applaud that."

"The thing is, Axel… " Lothar hesitated and began again. "It doesn't matter to me personally what you say or do. You are my friend, always. But not everyone is as happily insulted as I am." He stopped again and rolled the cuff of his shirt thoughtfully. "You cannot write everyone off. I won't let you. You cannot live by mistrust." He glanced at Lyddie.

"I don't mistrust them," Axel said, referring to the newcomers. "I merely detest them."

Bewildered, and wounded again by Axel's scathing judgments, though they had not this time been directed at her, Lyddie looked from Axel to Lothar. "Congratulations," she said weakly. Then, raising her umbrella, she hurried down the steps and fled into the rain that had begun to solder the sky to the ground.

7

A FEW DAYS AFTER HER VISIT to the gallery, Lyddie went to Axel's flat in Wedding. He buzzed her in at street level and she found the inside door open. "May I enter?" she asked, peering in cautiously.

"Please yourself," he said, returning to the armchair where he had apparently been reading. He took a pouch of tobacco and papers from the pocket of his shirt and rolled a cigarette.

Staying close to the doorway, she said, "I don't know whether you mistrust me or merely detest me. But I've come to apologize, Axel." She walked to the window, beyond which the working-class district stretched out in unrelieved sameness.

"Have you ever, in your beautiful life, done anything worth apologizing for?" he said, mildly amused.

She said, "I'm tired of your theories of my innocence. I know I acted badly when I left here three years ago and didn't explain."

"You found a life for yourself, Lyddie. Perhaps you've discovered the freedom of having no allegiances."

Allegiances. The last time Lyddie had spoken that word was in a pledge to the American flag. "I didn't owe you any allegiance. What can you even mean by that?" Axel's living room was small and void of decor, setting in sharp relief the ratty orange armchair in the corner and the TV tray sporting a dead philodendron.

"No. Of course you didn't. On that we agree."

"But that doesn't mean I don't have any."

"So, you do?" Axel said. "To whom?"

Lyddie was silent. She couldn't really say "to Phelps," having presented herself at the flat of the man he had warned her to avoid. Having left home without evidence that Phelps was dead. Hadn't it occurred to her that she might go to Iraq to search for him?

"I need to use the bathroom," she said, feeling her chest tighten and wanting to remove herself from Axel's scrutiny.

Axel hesitated, and Lyddie followed his gaze to the closed door down the hall. "Can you wait?" he said.

She looked at him in disbelief. Just as she was going to ask if the bathroom were in use, she heard a scratching sound at the door, and a whining.

Axel looked at his watch. "You can help. Work off some of your innocence." He went to the door and opened it, at which point a longhaired beige mutt darted out and leapt up onto the couch and then the desk, knocking over a stack of books and sending papers in every direction.

"Christ!" Axel said, lunging for the dog as it jumped over the back of the armchair. It slid from his grasp and raced down the hall. He cornered it in the bathroom again and picked it up. "Grab the leash," he said, heading for the door to the landing. "We're going for a walk."

The street of the working class neighborhood was lined with tenements. A stronghold of Communism before the war,

Wedding remained one of the poorest areas of the city. Axel opened the driver's side door of the white Trabant parked at the curb and held the dog while Lyddie got in on the passenger's side. "I thought we were walking the dog," she said. She reached over to pet the animal and it nipped at her. Axel tossed it into the back where it sprawled on the seat, and he turned the key in the ignition.

They drove for a few blocks in silence, past empty lots and massive postwar concrete apartment blocks, a landscape in grays. "Your dog is not very friendly," Lyddie said, examining her hand.

"She's not my dog," Axel said.

Lyddie smiled at the Monty Python allusion, but realized quickly that it was unintended. Axel didn't smile. "Whose dog is she?" Lyddie asked.

"My neighbor's." He pulled the car to the curb in front of a butcher shop.

"What are we doing?"

"You are going to help me find my lost grandfather, Gerdot. My mother now believes he may live in West Berlin." Axel explained that he had found four possibilities in the telephone directory. He referred to them as Gerdots I, II, III and IV.

"Why don't you just call them up?"

"He was a Nazi, to whom my grandmother, a Jew, was prostituted," Axel said. "If I were he, I would not admit to a stranger on the telephone that I was the man in question." Axel said he had thought it better to try to observe each of the Gerdots in a preliminary way, in hopes that some distinguishing feature would confirm an identity. Or something would disqualify the man—age, perhaps. The first Gerdot had, indeed, been too young, in his early forties by Axel's calculations. The second Gerdot—that was a story. "After the second Gerdot, I thought

I might give up," Axel said. He stopped at a cross street and looked at Lyddie intently.

"What?" she said.

"Nothing," he replied. "I became distracted. You know. With questions and uncertainties. But now I've decided to finish." He told her that the size of Gerdot III's hand as he worked the key on the mailbox and leafed through a stack of envelopes at the post office had been impressive. And his age seemed about right. So now Axel was ready for the next phase of his program.

"He was a Nazi?" Lyddie said.

"The one I'm looking for, yes. He was."

Lyddie was uneasy. To what sort of retribution was she going to be an accomplice? "Why are you looking for him, if you know that?" she said.

"So. While I am talking to him, you will look for the family resemblance. The eyes? The chin? Anything you can notice. In just a minute or two, at eight thirty or so, Gerdot III will emerge with a small terrier, which he will walk in the empty lot next to that building. Once the ice is broken with talk of canine habits, we will ease, quite naturally, into this other business." They sat for a few moments in silence. Then Axel said, "My mother claims that this Gerdot was her father, though I don't know how even her mother would have known that, since all of the Nazis used her. He is the only family she has. I will investigate. I owe my mother that much."

Lyddie studied Axel's features, searching for a crack in his strange officiousness, but finding none, she said, "Axel, this is pretty crazy. I don't think I can help you."

"You may not understand," he said, "but please. Don't say that I am crazy. Hold the dog while I apply the collar and the leash. I have bought these myself. Or no," he said, looking at her hand where the dog's teeth had left a red mark. "I will hold the dog. You fasten the collar." He gave her the little red collar and she unbuckled it. Reluctantly, she put it on the dog.

"That's as tight as it goes," she said.

"Good. Very good," Axel said.

The first surprise was that when Gerdot III came out with the terrier, he was not alone. He was with another man, slightly younger looking. The two men headed for the weedy lot and began their rounds. As they approached the near side, marked by a set of dumpsters at the corner, Axel slipped out of the car, the little mutt in his arms, and established the dog on the sidewalk. He waited for Lyddie to join him. Then he walked in the direction of the lot. Seeing the terrier, Axel's dog began to tug furiously at its leash and pulled Axel toward the pair of men. "She is eager to make friends," Axel said as his dog, lifting a leg on the dumpster, displayed a healthy-sized member and then began sniffing the tail end of the other dog.

"He, I think," Gerdot said. The man was fairly tall, nearly Axel's height. But his face was long, creased deeply at the mouth and drooping into heavy jowls. Lyddie examined Axel's face— the upper lip that stayed down, leaving the task of expression to the rest of it. Given what happened to a face over fifty years or more, it was hard to tell if there might once have been a resemblance between this Gerdot's face and Axel's own. "Yes, of course," Axel said. "Your dog is a female?"

"Renée," Gerdot said as Axel's dog attempted to climb aboard and Axel jerked the leash violently. "You live nearby?" he asked.

"I'm walking the dog for my grandmother. She's a couple of blocks over," Axel said.

"I've never seen your dog around," the man said warily. His teeth looked artificial. Axel had good, strong teeth. But none of that meant anything, really, since, as Axel had explained, he might even have the right Gerdot and no shared blood. This Gerdot might merely be the one who had claimed the unborn child as his own or had been told it was his, given his grandmother's assigned role. "You know, this lot is private," Gerdot said. "I have permission to walk Renée here, but it isn't open to the public." The man indicated a private property sign posted on the exposed side of a pre-war building.

"I see," Axel said. As he backed away, he stepped in a clump of dog shit.

Lyddie wondered if Gerdot detected Axel's East German accent and rumpled clothes or merely perceived his rather obvious discomfort and his lies. She shuddered to think what Axel might say next.

Gerdot and his friend set off on another round of the lot. "Excuse me," Axel called out. "You remind me terribly much of someone my grandmother used to know." Teeth notwithstanding. He took a few more steps in their direction.

"She lives nearby?" the man called across the gravel and weeds between them, stopping for a moment.

"Unfortunately, she's not living anymore," Axel said, looking as if he were trying to read the man's face, to see if he might find there any evidence of an effort to atone for Nazi atrocities. Then he realized his mistake. The woman could hardly have a dog if she were dead. But before he could revise his story, the mutt had wriggled free of its collar and bolted toward the street. Lyddie heard the squeal of brakes followed by a thump and then another thump as the little dog landed on the pavement near the Trabi. The car slowed down but didn't stop. For a moment, the four of them looked at one another in horror.

"There's something about you that's not quite right," Gerdot's companion said, looking Axel up and down. "And that collar—it was too big for the dog."

"Leave it, Frank," Gerdot said. "I'm sorry." And he looked as if maybe he really was. He looked visibly upset. About the dog. "You'd better go pick him up," he said to Axel. Then Axel and Lyddie watched as he disappeared inside the building with the other man. A minute later, the lights went on in a room on the second floor.

Sitting in the driver's seat with the dead dog in his lap, his own head nearly touching the top of the car, Axel looked cramped. He opened the door again. "That BMW," he said to Lyddie, "was the only car to have traveled the street in the ten minutes we were here." He sat stroking the coarse white fur of the little mongrel. Lyddie was trembling. She followed Axel's gaze to the lit window of the flat, where they saw Gerdot III in Frank's consoling embrace, which ended with Frank's pulling out the tail of Gerdot's shirt.

"Jesus!" Axel exclaimed. He scanned the street and, seeing no one, he got out of the car and carried the body of the dog to the dumpster. "What are you doing with him?" Lyddie cried through the open window. The dog looked heavier than when he had picked it up before. Axel raised the lid and dropped it in. Then, obviously stricken with guilt over his neighbor's inevitable grief and the crime he himself could not own up to, Axel slammed the car into first and removed himself from the scene.

"Did that seem like my fault? Please say it did not," he said.

"Why did you throw the dog out?" Lyddie said.

"I can't return it now, can I?"

"No, but your neighbor—she may have wanted to bury him. Now what will you tell her?"

"No more than I've told her already."

"Which was...?"

"What do you think? She is not in the dog-lending business."

"God, Axel."

"The only car on the entire fucking street."

"Let me out."

"Right here?"

"Please."

He stopped the car but she didn't get out.

"I think what you just did qualifies as a crime," she said, nodding in wonder at his wholesale indiscretion.

"Oh, Lydia, please," he said. "Do you ever wonder how many crimes one life is made of? Is it a crime to want to know who you are? To want to know who it was that made you that way? I am made of Jew and Nazi. I am the victim and the perpetrator. Analyze that for me, Miss America."

They drove along for a while in silence, not in the direction of Axel's flat.

Lyddie said, "Don't you think that what you do, more than where or who you come from, is who you are?"

"That's a very American idea. *Be yourself!* And what does that make you right now, in light of what you're doing here with me?"

"That makes me afraid of you."

"Still?"

"All over again."

"So get out. Be done with me. I'm sorry I ever told you anything about my deranged existence. You had a very nice life, Lyddie, I'm sure, in the States. Go back to it."

"Sometimes I wish I could go back to it. But it's not there anymore." Lyddie looked out the passenger window; pressing her forehead to the cool glass, she tried to empty her head of the chaos there.

"And maybe it never was what you thought it was. Or wanted it to be."

"I don't know what you mean by that."

"I mean Phelps."

"It's not just Phelps. It's a whole life." How long ago had Axel's grievances and his need begun to carve out a chasm in her no ordinary happiness could fill? "I can't become again the person I was."

"I am sorry about Phelps," Axel said.

"Why did you call him?"

"It doesn't matter now. Do you want me to take you back to Charlottenburg?" he said.

"Can we bury the dog first?"

"Yes," he said. "We can bury the dog."

So Axel climbed into the dumpster to retrieve the dog, and he drove with her out to the periphery of the city and along the quiet, leafy streets of the Grunewald district, past baroque mansions and houses in the International style. Axel said that in that forest, Berlin's Jews had been collected for the death camps. The stately architecture and lush stands of trees reminded Lyddie of a turn-of-the-century sanatorium, the aesthetic grandeur of it matched in scale only by the madness that it had harbored.

They parked the car at the curb and began to walk. "As my stepfather said, trees are good for two things," Axel said. "Burning and hanging. If you do it in the right order, you can use them for both."

"But they're also good for walking under in the rain," Lyddie said. A fine rain had begun to fall. Axel walked in the gutter at the side of the street, carrying the dog, which he had put in a plastic bag that was too small, so that its head and one of its paws hung over the side. Grabbing the sleeve of his jacket, Lyddie tried to pull him toward shelter, but he shrugged her away.

"Everyone but my grandmother they brought here eventually," he said, oblivious to the runnel he was walking through. "Everyone who didn't flee the country in time. They kept her for sexual favors. If I cannot find the one man who is my grandfather, then my grandfather is Nazi Germany. I would prefer to find one man. I can then tell him my opinion of him." They walked a long path to the top of a hill, quiet and wooded.

"It's beautiful here," Lyddie said.

"Devil's Mountain. You know what it is made from?" Axel said. "Broken bricks and dinner plates and plaster from rooms where people lived and where they died. It's a whole city piled up like the mess a dog leaves."

He set down the bag and caught his breath.

"So there is the dog," he concluded.

Axel used the heel of his boot to scuff a hole beneath the previous year's leaves in the moist soil. Lyddie got down on her knees by his side and dug first with a smashed Coke can she found nearby, and then with her hands. As she dug, she cried. The hole was not deep enough, not nearly big enough. She dug until her hands bled, encountering fragments of the past, and she cried until it seemed her insides would be turned out. Axel stopped and stepped back away from her. After a few minutes, he said, gently, "Lyddie, that is enough." He removed the wet little carcass from the bag and handed it to her so she could set it in the ground. Then he helped her up and began grading the dirt on the top of the hole with the side of his boot. He tamped it down and, facing her, he pushed her hair aside and wiped her tears. With one muddy thumb, he made the sign of the cross on her forehead.

They walked back to the car. Still feeling the pressure of his thumb, Lyddie said, "Tell me something from the Desert Fathers."

He told her this: "An old man was asked by a brother, 'If I see the sin of my brother am I to despise him?' And the old man said, 'If we hide the fault of our brother God will also hide our faults; and if we expose our brother's faults, God will also expose ours.'"

LYDDIE WENT BACK TO THE FLAT and filled the long, generous tub, adding the Dead Sea salts Sabina had given her. She let the water lap at her breasts, which floated like buoys on the surface, and at the taut swell of her abdomen. She saw it rise from the weedy estuary between her legs. The ceiling of the bathroom was so high and the bathroom so spacious that the steam of the bath did little to cloud the immense windows she faced. At the end of the room opposite the door, two black panes reached at least six feet high and three feet across. Lyddie had asked Sabina how not to be seen by the entire neighborhood. She might have anticipated Sabina's response: "No one is watching you." She felt hopelessly small, exposed to the darkness. She turned the faucet back on, then off again, listening to the absence she knew would be Phelps. Sometimes, she talked to him. Sometimes she made him talk back.

"I'm not trying to bury you," she said. "I wish you could somehow let me know if you are alive."

"I know," he said. Just as she was beginning to feel comforted, he added, "Even if at times it's easier to believe that my absence is convenient for you."

"That's not fair," she said.

"Why not?"

"He tells me things," she said. "And each time he tells me something, I care for him more."

"Lyddie, you've got a face that makes people want to tell you things."

"It never had much of an effect on you," she said to Phelps.

"That's because I never had much to tell."

"So why the policy?"

"The policy?"

"Sparing the other person what you were feeling at the moment. Harm that couldn't easily be undone."

"That, Lyd, was to spare me your honesty."

"See, that's a problem," she said. I don't think you ever loved the part of me that you were afraid of."

It was quiet again. Lyddie washed quickly, climbed from the tub and covered herself in a thick towel.

8

BEFORE DAWN, HOLDING A FLASHLIGHT in one hand, Dimitri rummaged through the assortment of gear stashed beneath the stairs at the bottom of the stucco house. It had been years since he'd looked at any of these things. Most of them had belonged to his son. Fins and spears for fishing, tackle, a mask. He should have given it away long ago, though at the moment, he was glad that he hadn't. He pulled the rubbery black wet suit out and laid it on the table, where it looked sadly eviscerated. Its foam had begun to decay and, like anything that spent any time in his house, it had a musty smell. Still, it had kept the contours of his son's body and was the most tangible reminder Dimitri had had of Theo in the fifteen years since his death. For a moment, it seemed so intimate with the young man's form that Dimitri wondered why Theo's wife hadn't wanted to keep it. But of course, she'd had no use for it. She had moved to Germany, the country her mother, a Jew, had escaped during the war. She was as eager to forget all things Greek as her own mother had been to forget Germany. Maybe the boy, Akakios, would come back one day and want it.

Dimitri had not shared Theo's love for the sea. The sea was unpredictable and didn't care a whit what happened to any of them. Dimitri's own mother lay somewhere at the bottom of it— who knew where?—her bones well seasoned with salt. At least if you buried something in the ground, the earth thanked you by growing something new in its place. The sea never thanked anyone. When his Theo was fifteen and Dimitri nearly forty, Theo had insisted on teaching Dimitri to swim. Dimitri had felt ill suited to the task, his arms short and ineffectual, his belly always wanting to turn him onto his back. He was unnerved by the crackling static he sometimes heard when his ears were under water, and it seemed that at any moment he would receive an electric shock. Even the sun appeared high-voltage when he looked up at it from his watery state of unease.

Theo, in return, had cared little for Dimitri's icons and oils. Dimitri wasn't the sort of father to insist that his son run the café or learn iconography just because those were the things he him-self did. Dimitri had thought Theo might make a great physicist or astronomer, or a marine biologist because he was smart—the one everyone on the island had said would go places. But Theo had barely finished secondary school when he had run off and joined the Merchant Marine. He'd come home long enough to create a child and to marry the woman who carried it. His leaves after that were brief and infrequent. Theo died ridiculously, in a motorcycle accident in Indonesia, in his thirty-first year.

Theo's son, now a man himself, might remember the empty boots that appeared every few months in the courtyard outside the room where his mother had slept, and maybe the salty smell that filled the room for a couple of days after the boots were gone. He wouldn't remember his father's face, except inasmuch as his own resembled it. Even at five or six, the child, Akakios, was as handsome and smart as his father had been. In his father's absence, he would spend the afternoons at Dimitri's side in the little workroom where Dimitri painted, taking in the smell of linseed and mastic. He had listened, absorbed, to the stories of the Desert Fathers that Dimitri told him. Dimitri had become like a father to him in those years. After his mother took the boy to Germany, he and Dimitri had exchanged letters for a while, but his mother had remarried, and gradually the letters had stopped coming. Dimitri told himself the boy had a new life. A new father. Maybe even a grandfather. He should let it be. As for his own son, Dimitri thought maybe death was the adventure he'd been searching for.

Why only now, so long after Theo was dead, should Dimitri finally find sympathy with him? He picked up the wetsuit by the shoulders and held it against his own body, letting it dangle there. Maroula padded downstairs from the bedroom in her nightgown. "You're sighing," she said.

Dimitri turned away, embarrassed to have been caught in his nostalgia. "Get ready," he said quietly, rolling the suit into a quick bundle. "We're going to paint."

"In that?" she said, indicating the suit, which Dimitri stuffed into a feed sack.

"We're trying something new," he said. "But we'll be back by the time the Swedes want their omelets."

Dawn had not yet begun to inspire patches of translucence in the darkness. The white cubic houses, transfixed in a wee-hour stumble down the mountainside, stopped just short of the stone passage that wound through the village to the café and emptied out onto the road. The yeasty smell of fresh bread emanated from Maria's bakery at the lower edge of town. Hers was the only light on that early, and just next door were the three churches that always, in the context of that smell, reminded Dimitri of three unbaked loaves, in descending sizes, one rising into another.

Maroula didn't complain about the hour. She disliked the work at the café, though she'd done it all her life, catering to locals and resident Germans and tourists, all of them disappointed, somehow, by the fact that she was not Dimitri and not her dead brother of so much promise. Dimitri knew she felt these things, though she'd never said as much. But she liked being the central figure in his icons. Saint Barbara. Saint Euphemia. Saint Cecilia. It flattered her that the paintings looked more and more like her.

Typically, Maroula didn't talk much as they loaded up the donkey and headed down the mountain. But once Dimitri told her what he was going to do, she was full of nervous excitement and questions. "Where is the boat?" "Are you sure you'll be able to breathe?" "Did you put the paints in?" "How long will you be gone?" "What if I tug the line and you don't come back?" She asked these questions in such quick succession that Dimitri was absolved of needing to answer all but the last, which hung in the air at his back. "If you tug and I don't come back, tug once again. Whatever happens, Maroula, don't jump into the water. If I go, it means my time has come."

Maroula laughed at him dismissively, as if she thought the idea of his ever dying were a joke.

The obsolete sailboat Dimitri had borrowed from a friend (it no longer had a sail and was not exactly watertight) lay at anchor just ten meters or so off shore and was their base of operations. In the early light, Dimitri and Maroula carried the rubber dinghy from the place where they had hidden it in a hollow in the rocks and used it to ferry them to the boat so that Maroula would stay dry. Maroula remained on deck, staying the slow seepage into the hull with a tin can and running the compressor while Dimitri, tucked like a sausage into the decaying wetsuit, descended the ladder then dropped, with the air hose, below the surface and allowed the weights to deliver him to the floor of the sea. Receiving his tug on the line attached to the weight belt, Maroula sent down the easel and the modified olive oil tin that served as a paint box.

The floor of the sea was a watery prairie of greens. On the bottom the currents charted big, sandy pathways—the parts that when Dimitri looked down from the rocks were bright turquoise. As the sun rose higher, the underworld evolved, green as if it were just now discovering the meaning of color and green were all the day had invented so far. Dimitri named it as he dabbed it miraculously onto the canvas: moldy saddle, grape leaf, chartreuse, green of raw caper, green of cured caper, green of unworn fatigues. His paintings were now all background. No subject. Almost immediately, he began to entertain the notion that, contrary to Orthodox teaching, we come from the sea and, according to a pile of evidence, will return to it.

The sea had swallowed so many dead over the millennia! Schools of sardines nibbled at Dimitri's exposed hands as he worked, and he imagined his own mother in the moments just after she had given up her breath but was still, perhaps, of the body, sinking in euphoric escape from the fire at her back when the Turkish army had burned Smyrna and forced thousands of Greeks into the sea. By now, she would have grown accustomed to that watery world, suffusing it with a motherly grace. Easy, the life below. The grinding in his knees and in his hip subsided and he painted only infinite variations on blues and greens, like Monet and his lilies in various weathers and times of day and moods. Monet in his old age behind the watery cataracts that eventually blinded him. As a present from a visit to Paris, Theo had brought Dimitri a catalogue from an exhibition of those late Monets, the pages of which now bloomed green and black with mold.

Underwater, Dimitri was an old man in the skin of a young man, both of them swallowed back up into the womb. He was altogether absorbed in the beauty of the seascape, himself its subject, when he felt the tug from Maroula, signaling that it was time to ascend.

WHEN DIMITRI LAID OUT HIS DELIVERY of icons for Stelios to examine in the back of the other man's little shop a couple of weeks later, he could see his friend's disapproval in the way his mouth began to pucker as he stroked the back of his neck. "They're Maroulas," Stelios said, shaking his head and pouring out a little raki, a shot of which he offered Dimitri. Dimitri put it back in a gulp. He pointed out that the tourists bought postcards with his own face on them. Just that. Why shouldn't they buy Maroula as the spiritual icon of the age? She was world-weary, yet still trusting. "Aw, Dimitri," Stelios said. "She's a good girl and all. But these are Greeks we're talking about. The Swedes and the French and the Germans aren't buying icons the way they buy postcards. Most of these I send to the distributor in Athens. Even if they don't know Maroula, there is no..." He hesitated, searching for a way to say what he needed to say. "No swoosh of the spirit here."

"Swoosh? Maroula doesn't have swoosh?"

"Sweep. Lifting to another plane. Out of this world."

"No. That's just it. She is in this world."

"That's just it," Stelios said. He pulled out a box of cigarettes, opened it and offered them to Dimitri. The two men sat and smoked in silence for a few minutes, as if to negate the commercial exigencies that threatened to ruin their relationship.

They had known each other since they were boys. "We, Dimitri, are in this world."

"Precisely," said Dimitri. Smoke rose around them like a sort of incense in the stuffy little room, leaving by the cutout window high up in the wall, and they took comfort in it.

It was a dismal business to be sure, Stelios consented. But if this was the way of the future for Dimitri... He had hoped Dimitri had understood what people wanted. An island version of the old standards. And Dimitri did understand, in a sense. Even when foreigners bought this stuff, they wanted Greece without the Greeks. No Maroulas. The Greeks were merely tolerated—accessories to a landscape and a pleasurable way of life. Remembering the underseascapes that lay in the bottom of the box, Dimitri thought maybe he was guilty of the same sin, a sin of omission. Maybe he, too, wanted Greece with no Greeks. Religion with no saints—or God, for that matter. At home, he had deliberated for days about whether or not to show Stelios the sub-marine paintings. It seemed he had little to lose. He was about to unwrap the first of them when the door to the shop jangled open and in came Politimos, who owned the fish taverna down in the harbor.

Politimos was the last Greek Dimitri wanted to see. Scooting his chair back toward the corner while Stelios went out to greet his customer, Dimitri heard Politimos asking for an icon of Saint Andrew, who was the patron of fishermen. So like him to try to amass spiritual protection for himself, thereby liberating him from any scruples he might otherwise feel he needed to exercise!

Dimitri and Stelios both had lived through enough with Politimos to know what an opportunist he was. During the war, when fishing was dangerous, he had stolen Dimitri's only goat and blamed it on the Nazis. Dimitri knew but couldn't prove it, even though he had later found the goat's hobble—distinct for the elaborate knot Dimitri always tied—in Politimos's courtyard.

Having made his sale, Stelios returned to the back room. "You aid and abet his hypocrisy," Dimitri said.

Stelios responded with a shrug. "I sell icons. It's what I do."

"You think he deserves the protection of the Almighty?"

"I think I deserve to make a living," Stelios said.

Dimitri rewrapped the Maroula icons and put them back into the box on top of the unopened sea grass icons. Stelios, though he might deserve to make a living, didn't deserve to see them.

9

HEARING VOICES, Lyddie hesitated on the landing outside the door to the flat. Alone and waiting for Sabina to let her in, she had the uncomfortable sense that she was cut off and falling, though she knew that once inside Sabina's kitchen, she would feel relieved and welcome. It had been three days since she and Axel had buried the dog. She wanted desperately to talk with Sabina. She was starting to feel her pregnancy too, and she was growing out of her clothes. Maybe Sabina had things she could wear. She should see a doctor or a midwife too, she supposed. What would become of her? Still, oddly, she felt no connection to the child. She could not imagine a life with it. Maybe Sabina could help her envision that life. And even more than needing to talk about that, she wanted to get beyond all of the ambiguities of the neutral zone between them. She wanted to talk about Axel.

Sabina came to the door and invited her in. When Lyddie entered the kitchen, she saw Axel's back receding down the hallway to the bathroom. From where she stood with Sabina near the idle washing machine, she heard the water running. Sabina looked unsettled. "We've just had tea," she said. Lyddie glanced at the shining surface of the table, the teapot and clean cups still on the tray on the counter where Sabina kept them. Lyddie winced. "He was looking for Lothar," Sabina added. "Have you seen him? Lothar, I mean? Have you been to the Turkish Market?"

"Do you want me to get you something there?" Lyddie asked.

Their questions slammed like doors in quick succession.

"I just thought I'd stop in. I've got to go to Hansaplatz for my research."

Sabina looked out the tall kitchen windows, casually, and into the chestnut trees. "So," she said. "You have my number. You can telephone me any time."

"Sure," Lyddie said, knowing she had been dismissed. That was Sabina's power. Just as she could make Lyddie believe in logical solutions, she could, almost without a word, make her feel not only unwelcome, but existentially ungainly, as though not only her presence but her very being required justification.

HAVING NO INTENTION OF GOING to the Turkish Market and little desire to do her work at Hansaplatz, Lyddie stopped by the flat at Naunynstrasse and found Lothar and Kristof as they were leaving for a late breakfast. She happily followed them to the Café Hardenberg, near the zoo. Inside, the aroma of coffee penetrated a scrim of smoke, and students from the Technical and Free universities ate brawny bread with cold cuts and cheese and drank cappuccino in cups the size of halved grapefruits.

Lyddie was still shaken by having found Axel at Sabina's place. She had thought Sabina might be able to tell her more about Axel than she herself knew. Being certain of that now wasn't much in the way of consolation.

"Lyddie, what's the matter? You're unhappy in Berlin?" Kristof said.

His broad smile made her feel silly for fretting. What was the problem, really? That she was jealous? Or was it that the jealousy had aroused her guilt over being in Berlin at all. Because she did want Axel. She wanted him as she had not wanted anyone but him before. He had taught her what desire felt like, and once she knew, try as she might, she had not been able to forget. Pregnancy, a natural culmination of the act of sex, did not make the desire for sex go away. Nor did grief banish it. "I'm fine," she said. She wrestled with her boiled egg, hacking ineffectually at the shell until Lothar took the knife from her with hands that, like Axel's, were stained by oil pigments, and he gave the egg a firm rap near the top. He lifted the severed portion and put it on her plate. Though her German had improved immensely in the time she'd lived in Berlin, she had never gotten the egg thing right.

"Look at me," Lothar said. Lyddie looked. "You are not fine," he proclaimed. Then he raised an index finger in her direction. "The chin. It has small impressions when you're worried. Is it Phelps?"

"I am looking at your arm, Lothar," she said, quite obviously shifting the subject along with her gaze. "I've always wanted to ask you what happened." When he had cut the egg, his sleeve rolled up, she'd had a good view of the torque of his right forearm at the elbow.

"Broken in an East German prison," he said, extending the crooked arm for her inspection. "It healed but it was not repaired." Lyddie was fascinated by its abrupt angle, by the provocation and abuse it had not forgotten.

"Why were you in prison?" Lyddie asked.

"I am an ax-murderer," Lothar said calmly. "Come. Smile, Lyddie. It's funny."

"OK, it's funny," she agreed. "What was the real reason?"

"The Party did not like the colors he painted with," Kristof said. "Colors of conflict. His paintings did not promote optimism."

"Optimism?" Lyddie said, breaking a hunk from a *Brötchen* the waiter had set before her and spreading it generously with butter. She could hardly imagine the Communists looking on the bright side of things.

"Someone told them what they wanted to hear," Lothar said. Kristof shook his head, making gashes in his napkin with his coffee spoon.

"What's wrong, Kristof. Is he lying? Who is 'them'?"

"The Stasi," Lothar offered. "The East German secret police. And I am not lying. They were interested in everything we did. We were endlessly fascinating. Even more than now." He grinned.

"So who told them?" Lyddie said.

"We don't know," said Kristof emphatically.

"An artist or a writer," Lothar said. "Someone who was part of our circle. Kristof says it cannot be, but I know it was. No one else could know. Someone I was drinking with late at night. Someone who was sleeping on my floor and was pissing in my loo. Do you know what it's like to discover something like that, Lyddie?"

Lyddie shook her head, feeling remotely uncomfortable. Her chest grew tight. "Not really," she said.

"Good," said Lothar.

Kristof continued with great concentration to tear at the napkin with his spoon. He seemed uncharacteristically remote when he spoke. "You are forever changing the pictures you have in your head, because they are wrong, in every detail. You're moving the old food around on the old plates, the schnitzel and the boiled eggs." He gestured at their table. "You listen again to each conversation and to who said at which moment, 'I must go,' and you try to remember where you thought that person was going, or to think where he actually went. Or she." He put down the spoon and rubbed his cuticles absently. "You begin to go back through doorways, into rooms…"

"OK, OK," Lothar interrupted. "Why must you go on? It's enough to say it never ends. And our friend is lucky enough not to have to practice such mental gymnastics. Lyddie, are you proud to be an American?" Lothar said.

Lyddie ignored him. Considering Lothar's words, Kristof concluded, "It's only that most of us are here now and, if you have been on the other side, then each day you open your eyes and you have to decide whether to trust everyone or no one."

"And so?" Lyddie asked.

"And so someone like Axel—he trusts no one," Kristof said. "Even on a good day." Lyddie's face flushed. "Perhaps you've noticed," Kristof added, seeing her expression. His smile returned. Lyddie felt again, as she had at Sabina's, reprimanded for her naiveté in believing that she might have shared any real intimacy with Axel. She would, of course, be part of the "no one." She would not be an exception.

"But Kristof trusts everyone," said Lothar, looking at his friend with an accusing smile. "Everyone except for the bank. Like an old woman, he keeps his money in the cupboard."

"It's all true," Kristof said with a smirk.

"What about Lothar?" Lyddie asked, addressing the question to Kristof but looking sidelong at his friend.

"Lothar," Kristof said, "gives not a rat's ass about trust. It's of no interest to him." Lothar grinned, and they all returned to the food they had been neglecting. Lyddie urged Lothar and Kristof to help themselves to the plate of cold meat, cheese and fruit she had ordered, but having taken the edge off with a *Brötchen* or two, they appeared to be content with infusions of caffeine and nicotine, and she laid into the food herself, at the same time digesting what they had told her. It was nearly impossible to imagine living as they had. And yet she did know what Kristof was talking about. The endless mental revision and review of a life in light of new information. New sensations.

After a few moments, she became aware that both Lothar and Kristof had stopped drinking their coffee and were watching her. "What?" she said, arresting a slab of bread with cheese and ham midway between the plate and her mouth.

Kristof looked at Lothar, who also smiled with some obscure pleasure. Lothar said, "It seems that you are very hungry, yes?"

WHEN SHE OPENED THE DOOR to the kitchen, Axel was sitting at her table. He had entered the building on someone else's coattails, and he said she'd left the door to the flat unlocked. It was almost an invitation.

Lyddie put down her bags and went to the sink, where she stood with her back to him. She turned to the stove, from which she took a pan. She filled it with water, lit the burner, and rummaged on the countertop for teabags. Then he was behind her at the sink, his big hands on her shoulders, which were bare in a sleeveless shirt. Pulling her hair away from her face, he caught a finger in the hoop of a silver earring. She put her hand on his, drew it down her neck. She inhaled sharply at his touch. The water on the stove simmered. His other hand under her shirt explored the curve where her breast met her ribcage and then down her midriff. He stopped at her bellybutton. "Lyddie?" he said, turning her to him. He lifted the shirt over her head and tossed it onto the floor. She looked down at her own body.

"Think of it as birth control," she said, her voice confused with her breathing.

He touched her there in wonder, and then he found her

mouth again and his tongue and teeth opened her like a forbidden book, the book of things past.

As if all of the years between the night at the library and the present had been a long foreplay, she urged him on. Still wearing his shirt, he lifted her against the refrigerator and they came quickly, like two people caught in the completion of a circuit. Afterward, they went to the living room and lay down on the floor side by side, she on her back, he propped on an elbow next to her. He ran his hands over the swell of her middle and said, "When did this happen?"

"Four months ago," she said.

"If I had known, I would not—"

"You would not have come here," she said. "You'd have left me alone. But I didn't want you to leave me alone." She bit his nipple, arousing him again. She threw her leg over his hip and sat up, taking him more slowly, attending to the innuendos of his body.

All night they drifted off and then awoke to discover one another again. "Tell me a story," Lyddie said as the first light came in through the courtyard windows.

"The only one I have right now is not appropriate."

"Why?"

"It has your husband in it."

"Oh," she said. She was quiet for a while. "Tell me, instead about Gerdot II."

"That one is not so good for now either," he said.

They lay awhile in silence. Then Lyddie said, "When have your stories ever been appropriate?"

"You think that they are not? I always choose carefully," he said, a bit wounded.

"OK. Maybe you shouldn't worry so much. Tell me about Gerdot II. If the listener wants to hear it, then the story becomes appropriate.

"So," Axel said. "Gerdot II was working at Preussag. It's a chemical company, you know, here in West Berlin. For many days I watched him go there and watched him come back home." Axel sat up in the dark, maybe thinking about how to continue. "When at last I invented a pretext for talking to him and I turned up at his house, I decided to take the bull by the horns, as they say. I opened with, 'Do you not feel guilt over what you have done?' And here's what he told me, Lyddie. 'On the contrary; I feel nothing but guilt. Why do you want to know?'

"So I said I was a social psychologist from the East, doing a study on how people deal with their sense of guilt. It was best for people to talk in the comfort of their home environments without much premeditation. I said someone who knew he was suffering had suggested he become part of my study."

"God, Axel. Do people really believe this stuff?"

"People, Lyddie, are desperate. Some are desperate to hide, but just as many are desperate to reveal themselves. In the absence of religion, they welcome a chance to believe and to confess."

"Gerdot said, 'So many ruined lives. At first I didn't know what the gasses would be used for.'

"'Many people felt that way,' I told him, calmly.

"He said, 'I suppose I didn't want to know. Then when I saw in the papers... The children's bodies in the street where they had been playing. The vomiting and the spasms. I put that together with the unmarked shipments from Dow Chemical that we'd been processing at work and sending there.'"

Axel told Lyddie, "I realized at that moment that we had crossed wires concerning our genocides. We were talking about two different wars. He told me that the pesticides he was supplying to Iraq were being used to exterminate 'two-legged pests.' Kurdish ones. Human beings."

Lyddie was quiet.

"I shouldn't be telling you this story," Axel said.

"That's why you called Phelps? To tell him his company in Tonawanda, New York, was secretly sending chemicals to Preussag in Berlin, which was turning them into chemical weapons and supplying the Iraqis? Were you accusing him of assisting in genocide?"

"Lyddie, I called to give him information I thought he should have. I thought he would want to know. And do you know what he said?"

"I do know. I happen to have been standing right there. He said, 'Thank you.' And he didn't mean it."

"He asked how I knew this information when nobody else knew."

"You never really gave him a reason to believe you. To trust you, Axel. Maybe other people believe what you tell them, but Phelps never did. And why didn't you tell me?" she said, sitting up beside him and throwing her hands into the air in frustration. "I'm very, very tired of everyone protecting me from all the bad things that go on and that really matter."

"It wasn't about you, Lyddie. And I was not trying to injure him or expose him."

"But that's the same thing he told me about you! Whatever it was that he knew about you wasn't anything I needed to know but was a warning I was supposed to heed. In the end, it had everything to do with me. Now, in this case, it matters whether or not I think my husband went there to do his research supported by Dow knowing that they were also helping to kill the Kurdish people he was working with."

"What did he warn you about?"

"Just that I should stay away from you. He wasn't specific. He wasn't one to circulate stories about other people. So what should he have told me?"

"I don't know," Axel said.

Lyddie studied his face, waiting for him to relent. Finally, she said, "What happened then with Gerdot II?"

"We met again, and he told me he'd left the East after being recruited into the Stasi's program for training the Iraqis. The East Germans were teaching the Iraqi intelligence how to keep detailed records of the atrocities against their own people. As you may know, Lyddie, my people were good at those things. It was an area of expertise."

Lyddie stood up and began to pace the living room. "I can't believe how horrible—so what you're telling me is the Stasi was training the Iraqis to document—Oh my God! And the Stasi let Gerdot come over here, even with what he knew was going on?"

"He escaped," Axel said, standing up to put on his pants. "Only to find that he had become, once again, a collaborator in the same extermination. Just from the other side. On the Preussag team. The side of the good guys. The West. Home of freedom and democracy and brotherly love. Your side, Lyddie. Our side."

10

LYDDIE NEVER KNEW WHEN AXEL would turn up at the flat on Kaiser Friedrich Strasse, but after that first time, it was often near dark. They rarely got out of the kitchen before they began to lose their clothes.

Axel didn't stay. He said there was integrity to her life that he didn't want to destroy. Nothing was being destroyed, she argued, unless she herself was destroying it. "Why do you come at night if you won't stay?" she'd say.

And he would say, "I like the dark in you."

But to Lyddie, it seemed sometimes as though Axel could not stop long anywhere for fear of belonging. There were things she couldn't imagine doing with him. Eating, for instance. He took his cue from the Desert Fathers. Eating was a concession to necessity—an animal need that he would not much be bothered about. She, being a pregnant animal, ate often and alone. Talking about the future was likewise off limits. It was tacitly agreed that whatever happened between them did not

exist beyond the time they were together, and would not become
something referred to outside themselves or observed by others,
a What's This Between Lyddie and Axel. When they were with
Lothar and Sabina and Kristof, they barely spoke to one another.

But alone, Axel sometimes told her about things he remembered from the East. So Lyddie came to know the dark in Axel too.

FOR INSTANCE: AXEL SITS in the reading room of the
Staatsbibliotek beneath a gaunt corolla of fluorescent bulbs.
On the table in front of him lies Stalin's *Dialectical and Historical
Materialism* along with his *Problems of Leninism*. It is Axel's job
to create what the authorities are calling a "corrective and in-
terpretive concordance" to the works of Lenin, Trotsky, Marx,
Hegel and Feuerbach on the concept of dialectical materialism.
Stalin's work will serve as the red-letter master text.

When he started, Axel went diligently about the work, deeply
absorbed in reading the authors that required corrective attention
and merely tolerating the Stalinist revisions he had to make. But
as the months pass and apparently no one so much as glances at
what he is doing, he realizes that he has been assigned this task
for his own edification. And so, seeing personal edification as the
end of his labors, he has begun to take liberties. He always opens
Stalin first. He never deviates from that protocol. He pours over
the text with great absorption. Then, in his notes, as connections
occur to him, he refers the reader to passages by German poets
such as Paul Celan and Ivan Goll, as well as Sergei Yesenin, the
young martyr to Soviet artistic freedom. He reads from Lenin's
notebooks, for example, "Dialectic is the study of why the mind
of man ought not to take opposites for dead, stagnant, but for
living, conditional, moving things converting themselves one into
another." Then, pausing for a moment to assimilate the idea,
which strikes him as pleasant, he makes a notation: "Blue of the

lodes in your mouth, / you gasp up pole after pole." The voltage of Celan always goes straight to his heart.

"Is that why they forced you to leave?" Lyddie asked him.

"As good a reason as any," he said.

"But what were the other reasons?"

"They didn't say. Maybe I perplexed them."

"Why did they ask me about you at the border crossing? Why did they still care?"

"They spy on a lot of people over here, Lyddie. And they never knew what to think of me. It is likely that they suspected I had not finished undermining their authority."

"What else do you remember?" Lyddie said.

"I remember the view from the window of the State Library. I'll draw it for you," Axel said. While she rummaged for paper and a pencil, he said, "I remember standing at the window looking out onto Charlottenstrasse. Behind me, I would hear the sound of human fingers flipping through the cards in the catalogues. I would hear that dutiful sound, and it ruffled something far back in my psyche. Some wish for sense and order not imposed by the State. My view across Charlottenstrasse gave me the bombed-out section of a building, next to which was…" Axel took the pencil and paper Lyddie offered him and began to draw a brick structure with a series of arches that were cemented closed like a vault, leaving only a tiny wooden door for access. "Stalin's door to the universe," he said, tapping at it. He put the pencil down.

"Was that why you dreamed of staying all night in the library? At Amerika Haus?"

"One of two reasons, he said," and they went to the bed in her room.

Axel tried to explain to Lyddie the way it was back then. He told her stories so compelling that she imagined she, too, had lived them. But at other times the stories made him seem only more distant.

AXEL IS NINETEEN AND HE and the others are making their way from the amber-walled Café Mozaic on Schönhauser Allee to Lothar's one-room flat. It is in the days just after the activist singer and songwriter Wolf Biermann has been forced into exile in the West, and the names of many among his friends have appeared on a document of protest. For the first time, they have been bold enough to protest Communist strategies openly, though they have lived a variety of subversions for as long as they can remember. As a result of the protest, they have been told that the Wiener Café, their favorite gathering place, is closed for renovations, and they have derived a certain vitality from knowing they are a force worth closing out. Everyone among them suspects the café will remain closed another six or seven weeks then open its untouched doors as if they had all learned their shabby lessons in Communism.

They are explaining this to Axel's cousin Nikos, who has been allowed to visit from Greece. Educated by monks during the military dictatorship, Nikos is no stranger to the fervent resistance and idealism of Axel's friends. He is sympathetic to their cause.

"You knew him when you were a boy? In Greece?" Lyddie said.

"Yes," Axel replied.

"And was he in training to become a monk?"

"He was a novice. But that's not so important to the story. What matters is his idealism."

The trains lumber down the stiff spine of the street, raised above Axel and the others on orange steel girders. As the group scatters, making its way beneath the crumbling lions' heads and dirty cherubs of the row houses on Griefenhagener Strasse, Axel watches Nikos, defined in the dark by the streetlamp's aureole beyond him, his broad shoulders and long gait making him look keenly alive. Beside him, Lothar reminds Axel of a charismatic shepherd, blonde curls catching on his collar, ratty green sleeves rolled to the elbow. They look, to Axel, as they walk slightly ahead—and it strikes him as odd that he should think of it in such a way—sincere.

"Like me," Lyddie said. "That's how you think of me. Not in the sense of soulful but more like naïve."

"Well-meaning," Axel says.

"It diminishes the importance of the person it describes."

"I'm not boasting, Lyddie, about who I was. Do you want to know?"

Once Axel has recognized their sincerity, the entire evening's proceedings take on an antic air: the heated discourse on true socialism, the six new poems Inge pulls from the pocket of her blouse and reads in a voice vacillating, like that of a dramatic lover, between anguish and ecstasy.

With ambivalence bordering on disdain, Axel reads one of his own poems, which are generally admired for their resistance to interpretation. No one seems to know what they mean, exactly, but for Axel they are always a relief—a way of closing the door on something that's trying to get out. Whether he is inside with it or outside with the others is a question he cannot answer. The poems have been published in the East, though judiciously, in very small numbers.

Inge tells Axel she'd give all six of her poems to have written the one he read. But Axel knows the poem is nothing. And he thinks she'd do better to keep hers to herself. He is a socialist, not a deluded idealist.

"Didn't you want to sleep with her?" Lyddie asks.

"Nikos took care of her. You'll see," Axel says.

When the wine bottle is passed from hand to hand and mouth to mouth, Axel's head begins to explode with an imagined cracking of teeth. Each drinker raises the bottle—Lothar, then Käthe and Inge and Kristof—and Axel stiffens with something resembling pity and something resembling disdain. He smokes furiously, and he feels the same discomfort he felt when he went to his first Young Communist League rally. There, he witnessed a camaraderie he despised like a suffocating embrace.

He is relieved when, later, through the closed door, he hears the sounds of Inge and his cousin making love in the next room. Nikos the novice. Nikos the mystic. His cousin's "sincerity" comes quickly into question. The sound of their lovemaking is one of the two things Axel will store in balance in his memory when his cousin is gone. The other is the pressure of Nikos's thumb on his forehead before they part, and the movement of the hand that makes the sign of the cross over Axel's own chest.

It is late when Axel and Nikos return to the flat and Axel closes the door behind them. In the dim light he sees his mother sitting in a chair next to the cupboard. A flat box lies open in her lap, and in the box, he knows, is an Italian silk scarf, the fringed one with the feathers on it. It was given to her mother by one of the Nazis. Axel goes to stand in front of her while Nikos hangs back in the doorway.

"Mama, you should be asleep. You're tired." She has dark circles under her eyes, and he sees that, just below, the skin is beginning to crinkle like lavender tissue paper. But he sees, too, that he has startled her into fatigue, its source not the hour but her being apprehended and returned to it. Axel shakes his head gently. "She was no Italian Princess, Mama. She was a Jew." His mother is obsessed, it seems, with her own mother's misfortunes.

"But for that one night, she would have remained a Jew." His mother said this as if *Jew* were something one could take or leave. Something one outgrew. They had never been practicing Jews. It had never seemed to matter to them that they were Jewish.

"You treat it the same way," Lyddie said.

"I'd have left it behind a long time ago if that were the case—except that would only mean I'd be more Nazi."

"Why do you persist?" Axel says to his mother.

"Axel," Nikos protests, in Greek, not following the conversation completely but getting the general idea. "Leave her alone."

Axel and Nikos both know the story. How the Nazis kept the girl, how she escaped them during an extravagant party on the Pfaueninsel, the Island of the Peacocks. She'd been got up as an Italian princess for their pleasure.

"She was my mother. Your grandmother—and Nikos's too," his mother says.

"Yes."

"And on that night, because the father of her child loved her, she was able to flee through a hole in a bad dream that opened onto the real world, and everything changed." It is as if she were reciting something from the Brothers Grimm—a tale Axel has heard since childhood.

"A bad dream created by madmen at Goebbels' party—any one of whom may have been your father. For that you came back to this country?"

Axel knows that buried beneath the scarf in his mother's lap should lie a picture of the girl—she is still a girl, really—with eyes that remind him of starlings on pale, frozen ground. His mother has been saving the picture for last, the way the Jewish girl might have saved a bit of chocolate, in the early days, or later, a hunk of bread.

"Gerdot was my father, Axel. He knew that she carried his child, and he—"

"Stop!" Axel shouts. Then, more quietly, "Mama, stop. Please!"

His mother is exiled by stubbornness and pride into silence.

"You can be so formidable," Lyddie said. "Couldn't you just have let her deal with her sadness as she needed to?"

Axel said, "When she behaved like that, I could not bear it. This Gerdot was someone she didn't even know. This "father" of hers. I had survived without two fathers of my own—first the Greek one, who died when I was small and whom I almost could not remember, and then the German one, who died when I was not much older and whom I could not forget. Why did she have to indulge this fantasy?"

Next, his mother will take the picture out. Axel knows because about her there is a remnant of confidence, allowing neither fatigue nor resignation to dominate, despite the gloom he has cast. It is the look he has seen in the eyes of "the Italian princess."

When she lifts the scarf to find the picture gone, Axel doesn't know which is more insufferable: the woman of a moment before, as pale as a bloated cabbage and fawning over memorabilia of a Nazi charade; or the woman before him now, believing nothing anymore and wearing the expression of someone about to bury a cat that's been into poison.

"Will you show it to me?" Lyddie said.

"Someday, maybe," Axel said.

ONE NIGHT AXEL AND LYDDIE pulled the kitchen chairs onto the little balcony adjoining the bedroom at Lyddie's flat. They sat looking down at the white and red lights of the traffic on Kaiser-Friedrich-Strasse.

"Have you ever loved anyone?" Lyddie asked. "A woman, I mean."

"No," he answered.

She let that information settle, waited for the ripples to die away.

"What do you think it is—love?" she said. "Is it a daily thing? I mean, if you love someone, then it's consistent? Predictable? Does it mean you can tolerate the routine of days together? Or is it the opposite. Is love when you can't?"

"I'm the last person you should ask, Lyddie," he said.

"Why?"

"I am the last. That's all."

Lyddie got up and went to the kitchen, then returned with two cold bottles of Heineken which she set down in front of them. Opening one and handing it to her, Axel said, "We live on the Devil's Mountain. Our lives are nothing more than colorful scraps atop that massive pile of waste. It is not only selfish but also delusional to consider your personal life of any importance. It is a luxury to insist on loving and being loved."

"You don't mean that," Lyddie said.

"You don't know what I mean," he said.

Anger and hurt welled up inside Lyddie. She thought she might know something about building a life out of ruin. "It's no more a luxury," she said, "than protecting yourself from intimacy. No more than pretending no one can really touch you." She remembered what Kristof and Lothar had said, about having to decide whether to trust everyone or no one. She felt suddenly and irrevocably part of Axel's no one. Or worse. The spoiled American girl who tried to stay out of the rain. She had not experienced enough of life to fathom the filth at the heart of it all. No matter that her husband had hidden the truth from her and then gone off and left her alone—maybe a widow and maybe just a cheat. She couldn't stop herself from saying, "Whoever it is—whoever betrayed all of you, Axel—doesn't deserve your protection. And doesn't deserve to share the blame with the rest of us."

Axel sat perfectly still. In a voice that sounded suddenly weary, he said, "Who told you that?"

"What does it matter?" Lyddie said.

"Who?" he repeated.

"Your friends, Axel, who also hurt sometimes. Kristof and Lothar. They talk to me, you know."

"About what is none of your fucking business," Axel said. He got up and walked out, leaving his beer untouched and Lyddie alone on the balcony. She heard the door to the landing slam shut. A minute later, she watched him cross Kaiser-Friedrich-Strasse without looking back up.

THAT NIGHT, LYING IN BED, Lyddie fought the hurt caused by the things he had said. She knew that she had fallen in the way of Axel's formidable argument with the world. Still, she felt diminished by him on his pile of rubble. That was what she was thinking when the phone rang. In a panic over her emotional state, Lyddie let it ring seven, eight, nine times. A conversation with Sabina or Lothar or Ray was the last thing she needed. She could barely deal with her own feelings let alone disguise them or interpret them for someone else. She picked up the phone.

"Lyddie."

It was Axel. "Yes."

"Please, talk to me."

"You called. Why don't you begin?"

"OK," he said. It was quiet for a minute. "There is a story of a certain monk—"

"Axel, no stories," she said.

"I didn't mean to hurt you. When you left four years ago, so soon after I began to know you, I felt the loss of you. I don't want you to go away again."

Lyddie thought for a moment, listened to his breathing. "Where am I going to go?"

"I don't know. Maybe I can…" His voice lost power, and for a moment she wasn't sure he was still there. "You are good, Lyddie. Maybe I can somehow…" Again, his voice trailed off.

She felt the duvet grow heavy about her. She thought she could hear the plants exhaling. She said, "What scares me is that I am falling in love with even your scorn." When she had hung up the phone, she sat for a long time at the edge of the bed, trying to locate herself in that room, in Berlin, in the city of things broken.

11

BADLY IN NEED OF DIVERSION, Lyddie spent the next few mornings revisiting some of the iconic Bauhaus sites. At Hansaplatz, a "living showplace" of the International Style, women flew by on bicycles, infants mounted securely in front. In every direction, monolithic apartment buildings designed by architects like Luciano Baldessari, Walter Gropius, and Oscar Niemeyer for the 1957 Interbau competition rose in tall, leafy arbors and sported the optimism of their utility in orange or yellow blocks of color on patios facing south. "Nature penetrates the city and offers the urbanite new charms." That was what Gropius said, though further along, the small white flat-roofed houses that typified the Bauhaus ideal looked squat and incidental in the focus of Lyddie's camera lens. Fences obscured some houses from view; the white facades of others had been violated by graffiti.

By the time Lyddie reached Gropius's high-rise entry on the corner of Händelallee and Klopstock Strasse, the optimism she had tried to generate in spite of Axel had begun to fade.

The lace in windows framed with alloy suggested retirement in Sarasota. The cactuses and dressinas displayed there, the macramé hangers knotted during long-ago vacations at the North Sea, the prisms and the greeting cards all cluttered the Bauhaus ideal. Gropius could not have foreseen this, she thought. At the Archive, she had seen a photograph of his study, its single table and chair highly suited to a man who stacked apartments on paper. She couldn't help believing that Gropius himself must have rented a big, dark storage warehouse someplace else.

The shutter of her camera clicked and purred as she documented the anachronistic certainties that beauty and utility were compatible. She did the work of an art historian, but she felt like a historical vagrant.

Afternoons Lyddie spent educating herself on the baroque architecture of Sabina's private life. Lothar was only the first of Sabina's lovers Lyddie had met. Others she was coming to know as bits of history that emerged in the course of a day or a story while she and Sabina washed windows or went to the market or took Ulla down to the canal. All became part of the cloud that surrounded Ulla's paternity. Ulla had, apparently, a biological father who no longer figured in their lives. She had a legal father, who lived in Düsseldorf, as well as a sort of acting father, who was Lothar. There were, in addition, incidental lovers who competed for Ulla's affections by taking her on outings and buying her accordions and tricycles.

Lately, Sabina's familial difficulties extended to her half-brother, Siegfried, who had become restless and aggressive. He was nineteen now, living at home with Sabina's mother, who Sabina said no longer knew how to "handle to him." Tall and strong, he sometimes used force to get what he wanted. He had left bruises on their mother's arms when he seized her in a fury one day over her refusal to give him money for the movies. It was hard for the woman to insist on anything. She had suggested that Siegfried see a therapist, but Sabina resisted that idea. "His problems are physical, not psychological," she said. "He has me to talk to, and I know him better than anyone." Something was out of balance, Sabina was certain. He needed to see a homeopath.

So on a mid-August afternoon that started out cool and cloudy, Lyddie and Sabina set out with Siegfried and Ulla in the direction of the hospital. When they reached the canal, Sabina handed Lyddie a bag of stale bread and said, "We should not be more than one hour." Siegfried gawked at the opposite bank, where two women had stripped down to their big brassieres and panties and lay sprawled beside shirtless men in the sun, which had come out rather suddenly and had apparently taken them by surprise. Behind them, as in one of Lyddies' bad dreams of public nakedness, the traffic on Paul Linke Ufer trolled past. Siegfried and Sabina turned toward the hospital.

"Ulla," Lyddie called. The little girl galloped along the bank, flinging her arms to see if she could make the swans notice her. "We break it smaller before we toss it, like this." Lyddie tore off a few bits of bread and flung them out onto the water. Ulla took the bag and ran down closer to the edge with it. The swans had moved in, dipping their heads to the water for the bread. Lyddie saw, just down the bank, the wheelchair ghetto she'd seen her first days in Berlin. The women were now watching her and Ulla unabashedly, like some weird Greek chorus summarizing Lyddie's lonely fate. They might as well have sung it openly: Your life is a shambles. You're destined for grief. In the presence of so many one-legged women, two legs seemed suddenly to Lyddie a comfortable assumption about what was normal—one she might need to abandon as she had abandoned so many others in the preceding weeks: that faithful meant loving one person your whole life; that love implied admiration, that a friend was someone you trusted.

When Sabina and Siegfried emerged from the hospital an hour and a half later, both looking worn, Sabina grabbed Ulla's hand and began walking back toward the market. "How did it go?" Lyddie asked.

"Who knows?" Sabina said. "She gave us some remedies to try." Siegfried took Ulla's hand on the other side. All along the banks of the canal, people were shedding their clothes. Sabina seemed agitated.

"Is something wrong, then, Sabina?" Lyddie asked. That morning at the flat, Sabina had poured the tea and arranged the bread and jam on two plates at the table but no sooner had she sat down than she'd gotten up and walked over to the sink, where she washed a few glasses and spoons and then stood gazing into space. Seeing an opened envelope atop a pile of mail, Lyddie had asked if there'd been bad news. In response, taking two apples from the countertop, Sabina had given Lyddie one and announced that they wouldn't have time for tea. Siegfried was waiting. "What was in the envelope this morning?" Lyddie said now, wondering if it were appropriate for them to talk about anything serious in the presence of Ulla and Siegfried, though neither understood much English, so it didn't seem to matter.

Lyddie was surprised when the story came spilling out. The problem had to do with Ulla's paternity. Sabina had apparently been interested neither in pursuing a relationship nor in raising a child with Ulla's biological father. Because the government had required a father's name on the birth documents, and a friend of Sabina's had agreed to serve, her friend's parents had thought all along that they were the child's grandparents. Now they wanted to put some land up near the North Sea in Ulla's name.

"Let them give Ulla the land," Lyddie suggested. "They might as well be her grandparents. She thinks they are. They think they are. What's the difference?" For her own child, Lyddie hadn't thought any further than the question of a father.

Sabina seemed not to have heard her. "When Wolf agreed to put his name on the birth documents... I don't know. The State needed a father, and I needed the money from the State. They never asked for grandparents," she said, her voice becoming more emphatic. As they approached the corner of Plan Ufer where it crossed busy Kottbusser Damm, Sabina stopped to look at the oil-on-velvet renditions of Christ and Elvis. Then they joined the line of people waiting to buy *döner kebap* at the snack stand opposite. The small, sallow-skinned man carving pork from the turning mound on the rotisserie wiped his forehead with a napkin. Sabina took an apple from her bag and shined it on her skirt.

"But you have them, the grandparents," Lyddie said. "Can you tell them the truth?"

Sabina's face changed then, the way the smooth sphere of the apple she held was surprised by the crisp edges of the first bite she had taken. "The truth?" Her eyes watered, and she looked at Lyddie, who had spoken back into existence a place and a time Sabina had tried to erase.

When Lyddie saw Sabina's expression, she felt like a child who had used a big word in the right context without really knowing what it meant. "There is more then?" Lyddie said, and Sabina lowered her eyes. Lyddie had learned that even when she thought Sabina had made a full revelation, some significant fact or detail, which would eventually change the entire picture, had been lost or held back somewhere in her cluttered heart.

Sabina gave the stuffed pitas to Siegfried and Ulla, who ate them as they continued along the canal. "I talked to Ulla's father last week," Sabina said. She was walking more quickly now, deliberately, as if she hoped, somehow, that she would lose the rest of them.

Picking up the pace, Lyddie did not hide her astonishment. "Her real father?" She hurried Ulla along with a hand on her back. They arrived at the market, and Sabina slowed as they entered the cacophony of Turks and Germans hawking vegetables and fruits and scarves imported from Indonesia. Sabina said nothing. "You didn't tell him," Lyddie said tentatively. "Is it someone I know?" It had crossed her mind that even Phelps might be Ulla's father. This possibility was one she could almost not bear to entertain.

Sabina stopped at a stall devoted to the sale of cinnamon and cardamom, curry and paprika, and she selected two bags of spices. "It's no one you know," she said, opening her change purse to pay, then moving on.

Lyddie relaxed a bit. "You did tell him," Lyddie said.

"Yes, though I don't know why," Sabina answered, fingering the sleeve of a leather coat as the vendor watched her carefully. "It has only made everything worse."

"Does he want to be involved with her?" Lyddie asked.

"Clearly no."

"You care about him, then?"

"Why do you ask?" Sabina said.

Lyddie shrugged. "It seems a logical question. Did you tell him because you wanted him to share responsibility for Ulla or because you wanted to be with him as well?"

Before she could answer, Sabina turned around suddenly and said, "Where are Ulla and Siegfried?" They looked back just in time to see Ulla reach high above her head and hook her fingers over the lip of a bucket of gladiolas at the stall of a flower vendor. The bucket tipped, sending a spout of water down into the child's face. The Turkish vendor made a heroic lunge to rescue the bundles of flowers and shouted in German at the child, who shrieked in surprise. Siegfried, who had apparently seen her before Sabina did and gone back, picked her up as Sabina and Lyddie hurried over. *"Nein,* Ulla," Siegfried said, gently. *"Was machst du?"*

Sabina took a scarf out of her bag and wiped at Ulla's face. She said in German, "Siegfried, why did you let her wander off?"

"She was with me," he said.

Ulla said, "I want to buy some flowers."

A quiet, rapid altercation followed, and Siegfried ended up sullen. In order to appease both Ulla and the vendor, Sabina opened her change purse and took out ten D-Marks. Ulla pointed at the gauzy, trumpeted stalks, the salmon-colored ones, which the Turkish woman wrapped in newspaper.

Overhead, the steely edges of the clouds caught the gleam of the sun. It was almost two o'clock and the booths were beginning to close. Lyddie could see all the way down the wooden tables of produce and clothing and spices to the rumpled banana man on the corner, still droning *Bana-a-a-nen. Drei Mark, fünf Mark!* Between Sabina and Siegfried, hugging the stalks of flowers, Ulla seemed to dangle from the huge bouquet as if from a bright parachute. Siegfried held her arm and guided her along the street. Lyddie thought that Phelps would have approved Ulla's choice in flowers. The salmon-colored Peter Pears. "Classics," he would say. With a tenderness that made Lyddie wince, Siegfried brushed back a wet strand of Ulla's hair that had fallen down over her eye. Lyddie touched her swollen middle.

Sabina said, "She is independent."

"Yes, I've noticed," Lyddie said.

"I suppose I was the same, in my way," Sabina said. "When I had just three years or so, my mother, she was dancing in clubs for money. She would leave me at home alone at night. The number for emergencies was the only number I knew—equal to your 911—and so one night when she left, I called that number and began to talk."

"Why did you call?" Lyddie said. "Were you frightened?" Lyddie stopped to buy a bag of peaches before they left the market and headed back toward Sabina's flat.

"I suppose," Sabina said. "'Oh I am all alone, ' I told them, 'and my mother, she left me here and I don't know what to do.' And so they traced the call and found me, and they took me from my mother. For many years, I lived with my grandmother."

"Did your grandmother love you?" Lyddie asked.

"Yes, of course. Just as my mother loves Ulla. Though my mother always, I think, hated me for what I did. But oh, she wants Ulla to stay with her the night, and she buys for Ulla a toothbrush and a cup to match at the KaDeWe and she takes Ulla to lunch. I don't know if I can love her or if I can hate her for that. But really it doesn't matter." Having arrived at the flat again, she dug the gigantic key out of her handbag and unlocked the door. "I know what it is to wish that you can begin again."

It was this tenderness, this sympathy in Sabina that would not allow Lyddie to dismiss her. The atmosphere of confidences made Lyddie want to talk about Axel. Still, she was afraid of what she might find out. Instead, she asked about the one-legged women by the canal. "Are they air raid victims? Were there land mines after the war?" Lyddie felt she understood as little about the impact of the past on this city and the people who lived in it as she did about Sabina.

"They're from the diabetic ward," Sabina said. "From the hospital where Siegfried and I went. It's there beside the canal." Sabina threw her sweater over the back of a chair in the kitchen and took Ulla into the bedroom to put her down for a nap. She called to Lyddie, "I forgot to tell you. There's a letter for you too—there beside the oven." Lyddie flipped through the pile of bills until she saw the letters of her name in a familiar scrawl partly obscured by a forwarding sticker.

"My God," she said aloud. And then again. "My God." She sat down at the table, examining the postmark. Recent. From Ankara.

"What is it?" Sabina called from the other room. Hearing no response, she came back to the kitchen to find Lyddie sitting with the unopened letter in hand, staring out the window, her mouth open as if she meant to speak.

"Oh, Lyddie," Sabina said. "Is he dead?"

"I don't think so," she said. "How else…I mean how else…" Her voice lost its way.

Lyddie handed the letter to Sabina. "Will you?" she said.

Sabina took a knife from the drawer and slit the envelope at one end, removing the letter—a single sheet of paper with Kebap 44 and an address in Turkish at the top. Lyddie took it from Sabina and read, herself, its painfully brief message. A message that left out almost everything—as if it had been written by a hostage. *Lyddie*, it said, *I'm alive. Don't do anything. Promise me. No longer at this address.*

What did that mean? And who had been looking over Phelps's shoulder as he wrote it? Did it mean Don't try to find me? Don't try to rescue me? Or did it mean Don't leave me. Don't give up. Don't do what you're already doing. The ambiguous command hung in her chest, as heavy there as an old tire, something that could be put to use but for what purpose? Probably not a journey. A life raft? A swing? The joy Lyddie had anticipated months before in her dreams of Phelps's reappearance eluded her. Scraps of it tore at her emotions, but quickly they settled out into a renewed sort of grief. Or anger. Phelps was still out there, somewhere—an anachronism forbidding her to act. He'd left her no way to ask for clarification. No way to resist him. He didn't need her. He needed to keep her innocent of whatever adventure or nightmare had befallen him. The note was unsigned.

And still, Phelps was alive.

When Lyddie left Sabina's apartment, descending the high, dank staircase and opening the heavy door into Forster Strasse, even laden with bags of potatoes and peaches as she was, she felt the world's insubstantiality around her, as if all of it—the great northern oaks, the Turkish women at the market, and the stone facades blunt against blue sky—were an enormous deception.

12

DIMITRI WAS TWO WEEKS into his undersea exploration. The water an oily calm in the morning before the meltemi wind kicked up its surface and interfered with the light, he had been in an ecstasy of slo-mo dabbing. He experimented in thicker application with a knife to represent the grasses that moved like a single body though the blades maintained their definition. And he was still trying to find a way to capture the medium of the water—translucent but more present than air. It was like trying to paint wind. The grasses were the best way, just as grasses in a field made the wind evident. But painting water without its surface was like trying to paint the spirit in the absence of the person on whose life it had wreaked havoc.

Feeling Maroula's tug on the rope, he closed the paint tin, tied the easel and the tin to their respective ropes and then removed the weighted belt and knotted it to the remaining line. He kicked his way up to the surface, climbed the ladder, and was heaving himself back onto the boat when an enormous boom shook the

cove, throwing him out onto the deck before he could get his footing there. Maroula, standing near the compressor in the stern,
lurched and stumbled over the coil of rope she had just arranged,
landing against the gunwale.

Sprawled on the deck of the boat, Dimitri cursed.

He pulled himself to his feet and looked across the cove to
see the blue and red Medusa III motoring in the opposite direction. All around him and Maroula, silver fish floated, their white
underbellies catching the gleam of the early sun.

Politimos. Always ready to adapt to circumstance! Now the
circumstance was that the Aegean, once the kingdom of bream
and sardines, swordfish and anchovies, every kind of fish in
quantity, was pretty well exhausted. It was harder and harder to
draw a good catch, and Politimos had a fish taverna to run. He
most likely would not collect even half of what he had damaged
or killed with the blast. There would be many more fish below
the surface, and he was too lazy to go diving for them. Only
the ones whose swim bladders had burst would float to the top.
Those were the ones he would gather.

But the law of silence governed fishing practice on the island,
mainly because no one really wanted the officials looking too
closely into his own affairs. If you turned someone in, you might
have your taxes audited, or find your own business destroyed by
rumors of rats in the kitchen. In fact, since the war, no one quite
trusted anyone else on the island. You looked out for yourself.

"Who was it?" Maroula asked, picking herself up off the
deck and remembering to haul in the remaining lines at the side
of the boat. The weight belt came up first, followed by the easel
and finally the canvas with a big tear up the middle, where it had
been punched through by the explosive shock.

Even if Dimitri were ready to die, the thought that anyone
else—least of all Politimos—should kill him or ruin his still fairly

decent life was infuriating. "The boat was probably stolen. Turks, I think," he told Maroula. He listened to the distant motor chuff around the cove as they washed down his gear in silence.

In the days that followed, Dimitri thought about turning the other man in. He was furious with Politimos not only for ravaging the sea but also for violating the space he considered sacred—the site of his morning painting ritual. To add insult to injury, that anyone would enter a cove in broad daylight in a boat with its name painted brightly on the back and toss a Coke bottle of fertilizer and kerosene overboard with another boat in plain sight made Dimitri almost certain that man must be enjoying the protection of someone other than Saint Andrew. Someone in local government, perhaps.

What was it that the Desert Fathers said? If we expose our brother's faults, God will also expose ours. And what were Dimitri's own faults? Well, right then he was lying to Maroula about Politimos, since he didn't want her spreading any rumors. Dimitri supposed that harboring a death wish was also something of a fault. A sin, even. And thinking too much about the dead. And taking liberties with orthodoxy, for instance in the Maroula desecrations. Once he got started, he could hardly make it from the post office, where he had picked up a letter, to the café, where he intended to read it—each step he took faulty in some way. Each a reason merely to work around Politimos, as he always had, in order to abide awhile longer in God's slackened expectations.

The letter had a Berlin postmark, but Greek script. Dimitri opened it carefully with a knife but left it on the counter in order to pick up the tray of Greek coffees Maroula had prepared and carry it out to the terrace. A few tourists sat waiting for the bus down to the harbor. It was high season—August—and business was steady, though there never were as many tourists up in Hora as down below in the harbor. Only those who wanted a more "authentic" experience bothered to make the twenty-minute bus trip up the mountain. In the morning and evening, Dimitri's clientele were mostly men from the village, who stayed inside smoking and playing backgammon while watching the TV mounted in the corner above the ice cream freezer. In the late afternoon, the terrace belonged to the foreigners—Germans and Scandinavians mostly, a French couple who returned every year, and once in a while an Italian.

Returning to the interior, Dimitri sat down at a table by himself, pushing aside the pile of newspapers with which he had been wrapping icons. He opened the letter and read.

My Dear Pappou,

   I apologize for my ragged Greek and for the many years since my last let-ter. I have read again the letters you sent when I was a boy. The Greek charac-ters appear strange to me here, too, like garden tools—hoes and scythes—like some code of my childhood that I am trying to break. But I find that I have forgotten little.

   You wonder, of course, why I write now and why I did not write for so long. The last letter was yours. In your let-ter, you said I was more like you than my father was. When we left Greece after my father died, my mother told me that she and I could live there until we both grew beards and we would not be Greek. It is true that she was not Greek. But am I not Greek?

   That, however, is not my subject. For as many years as I have not written, we have been searching for my mother's fa-ther. I believe you knew my grandmother

```
Frederieka when she first came to your
island. I wonder if you know, perhaps,
more than I do—or more than my mother
does—about her and the man who was the
father of her child, that is, my mother's
father. I sometimes think my grandmother
told my mother stories in such a way as
to soften the impact of terrible events
in relation to that man's identity. Would
you kindly tell me what you know?
    I am now a painter. And I have not
forgotten the stories you told me. I find
myself telling them lately.

                    Sincerely, Axel (Akakios)
```

The room was dark, lit only by a stripe of sunlight that came in through the doorway. Dimitri could feel time passing in the click of the ivory backgammon pieces around him. If the boy were there, where would he sit? Inside with the Greeks, or outside with the sun worshippers, drinking Heineken or Amstel? Just two weeks before, Dimitri had wondered if the boy would want his father's diving suit.

Like most Greeks on the island, Dimitri had tried to put the years of the Nazi occupation behind him. And then the years of the military junta. There were things, of course, that he could not forget. Like knowing that he had been betrayed by someone of his own village. How it irked him to hear Politimos asking for God's protection.

Dimitri did remember the arrival of the German Jew, Frederieka, just before the Nazis had come to the island. She was pregnant and afraid. And beautiful. What a will to live! Even now, Dimitri could not think of her without a shiver that shot from his solar plexus down to his gut. His father had given her shelter and she and Dimitri had spent evenings sitting on the rooftop, he teaching her Greek words, beginning with the names for the foods he would coax her to eat. At first, she had hoarded the things they gave her, bread and sweets, olives and cheese. But she had learned quickly, and he had watched in wonder as her belly grew, one moonlit night followed by another. She had told him how she'd been costumed by Nazi officers to look like a contessa for the party they'd staged on the Island of the Peacocks, celebrating the Nazi alliance with the Italians under Mussolini. She told him it was seeing herself dressed that way—the fountain of beads on her forehead, the glimpse she caught of herself in the surrounding water, and the quickening of the child in her womb—that would not allow her to be a whored Jew any longer, or to become a dead Jew.

The war had not yet begun, but Jews had been dispossessed and many had fled Germany's borders into the neutral territories of Austria and Poland. The daughter of early refugees, she had been retained for the pleasure of the Nazis. And she had seen friends disappear.

The Nazis had stocked the party with film stars and celebrities to help them play at being Italian lovers, Italian fascists, cardinals and pontiffs. Goebbels had taken on the ogival headgear of a cardinal. He flapped his wings, strutting and stumbling after a peahen. His red face, she had said, bobbed over the crowd like a strawberry in a bowl of champagne. How many of these details had she been able to convey and how many had Dimitri filled in himself?

She had waited until the Nazis lay with their pink fingers spread in the grass or over their faces and their very white skin haunted the grounds where they slept drunk. Then she stole a wallet and bribed the boy loading the truck with statuary to help her get to Milan. Pretending she was deaf and dumb, she hadn't stopped until she'd reached Dimitri's island.

But Frederieka had married another boy from the village. Then Dimitri's son, Theo, had married Frederieka's daughter, Frosso.

Dimitri pushed the letter from Axel aside and reached into the box of icons beneath the table. He opened the *Kathimerini* to a story about a boatload of Kurds who had washed up on a neighboring island, and laid the icon on it, pondering his response to Akakios. Or Axel, as he called himself now. He wondered if he should tell the boy that story. Dimitri began the letter.

```
Dear Axel,

    Have you ever seen the floor of the sea?
I have been there recently and it is really
quite extraordinary.
```

He was distracted by a conversation out on the terrace. "Do you go to the back and choose your own fish?" a man asked. Dimitri got up from his chair and walked over to the doorway. They were tourists, talking about eating at Politimos's place down in the harbor. The woman said, "No, but maybe you can if you ask." Dimitri knew there was a reason Politimos wasn't displaying his fish to his customers. The fish Politimos pulled into the harbor and served at his taverna would be ragged looking these days: mullet and snapper with ruptured blood vessels, broken bones—evidence that he had grown impatient with the sea. Dimitri burned to tell the tourists the price of their pleasure, but he resisted. He sat down again and addressed himself instead to Axel's questions.

```
    I don't know if the past can ever be kind
to us. We cannot shape it as we do the
present.
```

He had always loved Frederieka more than his own wife, more than life itself. Maybe he was as little to be trusted as Politimos. He knew God had most likely forgiven him, if God cared at all about such things, but forgiving him was like pouring honey down the gullet of a goat.

Dimitri wrote for twenty minutes or so, telling Akakios little of this but some of what Frederieka had told him: that the father of the child had loved her. That he was a Nazi but was not like the others. Then he returned to the task of wrapping the icons on the table. He paused to examine his copy of the island favorite, depicting the storm-tossed arrival of an abbot and monks from Patmos to the monastery on the face of the cliff near Aghia Margarita. It sold in the local shops nearly as quickly as it could be reproduced. The men in the boat were praying for deliverance from great, stylized waves rendered like the leaves of an artichoke. Dimitri painted these icons without life models. Occasionally, he relieved his own boredom by changing the faces of the men in the boat to those of his friends on the island. When he was feeling particularly impious, he used even less likely models. The icon in his hands, for example, featured Politimos as the abbot. It was a joke only locals would appreciate. What would Stelios have to say about that? He hadn't responded well to the Maroulas. Dimitri wrapped the icon and placed it in the box along with the others. He sealed the letter he'd written and copied the address out of a little book he kept in a drawer of the table. Then he retraced his steps to the post office to mail the letter and continued on to Stelios's place with the box of icons.

13

LYDDIE WENT TO AXEL. When he opened the door of the flat, she fell into him, sobbing. She told him about the letter from Phelps. The postmark meaning Phelps was alive. That Phelps had sent the letter at all meant he had not willfully abandoned her. That he had not signed it or written more meant he was most likely in danger. That she was there with Axel meant that she had not been patient. She had run out of patience, and was tired of its representing virtue. Axel said that what had happened was good luck, the child's father coming back from the dead. It was certainty where there had been only uncertainty before. Every child deserved that. "But the child's father also happens to be my husband," Lyddie said. "He disappeared for over four months under a premise at least slightly falsified and then sent an unsigned note. That won't buy the baby a shirt or take him to the zoo. And what is this you and I are doing? It's something different than when we began."

"Maybe he is making right the wrong he helped to perpetrate."

"Why would you think that?" Lyddie said. "Let's face it, Axel. He's given none of us the satisfaction of knowing what he's doing or why." Axel wiped her face with a wet cloth and for some reason brought her a comb, with which she combed her hair. Lyddie stayed with him that night and was awakened by his nightmares, which she suspected were the reason he never wanted to stay the night at her place. "What are you dreaming?" she said, waking him. "Tell me."

Axel dreamed his teeth were crumbling in his mouth and he was swallowing them. He dreamed he was driving the Trabi but was cramped in its compartment because the back was occupied, floor to ceiling, with the carcass of a huge animal he had slaughtered illegally. The odor was less than pleasant. He could think of no way to get rid of the carcass except to eat it, and so he returned to his flat where, night after night, he sawed it up into cutlets and shoulder roasts, enough for a party of eight or ten, but he ate alone, and he ate until he didn't have the heart to go on eating.

During the day, Axel ate almost nothing. It seemed to Lyddie that he needed her and she was glad for that. He spoke to her of his demons. She told herself it was for him that she stayed the next few nights, though he listened to her, too.

Axel watched Gerdot IV, who came and went from his flat, once to the library, where he sat reading Schiller; once to the liquor store; and another time to the pet store, where he surveyed all of the birds and the reptiles, asking the clerk numerous questions about the requirements of each, but in the end left empty-handed, as if he had merely been looking for conversation. The longer Axel delayed contact with him, the more unnatural he felt lurking around the neighborhood of the man's flat.

Seeing that it was no good for Axel to search for Gerdot, Lyddie tried to persuade him to give it up. She remembered the guards' interrogation of her at the border four years earlier, and she said it was no wonder the East Germans thought Axel was spying, the way he followed these Gerdots. If he'd given them little reason to think so then, he was giving even the West Germans cause to wonder now. Furthermore, as Lothar had pointed out to both of them, nobody was born a Nazi. It was a political party, not a chromosome. You joined, or you didn't. Who in Germany didn't have a grandfather who was a Nazi? There must have been hundreds of those men—thousands of them still living. As for being a Jew, Axel didn't really embrace that heritage except in the form of this obsession. What about the Greek in him? Lyddie asked.

And yet, Lyddie thought about the part of her own child that was Phelps—Phelps, who was alive somewhere, and maybe in danger. That part possessed her still in that her unborn child half belonged to him. She herself was made up of obligations to absences. The Phelps whose hand had written the letter had displaced, now, the Phelps with whom she had argued and the one in whom she had confided over the past few months. The real man, who was apparently alive, he had blundered into Lyddie's consciousness in a way that left only silence. He was a man of few words. The dreams she'd had of his death stopped abruptly, and the nights were long and narcotized with this new reality.

One night Axel woke Lyddie with a cough. He sat up in bed and when the coughing stopped he said, "I went to mail a letter at the post office in Prenzlauer Berg." He was tired now so reverted to German. "*Ich trug keine socken.* I was wearing no socks. It was winter. The snow was falling wet and fast from a sky gray and finite. He snatched my letter—the guy working there—and then his eyes fell to the hems of my pants. He was staring at my chapped ankles. 'You need socks,' he said. I said, 'I have chosen against socks.' When the worker laughed, his gums showed, along with the dark rims where the plate of his teeth met them. 'Socks are not a choice,' he said with authority. 'You shaved this morning. I commend you. That was a choice, perhaps. Your ankles are roasting now in the warmth of the office. They were pink when you came in, but they have gone as white as pork bones.' At last," Axel told Lyddie, "the clerk's eyes met mine. 'You think you have made a choice,' he continued, 'but what you have made looks to me like another man's dinner.' The clerk laughed again, breathily with his neck and shoulders, and then he began to cough." When Axel awoke, the coughing was his own.

He got up to open the window wider and then walked to his desk, where he turned the lamp on and sat, sweating, in front of the typewriter, waiting, it seemed, for the words to come. He had told Lyddie they rarely did anymore. "Axel," Lyddie said, "It's three in the morning." He typed a few words then dropped his hands into his lap.

He walked over to where he'd left his pants the night before and pulled them on. He began searching for his shoes.

"Where are you going?" she asked groggily.

"I will speak with Gerdot."

"Which Gerdot? They'll all be sleeping."

"I must," he said. "If I don't I will go mad. Gerdot III and the dog give me nightmares. I need to replace him with another."

Lyddie threw her legs over the side of the bed and sat for a moment, drowsy, trying to get her bearings. She pulled on the jeans she'd worn the day before. Unable to button them, she slipped the black maternity top Sabina had given her over her head and then pulled it over the partially zipped pants. "I don't want you to go alone," she said.

He was watching her in the pale light of the desk lamp. "You need different clothes," he said.

"I suppose," she said. They hadn't talked about the pregnancy much until she'd told him about the letter from Phelps.

"And you need to take good care of yourself."

"I do. I mean I take good care."

"No. Not really," he said. "You try not to think about it. You can't not think about it anymore. You've avoided things you can no longer avoid."

"And you are scavenging for the remains of things that are best avoided."

Rather than take the Trabi, they walked. Outside, the air was fresh and cool. The windows were mostly darkened, except for an occasional living room lit by a TV screen and an insomniac. Axel said, "It's not scavenging. We are like night managers. You and I oversee the turning of the globe from the dark side." He was vigilant, taking in the gleam of hubcaps and the corrugated slouch of empty cardboard boxes and the dog shit beneath a row of bushes. He threw an arm around her shoulder and pulled her to him, inhaling. "Your hair," he said. "It smells faintly of lichens. And fresh bread." He let her go.

Lyddie said, "Axel, even if you don't avoid the past, you can't change it. If you ever become a father, and then a grandfather, then you can decide what a father should be, and what a grandfather should be. You can be that for someone else."

"Have you decided what a mother should be?" he said.

"This is about you," she said.

"You are going to be a mother. I am not going to be a father."

"I never thought you were," Lyddie said, defensive. She had not given license to the shadowy feeling that Axel had more claim to the child in her womb than Phelps did, dead or alive, since she had made love with Axel more than with Phelps in the baby's presence. But there the feeling was, caught like a bone in her throat while she insisted she'd eaten no fish.

"I mean I never will," he said.

"How do you know that?"

"I am unable," he said. "An illness when I was a child."

They walked more quickly along the drab streets of Wedding. Driven by some fury inside, Axel guided them toward the Tiergarten with its great trees full of four-a.m. wind, the sky an eerie, warm mauve of street light and city neon refracted. At the corner of Altonaer Strasse, they caught a glimpse of the winged figure of victory atop the tall column of the Siegessäule, which looked spitefully toward France. Approaching Händelallee, Axel checked his watch. Four-thirty. He indicated to Lyddie the building across the street. Lyddie stared in amazement. "That's his car, there," Axel said, indicating a pumpkin-colored Audi parked on the street directly in front of them.

"This is where Gerdot lives?" she said. "In the Hansaviertel?" Axel sat down on the wet grass of the Tiergarten. "I've been here," she said. "I've always wanted to see inside these places."

"This one was designed by Walter Gropius," Axel said.

"Yes, I know," Lyddie said. "Shouldn't we wait until daylight?"

"We will arrive like a dream," he said.

They climbed the steps to the third floor and hesitated in the hallway. Axel knocked. The Gerdot who answered looked so shocked to be visited in the middle of the night that he had forgotten to take the precaution of asking who it was before opening the door. The freckled pink skin on his forehead was fragile and papery. Backing into the room in his pajamas, he looked as though he had seen a ghost. He smelled of whiskey.

Axel extended his hand. "I'm Axel Herzog." Gerdot did not offer a hand in return. His hands were, in fact, shaking so badly that Axel may not have been able to seize one successfully had it been offered.

"What do you want?" Gerdot said.

"May we come in for a few minutes? We merely want to talk."

"Who are you? Are you with the leaseholders' association?"

The whiskey bottle sat on the table, empty. "I would offer you whiskey," Gerdot said, following her eyes, "but the liquor store is closed."

The very ordinary living area was distinguished only by the unusual geometry of the floor, crosscuts of two-by-fours juxtaposed mosaic-style. There were no doilies, no afghans draped over the tubular steel chairs in the kitchen, which itself was square and yellow—a color reputed to collect light. Gerdot drew his upper lip downward as he raised his eyebrows. When Lyddie and Axel didn't go, he moved reluctantly to the interior of the flat and sat down in an armchair near the living room windows, leaving them standing. Axel said, in his best friendly detective voice, "We're wondering about a Jewish girl named Frederieka." He took a picture from his pocket and showed it to Gerdot. It was the one Lyddie had seen in Axel's book at the gallery the night of the opening. "Did you know her?"

The look on Gerdot's face at that moment reminded Lyddie of an expression she'd seen on Axel's—the look that, like a screen door open to let a dog out, dismissed any niceties you might have prepared. Gerdot took the photo from Axel and walked to the window. He gazed out on the Tiergarten, where he seemed to see something in the darkness of its billowing greens. Axel walked over to him, and Gerdot handed the photo back, not looking at it again. "No," he said. His mouth twitched.

"A long time ago, perhaps?" Axel said. He watched the other man's face.

"How would I remember?" Gerdot said.

"But how is it that you do remember?" Axel said.

Gerdot looked to Lyddie for a way out, as if she might defend him. His lip trembled. "I asked God to send someone," he said.

Axel and Lyddie were silent.

"Maybe I saw her at times, but I never had her. I would never have accepted a gift from them." He walked across the kitchen and opened a drawer.

"A gift from whom?" Lyddie asked from across the room.

Now with a small packet of papers in his hand, clipped together, he answered. "From the Propaganda Ministry. To surviving members of the Prussian Academy—those who had received our letters of racial purity. We would see her at meetings of the KDK, the Fighting League for German Culture. 'The beautiful aberration,' they called her." Gerdot had begun to regain his composure. Axel looked at him as if he were the Ministry of Death incarnate.

"When was that?" Lyddie asked, trying to give Axel time to plot his next move.

"Great God, that was a world ago," he said, suddenly dismissive. "Things were seen in a different light. But can I offer you a drink?" Gerdot walked again to the cupboard, which he opened in vain. Did he think they had finished with the subject of the girl? He came back to the table, the little papers still in his hand, which was now shaking violently. As he sat down and removed the clip, the papers, which looked like labels, scattered. Lyddie followed Axel's eyes to Gerdot's large hands, the pinky fingers bent sideways so profoundly at the distal joint they looked as if they had been broken.

Axel seemed uncomfortably conscious of his own hands, which he kept in his lap, and Lyddie wondered if he had noticed. She picked up a couple of the papers and said to Gerdot, "Did she carry your child?"

Axel looked astonished at Lyddie's boldness. Gerdot had claimed he'd not had relations with the girl. But had Axel not noticed the fingers? From the start he'd told her to look for the family resemblance.

"They finished her," Gerdot said, skirting the question. "She disappeared." He used the euphemism with such understated calm that Lyddie was nauseated. Her hands went to her belly. Then she walked to the sink and threw up in it. For the first time since she had decided not to abort, she felt protective of the fetus she carried. She knew something Gerdot did not: that the child had survived. The girl had escaped. But Axel looked less and less like he wanted to be known to Gerdot.

"Look at it. Please," Gerdot said, indicating the paper in Lyddie's hand. "It's something I want to give you. Something I promised her."

The papers were, all of them, labels from whiskey bottles.

"People die," Gerdot said, "and then there is only guilt. I want to be done with it." He sat down at the table and pulled a blue and white handkerchief from his pajama pocket to wipe the sweat from his upper lip. "The land we had, my wife and I, was in Westphalia," he said, "and we lost it after the war." Holding one coupon aloft, he said, "You can redeem me."

Lyddie handed Axel a label and in silence examined the one in her own hand. It entitled the possessor to one square meter of barley field, which he could visit in rubber boots provided by the distillery. She gestured to the pile on the table and said, "There's a lot of land here." Gerdot had been drinking steadily in service of the absolution Lyddie doubted he deserved.

He stuffed the coupons inside an envelope and waited for the hand that held it to stop its violent spasm. Then he handed it to her. "You are a stranger. I will not see you again," he said. Lyddie could think of nothing to say. Only the aphoristic wisdom of the Bauhaus, the articulation of a psychological physics, pattered inside her head: *A charity appeal mailed in a light-blue-green envelope will command a surer philanthropic response than one sent in a white envelope. A telephone bell ringing in a white booth will seem louder than the same bell ringing in a purple booth.*

Then it was as if, for Gerdot, the screen went blank. "You say you are with the Association?" he said.

"We don't want your land," Axel said. "We're collecting for peacocks." He stood up from the table, disgusted, and shoved the chair back in with his foot. "And some topiary. We're asking each resident to give 200 D-marks." He waited for Gerdot to go to the credenza and return with a stack of bills.

Outside again, Axel walked so quickly that Lyddie had a hard time keeping up.

"Does that seem about right?" he said, trying to control his anger.

"Does what?"

"Two hundred D-Marks for a fuck in 1936. Somehow I'd always imagined they paid her. But she was a gift." He waved the handful of D-marks. "This, Lyddie," he said, "is my inheritance." He stopped walking. "He asked God to send someone. The coward!" he said. "Expecting God to do his dirty work."

"I know. And the fingers," Lyddie said.

"What fingers?" Axel said.

Axel hadn't seen the little fingers.

"Oh, Jesus, Lyddie, I don't know if I can bear any more."

Lyddie hesitated, but he seemed to be waiting for her. She took his hand and separated the pinky from the other fingers. "Did you ever break this?" she said. Both pinkies were the same.

"No," he said. Then, understanding what she might be suggesting, he said, "He had my fingers?"

Afraid of his reaction, Lyddie stared at the sidewalk.

"What a pathetic fucking liar," Axel said. "I sat there listening to his obnoxious lies, and I almost believed him. I hoped there was no blood we shared."

"He may have cared for her," Lyddie said. "And he's paid more than two hundred D-Marks. He thinks she died. He's clearly all eaten up by guilt."

"So there he sat, larded with years of his own gory forms of indulgence! Suicide would have been more prudent." Axel's fury continued to escalate. "Well, perhaps God has sent me," he said. He looked as though he wanted to crawl out of his own skin. "I had a knife in my pocket the whole time and I should have used it. Or given it to him and hoped he'd know what to do with it. Why didn't you tell me when we were back there?"

"Please don't talk like that," Lyddie pleaded.

Axel stopped in the middle of the sidewalk and looked back toward the complex.

Then he began walking in that direction, back toward Gerdot's building. Lyddie froze. She didn't think him capable of killing anything. Even the dog, he had suffered over. But he seemed crazy with this new knowledge and with Gerdot's failure to own up to what he'd done. At the curb about ten yards short of the building, he stopped beside the pumpkin-colored Audi and began slashing at its tires with a vengeance, moving from the driver's side back, around the rear and then to the front seat on the passenger side, where he hesitated and stopped breathing long enough for Lyddie to know that the heaving and the gasping she'd heard were mainly his. The tires merely sighed as they relaxed onto the pavement. The streetlight illuminated the passenger seat, where Lyddie could see that Gerdot had left a plaid wool cap and an advertising circular. Axel allowed his breathing to slow and quiet. He looked at Lyddie, who watched from near the hedge. Pocketing the knife, he left the last tire with its worn tread and inflated optimism untouched.

Axel walked calmly back to where Lyddie stood. She said, in a voice that was grainy and exhausted, "What made you stop?"

BACK IN AXEL'S ROOM, they opened the window and lay down on the bed. It was light by then, cool and gray outside.

Axel said, "They slept under billions of stars."

"Who did?" Lyddie asked.

"The Desert Fathers," he said. "And sometimes they acted in error but they were forgiven by good men like Macarios."

"Why? Why were they forgiven?"

"It was their deepest intention to live simply and by the truth, if ever they found it."

Axel told Lyddie he felt an uncomfortable tingling in parts of himself that had been asleep—a sensation that heralded not only desire and anger, those sado-masochistic bedfellows, but now pity and grief and remorse, like a three-legged dog that laps sloppily at the faces and hands of those who don't necessarily want it around. He said, too, that maybe there was something worse than not knowing who your grandfather was. As if by way of apology, perhaps remembering their talk about Phelps, he said that maybe certainty was not an answer to the most difficult questions. "That's why" he said, "I stopped before slashing the last tire."

"The Desert Fathers are more your kin than Gerdot is," Lyddie said. Despite the genetic evidence, she was sure that Axel could not afford to participate in the sort of ruin to which Gerdot had succumbed.

Axel said, "Seeing him at the table, so afraid that someone might ask something of him, I saw a man almost as incapable of moving on as I am."

14

LYDDIE CLOSED THE NEWSPAPER that lay on the table in front of her at the café in Neukölln where she and Axel sat waiting for Lothar to show up with the keys to the flat they were helping him paint. Lothar had come up short on time and labor for the job, and Lyddie needed money. Axel sometimes helped Lothar when there was enough work for both of them.

The newspaper headlines read *700 East Germans Surge Across Austrian Border!* The Ossies had gathered under the pretext of holding a "Frontier Peace Picnic" and then made an exodus. Lyddie found it thrilling, this massive breach of the Iron Curtain. For the present, those who left the DDR illegally by "vacationing" in Hungary, even if they made it into West Germany, would not cross back through the East to reach West Berlin. So West Berlin, insulated by the Wall, remained relatively untouched. Still, it seemed only a matter of time before the East Germans would reach there. Axel pushed the paper aside. He signaled the waiter for a refill on his coffee and asked

Lyddie if she had seen the article about the blind—the people whose vision had, on account of medical advances, been quite suddenly restored. "Most of them," he said, "found the experience of sight terrifying."

No, Lyddie hadn't seen it.

Axel said, "Trees, which had been just smudges of green, became, in full definition, terrible." He was looking up, now, into the chestnut tree shading their table. "Their millions of leaves were threatening, the world relentless as it forced itself on the eye."

"Did they adjust?" Lyddie said.

"They wanted to go back," Axel said. "They wanted to not see." He took her hand and they sat in silence.

Chestnuts dropped dully on the sidewalk. A pair of small boys walked past, making farting noises with their armpits. Inside the café, someone had set up a TV on the bar, and Lyddie and Axel heard an East German woman talking about bananas.

"Ossies," Lothar said, approaching the table from the street in his white painter's clothes and acknowledging the newspaper on the table. "Arriving now in masses."

"Yes," said Axel, letting go when Lothar looked at his and Lyddie's hands, and shifting to German, as he and Lothar did when they argued. "And bringing the stink with them. What do they want, anyway?"

Lyddie, keeping up with them, said, "Don't you think others have a right to the freedom that you enjoy?"

"Who said we were enjoying anything?" Lothar said with a grin. "Let's go. The stuff is all at the flat."

Axel gulped the remainder of his coffee, stood up, and grabbed the paper as they left. "They blunder over here with a couple of suitcases like the chicken crossing the road," he said, catching up with Lothar. Then he addressed Lyddie in English. "Do you know that specimen of American humor? Why did the chicken cross the road? I saw that written in English on the Wall near Checkpoint Charlie."

"Our reasons were better?" Lothar said in German. He worked the lock on the outside door with the giant key.

"Your reasons. I recount for you a bit of recent history. I was asked to leave. You are the expert on choice."

They climbed the stairs and Lothar unlocked the flat, which was empty. Inside, he wrenched the lids off a forty-liter bucket of white paint and a forty-liter bucket of varnish. "I wouldn't call it choice," Lothar said, "when the alternative was to vacation in the lovely facility at Hohenschönhausen. If that is where I was for my very long holiday. I'm not certain, because, Axel, the Black Maria they took me away in had no fucking window."

Beginning to stir the paint with a stick, Lothar looked up at Axel, who was still standing near the door. "Are you going to work or would you prefer just to reminisce about old times?" he said. "Lyddie, grab those ground cloths and spread them out along the wall for me. Axel, you can wipe down the floor in there with the tack cloth." He gestured toward the main room. It was rare for Lothar to show his irritation with Axel. He had long before, it seemed, developed some method for not judging Axel on the basis of his insensitivities. But Lyddie knew from the discussion at the gallery that Lothar, too, was feeling invaded by the current immigrations, so it would be difficult for him to avoid being stung by the barb in Axel's words.

Almost in spite of himself, it seemed, Axel continued. He often tried to prove that the sincerity he witnessed in his friends, even long ago, was a fleeting emotion. "What happened to the Socialist cause of reform?" he said. Addressing Lyddie then, he said in English, "When it required sacrifice on his part, he cashed in his coupon for a lifetime supply of bananas." Axel went to the kitchen to get the package of tack cloths they had bought the day before. Returning, he met Lothar face to face in the hallway.

"If I am one too many East Germans living in the West, you, Axel, demonstrate the glumness and provinciality of at least ten. If the Socialist cause is gone, it is your friends against whom you sharpen your edge. If your friends go, then you will divide infinitely against yourself. I hope your half-life is long." Lothar shook his head and continued into the bedroom with his roller and paint pan. "And speaking of time," he called back, "we have exactly three days before the new tenants arrive and it takes twenty-four hours for the floor to dry after one coat. We haven't started and we need three coats. Can we please finish this place without banishing one another?"

Returning to the far corner of the living area, Axel knelt and began to rub down the freshly sanded oak floorboards. "Maybe I just need to get out of here," he said thoughtfully, in English again, his voice carrying through the empty flat.

Lothar called from the other room in German, "Where else would you find anyone who'd tolerate you, let alone give you work? You're getting pretty crazy, Axel. You know that, right?" He walked back to the living room to look at Axel, whose progress across the floor on his knees was like that of a penitent. Lyddie, following in Axel's wake, began to apply a coat of varnish. She avoided looking at Lothar, who had seen her hand in Axel's. "I mean I think you're a really incredible poet and all, but you're a little demented. Back me up here, Lyddie."

"Why do you say that?" Axel said, looking up from his labor.

"Oh, for instance, the woman from next door who showed up at the flat yesterday and accused you of killing her dog. Did you get my note? In my mind, Axel, the evidence against you lay less in her accusation than in my sudden and unprecedented inclination to believe it might be true. Yes. That my own friend from childhood, whom I have always and forever defended, might well have been responsible for the death of that innocently mangy creature some five or six weeks back."

Lyddie, making long, smooth strokes as Lothar had instructed her, felt all at once empathy with Lothar and guilty complicity with Axel. Axel rubbed at the floor steadily and with great care in large circular motions, not looking at her. He tossed the first soiled cloth over toward the door and began with a clean one. "Technically, her dog was hit by a car," he said.

"But you see what I mean, Axel. I could picture how it might happen. How you might involve yourself. And that troubles me." He went back to the bedroom and turned on the radio of the boom box, which was tuned to a station doing a special program on polkas and funk.

"My God," Axel said. He poured some varnish out of the bucket Lyddie was using and began applying it in the other corner. He worked steadily, inhaling the resinous smell of the finish. "What did you tell her?" he asked finally.

"What's that?" Lothar said.

"What did you tell the neighbor?"

"Oh, she won't be back. But that's hardly the point. If you left, you'd merely be running from yourself." Lothar was quiet for a few minutes. Then he said, "You know, I came to the West to get away from the Ossies. And now they're coming here because for some reason, in its old age, Hungary has loosened its asshole. Neither of us likes it. But I mean it, Axel. You need your friends. When was the last time you cared about anything important? Or even cared about anything? Give me a date."

"November 1968," Axel replied without hesitation.

"That was one hell of a long time ago, my friend," Lothar said, falling silent.

WHEN THEY HAD PARTED WAYS with Lothar, Lyddie said, "Axel, you were only nine years old."

"We were living in the flat on Raumer Strasse in Prenzlauer Berg," he said.

They rode the U-Bahn to Wedding in silence, though the subway car was nearly empty. Axel seemed to be letting the train take him back to a lost time and place that he had, without premeditation, spoken back into existence. 1968. They climbed the stairs to his apartment and he sat down in the kitchen. "It was cold out, late November," he said, "and I was chilled from my mother's scrubbing. My hair was still wet and it felt like it was freezing to my scalp."

"Yes," Lyddie said. She stood in the doorway, listening.

"My stepfather led me along Schönhauser Allee toward Senefelder Platz. Many of the upper storeys of the buildings stood vacant, the ones who had lived there having moved into 'palaces of the people.' They were the new highrises the state had built at places like Lenin Platz and Marzahn. But my stepfather had not put his name on a waiting list, even though our flat was crowded and it had no central heating or hot water. We passed the storefronts where my mother waited in line each day for bread and meat.

"'Papa, why don't we move to Marzahn?' I asked. My hair was freezing, and the damp air invaded my trouser legs and coat sleeves.

"'This is where we live, Axel,' my stepfather said.

"You know, in the East was built this elevated rail line, which we called The Municipal Umbrella. I remember we were walking in its shadow and I walked faster to reach a patch of sunlight. I knew we were going to the Jewish Cemetery. I don't know why I insisted on going there with my stepfather. Perhaps I did not want him to be alone in that place. Each time we entered the little oasis of death, dense with trees, I wanted to run.

But my legs felt slow and heavy. It was as if I were dreaming. Only my love for that man in the rumpled loden coat helped me overcome first the impulse to run and then this terrible paralyzed feeling."

Lyddie asked no questions. She let Axel talk. He was somewhere else. A boy again. And she knew the story he was telling would be a kind of key to all of the other stories he told. Even the stories he didn't tell. There was a part of her that wanted to cry out *Stop!* but she listened instead.

"My stepfather was a quiet man. He rarely talked, and when he did, he rarely spoke about politics or personal history. He worked as an engineer. What I knew from my mother was that at the age of fourteen, when the Soviets crossed the Oder and were advancing on the city, he had been handed a Panzerfaust bazooka and sent with his mother and older sister to fight at the front. Somehow he came out alive. His mother and sister were not so lucky. He had been twenty-two at the time of the Workers' Uprising against the Russians but he did not join in the uprising, though he was working on a municipal project on Karl Marx Allee.

"So when he stopped at the gate of the cemetery and he addressed me, I was surprised. 'Listen,' he said. 'The Jews were killed by the Nazis. You understand that.'

"I knew that I and my mother were Jews, at least partly. And that we were also Nazis, partly. She never said it like that, but I knew. 'In the days at the end of the war,' my father said, 'when the city was beseiged by tanks on the ground and bombed from morning until night, they sent even women and boys to fight, though it was clear they were going to be slaughtered.' I knew this too, but I listened with care for any new detail my stepfather would give.

"'If the instinct to survive was strong enough in you,' he

continued, 'and if you were wise enough to see that the Nazis were defeated or you believed they were wrong and you tried to run away and hide among the dead, you were hung from a tree in this cemetery by the Nazis as a deserter. Many trees in Berlin had been cut down for heat, but these, with a purpose, were left standing.' The densely planted trees inside the gate looked terrible to me—sinister and capricious. I was trying to sort out who was this 'you' that my stepfather spoke of. Where would I have been? On which side? I wanted, always, to believe I'd have turned on the Nazis and the Russians.

"'Did you run, Papa?' I asked.

"'No, I did not,' my stepfather answered. 'But if you didn't run from the Nazis, and rather your fear made you fight, then when the Russians came, they hung you as a Nazi from the same trees.'

"'But you escaped,' I said with relief. We had not entered the cemetery and my shoulders and neck began to relax as we stood in the sunlight.

"'I am talking about allegiances. Do you understand?' he said.

"I nodded, though I was not at all certain I knew what my stepfather was trying to say. I was used to his conversations that left out so very much, and I knew it would be of no use to ask him to explain further. My stepfather had stopped talking and he put both hands into the pockets of his coat. He was distant. I stayed at his side, and I remember leaving my own hand free should my stepfather want to hold it.

"We did not go into the cemetery but instead we continued down Schönhauser Allee to the statue of Alois Senefelder, inventor of the lithographic process. He knew that I loved this monument. I approached the statue of the seated man and ran my fingers over the letters set backward at its base in imitation of a lithographic block. Though I knew that the letters said Alois Senefelder, I deciphered them anew. 'Allegiances,' I said to myself."

Axel got up from the kitchen and walked into the other room. Lyddie followed. She watched him shuffle through the morass of newspapers and papers on his desk, looking for a clean sheet. Still smelling of paint thinner, he sat down in front of the typewriter. He found a piece of paper, which he set aside, and he pulled a saucer toward him. He took a pouch of tobacco from the pocket of his jacket and rolled three cigarettes, lining them up on the saucer. He pushed the typewriter back, stood, and walked to the window, where the working-class district stretched out before him in unrelieved sameness. "Why don't I move away from Wedding?" he said aloud thoughtfully, as if Lyddie were not there. "Because Wedding is where I live."

He seemed to take comfort in the smooth tautology of the moment, completed not in his own voice but in that of his stepfather. He walked back to the desk, lit one of the cigarettes and smoked it hard. He pulled the typewriter back into the small clearing he had made and inserted the piece of paper, on which he typed carefully, watching his fingers. Lyddie saw a word forming above them: ALLEGIANCES.

Axel returned the carriage and typed more fluently: My father hangs himself from a tree.

Axel smoked again, and then, as if he were unaware of her presence, scrolled the paper out of the machine and turned it over so that it lay back-side-up on the table before him. He ran his fingers from right to left over the impressions made by the keys.

"Axel?" Lyddie said.

"My legs refused to carry me away from the place where he had hung his coat from the limb of one tree before hanging himself from that of another. After that, I stopped caring about nearly everything."

Lyddie kissed his hair and his neck and the love they made on the bare floor was needy and full of hurt and exhausting, as if they were acting out on each other's bodies the history of their losses.

15

LYDDIE RETURNED TO THE FLAT on Kaiser-Friedrich-Strasse, and for the next few days, she kept her distance from Axel. One afternoon she walked the tree-lined paths of Charlottenburg Palace, just two blocks from her flat, while the sky roughed up into a black-gray as dense as an animal's hide and the wind tore water from the orderly trajectories of the fountains. Fuchsias tossed like chandeliers in a room where the windows had been left open. Lyddie thought about Axel's stepfather hanging from a tree, the small boy gazing up at him. She thought of Phelps standing in a wood near the edge of a mass grave, watching his Kurdish friends take bullets while a tiny blastocyte manufactured itself inside her. While she grew plump and multiple, Phelps became thin and desperate. Desperate to protect the secrets he had kept from her. Had he known about Axel's dark past? Did Sabina know? Was that why he had tried to scare her off? Or had he merely, out of jealousy, manipulated her lack of information so that she couldn't make her own decisions.

She thought of Phelps losing his mind while she and Axel kept at it with one another. And she thought of Axel, who maybe did care about nothing and no one. Anymore. Axel, whose heart kept breaking.

Lyddie breathed the heavy air, moving slowly in its amphibious spaces and welcoming the inevitable. Just as she hit the cobblestones of the open courtyard on the street side of the palace, the rain came, spattering her face and arms and then driving at her in sheets. She felt the rounded cobbles with the bones of her feet through her shoes as she ran. Reaching the entrance at last, she stopped to look back over the statue of Frederick the Great, drawn up from the seabed where it had lain for safe keeping during the war.

Inside, she drifted on the tide of language that washed in around her before she began separating Finnish and Dutch from French and Japanese. Noisy with the excitement of rain, of being wet there in the palace, people exclaimed over their own bodies in wonder: men wrapped like seals in the thick, wet folds of their t-shirts, women in soaked dresses that contoured their thighs and breasts. Lyddie's pregnant belly drew smiles.

The guide began the tour with a comparison to Versaille—a mistake that was universally understood, as people were already extending fingers to touch the faux-marble finishes. Lyddie wished for the bombed palace, its dome broken to the thick sky. She wanted the ruined damasks and the wind-chapped mantles, the walls blackened irreparably, even on the calmest of days, even under the vigilance of stars and a well-monitored peace. She was strictly anti-reconstructionist.

Another day, Lyddie took her sketchbook and rode the train out to the Grunewald where, walking with Axel six weeks before, she had seen several houses in the International Style. There had been a time when the Bauhaus design of the house she stopped to sketch might have seemed like an absolute: the almost Pleistocene simplicity of the facades; the flat, eaveless roofs; the universe in which there was no weather. Long, long ago there had been days when she could ask a question and the world would give a straight answer. Not always the one she wanted. But an answer. Maybe the world remained simple, and it was she who had grown difficult. Maybe she wasn't asking the right questions. Not asking had her husband believed that Dow was helping to kill the Kurds, and if so, why had he gone to Iraq anyhow? But asking instead why he never thought she was capable of handling the whole truth.

The sure, flat lines of the roof where she began her sketch gave her a nostalgic satisfaction. She lingered at a window with no cornice; above it, the white stucco had been streaked permanently where rain and snowmelt, finding no gutter, had run down. These houses were contracts to be read once and adhered to, no matter that the leaves came and went from the trees, no matter that people's lives refused to follow blueprints.

Now every belief seemed untenable, every desire misguided. She had tried to be, if not more responsible, then more responsive to something deep inside. Architecture was, for Lyddie, its own metaphysics, each building an argument about the nature of being. It was a pattern for the rubble over which history and obscurity would quarrel when the rest of us had finished our own quarrels with the unknown. Was there no architecture for these days? She couldn't stop loving Axel, even knowing that Phelps was alive. She waited for the joy over Phelps's survival to overtake her, but it did not. She had telephoned Ray and the Department of State to say that Phelps might be a hostage or a prisoner. She had told them, against Phelps's wishes, about the note. Even that he might know some things that Dow would rather he not know. Ray had pleaded with her to come back. Together, they would harass the authorities. But Lyddie said, "What if he doesn't want to be found?" and Ray had hung up on her.

A light drizzle began to curdle the lines of Lyddie's sketch. Lyddie watched it happen for a few minutes, curious at nature's revision of her careful work. A woman with a long pair of scissors came out of the house and clipped three roses from a bush in the yard. She stared suspiciously at Lyddie, whom it was clear she thought was no more than a trespasser or a vagrant, up to no good. The shower grew heavy, releasing into the air a sumptuous fragrance of honeysuckle and earth.

AXEL AND LYDDIE WENT in the Trabi to the flea market, where Axel wanted to pick up an armchair he had found there. They parked the car and walked East down 17 Juni to the River Spree, along the way trying on old men's coats and bizarre eyeglasses and hats with plumes, as if scavenging in the closet of history, nostalgic for lives they would not have, alone or together. At the near end of the bridge, a thirty-foot statue of Sophie Charlotte towered over an assortment of teenagers and peddlers gathered at its base. An old man leaning against Sophie's gown played "Good Night, Irene" on the accordion. When they found the vendor they were looking for near the bridge, Axel sat down in the chair and said, "It reminded me of a chair my mother had." The chair was a sea-foam green, its upholstery stiff and nubbly. Lyddie thought how suddenly forlorn Axel looked sitting in an armchair in the middle of a major thoroughfare. "Will you do something for me?" he asked. "I think you need an assignment."

"I might," she said, though she could not, at the moment, think of anything she would not do for him. Was it for him that she was turning her back on Phelps?

"Would you go to the East for me? I'll give you my mother's address. I want you to take her a message."

"Can't you visit her? Ever?" Lyddie asked. She shivered a little. It was the end of August. The weather had turned cool overnight and she'd thought little about a change of seasons when she had left home. She didn't have anything warm to put on.

"Not in East Berlin," he said.

"What is the message?" she said.

He scribbled an address on the back of a slip of paper he pulled out of his pocket and handed it to her along with an envelope. "Please ask her to open it when you have gone. Her name is Frosso."

Afterward, loading the chair into the trunk of the Trabi, Axel lifted out a pile of newspapers and found an old gray-blue broadcloth jacket. He handed it to her. "Put that on, if you like," he said, holding it by the shoulders and shaking it out a little when she hesitated.

LYDDIE CROSSED THE BORDER without incident and bought a few postcards; then she found on her map the address in Prenzlauer Berg that Axel had given her. She was glad to have Axel's jacket, not only because the air was damp and cool but also because it felt like a buffer against the barely restrained hostility pervading the atmosphere in the East.

She boarded the elevated train in the direction of Griefenhagener Strasse. She was nervous carrying a message into Communist territory, especially since she didn't know what it said. And if, on her return, she were asked if Axel had asked any favors of her? What would she say? To make matters worse, Axel's mother wouldn't be expecting her. Once in her seat, Lyddie sank a hand into the deep pocket of the jacket, searching for her map, which she pulled out along with a well-pressed handkerchief, a couple of receipts, and a very fine silver pen, none of which belonged to her. She admired the pen and used it to circle on the map the block where Axel's mother lived. The rest of the train ride she spent trying to decipher the faded German on the receipts and to figure out what Axel might have bought the last time he'd worn the jacket. It wasn't difficult to picture him walking these streets, waiting in line at the markets along Griefenhagener Strasse. She made out the word *Schnitzel* and the date 1979. It must have been ten years since he'd worn the coat.

Having located his mother's building easily and entered at street level, Lyddie climbed four flights of steps and then paused on the landing to catch her breath. Landings, Lyddie was certain, were among the loneliest places in the universe. You have arrived, but you have not been admitted. Nobody knows you are there. Maybe someone will come, and maybe no one. Maybe someone is staring at you through the fish-eye scope at the center of the door. She gathered her courage. Her knock was answered by a woman's voice. "Frau Herzog?" Lyddie said. "Frosso?"

"Who is it?"

"I am a friend of Axel's," Lyddie said in German. The door opened a few inches, and peering out from the crack was a woman with the dark hair of someone who looked much younger than Lyddie had expected Axel's mother to be. Lyddie greeted her. "I'm Lyddie," she said.

Frosso nodded, opening the door guardedly for Lyddie to enter. She gestured to the couch, which looked as though it had come out of a 1950s sitcom set. A pair of philodendrons grappled with one another on a TV tray near the window. Frosso's face was lovely, her features dark and strongly defined. Lyddie sat down, still wearing the blue coat, the map and pen in her lap. "I'm visiting from West Berlin. Axel sends his greetings," she said.

"He is well? He is eating?"

"He is well. Yes."

"He is not eating, then," Frosso said.

Lyddie smiled faintly. Frosso sat down in a chair opposite her. "The jacket is his. The child too?" she asked.

"No," Lyddie said. She stood and crossed the room to hand Frosso the envelope from Axel.

"Thank you," Frosso said politely. She looked in thinly veiled despair at the envelope, as if what it held could not possibly be good. Then she went to the kitchen and, returning with a knife, slit the envelope along the end.

"Oh!" Lyddie said. "He would like for you to read it in privacy. After I've gone."

Frosso's face was carefully composed around the mouth. "Has he found my father?" she asked.

"I'm not sure," Lyddie said, having no idea what Axel had told her in the note.

"Strange," Frosso said, shaking her head, then looking at Lyddie. She looked so long that Lyddie wondered if it was the apparition of herself in Axel's coat that she meant was strange. "Once I thought I would give anything to find him."

"And now?"

"What use? I would not give up my son to find my father. That was not what I wanted."

"Axel speaks fondly of you," Lyddie said awkwardly, for lack of anything else to say. She had been under the impression that Frosso had pressured Axel to find her father. The truth was that Axel hadn't spoken of his mother much at all, aside from telling the story of her and the scarf, which both galled him and, it seemed, inspired him in his search. Lyddie had sensed, nonetheless, that Axel suffered over his mother and wanted her happiness. He had taken the photo of his grandmother from her to protest her sentimental reconstructions of her own history, but then he had tried to use it to help her find her father. Now Lyddie saw something in Frosso that helped her understand

Axel's distress. Just beneath her nearly passive countenance flashed a trace of emotion so intense that it seemed only to await its occasion. More than her naturally dark hair, it was this that made Frosso look younger than her years and distinguished her from the East Germans Lyddie had seen on the train on the way over or in the state-operated restaurant four years earlier. The others seemed resolute in their sobriety, resigned to the drabness of their lives, the utility of bowls and spoons.

"Tell me," Frosso said abruptly, "something so I know I can trust you."

Lyddie looked alarmed.

"Something, I mean, about Axel."

Not sure she wanted to be trusted anymore, or was worthy of trust, Lyddie said, rather tentatively, "Well, you know I am wearing his coat."

"I see," said Frosso. She stood and, as if she didn't have time for such foolishness, began using the knife to snap some leggy pieces off of the wandering jew.

"And…" Lyddie said, painfully aware of the resemblance between her feeling at that moment and the way she felt when Axel said something dismissive, "He is afraid to…show what he is feeling." Frosso returned to her chair, which, with its wooden arms and worn green upholstery, looked uncannily like the one Axel had picked up at the flea market, as if the two had been a pair divided when the wall went up. "Why is he afraid?" Lyddie said.

Frosso's face softened from resistance to sadness. "I will tell you this, Lydia: he is not an enemy of the people. Take that news back with you. He should not live in dishonor." Lyddie thought it almost laughable that Frosso believed anyone in the West cared what the Communists called Axel—Enemy of the People or Superhero among Gods. It made Frosso seem suddenly naive.

But Frosso looked at Lyddie directly, and Lyddie fidgeted with the pen, twisting the upper portion. "His friends—they chose to leave their country. But not Axel. What did he do? He did nothing!" Her voice was rising now and her eyes filled with tears before she lowered it again. "In truth," she said, raising an index finger, "I think Axel cooperated more than any of them. Do you understand me?" Lyddie nodded, though still unable to rise to the pitch of Frosso's emotion. How could she tell her, without insulting or discrediting the Communist government, that no one thought ill of Axel in the first place? "He is a smart boy, and his research at the library was good. Once, they allowed him to cross the border, to take me to the Pfaueninsel, in the West, you know it? He asked them, and they allowed it. It is the island my mother loved, with the peacocks. The island from which she escaped. Now," Frosso continued, "I don't believe anything they say. Nothing. So tell Axel this, please. Do you understand me? I want to leave this place. I need Axel's—" Frosso stopped abruptly. "What is that?" she said, indicating the pen in Lyddie's hands. "Why do you have that?"

"What do you mean?" Lyddie said.

"Open it for me, please." Looking stern now, as though Lyddie were trying to resist her, she said, "I mean you will please open it for me. Screw it open." Baffled but following her instructions, Lyddie gave the pen a twist and it sprang open on top of the map she held in her lap. She looked in amazement at the pieces lying there, some of which did not appear to be standard pen parts.

What happened next was a blur. As the implications settled in around her on the way home, it was hard for Lyddie to reconstruct the actual sequence of events. At first, she had been immobilized by her own shock that she'd found actual physical evidence of Axel's having been bugged, however many years ago. She knew what Lothar had told her about the Stasi's interest in them, but it had seemed so remote. Being in the East now was like being in a time capsule. She was so absorbed in this sensation that she was broadsided by Frosso's anger, the subverted emotion that had finally found its occasion. Frosso threw Lyddie out onto the landing in a torrent of German, and Lyddie was back on the elevated train, sobbing in a car full of strangers, before she understood that Frosso thought the pen was hers—believed that Lyddie herself had been recording their conversation. What Frosso had said about the Communists would, of course, have been damning. All the way back to Charlottenburg, Lyddie fingered the parts of the pen in the pocket of the coat, though she didn't dare take them out to examine them further. After she made it through Checkpoint Charlie, she realized how risky it had been to cross the border in possession of them.

By the time she got back to the flat, she was exhausted and in a complete state of alarm. She felt terribly wronged by Frosso's assumption, but she couldn't imagine upsetting Axel by telling him about the incident. He seemed to have trouble enough moving beyond the past. Still, Frosso would be anticipating repercussions. Somehow, again, Lyddie had been caught in the middle of a mess that didn't feel at all like the long-ago past. For the first time since she'd arrived in Berlin, she wanted nothing more than to go home, whatever was left of it. To make matters worse, she had promised to keep Ulla that night while Sabina went to Bad Bramstedt to see about the land the "grandparents" wanted to give her. Sabina was waiting for her at the flat when she arrived and had time only for last-minute instructions. "I'll be back around noon tomorrow," Sabina said. "I forgot to bring her books, but she'll play with just about anything. *Tchüss!*" she called, halfway down the steps and blowing kisses.

Lyddie was spent, too distracted and preoccupied to play with Ulla. It was enough that Axel had been nearly destroyed by this business of trying to find Frosso's father, which no longer meant anything at all to Frosso. Add to that the terrible misunderstanding that had taken place. Unable to think straight, Lyddie sat down on the davenport with Ulla and opened a big volume on the architecture of cathedrals that she found on the bookshelf. She read the captions aloud to the child. She pronounced the German sentences with feeling and listened with care to Ulla's German chatter in response. She looked where Ulla pointed. Ulla said, "Why are the women sad?" and Lyddie shrugged. Too hard a question. She read, "The elevation of the nave is as somber as that of Magdeburg Cathedral: there is no triforium and the windows are small and Spartan." Ulla said, "Your arms are not puffy and soft like my mama's" and Lyddie read, "The north tower was raised to its giddy height asymmetrically and regardless of the substructure, accompanied by four side-turrets spiraling up on their own." The world was all askew, and none of the answers matched the questions.

Still, there was an intimacy between Lyddie and Ulla; Lyddie felt it in the way Ulla regarded her. As they looked together at the book, the photographs reminded Lyddie of Axel's painting in the exhibition at the Albright-Knox. The gutted cathedral full of broken-down cars. The faulty transmissions and cracked engine blocks of history. She remembered what Lothar had told her about the Trabi repair shop and Axel's despair over his car. There was the spirit's need and then the pileup of days that just kept finding new ways of saying no. Standing before Axel's painting, she had felt that paradox fully—been present in it. Axel was the catalyst for her experience of the world. She would not for anything unknow what she'd come to know. Axel. All of Lyddie's anxiety returned when she thought of him.

She must have said his name out loud, because Ulla, who she thought might be drifting out to sleep, said, "Axel is quiet, like you, Lyddie."

"Is he?" Lyddie said.

Ulla nodded. Then, turning to look into Lyddie's face, she said gravely, "Does talking hurt you?"

"Is that what Axel said? He said it hurts?" Lyddie asked.

"He said it can hurt people."

"But how, Ulla? Talking is good, no? Would you like to talk?"

Ulla shrugged. Though Lyddie's chest had begun to tighten and she felt a kind of panic rising, she asked, with exaggerated calm and a sweetness she'd heard in Sabina's voice when she dealt with the child, "Does Axel come to your house often?"

"No," Ulla replied.

"When do you see him? When did he tell you that?"

"At Lothar's," Ulla answered. Lyddie knew Ulla stayed there overnight once a week.

Lyddie sat with the child in her lap long after the little body slumped casually and the lips loosened in sleep. How innocently it seemed Ulla had given away Axel's secret. But then, it hadn't been Ulla at all, really. It had been Axel's own mother. Axel was more cooperative than the others. And, of course, the pen. Lyddie stroked Ulla's hair and began to hum softly against the chaos that had begun to break loose inside. Axel had talked, wasn't that it? In the East. He had talked. Hush, Ulla. Why had no one seen it? He still followed people! She had helped him do it. Lothar had told her that what had happened to Axel wasn't particularly bad, but she knew now that it was very bad. It was some kind of evil. He was. Yet as soon as she thought this she knew it wasn't true. How to do things like what it seemed he had

done and not be evil, she didn't know. She had no idea what he
had thought he was doing. But she knew, almost beyond a doubt,
that she'd begun to unravel the mystery of him in the present:
his desperation and his scorn, his passion and his resistance.
She'd begun to understand the story he had told—about the
monk who violated his austerity diet with honeycakes brought
to him by another monk. Axel was protecting himself, in advance, from her judgment. Despising himself for the pleasure
he took in her.

After she put Ulla down on the bed, Lyddie went into the
kitchen and made tea. Her sketchbook lay open on the table
and she flipped absently through her various "takes" on Berlin.
Though Lyddie had suspected, once, that Sabina and Axel were
lovers, what Ulla said dismissed that notion. Could she feel relief
to know Axel wasn't Sabina's lover, just a Stasi informant? If
that was what he was. She lay down her pencil and, drinking her
tea, did nothing for half an hour or so. Her having been with
Axel—a man she now believed had worked for the Stasi; having assisted him in his stalking of Gerdot; having shared, somehow, his anguish and his want; and having loved—loving?—him
made her feel that she was standing alone in that gutted cathedral. The parts of cars that had once added up to something
useful lay abandoned around her.

She really did want nothing more than to go back home.
But home wouldn't know what to do with someone like her.
The new suspicion that Axel had betrayed the others, rather
than making her feel angry or deceived or hurt, seemed to void
the shaky contract she had made with her own life. Phelps—
were he in fact alive and no matter his sins of omission—could
never love the part of her that could love a man like Axel.
Hadn't she, at bottom, known from the beginning that Axel
was capable of treating people like curiosities and then spitting

them out when he was done? So though she couldn't know what she thought she knew and be in love with Axel, the love she had had for Phelps, even if she could find a way to forgive him, assumed a simple heart on her part. And even when she had discarded this love for Axel, as she knew she must, it would have expanded something in her that would be left open and empty and could not be filled by Phelps or by nostalgia for who she thought Phelps had been. She ripped out the sketch of the house she'd made the day before and tore it into small pieces. Not knowing with whom she should be angry, or how to go on thinking what any of it meant, she felt herself letting go of every answer she ever thought she'd had, torching the blueprint of a life she'd worked at faithfully.

WHEN SABINA RETURNED THE NEXT afternoon in a state of nervous anxiety, Ulla was napping. Sabina's mother had left several frantic messages with Sabina's neighbor regarding Siegfried, who, in his fury over a curfew she'd imposed, had kicked a hole in the living room wall. Sabina insisted that if they were patient, the homeopathic remedies would do their work, but her mother said she couldn't handle Siegfried in the meantime. They had talked about the possibility of Sabina's taking him somewhere for a few weeks.

To make matters worse, the "grandparents" in Bad Bramstedt had told Sabina they would have the papers for Ulla's land prepared in a month. They wanted, when Sabina was ready, to put up a cottage there. Sabina could bring Ulla for the northern *Luft*, which the doctors had said would help the asthma she'd had since she was a baby. "There are days," Sabina said, "when I feel that Ulla and I are stepping into a fairy tale, one that I myself have written. The ending is not happy." Sabina had seen the land, where a light wood of larch and hemlock spilled over into a small meadow. "When I think about walking with Ulla," she said, "picking morels as we make our way to the cottage, I imagine, also, the wolf dressed like a grandmother who is waiting for us inside." She told Lyddie she never pictured the wolf eating them, but rather caressing Ulla, its dander arousing her allergies, which would bring on an asthmatic attack. Sabina laughed at herself over this. As far as she could tell, there was nothing about the grandmother to inspire such apprehension. Except, of course, that she wasn't the real grandmother. And that had begun to trouble her when it came to the question of an inheritance.

Lyddie was surprised at the way Sabina so easily grafted her adult experience onto a child's tale. As if the child of twenty years before had never moved from her vigil beside the telephone in that flat in Neukölln, where she had first begun to manufacture her own destiny.

Sabina sat on the sofa in the living room of Lyddie's little flat. She took off her shoes and curled her legs under her. Through a large window, Lyddie watched a man in the flat across the courtyard ride his exercise bicycle in his underwear. Sabina said, "I've decided to leave here for a while. Siegfried needs it. And I need it."

"Leave?" Lyddie said, shocked. If anyone left, it needed to be Lyddie herself. She didn't think she could handle being left, again, even by Sabina. "Where will you go?"

They heard Ulla awake, talking to herself in the other room. Sabina went in to get her. "Maybe Spain. Or Greece," she called from the bedroom. "Turkey? Somewhere the weather will be fine and to live is not dear. Not for permanent. Just for a time."

To live is not dear. Strangely, though the bottom seemed to be falling out of Lyddie's life, her entire existence truly ungainly, Lyddie felt that to live was very dear. After Axel had scolded her for neglecting herself, Sabina had taken her to see the midwife at the hospital clinic, and they had seen in the sonogram the baby's luminous head, its sweet forehead and nose in profile. Each day that it grew, it inhabited her as a persistent and subversive optimism, oblivious to the ambiguities and terrors of the world awaiting it.

"You should come along," Sabina said. "How long do you plan to stay here?"

"I don't know. I thought I would go back to my own life—my other life—before the baby came anyhow. That I would live out my curiosity and—" She stopped herself from talking about Axel.

"How are you handling to this news about Phelps?" Sabina asked.

Lyddie said, "It's not at all specific. I don't know if he's a hostage or if he's taking an extended holiday."

"He's alive rather than dead. That seems significant. And when they take hostages, the point is to tell someone."

"A prisoner then. They don't announce prisoners."

What would you do if you knew he wasn't coming back, or not for a very long time?"

"If I could help him I would. But I can't. I would go to Greece with you."

"And if you knew that he was returning to your house in Buffalo tomorrow?"

"I think I would be more happy than you can imagine that he had his life back. I would want to talk to him again. And still, I would go to Greece with you." For the first time, Lyddie realized that she had left Phelps, whether he was dead or alive. She was leaving him not for Axel, but because she was a different person than the one Phelps had tried to love. He had directed her life and now she would live out the part of herself he had not been capable of loving.

"Would you tell him about the baby?"

"I can't say. I would want to do the right thing, but I would not want his love for the child to control me."

"There is no right thing, Lyddie. You have to follow your heart."

"What if your heart is like a divided city?" Lyddie said. "What then?"

16

THE SEA WAS CHOPPY and the boat thrashed at anchor, but Dimitri wanted to see the bottom even in weather, so he went below against Maroula's wishes. Dear Maroula! The whole business of the icons seemed like a charade next to the wonders of the deep he had begun to explore—the fringed geography of sea grasses, each day their color rendered differently according to the sky and the currents. Each day issued its unique invitation. Dimitri was anchored before his easel by a weighted belt and breathing through the air hose, monitored from above by Maroula, when the body drifted past. His first thought on seeing it was that the heavy, floral Maroula had jumped in.

But the body, which turned now onto its side, one waxy arm rolled beneath it, the other outstretched toward him, reprimanded him.

Dimitri gave an I'm-OK-Are-You-OK tug on the main rope and waited for Maroula's response. She was, apparently, there at the surface. As the ghastliness of the scene before his eyes impressed itself on him, he wondered if the pressure had done something to his brain. He thought he might be hallucinating. The phantasm was not unlike one he had manufactured in his sleep innumerable times since his mother's drowning over seventy-three years before. Had his mother now, in fact, visited him? She was bloated and waxy, her demeanor languid. A school of sardines flashed toward her and lingered around her face, where Dimitri thought they might be nibbling at her eyeballs. In recent years, in his dreams, she had approached but been unable to recognize him behind an old man's white mustache. Now she bumped along the seabed, jostled and rolled by the current, and she didn't so much as glance in his direction. Her dress was ripped, her skin torn bloodlessly at the shoulder, flubbery like a piece of chicken meat soaked in warm water, or the flesh of a fish caught by dynamite. Dynamite! The thought shook him to his senses. He was not hallucinating. What he had discovered was not his mother but the largest victim of Politimos's recent fishing campaign. He himself had narrowly escaped being blasted out of the cove. Here was a real woman who'd apparently taken a dip in her dress in the early hours but had not been so lucky.

Dimitri closed his eyes then opened them, giving the body several opportunities to disappear. When it did not, he tugged twice on the buoy, signaling to Maroula that he was ready to surface. If the body were real, it would do the same in another few days without Dimitri's help or Maroula's. He would meddle no further with the dead. Once he had surfaced, not wanting to alarm Maroula (who was prone to religious histrionics at the faintest hint of the supernatural), Dimitri did not mention his experience below. Instead, he suggested they go home immediately. It was quarter to eight; they would be expected at the cafe.

Before they left, Maroula climbed so high up the mountain

to find a suitable place to pee that Dimitri thought she would relieve herself at the feet of the Almighty. She stumbled among the weeds and rocks until she reached the stone goat shed almost halfway up. Stopping to peer inside, she jumped backwards and shrieked.

"What is it?" Dimitri shouted.

"It is occupied!" she said.

"Of course it is."

"By men!" she said, hurrying back toward the beach. "They have dark faces and their eyes are very white!"

"Stay here," Dimitri instructed, going up to investigate. Seeing him approach, five men crawled out of the shed and began to scramble farther up into the barren landscape of thyme bushes and spiny spurge. Their clothing was torn, their black mustaches well established amidst scruffy beards. Dimitri called to them in Greek, but they disappeared over the top of the mountain. Observing their frightened retreat, Dimitri put two and two together. For Maroula's sake, he came out with five. "Demons," he told her when he came back down. Perhaps it was because she had revealed her bottom so close to heaven that she had called them out. The best thing to do was refuse to acknowledge them. Never speak of them. He crossed himself and she did likewise.

As he mounted the donkey to depart, his chest heavy with what he had seen, Dimitri removed his white handkerchief and waved it in the direction of the men's retreat, hoping that they were spying from someplace close by. Maroula plodded on ahead. Only after dark would he return to that place and call to them in Turkish, a language he hoped they'd understand.

Dimitri's wish was simple: to die with dignity before it was too late. Why, he wondered, should it fall to him to supervise so many foul-ups? First there had been Maroula's mishap with the oils— though he admitted to also having been distracted from his aim by the beauty of the undersea world. Then Politimos had come on the scene with his blow bottles, arousing in him an annoying will to survive. Was he now being called upon as an ambassador to foreigners arriving on Greek shores with a passel of needs?

The body had been one of their party. He would have to return to the cove in daylight to look for it, without Maroula. It was important that he get to it before the Coast Guard did. The local officials were anything but tolerant of such arrivals. Once before, Dimitri had seen refugees detained in a local building for more than a month. They were released in the end and instructed to get out of the country within two weeks, unassisted. And current officials were not disposed to benevolence in affairs involving Turkey. They might even have Coast Guard Ianni escort the refugees back to whatever violence they'd temporarily escaped.

That night, Dimitri hurried the last of the tourists, an American woman and a German woman who had arrived a few days earlier, off the café terrace shortly after ten. Returning to the cove on his donkey, he used his flashlight to peer inside the goat shed, but no one was there. "I've come to help you," he called in Turkish. "Where are you hiding?" Still no one came. He heard only the sea lapping at the shore. From the side of the hill, the water looked black and impenetrable. Dimitri left the bundle of bread and cheese and goat meat he had prepared after closing up the kitchen at the café; then he went down to the beach and waited with his back to the mountain. A few minutes later, he heard a whistle from behind him, and three men came to him out of the darkness, licking their fingers. "More black pepper next time," one of the men called out.

Dimitri replied, "Where are you from that you ruin your goat with so much pepper?" They weren't standing close enough that he could read their expressions. "The goat seasoned itself," he said. "You're in Greece now."

"Then I guess we made it," said the burliest one, stepping forward.

The others followed, and each of them in turn shook Dimitri's hand with a formality suggesting they considered him more than their waiter for the evening.

"What happened to you?" Dimitri asked.

"Last night, in rough seas, the trafficker ditched us. Some, we think, drowned."

Dimitri told them about the body he had seen, and they murmured their dismay. "How many of you now?" he asked.

"Fourteen. All hungry," another man said. His voice was weaker, and he smelled rank.

"And who is waiting for you on this side?"

The men were silent.

"We're Kurds," a gangly teenager said, finally. "No one is waiting for us."

Somebody had taken them for fools, and maybe that somebody was right. The way they had put their lives and the lives of others in the hands of a virtual murderer, nearly met their death on the rocks, and then come down from the mountain licking their fingers and asking for pepper, Dimitri had to wonder if they fully appreciated the unlikelihood of their survival. They were almost as foolish as he himself could be. He examined their faces, coarser than the Greek faces he knew.

Dimitri turned to the donkey and unfastened the jug of fresh water he had brought down. The men passed the jug around, drinking in savage bursts and then gasping for breath. Even if he never saw them again, he would paint their faces. He would paint them in their storm-tossed boat. Maybe their trafficker as the abbot, if he turned up. (The trafficker, it seemed, always survived.) What was the point of that, Stelios was sure to ask. Dimitri would tell him: God's wasted mercy.

PART II

1

PAST THE VILLAGE WHERE WHITE houses levitated above
the road, the lapis dome of a church rose on a sky of a more
reticent blue. The convulsed geometry of the mountains had
been softened little by millions of years of wind and weather.
Only in the village were there eucalyptus and plane trees. Lyddie
thought she had arrived. But the driver motioned further on up
the road—a gash disappearing around the side of the mountain.
The truck bumped along for another thirty minutes until the
mountains emptied out onto a plain where late-season fields lay
golden and dry. In the near distance, the turquoise sea completed
a trinity of blues. The driver pulled off the road and looked at her,
drawing his mouth into a shrug that suggested he had lived up to
his part of the bargain.

"Akladi?" she asked. She had seen the name of the village
on flyers posted in Hora and had been told she would be welcome there.

The driver nodded and she stepped out.

Where she had expected loud Greek festivity—women dancing to the music of a fiddle, raki tipped to the great mustaches of the men—there was nothing. The pickup pulled away, leaving her in a cloud of dust.

The profound silence around her could be perceived only as space—an immense volume of blue sky and of field. Coaxed by a light wind, a few aluminum cans and paper napkins skittered along.

She squinted into the sun. There was no church, no village of white houses. In the dry field next to a white building that looked like a taverna closed for the season, a donkey pressed close to the shade of a ragged juniper. Peering through the open doorway, she saw nothing at first, and then, as her eyes adjusted to the dim interior, two shallow marble sinks. Beside them, three-foot stacks of dirty porcelain plates and bowls towered precariously, monuments to the day's indulgences. Garbage containers were heaped with bread and bones. Lyddie paid homage to an old sensation: that life had happened in a room just beyond the one she had entered, a room caught in another time.

She wandered out to the road. The last village had been seven or eight miles back and there wasn't a car in sight. She pulled out the little xeroxed map she'd bought in the harbor. Along a footpath leading north from Akladi was a symbol indicating the "hermit rock beds" she'd heard about in the village. On the map, it looked as though the main footpath back to Hora, where Lyddie had rooms with Sabina and Siegfried and Ulla, would branch off at the site of the rock beds from the path she set out on. Thinking of the Desert Fathers, she made her way along between two stone walls traversing the slope of the field. Sweat began to trickle between her breasts and the exertion felt good. She welcomed the return of the sensation that she was strangely beyond the polarities of beginnings and endings. She was alone, but alone was not the opposite of together. It might as easily be the opposite of water, or of sky, or pickup truck.

But when the elevation rose again and the scrubland of low, spiny mounds stretched out before her, Lyddie began to feel more intimate with the ascetic experience than she'd ever wanted to be. And a strange ascetic she made, pregnant and beginning to feel encumbered. The scrub along the path had been chewed down to the root by goats. At times, she saw where the mountains ahead collapsed to the sea in a pandemonium of blues. Then the path bent away and the sea was obscured again by the rise of the land. In less than half an hour, she had drunk her liter of water and was flushed and sweaty. The hermit beds were nowhere in sight. Had she missed the junction?

The path eased out onto the edge of a bluff and began to follow the rugged shoreline. By the time Lyddie saw a track leading downward, she was almost desperately overheated. It occurred to her that if she could make it to the water to cool off, she could navigate with a clearer head and finish the journey to Hora after the hottest part of the day. If she didn't, she might well become dehydrated. The map indicated a cove named Paradise; the symbol, a figure doing the crawl, suggested it would have a beach.

But as she began to negotiate the steep track down, not without some difficulty, she began to worry about not being able to make it back up afterward. Though she was still quite fit, the hike would have been challenging even had she not been pregnant. After ten meters or so, she felt vertigo and panic, and she scrambled back up the path. She also remembered the cardinal rule of the sea: Never swim alone. She could have waded and splashed, if it were, indeed, a beach as marked and not just rocks from which one might jump or dive, but she was afraid to go down. The sun, the salt air, her fatigue—all made her aware

of her body's architecture. Even the body carried the design of
its own ruin. In the courtyard of the ribs. In the tracery of the
nose and mouth that opened onto blue space. The vertigo made
her head fuzzy and the panic made her feel that she needed to
shit. She was almost unaware of the thorn bushes she blundered
through but not of the sun's assault. She stumbled across a ditch
and hiked another twenty minutes in the heat before collapsing
on a stone wall beneath an olive tree. Blinded by sweaty tears,
chest heaving, she plucked a small, green olive from a low-hang-
ing branch and bit into it. Its bitterness excavated her mouth.
She spat, chastising herself for all of the ignorance that had
brought her to that place. For hitchhiking alone, for having followed Sabina to that island, for loving the Desert Fathers as a
way of not loving the one who told their stories. Loving, instead,
austerity. Refusals. The outer limit of human survival. And then,
perhaps, for having wandered beyond that limit. She had failed
the cosmic quiz: What is the opposite of alone, Lyddie? Not
pickup truck. Together. With whom she did not know.

She squatted under the tree to relieve herself and was surprised to see that what she had thought was sweat in her underwear was in fact blood. And then, before she could even think
what was happening, she felt a large clump pass and some clots
of blood, which she saw on the ground. A savage taste gnawed
its way up her esophagus and she fell back against the tree.

She must have passed out for a while. When she woke, two
flies were crawling over the fetus, one scaling its tiny foot, the
other probing a nostril. It looked fully like a baby, though no
bigger than a sweet potato. Lyddie waved the flies away and
lifted the baby, still attached to its placenta, in her hands, horrified. She wanted to back up a few steps, a couple of hours,
a month, a year, to a time when what had happened had not
happened. A time when she was not so thirsty. The thing was

that the child was bloody now and not moving at all. She wanted to have stayed at home and never have come to this place,
to have never left the greenhouse where her problem was grief
that she had played no part in bringing on herself. Her problem
was plants, wilting or dying. Venus flytrap. Heliconia. She had
thought the child had a will so strong it would live in spite of
her foolishness, as it had from the start, but it had been weak.
Pitifully small. It had needed care and she had ignored its need.
Had she some water, she'd have washed it. Phelps would hate
her now. Would hate her. The cramps came over her again and
she tried to breathe deeply to manage the pain. He would hate
her if he were indeed still alive and capable of hating. Because
death could happen quickly in uncharted terrain. Maybe Phelps
was dead now and the baby too and maybe dehydration and so
much blood loss would be the end of her. So this is how it happens, she thought, calming now. How strange. Even the pain felt
distant. She was ready to accept her own imminent death. But
a moment later, unable to handle the irreparability of what was
happening—had happened—the baby in her lap, she got to her
knees and then crawled over to a stone, the fetus in one hand
and, laying the umbilical across it, used a sharp rock to saw it
off. She knotted it and then held the fetus and hummed. Was it a
fetus or a baby? She cried wretchedly over its tiny ears, its cheesy
skin. Again she drifted out of consciousness.

LYDDIE DID NOT THINK SHE could carry the baby with her.
That would make her feel like a madwoman. And she did not
think that she could leave it. She hummed to herself—a song
from some other life—to try to stop shaking. The sun had
dropped while she slept and the air had begun to cool. At last
the moon came up, silvering the landscape. From across the
valley, the sonar blip of a cuckoo located Lyddie on the stone

where she sat. She listened for a while before the other sound came—a wailing so strange and out of place she thought it might be a kind of mirage. It should have come from the baby but the baby was dead. She had to tell herself that again. A coyote? The wailing returned, metallic, hollowing out her chest like wind in a bucket. And then the sound seemed less a thing to fear than a thing to follow.

She thought about digging a grave but the earth was too hard, and she remembered burying the dog with Axel. She could not bury her baby like a dog. Phelps would hate her for that too. She could never face him now, even if she wanted to. She stood and looked around. Seeing a socket in the olive tree, she wrapped the baby in the bloody underwear and laid it in the hollowed place. She stuffed the opening with weeds and stones, making a nest around the little body, and then cleared a place around its mouth. She threw the placenta into the weeds.

Exhausted and still stunned, Lyddie began to pick her way among the stones. She was bleeding but the baby had the underwear. Maybe she should have wrapped it in something else. She stopped and tore a piece from her skirt to try to stem the flow of blood. Above where she stood and farther along the side of the mountain, in the moonlight, she could see what, in her earlier panic she had not been able to see before: two stone walls cutting a diagonal against the horizontal terraces. If she could scramble that far, it would probably be a donkey path. Donkeys, unlike goats, had destinations. The bawling continued—that was it—crying—and she stumbled into the sound, pulled by sadness and fear and moonlight. By the time the crying stopped, the path had broadened and paving stones shone underfoot. Just around the curve of the mountain, she heard the sound of water burbling over rock. The houses of the village were mostly open to the sky, their roofs caved in, stone walls and windowless arches broken off and exposed. At the top of the village, big stone laundry sinks stood intact. Spring water flowed along a small sluice connecting them. Lyddie cupped her hands for the cool water and drank. Then, exhausted, she stretched out on a smooth, stone bench, wondering if this were the place she would leave her own bones. The moon blasted through three tall cypresses above her.

2

A SINGLE, CURT CICADA startled Lyddie awake. *Tssst! Tssst!*
The air smelled sumptuously sweet—honeysuckle and the
warm, powdery snuff of jasmine—but with a funky undercur-
rent. On opening her eyes, she found herself gazing directly at
the crusty knees of a donkey. She sat up on the stone bench, trying to remember where she was, how she had come to be there.
Though it was still dark, the sky had begun to soften about the
edges of morning. Water burbled nearby and all the unease of
the previous night returned when she saw the old man who had
apparently been addressing her.

"For what you come here?" he demanded gruffly.

The interrogation from behind the drift of his great, white
mustache made her feel as though she had awakened into an
afterlife: one in which she would surely have to plead guilty. She
was deliriously tired, and thirsty again. "The feast…" she said.
"At Akladi." And then I lost the baby, she thought but did not
say. All night, the tiny homunculus had dallied in her sleep.

"How you come from Akladi? *Me ta podia?* With the feet?"
he said.

Sitting up, Lyddie felt lightheaded. "By thumb, and then on
foot," she answered. "I walked here from Akladi." She realized
now who the old man was. She hadn't recognized him in this
strange place and without his beret, which she now saw he had
in his hand. He put it on, as if to confirm his identity.

Lyddie and Sabina had been well out of the harbor at
Piraeus when Lyddie had asked how Sabina knew about the island that was their destination. The answer was Axel. She knew
of it from Axel. The ferry had ploughed on ahead. It would
not reverse its engines. Its enormous, coiled ropes would not be
thrown down to the quay, nor would the huge ramp descend,
scraping the concrete, just because Lyddie wanted to get off.
Out in the middle of the Aegean, there was no quay.

Axel had told Sabina about the island where he was born.
And though they had not been given an invitation to visit,
Sabina had used the coordinates of Axel's life to chart her own
course and Lyddie's.

They had met Axel's grandfather, Dimitri, on the terrace of
the little bus stop café in Hora, the village from which Lyddie
had set out the morning before. "You search hermit beds?" he
said now. "God damn that Axel. He tell anybody everystuff."

"Not Axel," Lyddie said. "I haven't spoken with him." All of
that seemed far away now. "You told me," she said.

"So, did I?" Dimitri said glumly.

He had told her there had been mystics right there on the
island. Their heads had left permanent indentations in the stone
where they'd slept. "We will go there one day, you with me," he
had told her. "Do not go yourself alone. We will go, but we wait
some time."

"Hey," Dimitri said, examining her more closely. "You OK?"

Now a breeze turned the leaves of the olive tree in the courtyard all at once to their silvery undersides, and something as delicate as the needle of a compass shifted inside her. It had to do with
the shirring of the leaves, and the breeze on her skin at the same
time. There was blood on her leg from the day before. But she was
alive. She felt it keenly. And her baby was lying in the hollow of
a tree. What had Dimitri asked her? Something about Axel. Yes.
God damn him. Had it not been for Axel's ascetics, perhaps she
would not have wandered into the scrubland so wrecklessly. Now
her loss bound her to the choices she had made.

"You come alone?" he said.

Lyddie nodded. "I went to the feast at Akladi but it was over.
Finished. I was trying to find my way back to Hora." She stood
up tentatively, as if to continue on her journey.

Dimitri scrutinized her now. "Greeks no go *me ta podia* every
donkey shit path on this island," he said. "Why *Amerikani* think
they can—" He stopped abruptly, staring. Lyddie followed his
gaze to the place where she had been sitting, the stone bench
covered in blood.

"Dimitri," she said. "I lost the baby. It came. Before its time,
when I was lost."

"It is living?" he said.

"No."

"Why this happen?" he said.

"I was lost and so hot and I had no water. It was stupid of
me to go alone," she said, increasingly distressed. "It didn't have
to happen." She told him how she had decided to find the short-
cut on the path back to town rather than wait for another ride.
How at first, being alone so far from anything had given her a
surge of pleasure. "I think I need help," she said.

"Tell me, then. You were to this village?" he said, indicating
the ruined houses, visible in the cool first light of morning.

"No," she said.

Dimitri was thoughtful in the wake of Lyddie's revelation. He removed his blue beret and mopped his head with a handkerchief. The donkey flicked its tail. "You need rest," he said.

"Do people live here?" Lyddie said.

Dimitri made a scolding click with his tongue and jerked his head slightly upward in the Greek way. The gesture looked like a yes, but the sound countered it.

At that moment, a siren of a wail rose up—the same sound that had guided Lyddie to the place the night before. *"Panaghia mou!"* the old man exclaimed, invoking the Virgin as he removed the beret again and rubbed his balding head. Lyddie looked in the direction from which the sound had come. Dimitri, vexed, stared up into the three cypresses that rose above her.

"What was that?" Lyddie said.

Dimitri picked up his olive switch and flicked the flies away from the donkey's hindquarters, as if hoping he might in that way also discipline the howl into silence.

Finally, resigned, he said, "More bad you know just a little." He stood and, taking the donkey by its rope, started down the path. Looking back, he said, *"Ella, Amerikanida.* Come. You can walk?" Lyddie drank again from the water spout then followed Dimitri and the howling, past houses built amphitheatrically down the mountainside and rooms occupied by honeysuckle vines. Whitewashed stucco long gone, dark stone walls and arches stood exposed. A Persian lilac graced a courtyard with its gold beads of fruit. The insides of the next few houses yielded a rusted oven covered with a durable piece of oilcloth and a room full of wooden chair parts. The insularity of the village, situated in one of the few places on the island from which the sea was not visible, must have had a hand in its depopulation.

Something bright caught Lyddie's eye—a red swatch isolated

against the village grays and browns. A geranium. Or someone standing in a courtyard. As they approached, it came into focus as a child's red shirt, hung on a line inside one of the otherwise abandoned houses, along with two pairs of men's trousers.

Lyddie proceeded cautiously behind Dimitri, blood trickling down her legs. Two men asleep in their underwear sprawled on the terrace of a little chapel, oblivious to the racket. One, like an Arab, wore a scarf wrapped around his head. The crying persisted, growing louder until, as Lyddie and Dimitri rounded a corner, it stopped abruptly in front of them, its source looking up with one blue eye and one brown eye, neither of which was wet. The child couldn't have been more than two years old. He didn't look Greek. His skin was darker, his almond-shaped eyes set deep with dark lashes. His mouth was pursed in a small down-turned slash. Lyddie saw that he had found the map of the island she must have dropped. He had folded it and he made it flap like a gull. Dimitri, shouldering a sack he lifted from the donkey, grunted at the boy to move aside, and the child ran off. The house Dimitri entered was one of the few still in possession of its roof. Lyddie hung back in the doorway, looking in. Several bodies—sleeping ones—occupied the floor of the room, which was bare except for a makeshift table in the center, where Dimitri left the sack.

As they continued along the path, Lyddie said, "Where are we?"

"Smardakito," Dimitri answered, tying the donkey to a tree.

"I didn't see it on the map," Lyddie said.

"Twenty years nobody don't live here." Dimitri descended the steps into a weedy square dominated by a plane tree, where a woman wearing a long, dark dress that covered her from the neck down to the feet looked up from her work among some old shutters and doors. Around them lay chair legs, wooden

pallets, and a rusted iron bed frame—articles of a life abandoned. Lyddie forced a smile and offered a greeting in Greek.
"*Yassas.*" The woman's eye's widened, taking Lyddie in. The
steadiness of her gaze made room for every possibility that
a stranger might represent: threat, friendship, exploitation,
enlightenment. Not releasing Lyddie from her gaze, she addressed Dimitri in a language Lyddie didn't understand but
which didn't sound like Greek. There was a rapid exchange
between them. The boy reappeared, a dirty pair of green
pants slung below his brown belly, but the woman paid him
no attention.

"These people," Lyddie said, "Are they mystics? Some
kind of cult?"

Dimitri's face softened, and he seemed to relax a little.
"Mystics. Yes. But careful," he added, seeing her look again at the
boy. "This one has the evil eye." The woman said something more
to Dimitri. "Go with her, Amerikanida. The women will help
you," he said. He picked up a hammer and began prying nails
out of the door, which had already seen at least two incarnations.

Inside the house where Lyddie had seen people sleeping,
two other women had begun preparing food. Briefed by the
woman whose name was Anya, they took her to the back of the
house where they had buckets of water so that she could wash,
and they brought her clean rags to catch the flow of blood. They
gave her something to wrap up in while they washed the blood
from her dress. In a language she didn't know, they made her lie
down on the cool floor and rest.

Dimitri came in twenty minutes later and sat down in one
of two chairs in the room—the only one that still had a seat. He
exchanged words with Lyddie's caregivers. "You cannot go back
now. You will stay here with them," he said.

"Why are they here?" Lyddie asked.

"They live as community. They need food. Need house. This village no persons don't use." Large circles showed beneath Dimitri's eyes. He stood with difficulty, his knees creaking. "And nobody else don't know about it."

Lyddie said. "Please don't leave me here." Dimitri walked outside but she got up and followed him. "Please, Dimitri," she said. "They'll come looking for me soon. Help me go back. I need to go." The baby's death seemed like more than a personal loss. Something she needed to report. To confess.

"Look, Amerikanida…"

"Lyddie," she said.

"OK. You listen Dimitri. I take you back to Hora. But you have choose. You help me, or you stay quiet. No American advertise," he said, wagging a finger. "Nobody don't know about this place." He looked at her legs, scratched from her scramble the day before, and shook his head, still disbelieving the misfortune that she'd found her way there. "You understand?" he said.

It seemed to Lyddie she had very little choice, or a false choice at best. She had stepped off the edge of the map of her life and would soon be forced to give up altogether on the idea that the truth was something that could be told. "I wish I understood better than I do," she said.

Dimitri looked up into the sky, as if for assistance or intervention. "I no can explain to you now. Please. They need help. You not listen Dimitri first time when he say you not go to Hermit Beds. And you gone there. Now you find hermits. So I ask you again something. I hope this time you listen me."

"How far is it to Hora from here?" Lyddie said, dismayed by Dimitri's lack of sympathy.

Dimitri checked the height of the sun, pale and composed like the yolk of an egg. "Forty minutes with the donkey," he said. "The road makes like so," and he formed a *C* with his thumb and forefinger. Pointing at the gap between them, he told her, "You found the short way—almost." He smiled then, and the old benevolence seemed to have returned.

"MY GOD, WHAT HAPPENED?" Sabina exclaimed when Lyddie found her and Ulla back at Rooms Fani Vevis, where they were staying together. The time Lyddie had spent lost in the arid backcountry seemed to her so surreal that had it not been for the continued bleeding she'd have thought she'd dreamed the baby's death. Ulla ran over and, to cheer Lyddie, flashed before her eyes the brightly woven bracelet Sabina must have bought for her at the boutique across the street from Dimitri's place. Lyddie forced a sad smile. She sat down on the bed and told Sabina the story of the miscarriage, carefully avoiding any mention of the village or of Dimitri.

Sabina looked away, wiping her eyes. Lyddie thanked her silently for not saying *You didn't want the baby anyhow.* In Lyddie's lap, her hands rested on her still-round belly. She swallowed hard, shook her head. She remembered that the baby had been a girl, and her breasts began to tingle.

"Sleep," Sabina said, turning down the sheets for her. "I'll go for the midwife."

"Why? It's too late for that," Lyddie said and dropped back onto the pillow. But Sabina went out with Ulla. Lyddie fell into such a deep sleep that Sabina seemed to return within seconds with another woman, who examined Lyddie and told them she just needed rest.

3

AFTER SLEEPING IN THE ROOM all day, Lyddie got up and, still feeling a bit ethereal, went with Sabina to the café for a late dinner. Siegfried was down in the harbor, or at the Poseidon, a club where he spent much of his time. Only very late at night would he return to the room next to theirs to sleep. Sabina had tied her hair with a scarf against the wind. Lyddie noticed how easily her carelessness in dealing with it translated to beauty. Lyddie pulled out a blue wooden chair and collapsed into it. "Mama, I'm thirsty," Ulla said in German. "I want to play with the lizards."

"The lizards are asleep. Why don't you sit with us and have something to drink, and then you can go find the other children?" Sabina said. Lyddie found assurance in the way Sabina answered Ulla's requests with a *ja* or a *nein*, a solution or a consolation.

Lyddie looked around. No Dimitri.

From what Lyddie could tell, the more he resisted them, the more Dimitri was loved by the foreigners in the village. His austere face, softened by the beret and by the kind, white slope of his mustache, had become, alongside the monastery and the headless windmills of Hora, an emblem of the island, appearing on postcards and in guidebooks. His was the face of unchanging Greek life, the life tourists came looking for.

Those who managed to eat and drink while sitting on the concrete terrace of Dimitri's place in Hora possessed esoteric knowledge regarding the mystery of service. When newcomers joined the party, no one moved with the intention of waiting on them. Even when he was there, Dimitri would appraise them passively while his daughter sat on the bench against the wall—implacable, a test of endurance for the thirsty. The refusal of her big, floral body spilled beneath her folded arms. It occurred to Lyddie that day that none of them, herself included, really knew Dimitri. What they knew was their own desire for enduring simplicity. Dimitri, however enduring, was anything but simple.

Sabina tossed her head back and pulled the scarf from her hair. She gathered the loose strands, twisting the scarf and the shank of light hair together and knotting them. "You have that look about you, Lyddie. Like something has gone loose inside," she said.

Lyddie looked up, caught off guard by Sabina's assessment. Losing the baby might have been enough to unhinge her, though Sabina couldn't possibly mean that. She also seemed to think that Lyddie's having had a miscarriage was beside the point. And yet so much had "gone loose" for Lyddie—so much Sabina didn't know about—that she couldn't imagine what the other woman meant. Everything she had done at every step of the way was the wrong thing. She felt too exhausted and edgy and tired with bleeding to do anything about it.

Lyddie was startled from her reverie by the crisp ching of breaking glass. Dimitri stood near the doorway empty-handed, having apparently come out of the dark interior and stumbled with a plate of food. People stared first at the meatballs that rolled to a stop at their feet and then, mouths still agape, up at Dimitri. Finally, to spare him the shame of being old, they closed their mouths and looked away at the sky, fermenting pink and ochre over the harbor in the distance. Maroula appeared with a broom and swept up the evidence as Dimitri disappeared inside. Reluctantly, as if she were serving mourners at a wake, Maroula brought out two plates of french fries. There was silence. After a minute or two had passed, people looked at each other again, but differently than they had before the plate was broken.

Dimitri came back out and sat down at a table of Germans drinking beer. He said something in Greek about *keftedes*, meatballs, then put his head down on the table and fell asleep. "What did he say?" Lyddie asked.

A big, ruddy-faced German with a shaved head translated. "There was a time when we would have crawled under the table after them, like dogs."

Lyddie watched the pulse at Dimitri's temple and saw the bones of his skull where his hair had receded.

"He is tired," a Scandinavian woman said, continuing the conversation in English. "He begins to forget things."

"He is a one-man history," the German said. "No wonder he is tired."

A one-man commune, Lyddie thought. "I'm tired, too," Lyddie said, standing from the bench along the side wall of the terrace and attempting to push past the bald German whose chair blocked her way.

He didn't budge. Instead, he said, "You simply have not had enough to drink. Werner," he called to someone sitting nearer the doorway. "Get our friend a Metaxa."

Lyddie protested, but the big German pulled her arm and she sat back down as Werner disappeared inside for the drink.

"What is Dimitri talking about, Ralph?" a woman asked him. He had apparently been living on the island several months of the year for a long time. He seemed to know a lot about what went on.

A blonde German with a receding hairline and a ponytail cut in. "He is talking about being hungry. The Italians were here. At the time of the Second War."

"The Germans too," Ralph said, "and for sure you know they were eating all of the *keftedes*." He looked around and laughed irreverently, with a deep, seditious *heh heh heh*. Lyddie wasn't in the mood for his coercion and his dark humor, but she wanted to know what he knew about the island. He explained that Dimitri's family had come from Turkey in the nineteen twenties, at the end of the war between Greece and Turkey. The Turkish army had burned the Turkish city Smyrna, now known as Izmir. "The Greeks who lived in that city," Ralph said, "they were hurried to go for swimming because the city was burning behind them. Only none of them knew how to swim." Ralph used his fork to convey a little bevy of fries to the edge of the plate and then watched them spill over onto the table. "Not funny, correct?" he said. "But all in the human family, these whores." He looked at Lyddie again, taking the glass Werner had brought and setting it emphatically in front of her.

"Yes," said the one with the ponytail. "We Germans too have problems of East and West. They say now that twenty thousand Ossies who "vacationed" in Hungary but didn't make it across the Austrian border refuse to return to their Utopian state." But Lyddie was still wondering what whores Ralph was talking about. Then it dawned on her that he meant horrors. Sabina looked as though she considered the demonstration with the fries wasteful, but no one moved to take any from the table, as if to do so would be tantamount to cannibalism.

"The Ossies leave happily," said Ralph. "The Greeks who leaved Smyrna were not so happy. They cannot even pretend to take vacation. You know," he continued, "the Allied Powers who told to the Greeks they can have this part of Turkey, these same ones stood on their ships and they watched the Turks throw the Greeks into the sea. They listened to the opera with very big sound so that the cries of the drowning ones cannot make trouble for their ears."

"Dimitri's family drowned?" Lyddie asked.

"Many relations, yes. His mother. And some uncles the Turks take to camps to shoot them."

The German with the ponytail volunteered with optimism, "But we have Dimitri sleeping fast beside us, so perhaps someone in the family was lucky."

"More lucky than the Kurdish who arrived from Turkey since two days or three. You have seen the boat, Ralph?" This was the Scandinavian woman.

"No," said Ralph, surprised and visibly sobered by this news of a more recent catastrophe.

"Kurds?" Lyddie said.

"Smash to smithereens," the woman said, looking at Lyddie. "It is an expression, yes?"

Lyddie nodded reluctantly, twisting a greasy napkin in her lap. She reached for the Metaxa and took a gulp, thinking of the men in their turbans, the dark-haired women who had tended to her. Of course they were Kurds. In her delirium, she hadn't seen it. Were they Phelps's emissaries in the surreal universe she'd stumbled into?

Sabina said with authority, "All are thought to be lost. Ianni told me yesterday. They have found no one."

"Which Ianni?" asked Ralph. "Fat Ianni?"

"Coast Guard Ianni," Sabina answered.

Dimitri snored lightly at the next table, his head on his arms. Lyddie wanted him awake so she could see his face. "A boatload of Kurds wrecked here? On the island?" she asked.

"In the night, they think, when the sea was high. But nobody seen it before the next afternoon. On the south side, near Aghios Nikitas. The boat went up on the rocks."

Lyddie took this in and watched Dimitri's sleeping face. Maroula lumbered out with two more plates of *keftedes* and some calamari and put them at the tables of the Germans.

"Maybe I go later," Ralph said. Tomorrow. He shook his head in disbelief. "When will finish this political mess?"

Dimitri lifted his head suddenly and, wagging a finger sideways, said in English. "Don't eat fish with Politimos!" He looked deliriously tired.

The Scandinavian woman, perplexed by the non sequitur, laughed out loud when she realized Dimitri's misunderstanding of Ralph. Her sun-scorched features suggested a hedonism approaching obscenity in contrast to the hard work of Dimitri's face and the blue of his beret. Dimitri raised a thick, serious eyebrow.

"Politimos?" Sabina said.

"The Captain. He owns the fish taverna down in the harbor," Ralph said.

"Why? Why should we not?" asked the woman.

"He take fish with big boom," Dimitri said. He put his head back down, and the others smiled sadly over his entry into the conversation, apparently relieved to let go the subject of war and exile. They began to speak German and English softly among themselves. Ralph and Werner got up and went across the road to buy cigarettes.

But Lyddie's discomfort grew. A boatload of Kurds? That, like the knowledge that the baby she and Phelps had made was dead, lying in a little nest of sticks, seemed as if it had materialized out of one of her bad dreams. Who were these Kurds? To which of the tragedies that had befallen her would they be the chorus? And Dimitri—what was he? Some kind of trafficker?

Moreover, Lyddie and Sabina had both eaten fish with Politimos, at his taverna in the harbor. How were they to know? The fish was good, its white flesh laced delicately with veins like that of a trout. She'd come to the island to escape one set of indiscretions and had, apparently, stumbled into the dead center of another. Without the child, she felt strangely cut loose. Strangely herself, falling headlong into something as inevitable and personalized as fate. She thought of the hollow above Axel's breastbone, so lovely at times it made her want to cry. She and Sabina were alone at the table now, and a question burbled up from somewhere deep inside her, from way back, when she'd first arrived in Berlin. When Phelps wouldn't tell her everything he knew. She addressed her friend softly. "Sabina, how well do you know Axel?"

Sabina, caught off guard, looked first at the calamari and then at the untouched plate of meatballs between them. "Well enough, I suppose," she said.

Lyddie proceeded carefully. "He can be so…aloof. Always protecting himself. I just thought that, if you were close to him, you might know… if something had happened to him, in the East."

A hank of Sabina's light hair fell just below her jaw, the slant of it repeated in her cheekbone. Sabina was beautiful in an off-hand way. Clearly she hadn't worked to make it so. But not everything about her was uncalculated.

"It doesn't concern me," Sabina said. "You shouldn't worry about him." She squeezed a piece of lemon onto the calamari between them; then she lifted her fork and bit the tip of a tentacle, chewing it with her front teeth in a way that tormented Lyddie. The sunburned skin of Lyddie's face grew hotter.

Looking up again at her, Sabina said rather buoyantly, "But it does worry you. You are attracted to him still?"

Lyddie's hesitation was enough of an answer.

A light wind swept in off the Aegean, lifting the napkins and fluttering the edge of Sabina's skirt and the tips of her collar, her hair. It made the nearby eucalyptus tree quiver like an eardrum. For a moment Sabina looked unsettled. "Ah, Lyddie, forget it. He is not for you," she said, shaking her head and smiling a little at the thought that Lyddie should suffer over Axel. "I don't say it to disappoint you, but I think he has not interest for anyone. It is his way." Sabina picked up the beer bottle, still dewy from its encounter with the heat, and she lifted her hair and held the bottle to her neck.

It hurt Lyddie, this way Sabina had not only of keeping her own secrets but of keeping Lyddie from sharing hers. "I wouldn't be here if I wanted him," Lyddie said, an edge in her voice. All over again, she wondered what it meant that she had enjoyed the taste of fish killed by dynamite. Maybe she was no different from anyone else.

Now the Germans went over and woke Dimitri, who had drifted out again, to count their beer bottles and tally their bill. Seeing that Lyddie and Sabina had also finished eating, Ralph said, "Tomorrow, I'm driving to the sea to look to the boat that is kaput." Dimitri stopped murmuring numbers in Greek, his finger resting on the lip of a bottle. He seemed to have lost count and, standing there like that, everyone waiting for him to perform a task of which he was suddenly incapable, he looked worried and old.

"Where did it wreck?" Lyddie asked, looking directly at Dimitri.

But it was Ralph who answered. "Around the point south of Aghios Nikitas. He paid Dimitri more than was necessary and waved off the need for change.

4

BY THE TIME LYDDIE AND SABINA went with Ralph to the site of the Turkish boat's ungraceful landing, the salvage operation had been in full swing for two or three days. The tideline at the beach was strewn with clothing, coffee pots, dishpans, and rope. Flotsam knotted a thick garland of Neptune grass that had been churned up and washed onto the sand. It looked as if a thief had ransacked the sea for something valuable, which it turned out the sea did not possess. While gulls picked at a soggy, broken box of cookies, a Greek shouted at two Albanians helping him load onto the roof of an old Toyota a raft-like segment of the boat. They had apparently carried it up from the other side of the point. The car's red paint was completely oxidized, and its shocks had given up a long time before. But the Greek man would have firewood—a rare commodity on a deforested island—through the winter. Ralph went over to talk with him.

Sabina scanned the goods eagerly as if she were at a flea market. She picked up a tin plate then tossed it aside when another shiny object caught her eye. "Why do you just stand there, Lyddie?" she said. "What are you thinking of? Do you need to rest?"

Lyddie watched as a Romani woman in a long, colorful skirt poked around in the debris, examining first a sweater, soggy and voluminous, which had a large hole in the back, and then a black shoe. The woman put on the shoe and wore it as she dug through the pile of Neptune grass, most likely looking for its mate. "No," Lyddie said, distracted by the woman hobbling through the wreckage in the black shoe, "I guess I don't need anything." And again she thought of the little body in its nest of weeds, the Kurds in their makeshift village. Sabina's bravado was, it seemed to Lyddie, predicated in a love of shiny things she thought were free. But it always turned out they had cost somebody something.

The sea was blue-gray and sullen out beyond a few greenish channels where the bottom was clear of sea grass. Ralph sauntered back. "This guy," he said, indicating with a thumb the Greek up by the Toyota, "he heard also that no one survives, except probably the captain, who is usually escaping in these situations."

Lyddie, however, knew now that there were survivors. They were being fed and looked after personally by Dimitri. They were up in Smardakito stoking a fire and banging out makeshift furniture, making do with the clothes they'd managed to keep on their backs. She stood very still, immobilized by the effort of not sharing that news. "You never finished telling us about Dimitri's parents," she said to Ralph.

"They stood in Smyrna one year after the disaster, and then the allies have a beautiful idea to exchange one-and-a-half million Greeks from Turkey for a half-million Turks from Greece. They decide to send these ethnic Greeks here. That is how Dimitri's family was coming. The uneven exchange leaves how many Greeks with no *keftedes*? I am happy to do the maths for you." He stared dumbly at his fingers, as if calculating. "One million," he announced. "Dimitri was a child at that time, on the side of the hungry."

Against the wide-open sky, the water rippled, tight-lipped about the bodies that had piled into it over the centuries. Lyddie heard its Miranda Warning: *You have the right to remain silent.* But remaining silent about so many things was taking a toll on her. And though her doubts about Dimitri's integrity had all but vanished, she was not comfortable with any of the secrets she so reluctantly carried.

"The most part of the boat is just around the point," Ralph said. "Shall we have a look?" The three of them wandered across the rocks. When they rounded the headland, the wreckage came into view. Having been dashed on the rocks in high seas at night, the boat lay in thousands of splintered boards, most of them bearing only traces of blue paint or varnish. It must have been in bad shape to begin with. A great section of the rail lay intact on a sandy area among the rocks. Ralph made his way down and lifted it, working his hands along its length so that it towered beside him. He smiled broadly for Sabina to take a photo as a huge wave came up from behind and wet him to the knees. He did not find it as funny as the Romani children did. They stopped gathering armloads of the smaller pieces to laugh at the bald spectacle before carting off their booty in the direction of the camp near the helicopter pad.

"Look! It's Ianni!" Sabina exclaimed, putting her camera away. The Coast Guard's inflatable tender came dashing in over whitecaps the wind had begun to raise. The motor having slowed, the boat settled lower in the water and approached cautiously. Lyddie hung back as Ianni leapt out onto the rocks, lean and tanned from a life spent in and on the water. Lyddie was fairly sure that Sabina had been sleeping with him. It bothered her to see

Sabina taken with such an obvious playboy. With his neat, round biceps and his pressed white pants, he was a parody of himself.

"Have you found anyone?" Sabina called out.

Ianni secured the boat and, fastening a couple of buttons on his Coast Guard shirt, said, "We are looking now for the dead. And the captain who abandoned them. By now for sure he is nearby, counting his money."

"You weren't able to rescue any of them?" Lyddie said, wondering still how fourteen people might have made their way to Smardakito without assistance.

"I do not say I am a superhero." Ianni paused, seeming to want someone to contradict him. Lyddie was glad Sabina didn't try. "The traffickers," he explained, "wait for high seas— Beaufort eight or nine—so we are not making patrol. Then they abandon the boat near shore. This way, when the boat is damaged, we cannot send illegal persons back to Turkey."

Lyddie watched the way Ianni leveled his gaze at Sabina's chest. "They are Kurds? From Turkey?" she asked.

"Or from Iraq. The boat, however, is Turkish." Ianni stooped to pick up a timber with both hands. "You can tell," he said decisively, rubbing a few fingers over its weathered surface, "because they take care for nothing, the Turks."

"My God," Sabina exclaimed. "Can you imagine? They are trusting this person, this Turk, who they believe will take them to a new life, and he is looking only after his own." Sabina's righteous incredulity struck Lyddie as odd, given the web of deceits Sabina herself had woven.

"I must go," said Ianni, stepping delicately through the rubble as if afraid he might soil his deck shoes. "Will I see you later?" he called to Sabina's breasts.

When he was gone, Lyddie shook her head in disbelief. "You can't be serious about him," she said. "Do you see the way he looks at you?" Lyddie and Sabina had always held against one another their own failures in love.

"I did not say that I am serious."

"He's using you, Sabina."

"Perhaps I am using him also." Sabina smiled, pleased with having said boldly something Lyddie would not approve of.

"I think Lyddie is right," Ralph offered. "Ianni is a *Nichtsnutz*. Sabina, you should use me instead. I offer myself." He raised and lowered his eyebrows in proposition, laughing subversively. "Think about it," he said, wandering off in his soaked pants to examine the wreck.

"What's a *Nichtsnutz*?" Lyddie said. "It sounds absurd."

"Oh, it isn't true. Ianni has a good job."

"A job he's not very good at," Lyddie said. She dug with the toe of her sneaker, exposing a timber buried in sand. "Maybe he should stop looking altogether. Sometimes it's when you're not looking that you find things."

"Lyddie?" Sabina said, examining Lyddie's face. Tired, Lyddie sat down on the rock. The waves from Ianni's boat still slapped at it. "Where are they?"

"Promise me you won't tell. Because I have to tell you, Sabina, though I am sworn to secrecy. I can't stand the way you idolize Ianni." Sabina had much finer men at her disposal. And she had, it seemed, disposed of all of them.

"Tell me," Sabina said.

She sat down beside Lyddie, and Lyddie told her how she had stumbled on the village of the refugees. Lyddie welcomed the relief of sharing how the women had cared for her after she'd lost the baby and how alone and afraid she had felt when she thought Dimitri would leave her there in Smardakito. She told Sabina the village was beautiful in a tumbledown way, that the women were bold and unflinching in the face of the disasters they had survived. Sabina listened in wonder. She seemed to hold Lyddie in higher regard for the experience she had had and for what she knew, and Lyddie took pleasure in her new authority.

It wasn't long, however, before it began to bother Lyddie even more that Sabina told her so little when she had said things she'd been asked to keep quiet. In light of the carelessness she felt was at least in part responsible for the loss of her own child, it bothered her, too, that Sabina could be so careless with the child she had. One afternoon when she and Sabina had come up from swimming at Aghia Margarita and had left Ulla at the room with Siegfried to nap, Sabina walked inside the café to get two more glasses of ouzo. When she returned to the table, an older Greek woman was climbing the steps to the terrace holding Ulla by the hand. "*Po, po!*" she exclaimed, breathing heavily. She spoke in Greek to Sabina, gesturing repeatedly up into the village then clucking and wagging a finger.

Sabina put out her arms to Ulla. "*Komm,*" she said, and then, in Greek to the woman, "*Efkharisto poli!*" Thank you! She remarked to Lyddie, "Four years old. She walked all the way to the end of the village and out the dirt road to where is the big road!" Sabina shook her head with pleasure and disbelief. The woman, returning from feeding her chickens, had found the child there, a kilometer from Rooms Fani Vevis. Ulla, with her golden curls and her cotton skirt and leggings, belonged unmistakably to Sabina. The woman wagged her finger at Sabina again in reproof.

Sharing the woman's disbelief, Lyddie said, "I thought Siegfried was looking after her while she slept!"

"Siegfried went down to the harbor," Sabina said. "She's OK. She is fine."

"You left her alone in the room?"

Sabina answered, "Once I left her at home in Berlin sleeping and when I returned, she was at the stove, making chocolate." Ulla was sitting on the bench by then and the woman had left them. Staring at the glass of cloudy ouzo in front of her, Lyddie waited for Sabina to draw out the lesson in that story, but Sabina merely nodded, as if the child's industriousness said it all. There was something missing in Sabina. Some failure to reach the obvious conclusions or to accept useful advice. It was related to her stubborn refusal to confide anything at all in Lyddie, who wanted not only to tell the truth but also to be told the truth. She wanted honesty, from herself and from others. At times, she thought it was all she really wanted. Lyddie exchanged a look with Dimitri, who sat alone at a small table just inside the doorway but had been watching. Already, she had let him down.

"I'm tired," Lyddie answered. "I think I'll go back to the room." She opened a small, woven purse to leave money for the bill. Its emptiness reminded her of another discomfort between herself and Sabina.

The previous morning, a five-thousand-drachma note had disappeared from the nightstand where Lyddie was certain she had left it with her key and a guidebook. It was not an insignificant loss—several nights' lodging—and Lyddie's funds were running low. Sabina thought Lyddie suspected she might have picked it up. By mistake, of course. Lyddie knew Sabina thought so, and in order to disabuse Sabina of this notion, Lyddie had worked overtime to vindicate them both. What was it about Sabina that made Lyddie feel she must labor so at innocence? Not just now, over this, but always. It was true that Lyddie wasn't as innocent as she had once thought herself. But Sabina casually obscured all of the questionable areas of her own life. The worst of it for Lyddie was the reality that sooner or later, she would need to begin borrowing money from Sabina. That would make her even more dependent on someone she could never fully trust. It also brought into very clear focus her own lack of a plan for the weeks and months to come.

"No worries," Sabina said, gesturing to the empty plates and glasses. "I'll get it and you can pay me later."

It was only the truth Lyddie wanted when, alone in the room, she opened the small cupboard where Sabina had tossed her clothes the night before and began turning pockets wrong-side out. Just the truth for once. Seeing the foldup bed next to the sink, Lyddie thought of little Ulla waking alone in the white room where Sabina had left her, imagined the coolness of the tile beneath her feet as she stood up, calling out in a voice small and uncertain. Lyddie worked her way through several pairs of shorts and then felt around in the pocket of a jacket. Each failure to produce the five-thousand-drachma note convinced her further not only how well, but also how deliberately Sabina had kept her secrets. She wondered what would become of Ulla and what she herself was doing with Sabina in that country foreign to them both. She yanked the jacket off its hanger and flung it across the room, where it knocked an empty yogurt container and two water bottles, one uncapped, onto the floor, sending a small stream across the tile to where she stood. She knew that one five-thousand-drachma note looked no different from another, that even if such a note had fallen from one of the books whose pages she fanned upside down or one of the envelopes she emptied, she'd have no indictment of Sabina's character. Still, she heaved up a whole pile of things from Sabina's suitcase, thrashing tank tops and socks and underwear into a messy heap and then kicking the suitcase onto the floor. It wasn't about theft or bad mothering or men. It was about the way Sabina refused to let her in. To make matters worse, she had a way of discouraging Lyddie from telling her anything but then breaking and entering unexpectedly into Lyddie's protected space.

Just as Lyddie tore the sheet off Sabina's bed, a breeze caught the top half of the door, which she had left unlatched, and swept it open, banging it against the roughly plastered wall. Lyddie spun around, the sheet wrapping her, just in time to see Siegfried disappear in the direction of his room next door. He must have come up from the harbor. How long had he been watching? Being "simple"—that was how Sabina put it—did not give him voyeuristic rights.

She dropped the sheet and walked over to unlatch the bottom of the door. Stepping out into the courtyard, she saw that the door to Siegfried's room hung open. "Siegfried," she called. He came to the door. "Why were you spying on me?" she said.

"What are you looking for?" he said, his voice high and warbling.

"Nothing," she said. "It is not your business, Siegfried. You should not be watching."

"Is it something of Sabina's?" he said.

Lyddie didn't answer. She turned and went back into her room, closing the door behind her. She looked around at the sad piles of clothes and books that had refused to give up any secrets. She did her best to straighten Sabina's things; then she walked to the sink and splashed her face with water. In the mirror, she saw white lines the sun had not found around her eyes, where she must have been squinting or smiling. It amazed her, given the range of feelings she experienced in a day, that anything of expression or emotion should persist long enough to become part of the skin. When she pulled the tube of lotion she'd bought that morning from a plastic bag inside the daypack that sat beside the sink, out tumbled the blue and white five-thousand-drachma note.

5

THE NEXT DAY, FEELING STRONGER, Lyddie set out to meet Dimitri before dawn. She followed the old path from Hora, carrying a daypack loaded with provisions she'd bought the previous evening and a blanket borrowed from Rooms Fani Vevis. She had walked just a short way when she heard a rustling in the dark behind her. She stopped and shone her light back, catching movement among the weeds—and something blue. "Who's there?" she said, remaining still. Half suspecting it was a sheep or a goat, a rag around its neck, perhaps, she repeated, "*Yassou. Is someone there?*" Cautious and alert, she shone the light again and saw nothing. She continued, tense now, aware of the remoteness of the village to which she was headed. She was relieved to find Dimitri waiting with his donkey in the place on the path nearest the rusted-refrigerator dump that they had agreed upon.

"*Ti kaneis? Kala?*" he said in greeting. "How are you?"

"*Kala*," she said. "Good. Just a little scared. It's still so dark." Now she could see that Dimitri himself looked worried. He knew about her expedition with Sabina and Ralph from the café to the site of the wreck. "Dimitri," Lyddie said, "I know everything."

"What you know?" he said.

"I know your villagers are not mystics. They're refugees. Illegal. I saw the boat."

"Ah. Yes," he said. He let her congratulate herself for a few steps before adding, "But maybe mystics also. Sufi, I think. They can be refugee and mystic, no?"

"They're probably Muslims. I wonder what they do believe."

"They believe life is more better in Greece, where in the moment nobody don't try to poison or shoot them," he said.

Dimitri said there were fourteen refugees in the village: eight men, three women, and three children, the smallest of whom had been orphaned when his mother and uncle had drowned. Dimitri told her he had seen the body of the mother when he was painting underwater. Lyddie imagined that the black shoe she had seen the gypsy woman scavenging might have belonged to her. And though she had not seen all three children to compare their sizes, she had encountered one who was very small and extremely unhappy. Now when she thought of the ragged bellow that had guided her to Smardakito and the boy with one blue eye and one brown, she pictured the woman in the cove, given over to the sea's indiscretions, oblivious to the boy's need, and still wearing the other black shoe.

"What did you do with the body?" Lyddie asked.

"At first it frighten me and I think, Just a phantom, so I do nothing. When I go there again, I cannot find it. Sometime a current wash a body in and out again. Where I see her, can be strong current nearby," Dimitri explained as they traversed the terraced mountainside in the morning mist, guided by the sonar blip of a Scops owl.

Lyddie stopped to pluck thyme from a thorny mound en-croaching on the path, which was not well trodden. "What happens when somebody finds it?" she said. As she walked, she crumbled the thyme into the palm of her hand and inhaled the crush of its scent; then she put it in her pocket.

Dimitri shrugged, performing a gesture that reflected, in the Greek vocabulary of the body, more an existential stance than a response to an immediate question. It was largely that shrug and his general benevolence, given the horrors he'd lived through—variations on war, exile, and hunger—that inspired Lyddie's trust in him at the moment. But even taking these things into account, she wondered about his suitability as director of their mission. He said, "I worry what happen when they not find the other fourteen bodies. But do I look like one who say the fortune?"

"Are we just going to hope they don't start looking for survivors?" Lyddie said, poised between optimism and doubt.

"You have better idea, Amerikanida?" He brought the donkey to a halt so that he could climb up and ride awhile. He looked surprisingly nimble as he mounted it to sit sidesaddle.

"Will the authorities really send them back to Turkey?"

"Maybe. Or they will lock them up some time, then force them to go out from the country."

Lyddie thought about Frosso's mother, a Jew, and the stories about her escape from Germany during the war. "Axel's grandmother came here, didn't she, in the thirties?"

Dimitri, up ahead, grunted.

"Did you know her?"

"Sure I knew her," he responded. "Not so big this island. Not big enough."

"Did you help her when she came here as a stranger? So they wouldn't send her away?"

"Yes, I help. I want her to marry. Her baby need a father."

Dimitri stopped the donkey for a moment and turned to look at Lyddie. "Why I tell you this many stuff?" he said, sighing. "In those years, danger was not so much they send her away. Long time she must hide when the Nazis come here." He made a skeeching sound in his cheek and the donkey began to walk again.

"You wanted to marry her?" Lyddie said, surprised at this part of the story, which she hadn't heard from Axel. Perhaps Axel and his mother never knew it.

"She was young and much beautiful. We live in Smardakito then," Dimitri said.

"You lived there?"

"Sure we did."

"And she said no?"

"My father said no because she have another man's child. Then she marry to another boy from the village."

Dimitri walked on ahead in silence. Lyddie couldn't see his face but suspected she had touched on a delicate subject. They rounded the spine of the mountain and forged their way through a derelict stretch of path overtaken by thyme bushes and by nettle, about which Dimitri warned her just as it brushed her leg. A moment later, her skin raised red welts that stung mercilessly. "Got it, did you, Amerikanida?" he said, turning when she cried out. She was reduced by the acidic sting to gasps and syllables of pained vowels. Dimitri brought the donkey to a halt and hopped from his side-seat the two feet to the ground. "When nature give a prick, it give something beside to make better," he said, scanning the weeds at the edge of the path. "*Pou enai…* Here!" he exclaimed. He ripped a few leaves from a plant growing low to the ground and handed them to her, demonstrating how to crush them and rub them over the skin. The needling began to subside, though Dimitri's botanical remedy stimulated painful thoughts of Phelps. Dimitri climbed back onto the donkey.

"Dimitri," Lyddie said, thinking again about the refugees. "I want to tell you. My husband—he was working with the Kurds in Turkey and maybe in Iraq. He was lost there, during Hussein's campaigns against the Kurds. I believe he may be alive. I know it's crazy. Impossible. But will you ask the refugees if they know anything about him?"

"*Malista.* Certainly. We will ask," he said.

"These Kurds plan to live here for how long?" Lyddie said.

"*Siga, siga.* Slowly, *pedhi mou,*" he answered. "Ask me what they will eat for lunch. Ah, *malista.* Then I tell you they will eat cucumber and fava and potato. It is what we have bring, *neh?* Here on *gaidaros, neh?*" He patted the saddlebags. Perhaps they make a long sleep in the hottest hours. And then they have for supper what you bring in your sack, Ameri..." He paused and corrected himself. "Leda. It is correct?"

"Yes," she said, before she realized he had meant her name and not the menu. She liked the error anyhow.

"So much I can tell you for certain," he said.

Lyddie was beginning to discover that Greeks generally didn't like to use the future tense, for either planning or prognostication. In time, the future would deliver itself as the present without their assistance, and then they could welcome it hospitably as a friend rather than a stranger.

After the three cypresses, they followed a passageway leading toward the open *plateia* and approached a house with a small iron balcony on the second storey. Dimitri tiptoed inside. Lyddie counted five bodies sprawled on the floor in sleep—four men, fully clothed and, curled on a rag rug under the table Dimitri had improvised, the boy she'd seen some days before. Two big clusters of garlic hung nearby—presumably for protection against the evil eye. One of the men rested his head awkwardly on a small dishpan. Pointing to the boy on the rug, Lyddie said, "He is the smallest, isn't he?"

"*Neh*," Dimitri said. "He is."

There on his little piece of ground, the boy looked as though he had just washed in with the Neptune grass, and he seemed all at once terribly lucky and terribly cursed. Lyddie hoped he did not have in his dreams the sorts of pictures that had haunted her own, though she suspected he might.

"We put the food here," Dimitri whispered, indicating the table. Lyddie found herself unable to form words at all.

"They cook on brazier. *Karvouna*," he said. "I have bring." He finished emptying the contents of the burlap sacks onto the table. "Only after dark so nobody don't see the smoke." Beside what he had brought, Lyddie's contribution of three zucchini, two bags of rice and a few pears looked small. Lyddie spread the blanket over the boy before they walked outside and, feeling the whisper of morning air and the light on her face again, she burst into tears.

"I shouldn't have wandered so far, Dimitri. I should have stayed in Hora——" her breath caught, "and taken care of myself and the baby." Then she was sobbing as she tried to explain how she had abandoned Phelps too by not going to look for him. He might that very minute have been in need, like the Kurds they had found. She sobbed from a chasm so deep she thought she would be swallowed by it.

Embarrassed, Dimitri proffered his sweaty handkerchief and looked off in the direction of the sea. "Don't you cry, Amerikanida," he said. When she neither responded nor took the handkerchief, he went to the donkey and doused the han- ky with water from a big plastic container he had filled at the sinks on their way in. He took it over to her and said, "*Ella*.

Come. Take it. Clean your face. Then we will go." The simple instructions calmed her and as she followed them, the spasms of grief subsided. As they emerged into the open *plateia*, Dimitri said, "And the husband of you, believe me, the Kurds will take care to him. These others God give us so we can be in charge. If you go there to Iraq, somebody else have to search you. You come here and you are helping. About the baby—blame someone else. Blame God because he make the day too hot. Blame the person who tell you about the feast but not say the time. Blame the Germans for their bad map. The Greeks for being lazy in the afternoon!"

Two women, their arms encompassing the huge bundles of sticks they carried on their heads, mounted the steps from the fields below the village. Lyddie recognized the older one as Anya, the woman who had taken her inside the last time she'd been there. The other, the younger of the two, looked as though she might be a sister. Her face, like Anya's, was defined by a broad, strong mouth and a long, elegant nose undulating at the bridge. The women put their loads down beside the plane tree.

"I want to thank them," said Lyddie, still sniffling.

Dimitri interpreted, and the women smiled. The younger woman gave instructions to Anya, who walked toward the house where Lyddie and Dimitri had left the supplies. Then she spoke with Dimitri, both of them looking at Lyddie. Dimitri told Lyddie, "She want to know how are you feeling."

"Much better," Lyddie said, wiping away a stray tear.

Anya took Lyddie's hand and clasped it warmly with both of her own while saying something to Dimitri.

Dimitri told Lyddie, "I say we must go soon. But she say you are guest. We have tea."

Lyddie wiped her face and met the younger woman's eyes, the whites of which were very white. The woman patted her chest and said, "Nuray." Lyddie nodded. On the ground before her, Nuray propped up a few of the sticks around a brittle and thorny piece of tumbleweed, then produced from nowhere, it seemed, three stones, which she placed at even intervals around the perimeter. Anya emerged with matches, a small pan of water, and four glasses, which Lyddie recognized as belonging to Dimitri's café. Nuray knelt and blew gently, and almost before Lyddie knew what was happening, a small fire had been summoned.

As the water began to simmer, both women looked Lyddie over carefully. Nuray smiled rather sadly, meeting Lyddie's eyes. It was as if she were not only searching for Lyddie's smile, which she found, but probing her sadness too. Lyddie found the little ritual strange, a reconnaissance mission accomplished without words. The woman patted her breast again and spoke, appealing to Dimitri to make her understood.

"The Kurds say, 'When you cannot build a village, then build a heart.' You see, Amerikanida, when they force these people out from their Iraqi village they go to live in the Turkish mountains."

The tea was strong and sweet, and Lyddie felt wide awake now. Alert through and through. Lyddie said, "Ask what area they've come from." Dimitri addressed the question to Nuray and then replied, "Bahdinan, in Iraq. Near the Turkish border."

Lyddie said, "Did she ever meet an American man there? He was studying traditional Kurdish medicine in the mountains of Turkey."

When Dimitri translated, Nuray shook her head. In the silence that followed, they drank the tea together. Lyddie patted her chest and said, "I want to help you."

On the way back to Hora, Dimitri rode the donkey and Lyddie walked ahead. The sky was overcast, so it wasn't possible to tell how high the sun was. Lyddie wondered if they might be seen returning to the village. As if in response to her thoughts, Dimitri said, "Leda, you go more fast. We don't arrive together, OK?" This concern reminded Lyddie of what had happened that morning.

"Dimitri," she said, "When I left Hora this morning, I think someone may have tried to follow me."

"You saw somebody? On the path?"

"No. I'm not sure. I felt there was somebody behind me. When I shone my flashlight, I saw something move away. Maybe it was just an animal. It was blue though."

"We have not the blue animal in Greece. You say to anyone what you find at Smardakito?" Dimitri asked gently.

Lyddie didn't want to lie to him. "Only Sabina," she said. "Dimitri, I'm sorry. I had to talk to somebody."

"*Panaghia mou!*" Dimitri exclaimed. "*Panaghia!*"

"I'm awfully sorry," she said.

"You are trusting this Sabina? She is good person?"

"She is a friend of Axel's," Lyddie said. That was about as honest as she could be at the moment, not wanting to *not* trust Sabina, and willing herself, against the evidence, to believe in Axel's integrity, because he was Dimitri's grandson. "I wish I hadn't told her," she said. "But I think she is good at heart. She promised not to tell."

He heaved a sigh. "It don't help to worry," he said.

"While I am confessing things," Lyddie said, I should tell you that I'll need the blanket back. Before I leave Rooms Fani Vevis," she said. "I borrowed it." She was thinking now, again, about the boy who lay beneath it and how little she could do to protect him.

"The blanket. I understand," Dimitri said, walking beside the donkey to give it a rest. "I have borrow many things. A dress my Maroula hang to make dry, brazier from courtyard of

summer Athenians. From my own, I 'lose' knives, pots, plates."
He laughed a little and looked at her to see if she would smile.
"Behind the forks at the café, people say, 'Dimitri get old,
Dimitri lose something more.'" He tapped the side of his head
with his finger, his blue eyes glistening. "When you leave Fani
Vevis?" he asked.

"Ask me where I'll go when I do. I can't answer either
question."

"Never mind," he said. "*Siga, siga*. Slowly. Just you don't talk
to nobody else."

"You're not angry?"

"Little bit," he said.

When they rounded the mountain, the sun was well above
the horizon. Dimitri stopped. "You know the way, yes?"

Lyddie nodded. "I can't continue to steal blankets and buy food
for so many. I want to help, but I don't have the money. They'll
need towels and soap and dishes and sugar. I can't even think how
much…If you think I have money because I'm an American…"

"No," he said.

"So what do you want me to do?" she said.

"Buy things," he said, summarily. "And you take to them.
Nobody ask why Amerikanida go out *me ta podia* into the mountains."

"Do you understand me, Dimitri? Buying is what I cannot
do. I'm not sure I can even pay for the room I'm sleeping in.
Whatever I used to have, I don't have anymore!" She couldn't
begin to think how much she had lost. She fought back new tears.

"No worry, Amerikanida. I have sell house in Hora to
Germans. I give money; you buy. In place small like Hora, Dimitri
no can buy many stuff. Then everybody say, 'Why he do this?'
And when I 'lose' many stuff, they see me to the grave." He
smiled. The wind howled.

"Why are you doing this, Dimitri?" Lyddie shouted.

"Ask me when will I die," he shouted back, turning the donkey and then giving it a rap on the behind with the olive switch.

6

THERE WAS WIND, RISING in the morning and dying off late in the afternoon, never disturbing the obsessive blue of the sky. The busses were late, often by hours. The island offered two places to swim—the pebble beach on the far side of the harbor, requiring a bus ride down the mountain and then a walk, and the rocks at Aghia Margarita on the south side below Hora, requiring the same, though the walk was steeper. When garbage washed up at the beach near the harbor, everyone swam at Aghia Margarita.

There was chicken or meatballs or calamari with Greek salad for dinner, unless one had money for fish down in the harbor, and that was suspect anyhow. The tomatoes in the salad were ripe and sweet. Sometimes there was dried oregano on the feta, sometimes not. If not, you could try asking for it. Always, the old people sat in the evening on the benches built into the stucco walls facing the widened dead end of the road where the busses turned around and the narrow stone-paved passageways disappeared into the white maze of houses. Dimitri watched over the tourists who drank together and laughed about the refusals of the village to accommodate them, about the delays and the heat. They became repetitions of the word *foreigner* in the simple vocabulary of the Greek day.

In the two weeks Lyddie and Sabina were on the island, the tensions that had arisen between them did not dissipate, though they lingered more as a consciousness of withholding on both parts than as outright antagonism. Lyddie had asked Sabina what she knew about Axel's past, but Sabina clearly wasn't going to say. Lyddie ached to tell Sabina what she thought she knew about his role in the East, but Sabina tacitly discouraged her confidence. Sabina, she knew, would only say she had no right to judge others. Each day that they sat at Dimitri's place in the late afternoon, the silence opening around them, Lyddie felt that what she had told Sabina, *I wouldn't be here if I wanted him*, was becoming more like the truth. Her grief over the loss of the baby bled over into her sense of Phelps's absence as final, somehow. And though she knew he might still be alive, she felt widowed by both him and the baby. Twice abandoned. And at times, twice guilty. But Dimitri was right. What could she do to help Phelps? She couldn't go to Iraq herself. By reporting his note, she had already violated his instructions for her not to "do anything."

Sometimes it seemed to Lyddie that she and Sabina had nothing in common but the ability to nurse a drink that gave itself up almost more slowly than time. Lyddie had more in common with Dimitri, when it came right down to it. They at least shared a cause.

One afternoon, Lyddie came back to the room to find Siegfried waiting for Sabina at the small, round table in the wind-sheltered garden. Siegfried was a strange creature, childlike and expectant in some ways, but physically a grown man. In his high, thin voice was the confidence that when he called Sabina, she would come, would put his food before him. Beside him on the stone patio sat a loaded beach bag.

"Yes, Siegfried. One moment," Sabina called out from inside his room, where she was apparently getting something from the refrigerator. Except for the sound of workmen slapping stucco over brick in the passage nearby, it was quiet in the garden, close to two o'clock. Siegfried held a small plastic bag in one hand. Bougainvillea and grapevines, dangling from a wooden pergola, shaded his face.

"Are you going to go swimming?" Lyddie asked him. She felt vaguely uncomfortable with him on account of the way he'd compromised her privacy a few days before and had caught her in her fury at Sabina.

"Yes," he said. "At Aghia Margarita." His eyes looked wildly blue under the influence of his blue shirt.

"Ah! *Hallo*, Lyddie," Sabina said, emerging with Ulla. She arranged on the table the Fanta from inside and the cheese pastry she had brought from the bakery for Siegfried. Then, looking more closely at Lyddie, whose face must have borne traces of her distress, she asked, "Is everything OK?"

"Sure," Lyddie said, "fine," forcing her gaze away from Siegfried's shirt but seeing it, still, at the periphery.

Sabina seemed to notice the bag Siegfried held but, shifting from English to German, said to him only, "You were at the Poseidon again last night."

"Yes, Sabina," he answered. The Poseidon, at a higher elevation, was visible in the distance over the rooftop of the adjacent building. By day, it looked decidedly drab, though at night the bar had a strange allure, its flickering lights and young crowd teetering on the edge of the villa's ruin. An empty swimming pool bordered the villa in the rear amid mulberry and lemon trees being taken over by honeysuckle.

"I think you cannot go there alone anymore," Sabina said. She shut her eyes tight for a moment, like someone trying to squeeze the truth into a smaller sum. Then she looked at him. "Siegfried, you must wait for a woman to show she has interest in you. You cannot force her."

His shame became visible. The night before, he had been brought to them drunk, the foulness of his cursing rendered absurd by the little snack Sabina had laid out. "She said she liked the music, Sabina. Sting. I was dancing, like everyone."

The wind had begun to pick up now and, coming in from the south, it shuffled the silences in the garden and twisted the towels that had been hung out by the proprietor that morning. Lyddie watched Siegfried. She had seen him in the furious agony his sexuality provoked, his entire body on edge, his eyes and lips glistening, his face already touched by the bewilderment and resentment of being rejected. Like a cat awakening the neighborhood with the high, human yowl of its heat, he made her nervous. Sabina said that in Greece, because he did not speak the language—did not, in fact speak much at all—Siegfried was not immediately perceived as strange on account of his voice, and he had become bolder.

Two more workers arrived and began to chip at the stone of a nearby passageway with sledgehammers and spikes. The noise seemed to add to the antagonism of the world as Siegfried perceived it. The anger rose in his face. "I cannot force her, Sabina, but she wanted it. I saw her in the empty pool with Ianni. They were in the deep part and he pushed her, against the wall. I thought she was hurt but then I heard her voice. She didn't know what to do but she liked it." Siegfried's bag hopped a little on the table.

"Coast Guard Ianni?" Sabina said.

"Divorced Ianni."

"What do you have?" asked Ulla, who had been busy with her cheese pastry. She sat next to Siegfried, her chubby legs dangling from the chair.

Siegfried did not answer, and Sabina said nothing. Her arms lay inert on the table, among crumbs and coffee rings. Two napkins lifted off and flew nearly straight up and away when finally she raised her hands to gather her hair. Lyddie wondered what she was thinking. Had she considered paying a woman for Siegried? What would keep her from it? Availability? Not ethical reserve, certainly. More likely the precariousness that sex would bring into his life—an instability Sabina knew he could not withstand. And the fact that he needed more than sex. Needed what Sabina, fierce in her loyalty, tried to give him.

"What is in the sack?" Sabina asked with more resignation than curiosity. Despite the wind, which was at her back, sweat began to form little beads along her upper lip.

Siegfried offered her the bag. "See for yourself," he said, still hurt.

She took it and looked inside. Troubled, she passed the bag to Lyddie. Out of the plastic, the black eyes of a tiny bird looked up in terror, like the currency of some feeling they all knew well but had removed from circulation.

"Maria gave it to me," Siegfried said. "She found it." Maria was an older woman from Hora who cleaned rooms at Fani Vevis.

"And what did she think you would do with it?" Sabina asked, irritation creeping back into her voice.

"Take care of it," he said. Siegfried took the bag from Lyddie and lifted the bird out, cradling it in his palm. "Take care of it," he repeated. "It is my responsibility now."

"You want to take care of it but you will only hurt it," Sabina said.

Siegfried looked intently at her, though she had turned her face from him, disappearing into the shadows of the arbor. "How do you know?" he said.

It was the first time Lyddie had ever seen Siegfried challenge Sabina's authority over him. In Berlin, he'd wanted to prove himself worthy of her affection and trust. Even the day Ulla had disappeared at the market, it was Siefried who ended up sulking while Sabina carried on as if nothing much had happened. He had a capacity for feeling that Sabina sometimes lacked. Now, when he addressed her, Lyddie saw in Sabina's eyes the same look of vulnerability and panic she'd seen that day a month before when Lyddie had asked her why she couldn't just tell the truth to straighten out the question of Ulla's paternity. That look alone could convince you that some mistakes were irreparable.

FOR TWO DAYS AND TWO NIGHTS, wind thrashed the tamarisks and howled through the chinks in the walls. It rattled shutters and hurled stones that pocked the stucco facades of the houses. There was no question of Lyddie's making the trek up to Smardakito with Dimitri; no question, even, of Dimitri's going alone. When Lyddie and Sabina walked the hundred yards from Rooms Fani Vevis to Dimitri's place for something to eat, the wind flung even their words away from them. Lyddie expected to see them later, nesting like senseless anagrams against the chain-link fence behind the gas station, along with water bottles and ice cream wrappers and the torn-out pages of Greek school books.

It was not the cool meltemi from the north. It was a thirsty wind in from Africa. At night the dampness it picked up invaded the linens. Lyddie would draw a sheet and a woolen blanket around her, happy enough at first for that comfort. But soon the clammy sheet felt heavy and close. She'd throw off the blanket, extending a bare calf beyond the sheet's edge. Finally, she'd toss the sheet too away in disgust, as, on the bed opposite, Sabina would pull the blanket up again, the dampness having settled onto her bare skin. All night the wind told lies their bodies made them want to believe.

Siegfried and Ulla slept late and played card games when they got up. All of them spent their days in the room or inside the café, eating, reading, writing postcards that would languish in a big bag at the post office until the boats were given permission to run again. Lyddie was troubled knowing that Siegfried had followed her, but since she couldn't go anywhere anyhow, she didn't bring it up with Sabina.

When she awakened at last to a morning of calm, Lyddie felt, in her first moments of consciousness, as if she had come into possession of a sixth sense finely attuned to the dimension of silence. Gradually, the fuss of a motorbike, advancing and receding as it negotiated the switchbacks on the road up from the harbor, leveled off into a steady whine, and the voices of Greek women, like cups full of stones and water, emptied their greetings into the clear morning outside the window. Lyddie rose and opened a shutter. The canvas awning of the Xenia, a bakery up the alleyway, hung from its moorings in three ragged strips. Slats of sunlight fell across Sabina where she lay on the other bed, asleep. A tassel of her golden hair spilled from the twisted sheet.

Lyddie sat on the bed, putting on her clothes from the day before quietly when Sabina's voice at her back startled her. "Listen!" Sabina said. "It is still. Lyddie, what are you doing? Let's go to the monastery, early, before it becomes too hot." Lyddie turned to see Sabina propped on an elbow, looking particularly vibrant. She couldn't immediately think of a reason not to go; she could go to Smardakito a little later, and

Siegfried was good with Ulla. "We'll be back before they get up," Sabina said, throwing off the sheet. "Come!"

They walked down the dirt track behind the radio tower for fifteen minutes until they hit the dirt road; then they started the long zigzag back up the steepest part of the cliff on the stone path. They climbed for twenty minutes in the heat before stopping in the shade of a solitary eucalyptus tree. The air was lucid, keen with the late-season sun. Far above them, the monastery clung like a stiff, white bandage at the midpoint of the precipice. Below, in the middle distance, the monks had built a cistern and etched a small garden from stone. Two long rows of melon and tomato plants suggested succulence amid the thistle and gorse dominating the escarpment. A thousand feet down, the sea began abruptly as a strip of turquoise near the rocks and extended outward to a deeper, lacquered blue. Already, like illuminations of a mystical text, the bodies of a few early swimmers drew a white calligraphy on the water's Byzantine calm.

Sabina's chest heaved, and she rested a hand on a sunburned knee. "What do you mean," she said, "you wouldn't be here if you wanted him?" She spoke as if the sea below and the sallow sky above were the only context her words needed. She looked at Lyddie. "It isn't as simple as you make it seem," she said, breathing hard.

Lyddie couldn't answer. It had been a week at least since their conversation about Axel. She had meant what she said, or had wanted to believe it. But being in the Greek landscape, she thought a lot about his Desert Fathers—the stories that seemed to have replaced the other kind of talking she was almost certain Axel had done. The story her heart told was a different one than the story her mind told. She couldn't recast her role with Axel as nothing more than that of a player in the ethical farce he was directing. "I'm doing what I want to do," she said.

She looked up at the monastery. Its multitude of tiny, hap-hazard windows gave it the appearance of a primitive cliff dwell-ing. Two gawky buttresses, almost vertical, reached nearly to the top of the whitewashed oddity, propping it against the cliff like a paper cutout. In Greece, an elemental spareness gave simple structures, like simple acts, a sacramental quality.

"'Tis beautiful, isn't it?" Sabina said, watching her. Lyddie nodded. She removed the water bottle from her pack and took a long swig, then offered the bottle to Sabina before setting out again up the path.

"Sabina, the last time I went to the refugee village," Lyddie said, pausing to catch her breath, "early in the morning," and she stopped again, looking back, "I think Siegfried was follow-ing me. I saw something blue—the color of the shirt Siegfried wears. Was he in bed when you got up that day?"

Sabina considered for a moment before answering. "I don't remember."

"He worries me sometimes," Lyddie said. "Did you tell him about the village?"

"No," Sabina said. "Lyddie, he's simply curious. He would not hurt a flea. You saw him with the bird. He wants to take care. You see the way he is with Ulla."

Lyddie had not forgotten, however, what Sabina had said to Siegfried about the bird. *You want to take care but you will only hurt it.*

Inside the monastery, the air felt musty and cool. From the cardboard box at the entry, Lyddie and Sabina took shin-length skirts and long-sleeved blouses, which they pulled on over their shorts. Though the garments had been provided for the sake of modesty, the effect was quite the opposite. The barrier of personal taste removed, their bodies were exposed in much the way the texture of the cliff was revealed by the smooth mason-ry flung against it. Sabina looked vulnerable and sensual, her

strong forearms bursting from the unbuttoned cuffs of the wrin-
kled blouse. The brown and olive skirt skulked unevenly, irreverently around her shapely calves. Lyddie became a girl again,
her arms unaccountably long in clothes handed down from a
stranger. She and Sabina laughed together at themselves.

Suddenly serious, Lyddie said, "Why did you think I cared
about Axel?"

"Are you joking?" Sabina said. "Your face, Lyddie, when I
asked you. When I look at the right moment, everything is there
in your face."

Midway up the tight coil of steps, they bent to enter a narrow passage that opened onto a cramped sitting room. A monk
in gray robes ushered them in. He offered them seats on two
wooden couches draped in tapestry. Sabina extended herself
graciously to her host, shifting from the English she spoke for
Lyddie's sake to Greek, which she spoke with convincing fluidity.
Lyddie laughed to hear that music, the same Sabina used for
English. It was Sabina's way with language to compensate in-
complete knowledge with musicality and confidence. Effortlessly,
she finished the Naxian liqueur and lemon sweets the monk had
offered. Lyddie took a small drink and coughed. She found refuge in a glass of water their host passed on a tray.

From atop a stallion in a photograph on the wall, a monk
with a long, pointed beard and a tiny, gray bun at the nape of
his neck, matching that of the monk who served them, looked
down. He seemed oddly chivalric against the barren landscape
in his exotic getup, topped off by what looked like a Shriner's
hat. His eyes were defiant. Centuries of monks looked down
from portraits at the hard-backed couch from which Lyddie and
Sabina looked up.

Lyddie, though she felt stronger than ever, was taken with a
desire to come clean. She had felt it when she'd met Nuray up in

the village. And now the face of the monk who served them and who sat with them, mostly in silence, seemed to have assimilated the entire range of human experience in lines of knowing and compassion. Perhaps it was merely what the sun had done to his skin. Still, she would confess everything—her unfaithfulness to Phelps and his withholding from her, the information she had about Axel and the fact that she had loved him in spite of it, her negligence with the baby—and all of this not because she needed or wanted forgiveness, but because she wanted to add the complexities of her being to the great human swirl of the monk's spirit. For the first time in weeks, she allowed herself to think of Axel and Phelps in the same frame. They surfaced in her consciousness as two monks tending a garden. She herself was far away, looking up from a medieval manuscript or out a window at the sea. Just then, she felt dishonest not so much toward Phelps as toward Sabina. And yet she felt, once again, that Sabina had forced her into that position.

When Sabina stepped through a tiny doorway onto a balcony, Lyddie instinctively hung back. Watching, she was struck by Sabina's face, looking out toward the sea beyond and below. At that moment, it seemed to her that all the things that happened were just stories we told or that others told about us. But faces were the truth, whole histories played out in moments of expression. And Sabina, with the sun and the breeze playing over her features in a sheer union of desire with fulfillment, seemed honest and innocently sensual.

Lyddie went out to lean on the wall beside Sabina, absorbing the exquisite turquoise shock of the sea below. They stood in silence for a few minutes before Lyddie said, "Sabina, I have to tell you. I was sleeping with him."

The look on Sabina's face betrayed not only her astonishment, but also her displeasure. At that moment Lyddie suspected that

Sabina knew about Axel's activities in the East. Which would mean that Lyddie had announced she'd slept with a traitor. "Just once?" Sabina asked.

"No. Not once."

"And he left you then…"

Lyddie interrupted. "No. Then I came here. With you. Sabina, " she said. "Perhaps you know…I mean, I'm not proud of what I did, in light of what perhaps we both—"

"Lyddie, no more," Sabina said quietly. Then, suddenly brusque and practical, she said, "'Tis your own affair. Surely you don't think I can be in a place to criticize you. You can sleep with the Pope, for what I care. Or the Patriarch." She smiled.

"Yes, but I wanted—" Lyddie said. She stopped this time on her own. Somehow it had not occurred to her that Sabina might be jealous of her. Lyddie wanted only to talk with Sabina about Axel. Not to argue, but for them to be two women sharing confidences against the inveterate calm of the sea, as it seemed they had been moments before. Now, suddenly, it seemed she was asking Sabina's permission to love Axel.

"No problem, Lyddie. Honestly," Sabina said. She looked almost supernaturally unmoved as she re-entered the monastery.

When finally she and Lyddie made their way back through the low interior passage, they deposited a few hundred drachmas in the box at the bottom of an ascending stair and followed it up into a small chapel at the top of the monastery. They paused briefly among the gold-emblazoned icons and the frescoes busy with tribulation and sacrifice. The room, flanked by rows of austere throne-like seats, was empty, except for a single, wizened monk sitting at one end. He gazed steadily at the floor, as if entranced. Each time someone entered, he looked up briefly, keeping a mental count, perhaps. Then he returned to his reverie.

A couple of minutes passed before Sabina handed her

camera to Lyddie and approached him. *"Papa,"* Sabina whispered, using the familiar Greek term. He looked intently at the floor, not hearing her, or not acknowledging what he had heard. *"Papa,"* she repeated. He looked up.

All at once, Lyddie found herself at the center of a new controversy, holding the camera that threatened to snap the picture of the monk with Sabina. The monk protested. The room was close and warm, the air like damp felt on Lyddie's skin and in her chest, and she wanted to be alone, anywhere away from Sabina. They were joined by a Swedish couple and another German, all of whom were amused by Sabina's boldness and the camaraderie she assumed in dealing with the stern, patriarchal figure. They fell into a surprised silence when at last Sabina told Lyddie to put the camera away and said something in Greek that brought a vague smile to the monk's mouth. It was that smile, and the way he studied Sabina's face for a moment before, with effort, he stood and walked across the room to a door carved with figures, that transformed the mood of impropriety and panic to one of sanctity and calm. In the days to come, it would be this scene that would come to mind when Lyddie asked herself why she cared for Sabina, and why she would make the choices she would make on her behalf. It was the inexplicable way her bungling was rewarded with beauty, as if Some Great Being had seen that her heart was in the right place and, willing to ignore the particular transgressions of her daily life, had seen fit to extend grace.

Opening the door, the priest removed a small brass censer. He fumbled with two or three matches before lighting it successfully. The scent that rose heavily in the wisp of smoke the old monk released in their midst was the woody smell of old apples, spiced with the flavor of words like *Rosicrucian*. The voice in which he chanted was as clear as that of a novice. He distributed the last words evenly, pausing before each member of the party: first the tall Swede, then the Swede's wife, who stood like a girl scout with her eyes closed, then Lyddie, and the other German—a man of about fifty—and finally Sabina, before whom he lingered, forming with his free hand the sign of the cross.

In silence, Sabina and Lyddie descended the monastery path and the serpentine dirt track and finally the rocks to the sea at Aghia Margarita. "Let's swim," Lyddie said. "Do we have time?" The water was warm, its surface slippery calm. Free of urchins and sea grass, the seabed refracted a diaphanous green-blue light. They took off their clothes and Lyddie dove from the huge rock plates; Sabina waded in from the pebble beach. The salt made floating easy.

When they climbed out and lay for a moment on the rocks to dry, they heard a voice from the water. Before them the Swede labored with fins to stay afloat, a snorkel and mask pushed up onto his forehead. "What did you say to the monk?" he called to Sabina. "He didn't want his picture taken with a woman, I suppose."

"He said that human memory is short," she answered.

Lying back down and leaving Sabina to the conversation, Lyddie felt like a figure newly scratched onto the clean slate of the rock.

"So, what was funny?" the swimmer said. Lyddie could see out of one open eye that the fins were pulling him down, and he was growing winded, but he lingered, waiting for Sabina's response.

"I said I have no worry to remember this, but I worry about the memory of God."

"Ah," said the Swede.

When Lyddie sat up again, she saw him swimming off, his white buttocks plying the smooth surface as he nosed with his snorkel in and out of crevices in the rock.

"And then he makes this" Sabina said to Lyddie, imitating the lilt of the priest's forearm swinging the censor, "to help the Big One remember us. 'Tis beautiful, Lyddie. Do you think He will?"

7

LYDDIE MADE SEVERAL early morning trips to Smardakito with provisions. Sometimes Dimitri waited for her with the donkey and they made their way together around the mountain to the sheltered fold in which the little village had come to life. Or Lyddie went alone. She didn't think Siegfried had tried to follow her again. Since Sabina hadn't felt she needed to speak to him about his intelligence activities, Lyddie had tried to do so herself. He disappeared into his room and emerged holding something in his fist. As if to placate her, he said, "I have the note for Sabina." He seemed so certain she would know what he was talking about that, despite being perplexed, she held out her hands. Into her palms like a well-prepared nest, he spilled his fistful of torn scraps, a few of which fluttered into the honeysuckle taking over the wall adjacent to the two rooms. "It was on the door," he said.

Back in the room, Lyddie threw the torn bits of the note—a jumble of German words—into the drawer of her nightstand.

She accepted it as Siegfried's offering of peace, probably something threatening or angry he had written and destroyed.

The inventory of goods Lyddie had supplied to the village
included two towels; a tube of toothpaste, some shampoo and
soap; white beans, pasta, coffee and zucchini; seven plates; and
two more blankets. Dimitri had shanghaied three chickens that
provided eggs and had "lost" one of his own goats for milk and
cheese.

Lyddie found herself extending her visits, staying in the
mornings to help the women sort and prepare the fava or the
chickpeas, learning from them how to milk the goat. Among the
women, there was Nuray, the one who wore Maroula's missing
dress. (Younger and less ample than the former occupant, she
gathered it around her waist with two rolled dishtowels knotted end to end and wore men's pants underneath.) Nuray was
married, though probably not yet twenty. Anya, the first of the
women Lyddie had met, was Nuray's older sister; she was also
married. And there was Sarya, their cousin, who was beautiful
in the strong, unstudied way that Lyddie thought only a woman
who has had to carry a machine gun can be beautiful. Sarya was
not married. Lyddie did not share a language with them, but to
look into the faces of such women was to cut through all of the
nonsense that clouded human experience. Lyddie felt herself
growing strong in their presence. Each time she arrived, they
greeted her with a kiss on each cheek. The men usually slept
later and worked separately.

Lyddie knew from Dimitri that the Kurds had lived for almost two years in the mountains to which they had fled to escape. Now they had just enough food to take the edge off their
hunger. Once again, death had sorted them out and left them to
go on against the odds. They had a remarkable way of inhabit-
ing fully and with ease the place where they found themselves,

an attitude that belied their transience. They were comfortable among the cicadas and the lizards—residents, it seemed, only of the earth itself. Yet in their eyes, Lyddie could see that they were fully alert. They could disappear in a matter of minutes if they needed to. And if they were to leave tomorrow, it would not change the fact that they had been in that place forever.

Often in the mornings, Lyddie would hold the child Bilimet on her hip to keep him happy while the others worked. Some of the women would point to his blue eye and then to one of their own brown eyes, wagging their fingers and making scolding sounds by clicking their tongues. They seemed to despair and to marvel over Lyddie's boldness in looking into the boy's face. It was hard for her to reconcile this cruelty on their part with the stoic beauty she saw in them as they went about their new, uncertain lives. Dimitri tried to explain to Lyddie the evil eye, against which each of the Kurds wore a small glass amulet in the form of a blue eyeball. Some of these charms Lyddie herself had purchased for them in the harbor to replace the ones lost at sea. Dimitri said that though the boy might not know he had this bad energy in the eye, still these people, like the Greeks, believed the power of it was great. He explained that they thought it was the boy's fault that his uncle and his mother were dead.

"That anyone so small…" Lost in thought, Lyddie looked off in the direction of the sea. "And what do you think?" Lyddie asked Dimitri. "Do *you* blame him?"

"Amerikanida, I must ask myself about the Turk who take their money and go from their boat when the sea is big. But this man they trust. They pay much money to trust this man. And what he can do against such power of evil?" As he said this, he indicated the boy, who sat nearby playing with two olive branches Dimitri had cut for him, and he winked at Lyddie.

Lyddie shook her head.

"Don't make judgment, Amerikanida. When the life is bad for very long time—not weeks or months, but years, not years but many hundred years—people must find how to explain. Why bad things happen? A very old idea, this. It make them strong to believe they can understand and push away the evil."

Dimitri told her, too, that Nuray had some news. One of the men, Anya's husband, had been a Peshmerga fighter against the Iraqis. Just a month before they had fled, he had met an American who had witnessed the massacre of one of the villages near Qaladiza. He understood that the man had been working with the resistance. Dimitri relayed Lyddie's questions: What did the man look like? (Answer: An American.) Why was he there in the first place? (Answer: The less known in these situations the better.)

Only once, wanting to be close to this news of Phelps, however lacking in detail, Lyddie went out to the village in the evening, carrying a flashlight, though she didn't expect to walk back until morning. Perhaps, like her, Phelps would gather with a group of Kurds around the dying coals of a brazier under the stars. Perhaps he and she were working for a common cause. Anya and Nuray and the other women squatted comfortably on their haunches; some of the men lay back with their heads propped on their folded hands. Lyddie sat on a rock, holding the boy Bilimet on her lap. Serhat, the thinnest of the men, sang for a very long time, his voice like a taproot going deep and finding water. Lyddie thought of the life she'd lost.

Phelps holds a hose that sends up an arc fanning out just before it falls over a row of tomato plants and, behind it, another of ruminating sunflowers. He waves the arc back and forth in the evening air, taking pleasure in the way the rain he makes follows, a little bit behind, as if he were teaching it the languorous movement of a dance. Watching him, Lyddie thinks that gravity is beauty—the tension between flying and falling. She tries to make Phelps speak. She wants to remember his voice. Again and again, into the chilly autumn air of the yard, she calls to him. But his words, the slant of his humor—they are lost to her now. Her own calling reminds her of the man from the island of Syros who passes through Hora these days with a bullhorn, hawking blankets and jackets–provisions for fall and winter. His voice is loud, with an air of electronically garbled urgency. No one ever seems to buy. Phelps turns off the hose and listens to the sound of water percolating through the earth. Then he walks to the back of the house, stamping his feet three times at the door before disappearing inside.

In the little group around the brazier, Lyddie saw that Nuray was watching her, and she followed the other woman's gaze to the boy on her lap, whose lids were growing heavy as he drifted off to sleep. "*Onun iyi bak,*" Nuray whispered.

"What does it mean?" Lyddie said.

Nuray smiled at her and nodded.

THAT ONE AFTERNOON AXEL SHOULD appear amid the small crowd of tourists and locals drinking beer and eating small fish on the crumbling terrace of Dimitri's café should not have surprised Lyddie, given his penchant for showing up unannounced. Looking brown and relaxed in a worn black t-shirt, he tipped his wooden chair back on two legs, leaning against the wall.

Before leaving the city, she had left his jacket outside the door at his flat with a note saying she'd be going with Sabina to Greece for a while. Now Lyddie took shelter against the high wall next to the steps, where he would not see her.

Across the street from where Lyddie stood, a young woman tied colored scarves to the plaster railing in front of her small shop. She knotted them so that they moved against each other in the wind like horses' tails in a battle.

First Lyddie felt desire for Axel, as strong as she had ever felt it, and then she felt the powerful reprimand of what she knew about him, the distance it put between them. Once again something had approached her from unfamiliar territory—something that reminded her of history in its power to subsume the personal and dump it onto the heap.

On his way down the steps, Axel nodded as he passed, then swung his leg over a motorbike parked near the wall she was leaning against. He started the engine and pulled away, but he wheeled around to her and, before roaring off up the island road, said only, "There's a wedding feast at Akladi. Tomorrow night. I invite you."

Lyddie had not tried in a long time to talk to Phelps, not even in her own head. He was, at best, out of touch with her situation, like someone who has been away a long time and fails to acknowledge that life has gone on. But seeing Axel again, she knew she was losing her bearings. She longed for Phelps's pragmatism to ground her, as it had used to. "You had reason to warn me away from him," she said. "I know that now. And I'm listening. Tell me what you think I should do." But Phelps was completely unreachable. It seemed the child may have been their only connection.

The next evening, in the windswept countryside at Akladi, she sat down across from Axel at one of the long tables set up outside the feast hall, where she found him drinking raki. The driver who had given her a ride had said repeatedly with great exuberance and spoon-to-mouth gestures, *"Fagito!"* He had used the same word Lyddie had heard on the way to Akladi the first time. She thought it meant feast, or the goat stew that simmered on the open hearth in the kitchen. Dimitri, too, had invited her to the wedding, so she told herself it wasn't for Axel that she had come. The magnified whine of the fiddle mesmerized her, and through the doorway, she watched the bride in a small ring of dancers pressed close to the band, their shoulders and arms revolving in the bright, artificial light. The loud and constant circularity of the music suggested no alternate route.

"Who got married?" she asked Axel.

"Nikos. My cousin." Axel indicated with a nod the handsome young Greek leading the circle of dancers. "This is the island of my mother," he said.

"Yes, it's beautiful," she said, remembering immediately and with considerable discomfort that the last time she'd said that about a place, it had not gone well. Teufelsberg. Devil's Mountain. Axel's pile of bitter memories.

Lyddie looked around at the faces in the crowd. "Who did he marry?"

Axel couldn't hear her. Communicating over the cacophony of Greek voices and the music, increasing in tempo and intensity, was difficult.

"The girl," Lyddie said more loudly. "Who is she?"

"She is from Syros."

Lyddie looked where Axel indicated. Dimitri sat nearby, among several old men, downing shots of raki near an eruption of oleander at the edge of the terrace. He saw her, and Lyddie merely smiled. Then she looked away, not wanting to betray too much familiarity.

"You know my grandfather?" Axel said.

"From the café," she answered. She wondered how much Dimitri had told Axel of his activities in Smardakito. "When did you arrive on the island?" she asked.

"Since one week," he said.

"You came for the wedding?"

"I am here for the wedding," he said, ambiguously. Axel

seemed tentative, as if he were afraid of saying too much. He let her establish the territory of their conversation.

"Does Sabina know you're here?" Lyddie hadn't mentioned to Sabina her encounter with Axel. And Sabina certainly hadn't shared the news of his presence with Lyddie.

"She knows," Axel answered.

Lyddie sighed and breathed deeply. The air smelled dry and powdery sweet. She remembered how bad a conversationalist Axel could be. And how jealous she could be of Sabina. Where to go from there? They had definitely lost ground since she'd last seen him. That had everything to do with her knowing much more about him than before, and possibly with his knowing that she knew. "What did you do today?" she asked, leaning in across the table so that he could hear her above the music and revelry, the rounds of ammunition being fired off in celebration nearby.

"I got out of bed at about seven o'clock," he said. "And I walked twenty meters and plunged into the sea." He looked out over the crowd and then at Lyddie, pausing after each entry, registering what he said with a nod. "I swam. I dove, six or seven times, deeper than yesterday. Then I practiced exercises for the breath. After, I went back to the house and put my clothes on."

"This could take a while," Lyddie said.

"You don't want to know?"

"I do. Please go on."

"Where was I?"

"You were getting dressed." She smiled. But his eyes remained serious. He seemed calm, but distant, as if he were afraid of her.

"I read two hours. Then I went to look for my cousin." Suddenly he was talking more loudly. The music had stopped abruptly and the lights had gone out. Faces were arrested mid-sentence. A group of Greeks playing charades next to Lyddie stopped with their hands in the air, their mouths open in surprise. Lyddie became acutely aware of something primitive in the landscape that surrounded the night gathering, something that in a gulp had muted the human sound. Then came the throbbing of cicadas and the crowd thrilling to its own magnetic clarity. Cries of pleasure and laughter rose out of the darkness.

"We came here to the village and after some hours, of course, I saw you," he continued quietly.

"You forgot to say what you were reading."

"*Paradise of the Fathers.* Come, let's walk to the sea," he said. They rose from the table and walked down opposite sides to meet at the end of it. Standing there for a moment, close to her, he looked into her face, and when she tried to look away, he touched her jawbone, turning it back to him, the way the guard at the border had done months before. "Your eyes. Something has changed, Lyddie."

His own eyes were intense, his face angular but softened by his high forehead. She had not noticed before how his hairline had started to recede at the temples. They began to walk as the lights came back on and the music resumed behind them. "I'm not sure if things have changed or if they never really were the way I thought," she said. "You didn't tell me you were planning a journey. There's so much you haven't told me. Sometimes I think you have cared for me and sometimes I think you have merely used me to convince yourself you weren't acting badly—stealing dogs, slashing tires, lying when the truth was hard to tell." She hesitated on the verge of naming the worst of his transgressions. "You pulled me down with you so you wouldn't have to be alone," she said, stepping back from that other accusation. "But as you told me, it's a luxury to insist on loving and being loved. I didn't think you meant that when you said it. I see now that you did mean it."

Axel ran his hand back through his hair in a gesture of patient fatigue, as though he had expected to have to deal with this charge. "I told you I thought I was wrong," he said.

"No," she said. "You believe that with your whole being."

"I was not, as you call it, 'using' you," Axel said quietly. "That first day I saw you at Lothar's house," he said, "I wanted to prove to you that life was not as simple an entertainment as you believed it was." They had come to the beach, where large white stones worn smooth by the sea had been thrown up to cobble the sand. Axel sat down on a rock and loosened his collar. Lyddie stood in front of him, her gaze dropping to the buttons on his shirt, which shone in the moonlight. "You looked so… sincere," he said. "I had set out to prove something to you, but I found that I wanted you. I wanted to be like you."

"Sincere? Like a greeting card? Or do you mean something more along the lines of gullible and innocent?"

"The irony is yours, Lyddie. You won't allow me to say what I have felt."

"And the day you asked me to go to your mother? What did you tell her in the note?"

"I told her her father was dead."

"You manipulated me into helping you lie to her. And now your mother thinks I—"

"I wanted you," Axel said, seeming to ignore the suggestion of reversed roles. "But I also wanted you to help me put that matter away permanently. It was destroying me and my mother too. You helped me to see that. Perhaps you have no reason to believe me, and if you cannot believe, I understand. I am not a person who has lived without error."

Error. That word carved out in the conversation a whole new chasm into which Lyddie wasn't ready to leap. It was as close as she'd ever heard Axel come to a confession. She felt her judgment easing. Maybe he had wanted her. She couldn't help but wonder if he also wanted Sabina. Maybe that was why he had come to the island. Lyddie looked at the ground. "And now?" she said, glancing up at him.

"Now?" he repeated. The moon lit a path across the sea. Lyddie considered the judgments she had made following her visit to East Berlin and the margin for error in each.

"Now what is it that you want?" she said.

She waited through a long silence.

"I want you to believe I am capable of good."

"Oh, Axel," she said, frustration and hurt mingling in her voice. If he'd said he loved her, then maybe what he wanted would be more possible. But he hadn't said that. He took a pack of cigarettes from his breast pocket and offered her one, along with the lighter. She turned her back against the wind and struck the lighter-wheel six or seven times before the flame leapt up and caught. "How long will you be here?" she asked, turning back toward him.

"I go to visit Athos in a few days."

She inhaled deeply, letting the smoke she wasn't used to excavate her lungs. "Who is Athos?" she said. She still had no idea how Axel felt about her. Only that he wanted her good will and trust. So far, everything else they had discussed was in the past tense.

"Athos, the monastery. In the north of Greece."

"What for?" she asked. "Will you do some kind of penance?"

"You think I'm in need of it." He said this without offense and was thoughtful for a moment. "Perhaps I need to be alone. No one leaves you alone in the way that God does," he said.

"I can do the same, if you would prefer that," she said.

"Please don't."

Lyddie felt something unraveling inside faster than she could stop it. She wanted him to touch her again. As he stuffed the cigarettes back into the pocket of his shirt, she turned abruptly at the sound of rustling in the weeds above them. Two goats appeared on the rocky bluff, their legs apparently hobbled, making their passage difficult. Their eyes snared the moonlight in the moment before they retreated, skittish at a human presence. Lyddie thought about the image of herself with Axel carried away in the black boxes of their pupils.

"What do you think of me?" he said. He looked directly into her eyes, his mouth dark on his face in the moonlight.

"There is too much I don't know," she replied. "And you're not going to tell me. Are you? I know that." The suppressed agony in his face at that moment was almost more than Lyddie could bear.

"Let's not forget about the Desert Fathers," she said lightly, looking away again.

"I never forget about them," Axel said. "There is little I would not give for their wisdom." He got up from the rock and walked to the sandy crescent where the waves broke softly. He slipped from his pants and his shirt and tossed them back toward her on the stones, his only invitation for her to join him. Then he dove into the moonlight that spilled across the water.

His swimming in the dark frightened Lyddie. While she waited for him to surface, she imagined his journey into the depths. She pictured him amid a mute congress of fish and sea plants, alive beneath the membrane separating water and night sky. She heard him surface with a splash. Again, he went down. In the held breath of his absence, Lyddie stood suspended on shore. Axel surfaced and dove, the distance and the darkness between them translating his movement alternately as exhilaration and desperation. She knew he dove deep. His absences were long and he surfaced each time near the place where he had last disappeared. Once, when he stayed down for nearly a minute, she called out to him, terrified. The void his absence created reminded her of one she had felt before, one that she knew his reappearance would not completely fill but that each absence made greater.

Lyddie turned from the water and began picking up smooth, white stones to calm her racing heart. Waves washed onto the beach. She did not hear him until he was immediately behind her. And then she tasted the salt on the arms that wrapped her chest from behind, the arms in which she buried her face. Through the linen of her clothes, the seawater from his body soaked her.

8

"Pappou!" Axel called out from the shed that he and one of the Kurdish men were converting to a latrine. "Why don't you come in here and do some digging?" Dimitri paused to watch a lizard explore the interior of the pot left sitting on the cold brazier the night before. Finding nothing of interest inside, the lizard ran out onto one of the handles and then sat, lifting its right front leg and limbering its toes in the early light. Axel stepped out of the shed, following Dimitri's gaze, and he pointed to something shiny on the ground near the cooking pot. He walked over and bent to pick up a silver hoop and wipe it on his pant-leg. "Who's been up here besides you?" he asked. Greek had come back to him easily.

Dimitri sat down on the edge of a stone well surrounding the old plane tree. "Your friend," Dimitri said.

"My friend."

"Leda Amerikanida. I saw you together at the wedding. I like her, Axel. Despite where she comes from. And the husband, who, incidentally, I don't think is coming back." He had felt a pleasurable shock at seeing Axel disappear with her that night.

"But what was she doing here?"

"She found the place on her own. What can I tell you?" Dimitri answered.

Axel took the shovel from Dimitri and went back into the shed where the Kurd was still working. Dimitri labored up the steps toward the spigot. He splashed his face with water and drank. When he returned, he stopped at the doorway and saw the Kurd looking Axel over appraisingly. Axel watched the Kurd's shoulders and arms as he turned to his digging and the muscles worked beneath his bare skin. Axel said suddenly, in Greek, "I, too, am a refugee." He tapped his chest. "I, too," he said again, with deep conviction. He tapped his chest so hard this time that the bones must have hurt. The Kurd shrugged, uncomprehending; then he spat into the dirt and wiped his mustache on his bare arm, leaving a glistening smear.

Dimitri said, "Axel, who are you talking to? He doesn't understand."

"Pappou," Axel said, "Like him, I came here hoping to start over." He chipped a little at the hard earth, his efforts seeming absurd compared to the other man's. The Kurd lifted a a shovelful of shale he had loosened. They could hear the voices of women up at the main house, laughing and then scolding the children in Kurdish. "I believe I have a daughter here," Axel said to Dimitri. The pile of dirt in the corner grew. "I know I don't seem like a father. I never thought I could be. Remember when the doctor said I would never father a child?"

"You know that Lyddie lost the baby, don't you?" Dimitri said.

"Not Lyddie's child," Axel said. "A living child. Three years old. And the mother of this child, she is certain that I am the father." Axel stopped digging for a moment to look at Dimitri.

"Still, I don't know what I thought, coming here like this after I said I didn't believe her. I said I wanted nothing to do with being a father. The day she called me to her flat and told me, I sat in her kitchen, unable to feel anything at all. It was the day after Lyddie first came to my place. We had buried a dog together. I could think of nothing but the smell of her hair. Like fresh bread and leaves."

Dimitri wondered if Axel did not care for the mother of another man's child more than the mother of his own. He remembered that feeling. He, too, had been a man of duty.

On an impulse, since they were in touch again and the boy had seemed interested in his past, Dimitri had written Axel, asking for his help. There was no one on the island Dimitri could trust except Nikos, and Nikos was all caught up with the business of the wedding. Maroula was needed at the café and was no good at secrets anyhow. She had, in fact, heard Dimitri tell the foreigners groggily that Politimos had been fishing with dynamite. A few days later, feeling heroic, she had made a trip to see the authorities. She told Dimitri proudly that evening that she had taken the bus to the harbor and waited at the Port Police for forty-five minutes but no one was in the office. She had left then for fear of missing the last bus back up the mountain before dinnertime. Dimitri didn't want anyone poking around in his business, which wasn't, at the moment, on the up and up. He had tried to explain to Maroula how dangerous it would be for his own restaurant if they reported Politimos. Maroula said Dimitri had already reported him to all of the tourists; wasn't that dangerous too?

Dimitri wiped the sweat from his forehead with a handkerchief and tried not to think about that. For the next few minutes, Axel worked intently with the shovel, having made his way past the shale to a slightly softer sediment below, and looking as though he were beginning to enjoy the ache in his arms and back. "Except," he said, the sweat now running down into his eyes, "I thought…" Here he paused again and stopped to take off his shirt and wipe his face. "I thought I could at least see the child again. Apart from Lothar. Not at his place, where I often saw her. I wanted this: to speak with her mother again. Though she knows things that don't cast me in the most favorable light."

"So you have a fresh beginning," Dimitri said. What could be better?"

Axel looked up from his work, thoughtful. "The ones who drowned," he asked suddenly, "were they family of his?" He looked at the Kurd as if thinking for a moment the other man might at least understand this reference to his own experience. But the man was addressing himself with hard-earned satisfaction to the hole and had stopped paying any attention at all to Axel. Dimitri clicked his tongue and jerked his head back in a no.

"There's a lot that could go wrong," Axel said. "To begin with, I'm not sure she wants to see me here. And the American, she's here too and probably doesn't think too highly of me. That kind of mistrust, it eats at you," he said, comparing the depth of the hole he'd just finished with that of the one the Kurd had retired from with a cigarette. He shook his head. "Not to mention the uncertainty of fathering generally." Propping his shovel in the corner, he walked out into the sunlight where Dimitri had begun to pull nails from an old board. "Well," he added, "if nothing else comes of my visit, someone will have a place to shit for a few days."

"You know, babies bring women with them," Dimitri said. "You asked in your letter about your Nazi grandfather. But the truth is, Axel, the one who raises the child is the father. The one who loves the mother. I'm not such a fan of genetic theories. I would have married your grandmother, Frederieka, if I could have. My father wouldn't let me because she carried another man's child. The child of a Nazi."

"That would have made you...my grandfather all over again, but in a different way."

"Except that you would have been someone else."

"I want to be someone else."

"You can't."

"For once, Pappou, I want to do what is right. It's so odd. To prove to Lyddie that I am capable of good, I would have to make a commitment to someone else that would hurt her."

Love and duty. Though Dimitri had spent nearly a lifetime of good days with Eleni, his wife, and he would love his children until the day he died, even Maroula, especially Maroula, he had never felt anything for Eleni like the love he'd felt for the Jewish girl those nights on the roof, teaching her the language of his thoughts and discovering the life force in her. He often wondered what his life would have been like had he disobeyed his father, who had never really liked Eleni anyhow. "Is it the German woman? Sabina?" Dimitri said.

"Yes," Axel said.

"I don't trust her," Dimitri said.

9

WERE IT NOT FOR the presence of the old monk at Sabina's twenty-ninth birthday on the cliffs above the Aegean, what somehow took on the flavor of ritual might have seemed mere caprice. The heat was bold by eleven-thirty, when the monks had finished their morning prayer and their gardening. Father Anastasios appeared, at first descending from the gardens below the monastery like a moat in the eye, his gray robes zigging and zagging with the path. Until he reached the territory of the goats and passed on down the cliff toward them, Lyddie had not believed Sabina when she'd said he was coming. Had Sabina told her about Axel's impending arrival—or at least that he was on the island—perhaps she wouldn't have believed that either. Still, it bothered her that she had been surprised. Kept in ignorance.

Lyddie sat beneath an olive tree that somehow, impossibly, was not losing its battle against the elements. Sabina laid out two beach towels on the narrow strip of ground that had been terraced from the reluctant earth centuries before. Ulla played among the stones; Siegfried sat on one of the towels, stiff and agitated, pulling weeds in clumps. Sabina watched the descending monk for just a moment now and then but looked back out at the Aegean each time, as if checking his progress against some correlative there. Lyddie thought about the last picnic Sabina had thrown—in the minefield at the Görlitzer Bahnhof. And her philosophy of life as a party you have to "wreck." The likelihood of anyone's "wrecking" this party was slim. Unless, of course, Axel showed up. Wanting Sabina to know that she knew he was around, Lyddie said, "Have you invited Dimitri? Or Axel?"

"Dimitri, no. And it would be a long way for Axel to come for a birthday party," Sabina said, apparently unsurprised by what Lyddie knew.

"Well, he's got his motorbike. It's not that far."

Sabina looked confused. Her face clouded. "Where is he?" she said.

"Now? I suppose he's down at the harbor. I don't know. Why didn't you tell me he was here?"

Sabina merely shook her head. "How long?" she said, looking confused. "How long has Axel been here?"

Now it was Lyddie's turn to be baffled. "He said you knew…"

"*Kalimera, Papa,*" Sabina called out, looking up to see the monk opening the little gate. Lyddie could tell she felt more than mildly slighted.

"*Mera,*" the monk replied in greeting. He sat down at a little distance from the towels. His worn work boots troubled the hem of his robes, which he rearranged over them. The rest of them waited for Sabina to do something. Lyddie offered to open the wine, but Sabina waved her off with a glazed expression. The cake Sabina had bought from the Xenia was beginning to bald on top, its icing forming a pool in the box. Lyddie suggested they eat it while they still wanted to. But Sabina remained impassive. She seemed not really to hear.

At last, she pulled a lighter from her bag and Lyddie sighed with relief. But Sabina's digging in the bag brought out onto the ground letters Sabina had picked up at the post office in the past week, and she saw them now, lying in the bare spot Siegfried had cleared. Lyddie reached out to put them back—letters from Lothar and from Ulla's legal father, Hörst, and from someone whose name Lyddie didn't recognize. But seeing the letters, Sabina stopped her. She picked them up herself, and looked at them with fascination.

"Sa-bi-na," Siegfried whined, drawing out the syllables with pleading, as if he were afraid of something. She seemed not to hear him. The monk had pulled out a prayer book and was fumbling through its pages, perhaps searching for words with which to break the spell.

Impulsively, with an air of amusement that flared up into disdain and settled into satisfaction, Sabina lit the lighter. "To human memory," she said. The little heap of letters blackened at the edges, the layers of paper resisting before bursting into orange flames.

"Jesus, Sabina!" Lyddie said, forgetting the monk's presence and remembering the conflagration at Sabina's last party. She knew that Sabina, too, must be thinking about Axel, though clearly without the benefit of wisdom gained from experience. "You'll set the mountain on fire!" Lyddie shouted. The truth was that the little blaze restricted itself to the clearing Siegfried had made, until, in a panic, Siegfried seized the open bottle of liqueur the monk had brought and attempted to douse the flames.

Everyone froze. A low, blue burn followed the path of the alcohol across the ground and into the dry brush where it leapt up. "Mama, *Feuer!*" shrieked Ulla, terrified. This time, it was the monk who came to his senses first and sprang to his feet. Hiking up his robe and gathering it in his fists, he trampled the flames with his work boots.

Sabina, clearly having lost control of the drama she had initiated, released a torrent of apologies in Greek. But the monk would not let her approach him. He waved her off, then walked toward the olive tree. In the perfect silence that followed, they heard the spatter of him relieving himself against its trunk.

When he returned, Sabina made a cut in the cake and lifted a slab, which she handed to him. Then she cut the rest of the cake and served it. It seemed to Lyddie that Sabina's theatrics had nothing to do with Ulla's fathers and everything to do with Axel, though she didn't understand why. But she knew now that the flare-up at the monastery a few days before had been more than a casual jealousy. And partly on Sabina's account, she felt guilty over having been with Axel again since then. Sabina avoided looking at her. She spoke Greek to the monk, while Ulla tried to get her attention by tossing handfuls of stones onto the beach towel. Absorbed in conversation, Sabina arranged and rearranged the stones in patterns by her knee.

The others, exhausted by the entertainment, dozed awhile in the shade the stone wall behind them had begun to cast. Lyddie lay on top of the wall, squinting at the sky as long as she could. Then she closed her eyes and tried to read with her skin the nuance of a breeze so slight it might have been a thistle exhaling. She must have fallen asleep, because when she opened her eyes again, her arms were a bright pink. The monk had gone. Beyond her, the sea had begun to turn over small, white flaps on growing swells.

That evening Siegfried went out without saying anything to Lyddie and Sabina, who were reading in their room. He didn't show up for dinner at nine. Sabina and Lyddie took Ulla and checked the souvenir shops and Dimitri's place, and they asked the bus driver if Siegfried had ridden down to the harbor. The driver could always tell you who went where, but he hadn't seen Siegfried. They went to the Poseidon, though it was early for the club crowd. Neither the owner nor the bartender knew anything.

"Where would he go?" Sabina exclaimed, wringing her hands. "He goes off by his own sometimes but I am certain where he goes. Always, I know this. So why is he going and he doesn't tell me?"

"He seemed agitated this afternoon," Lyddie said. "At the picnic." Not wanting Sabina to feel responsible for what had happened, she didn't elaborate. They asked Ralph to take them in the car down to Aghia Margarita, and when they didn't find him there, Ralph took them to the harbor, where they looked in every taverna and café and even walked around to the far side where he might have taken a swim from the rocks known as Plakies. By dark, Sabina had begun to panic. He could only be lost now. Or drowned. They stood with Ulla up on the hill above Hora by the headless windmills, where he might have gone to watch the sunset. From there, they could see down into the courtyard of Rooms Fani Vevis, in which Siegfried's blue shirt hung drying. "Wait!" Lyddie cried. "Remember what I told you? That he tried to follow me out to the village?"

"Why would he go there?" Sabina said.

"No idea," Lyddie said, already starting down the hill and waving Sabina and Ulla along. "Curiosity, maybe. But don't you think it's possible?"

"Can Ralph drive?" Sabina said.

"It would be faster to walk. We'll need a light. Do you have a photo of Siegfried? No one out there speaks English."

"I have his passport," Sabina said.

They stopped to talk to Fani Vevis, the proprietor of their rooms, who agreed to look after Ulla. Then they hurried to the edge of town. Lyddie knew the path well, and they made their way along, not needing the flashlight Lyddie had brought, since the moon was bright. Lyddie tried to calm Sabina with assurances she knew were risky. All the way, they haunted the darkness calling Siegfried's name.

When at last they arrived at the village, it was quiet. Descending the steps, they called out his name. They saw light inside the house that served as the pantry, which was unusual, given that the Kurds typically sat outside around a small fire until very late. While Sabina waited, Lyddie peered in to find all of them gathered in a circle on the floor. The children were asleep under the table. "*Yassas,*" she said, looking around at the faces in the circle. They had taken to using Greek as the language of their greetings with her. But no one answered. Lyddie spotted Nuray on the opposite side of the room. Beside her was her beautiful cousin, Sarya. Nuray sat with her arm around Sarya's shoulders. Sarya's face was scraped, her clothing torn and stained with something that might have been blood. The rapt attention of those in the room was divided between Sarya and Lyddie herself. "What happened, Nuray?" Lyddie said, alarmed. She pleaded, "Please tell me what happened!" Nuray merely indicated Sarya with a nod, and then, as if ashamed, gazed at the floor.

Lyddie did not want to take out the passport with Siegfried's picture on it. She herself was afraid now. Whose blood stained Sarya's dress? Lyddie remembered Sabina's talk with Siegfried in the garden at Fani Vevis the day she had caught him trying to follow her. You must wait for a woman to show interest. You cannot force her. Lyddie began to retreat. "Sabina, come," she said quietly, urging her away from the house.

"Listen," Sabina said, holding up a hand to stop Lyddie.

It was a high-pitched whine, not like the low, mournful howling of the boy, Bilimet.

They walked toward it, climbing back up from the village to the main path and then continuing in the direction opposite that of their approach. "Sabina," Lyddie said. "I think Siegfried may have hurt someone. One of the women."

"No!" Sabina said, her voice already capitulating to the horror of this new possibility. "He could not. No, Lyddie. No." She was losing her composure now.

"Listen to me, Sabina," Lyddie said softly, grabbing her friend by the arm to stop her and then taking her other arm and turning her so that they faced one another squarely. "There was blood. I don't know whose. Something has happened, but they didn't have the language to tell me."

"Oh my God!" Sabina could no longer hold off the tears she'd held back all evening. "What has he done?"

"Come. He needs you," Lyddie said. In that moment when they knew they would find him, they were more afraid than they had been in his absence all evening.

"Lyddie, will you go before?" Sabina said.

"You call him, Sabina. He'll listen to you."

"Siegfried," Sabina called tentatively, "Siegfried, where are you? Tell me where you are." She called more softly, carefully now, as if both wanting and not wanting to know. A hundred yards further down the path, the whining stopped.

Lyddie scanned both sides of the dirt track with the flashlight and she and Sabina moved more slowly. On the left, Lyddie illuminated a vertical expanse of stone, and then a shoe, and finally Siegfried, who had found the hollowed-out beds in the rock about four feet up that had eluded Lyddie almost two weeks before. Sobbing, he looked frightful, his hands and face bloody. "Oh my God, Siegfried, what has happened?" Lyddie said.

"Sa-bi-na," he called, ignoring Lyddie. "Where is Sabina?" Then, seeing her, "You burned your lovers, Sabina. You didn't need them anymore. You are so very selfish. So selfish," he said, his voice smeared thin and tight in his throat, then breaking up as he began to cry again.

THE NEXT MORNING WHEN DIMITRI returned from Smardakito, he told them how Siegfried had come upon Sarya at the top of the village just before dusk. She had been gathering wild fennel, using a knife to cut it. Siegfried had tried to force himself on her, but she had used the little knife against him, slashing at his face and arm. Though the Kurds were upset, they had asked Dimitri not to report the incident. Sarya, they said, had defended herself well. And illegal immigrants had no rights.

"Dimitri," Lyddie said, "I don't think Sabina told Siegfried about the village. She said she kept her promise." Sabina had sworn this the night before when she and Lyddie had taken Siegfried to the pharmacy to find a doctor who would stitch him up. Sabina had made up a story about his having cut himself with a bread knife. "Still, one way or another," Lyddie said, "it's my fault he knew. He must have followed me out there. I don't think I should go there anymore."

"You know what Abba Mius say to the soldier who has worries about what he done?"

"No," Lyddie said.

"He say, 'Tell me, My Dear, if your cloak has rip, you throw it out?' and the soldier say, 'No, I mend it.'"

Lyddie said, "Abba Mius—was he a Desert Father?"

"Yeah," Dimitri said, sounding very American, but with a nod on the bias, in the Greek fashion. A nod involving a concession. "They need your help. But take care, Lyddie, so Siegfried not come again. And he not talk to nobody."

SULLEN AND SEEMINGLY ASHAMED, his chin and his forearm bandaged thickly, Sabina kept Siegfried under house arrest at Fani Vevis in the next days. He didn't resist. In fact, he seemed to welcome Sabina's attentions. Lyddie, afraid of him, would not stay with him alone except to sit in the courtyard in daylight while he stayed inside. Maroula helped by bringing them food and sometimes sitting with him for Sabina. Of the three of them, she was the only one really big enough to restrain him if need be. Sabina felt he shouldn't make the journey back to Berlin in his current unstable condition. She also admitted that he was less than predictable; she might not be able to handle him alone in transit. And yet, staying on the island, he was a danger in more ways than one. Not only might he try again to hurt someone. It was also clear that he knew about the refugees and might talk. After much deliberation between Sabina and Lyddie, Sabina called Lothar, who agreed to come to the island to help her take him back when he was better.

It was Lothar who gave Sabina the news that Phelps had called—he'd made his way through Turkey and into Greece. Lothar had told him where Lyddie and Sabina were staying. He expected they would hear from Phelps soon.

Lyddie's shock was absorbed into Sabina's almost supernatural calm. What they shared was a feeling that the situations in which they found themselves were so far out of their control and beyond their imagining that they might just as well merely dwell in them as an existential condition as try in any way to understand or react. That night, they left Ulla and Siegfried, still recuperating, asleep under Fani Vevis's vigilant eye while they went down to the harbor. They sat together at the quay on the south side, setting afloat, in boats made of paper, lotus-shaped candles Sabina had brought from Berlin. Lyddie prepared to break a long silence, composed of all that was ever deliberately left unspoken between them.

"Have you ever lied to me?" she asked Sabina suddenly.

Sabina's gold hair caught the flare of the candles, shimmering a little. She sat motionless. "Yes."

Lyddie ran her fingers over the pebbly concrete, as if trying to read its Braille in the dark. "And why did you? Am I any worse off for it?"

"There was something I wanted to believe."

"And did you?"

"I suppose I did."

"Would you lie to me now?"

"We speak two languages, Lyddie, and there is no book to tell us the difference. We might as well be lying," Sabina said. She began to rock gently toward the water.

"So that's the way you lied to me?"

"No. That is the reason it doesn't really matter. Still, in some ways I wish that I did not."

The waves from a passing ferry capsized the paper boats one by one and doused their candles. Lyddie longed to speak effortlessly with someone. She was tired of ambiguity, of her questions being turned on themselves, magnified like clear drops of water suddenly aswarm with microscopic and potentially harmful organisms. Nothing was simple anymore. The process of making room for truth as a quotient divided infinitely against itself made her chest ache.

That night when they got back to the room, Fani Vevis had left a telegram for her on the bed. There was a phone number for her to call at ten. Ambivalent, she walked out to the edge of town near the radio tower and the empty fountain. She stood a long time looking up at the stars before she got the courage to approach the pay phone and dial the number on the little paper. It rang a long while, and then it was Phelps, saying her name, saying "Is that you, Lyddie?"

"Phelps," she said, "I've had no idea—what were you going to say?"

"I'm in Greece," he replied, his voice sounding distant and small. "No idea?"

"Really?" she said. "Yes, well, where you…I mean I've been crazy with fear…" A bad connection caused an awkward delay in delivery of their words, and they stumbled over one another's false starts. Lyddie kicked at the dirt. Candy wrappers and crushed cigarette boxes skittered around the empty fountain a few feet away at the center of the square. Seizing the silence, Lyddie said, "I really want to talk to you. I want to tell you everything." She spoke much more deliberately than she meant to. "Can you hear me? I don't think…"

"Are you with him, Lyddie? You were determined to be with him. And you never really—"

"It's you I want to talk to—" she started. "Never what?"

"Wanted the baby."

"A baby."

"I found the pills. Did you think I would wait forever?"

"But I stopped taking them. There was a baby," Lyddie said. I guess Ray told you. Still, I'm the one who's been waiting."

"Let's go home, Lyddie."

"I don't know if I can," she said. "Why now?"

She waited through a few seconds of static before she realized the line had, in fact, gone dead.

10

THE HOUSE WHERE AXEL STAYED—on the north side of the harbor, beyond town and looking out to the sea—was elemental, simple. It had a rectangular cistern at the front, which he told Lyddie was for gathering rainwater. He had water at his doorstep.

The afternoon he first showed her the place, he stood at the edge of the little cistern and considered aloud the contrast between his own situation and that of the Greek monk Ptolemy, of whom he had been reading in *Paradise of the Fathers*. Ptolemy lived in the desert at Wadi-an-Natrun, a valley two days by camel from Cairo. In that part of the desert the rocks were so steep they said you could not live there. The place was called Klimax, "the ladder". Water was sixteen kilometers away. So Ptolemy set out sea sponges at night to collect dew in January and February. These sponges he squeezed into a jar, and in such a way he managed to drink. But in the end he went mad and retreated to the city, where he lived in decadence the rest of his life.

"I don't want to go mad," Axel told her.

"You have a bit of Paradise right here," she said.

Later, Lyddie sat on the bed in her room and cried. She cried convulsively, not so much for what she felt, but for what she knew she had not felt before. Her life had been like a house not designed with her in mind. She had cared for it and lived in it, but never really felt like a presence there. Now, though her life was complicated and unpredictable, she felt fully present in it. She looked at herself in the mirror of the armoire. Unfamiliar with her own beauty, she was startled when she saw it there. Perhaps she was going mad, and in her madness, she looked directly into her own face, seeing it as if for the first time—as if it were an answer rather than the relentless question it had proven in the past. She looked without judgment and without perplexity. The sun on her skin and the crying itself had made her eyes bright, gazing intently out from black lashes clumped below. From a deep bluish rim around the iris, she plunged through the striations of sea green toward the pupil, that perfectly formed darkness at the center.

Lyddie imagined that by the time the monk Ptolemy descended his desert rock to collect the drops in the jar, the cells of his body would be caving in with thirst. His ascetic resolve would fade with the pleasure of drinking, the moisture of nights and seasons on his lips and tongue. The water would taste of lemon balm, which grew in the garden of the wife he had left in Alexandria, ninety kilometers and a lifetime to the north. Or in the garden of the woman he had never had. Either way, he would long for the less ambiguous days of his asceticism, when the dew he had collected tasted of nothing but the sponge itself.

Axel said that such a man walked away from a debt to a sultan or a merchant in the city to live in a desert cell. But who could say how it happened for others, or at what moment long-ing became the practice of longing, a rejection of the gifts that arrived like cast-off aromas on the moisture of a desert night? A glass of good water, had he drunk it, would have obliterated the monk Ptolemy, wrecking the ascetic edge with its pleasures.

Or it would have saved him, perhaps in the same way.

THE MORNINGS SHE WENT UP to Smardakito were reminders of how good it was to move beyond the personal. Nuray and the oth-ers did not seem to blame her for what had happened to Sarya. Each day Lyddie saw as a chance to mend the torn cloak of the day before. Phelps was alive now. She knew that for certain, and she felt the happiness of believing she would have a chance to talk things out with him. To understand and be understood. Maybe even to be forgiven. One night, Lyddie took from the drawer of the little table in the room at Fani Vevis the scraps of the note Siegfried had torn up, and she tried to piece them together, but she found the task impossible, as the note was in German, the writing bold and angular, some letters jutting into other lines and canceling the letters there. Not wanting to cause any more sadness over Siegfried, and at the same time not fully convinced she owed Sabina anything, she put the note back in the drawer. The nights when Lyddie walked with Axel and he ran his hands up her back and around to the sides of her breasts—the nights they made love against a rock or in the sand, Lyddie thought of Ptolemy in his desert, almost mad with thirst and looking for God. She thought too of Phelps, taking his first draft from the hose in the green-house back at home, the cool water spreading where his mouth entered it. When she asked Sabina if she still loved Lothar, Sabina said, "Like a brother, perhaps. One you take care for but who makes you angry also."

Lyddie said, "Yes, but you wouldn't make love to a brother."

Seeing Sabina's alarm, Lyddie reassured her. "It's all right. Lothar told me."

"Told you what, precisely?" Sabina asked.

"That you were sleeping with him again," Lyddie said calmly.

"My brother?" Sabina said.

"Don't be ridiculous, Sabina. With him. With Lothar. Before we left to come here, he told me," Lyddie said.

Then Sabina said, "Oh. That's true. I was." In the garden at Fani Vevis, Sabina opened cans of food for six or seven stray cats with pointed, inbred faces and a cursory covering of fur. Lyddie leaned on the stone sink and watched. "And what about Axel?" she asked. "You slept with Axel too, didn't you?"

Sabina put the cans down and sat at the table to watch the cats attack them. "Sleeping with Axel," she said, "it frightened me." She spoke slowly, finding what to say just before the words came out. "It felt so… unconnected to anything that happened before or after. As if I am an island, and he makes a crash landing. Perhaps you understand. It felt, in a way, like the only thing that has ever been real." She looked up at Lyddie. "It was a long while ago. But I needed Lothar after that. You can imagine."

Lyddie could imagine, easily. Lothar, for all his sarcasm, was a sweet man. Still, that didn't settle anything. Lyddie was careful about what she said next. "Just once?" she asked.

"Yes."

"But you still want him now, don't you? You keep your door open for him?" The cats ate greedily and then licked the tins.

"He will go out or he will come in. As he wants. No one can change him."

"But it hurts you, doesn't it? This freedom of his?"

"Great God, Lyddie!" Sabina stood abruptly and collected the tins, dropping them into a plastic bag with a clatter. "There is nothing that will not hurt you if you give it a chance. It hurts me. Yes, it does. It hurts so much that sometimes I don't know how I can endure it. Is this what you insist to hear from me?" Her face was all agape, surprised into honesty, but only for a raw instant before it composed itself again. She said, "Would it be different if I tell you that he is Ulla's father?"

"Axel? Her father?" Lyddie exclaimed. She felt her history with Axel come to an abrupt halt. It struck her as outrageous that he should share a child with Sabina. But Sabina had certainly trumped her with this claim. In fact, after the initial shock, she couldn't help but wonder if Sabina had invented it in order to have the advantage. "You told me her father was no one I knew," Lyddie said, tentatively.

"Maybe I was lying."

"Then maybe you're lying now."

Angry, Sabina hurled the cans at the garden wall and the cats scattered, except for a black and white one that rubbed against her ankle.

"It's just that Axel told me…" Lyddie said calmly.

"Yes? He told you what?" Sabina said, curious, though still indignant.

"That he couldn't be a father."

"Miracles happen." Sabina shrugged and punted the last cat so that it scampered away.

"Actually, you've said they don't." Lyddie was thinking of the unlocked cigarette machine and the windfall of cigarettes—Sabina's example of what wouldn't ever happen again.

"So, somebody made a mistake," Sabina said. "I can tell you that doctors are not perfect. Or Axel lied. Do you really believe everything that he says to you? You think he was thrown out from the East because he was a Boy Scout?"

Enticing though this opening was, Lyddie refused to change the subject. "Did you tell him he was Ulla's father?" Lyddie said.

"He wouldn't take that lightly, Sabina." In Sabina's silence, Lyddie remembered seeing Axel's back disappear down the hallway at Sabina's flat the day she had stopped by seeking her friend's sympathy and advice. "Did he believe you when you told him?"

"Enough!" Sabina shouted. "I surrender! I know you have been with him again, Lyddie. There is no need to prove you have a right. He has made clear he has no feeling for Ulla or for me. But he will hurt me with or without your permission."

WHEN AXEL ASKED LYDDIE TO WALK with him around the headland on the north side of the island one evening to see the house his German grandmother had lived in, Lyddie agreed, only because she was afraid for him. Though she knew that she risked hurting Sabina further, she needed to know what he thought about Sabina and Ulla.

From high above the port, they watched the few vehicles that had come to meet the ferry pull away, headlights cutting a narrow swath in the gathering dusk. Then there was only the churning of the water behind as the boat eased out of the harbor.

Axel decided that, rather than taking the serpentine road up and around the mountain to the vacant house, which his uncle looked after, they would go, in his words, "as the crow walks." For a while, they followed what was little more than a goat path; then they lost their way as they tried to traverse the valley. Axel oriented himself to the sound of the sea and continued, scrambling over stone fences. He led her with his voice, saying "Ella, Lyddie. Come." And when he saw the trouble in her face, a trouble she knew had to do with her dependence on him in the rugged nightscape, he said, "What is it?" but before she could answer, he exclaimed, "Ah!" turning her around to look. "The moon!" And there, over the sea, the moon had come up as orange as a pumpkin. "That moon," he said. "My mother told me that it made my grandmother remember, always, the Pfaueninsel, the Island of Painted Birds. *Pagoni* they are called in Greek. I don't know what you say in English. It was a place she saw many years before, far away, at the beginning of the war. His voice faded in and out as he stumbled across the field ahead of her.

When they found the little house, set steeply into the hillside overlooking the cove, Axel said it was too dark to make their way back and they should stay the night. They could walk up to the road and catch the first bus in the morning.

Lyddie wasn't happy that he'd brought her to a place she couldn't get back from. Either he was Ulla's father or Sabina loved him enough to want to make him believe he was. Knowing these possibilities, and knowing that Phelps was in Greece, Lyddie didn't think she should spend the night with Axel. He unlocked the top portion of the door; then he reached into the darkness and released the bottom half so they could go in. The little house smelled of camphor and mold. Axel opened the shutters and found a flashlight in the cave-like kitchen downstairs, which he turned on in order to rummage through a drawer for a mosquito coil. Upstairs, he lit the coil and set it on the table that occupied the central room, then he led Lyddie to a bedroom no bigger than the double mattress that occupied it. Axel pulled back an old printed sheet, the purpose of which was clear when the plaster fallout it had collected rattled to the floor. First taking off his shoes, he lay back on the mattress, his knees still bent over the end of it. He fell asleep instantly, the way a child might. Too troubled to sleep, Lyddie sat beside him. Taking off her shoes, she pulled her knees up to her chest. All around them, cicadas pulsed loudly. Worse than spending the night with him, given Sabina's new claim, was the isolation

she felt watching him sleep—his self-absorption and ambivalence toward her. When she said his name, just loudly enough
not to be heard, he reached for her arm and pulled her toward
him. "*Ella,*" he said.

She pulled herself back up and said, "Axel, why did you
come to the island? It wasn't for the wedding, was it?"

Axel sat up groggily. "The air is close. Let's go out." He led
her to the balcony and they sat propped against the door-frame.
"I want to tell you the truth, Lyddie. And the truth is that I must
not tell you."

"Did it have to do with Sabina?"

Axel was silent. "What do you mean?" he said, finally.

"I want to know if you came here because of Sabina—and
because of what she told you. About Ulla."

"I came here to begin again," he said, "the way my grandmother did. I came because I believed, after I saw how Gerdot
had wasted the part of his life that might have been better
than the very bad part before, that perhaps I did not have to
be like him."

Axel spoke in a tone he had until then reserved for the
Desert Fathers. Or the night they'd spent in the library. He was
unguarded, hopeful, in a way he had once been on her account.
Except that now, it seemed she could only get in the way. If anyone could help him start over, it would be Ulla. Lyddie remembered the helplessness in his face the day he had lit the drink in
Ulla's hand and the fire had spilled out onto her. With all of the
intensity he had once directed to finding Gerdot, he seemed to
be searching now for a way to put out that fire.

Axel dug into his pocket and pulled out a silver hoop, which
he held up in the moonlight. "I found something that belongs to
you," he said, handing it to her.

"Where did you find it?" she asked, surprised that he would

know it was hers, since she had stopped wearing its mate when she'd lost the one he held.

"Smardakito," he said.

"So you've been there. You know, she said."

He nodded.

"Your grandfather is a wonder."

"Shhhh," he said, smiling and closing his eyes. He fell asleep against the doorjamb. After watching him for a few minutes, Lyddie led him back into the bedroom, where she left him to sleep. Though Axel hadn't approached Sabina, Lyddie was certain he would. He seemed to want to set things right all around. And maybe he would want to be with Sabina.

In the main room, Lyddie fished around in the old desk for a candle and some matches. Though no one stayed in it, the house was still furnished, probably as it had been when Axel's grandmother and mother had lived there. A wooden buffet dominated the main room, the floors of which were concrete. On top of the buffet was a large, rolled Turkish rug, which, during winter, must have insulated the floor. Opening the door on the left side of the buffet, Lyddie found a candle in a wooden spool for a holder; she lit it and surveyed the contents of the other side: a stack of pressed linens. Removing some sheets, she did her best to make a bed of the wooden sofa against the opposite wall.

Not at all tired, she wandered into the next room, where she found a coal-burning stove, a cot-like bed, and a wobbly wooden desk with a key. She set the candle down on top of the desk, turned the key and pulled hard. The little wooden leaf dropped to reveal a series of cubbyholes. Lyddie pulled out the chair and sat down in the flickering light of the candle. They had left the shutters open, and a breeze came in behind her. She reached into the first cubbyhole, which produced a swatch of dark hair, a set of orange worry beads, and some rubber bands. She examined them

and returned them to their place. From a second cubbyhole, she
pulled a little stack of papers. On top was a photograph in which
a small boy, scowling, stood beside a man in uniform, as if he had
been commanded to pose. The man, on the other hand, looked as
though he were a stranger to such dissent—used to having the world
agree with him. He had an air of remote confidence. She turned
the photo over. It said 1964. Axel would have been five years old,
about the size the boy looked. On closer observation, the papers
beneath the photo appeared to be receipts. There was also a folded piece of newspaper. When she opened it, a powder that looked
like graphite spilled out. She tried to brush it into her hand, but it
smeared onto the desktop. Now she had made a mess. She looked
at the news article, which had a photo of the same man and then a
short article in Greek. For all she knew, she'd spilled the remains of
Axel's father, kept and forgotten in a place that someone had meant
to return to. She wanted to think it was merely pencil shavings, but
the powder was greasy, as she imagined ash from a body would be.
She had that all-night-in-the-library feeling about being where she
shouldn't be, doing what she shouldn't be doing. What right did she
have to be tampering with Axel's past? She went and got a Kleenex
from her bag and used it to wipe up the gray smear.

Just before dawn, an explosion shook the ground, caroming off
the face of the island from the cove. Lyddie bolted up from the little
couch where she'd tried to sleep. Axel stumbled in from the other
room. He opened the door, and standing there in the aftermath,
he ran his fingers back along his scalp, lifting the wavy, dark hair
away from his forehead. "Do you feel how it wakes the heart with
a shock?" he said. The sky had begun to turn pale, like a stunned
fish gone belly up.

She'd been awake nearly all night, and now she merely felt
tired. "It must be Politimos," she said. "Fishing with dynamite.
Dimitri told us about it." A smoky, sulfurous smell was perceptible

in the air. "Axel," Lyddie said. "I'm going back by the road. The bus should come along soon."

"Why did you sleep here and not in the bed? I will come with you," he said.

"No," she said. "Please. I need to be alone. Away from you."

Along the road back to Hora, lizards scattered to the dry brush in a reverse wake, preceding her motion. The static of cicadas attuned itself to an ancient and familiar frequency. Though Axel had not affirmed that he'd come to the island for Sabina, he had not denied it either. He wanted to begin again. Lyddie wanted him to have that chance. What she wanted for herself didn't matter so much anymore, though she loved him, at that moment, almost desperately. After an hour or so, the bus came and she let it rumble past. When it did, she saw his face at the window, looking out. He tried to open the window but couldn't. She felt more alone than she had ever been: alone because Phelps had made her so, and the baby had; alone because of Axel.

Still, she would step aside and allow things to fall as they would. She would not interfere. Her legs ached from the previous night's ascent and the physical pain felt good. As she walked, she counted the breadbox-style shrines on metal legs at the roadside, the contents of each like that of a miniature garage sale—a curious attempt to reshuffle the contents of a life into something of meaning. Virgins and saints crowded at the back amid miniature hurricane lamps, bottles for oil, and the dubious bloom of plastic flowers. Though she suspected the shrines might commemorate highway deaths, she preferred to think of them as stations on a journey.

LYDDIE AVOIDED GOING BACK to the room until late at night. When she got into bed, she thought Sabina was already asleep. She lay in the dark, thinking. She was surprised to hear Sabina say her name. "They brought the bodies in from Ormos Stephanou this afternoon," Sabina said. She spoke quietly, so as not to wake Ulla.

"The man and woman who drowned? You saw it?" Lyddie said.

"The woman. I asked. She was wrapped in canvas." Sabina seemed as though she were still in a state of shock.

Lyddie's own eyes had adjusted to the dark, and she saw Sabina's hands where they lay on the sheet of the bed next to her own. She imagined Sabina's fingers wet and salty from contact with the other world. "Why would you want to see her? They let you?"

"Coast Guard Ianni. I wanted to understand what the body is—what it is without the will. And I wanted to know how the sea…" Her voice trailed off, as if asking Lyddie to understand without her having to say it all. "As you know, they were Kurds. Ianni said he thought the others should turn up soon."

"What will happen when they don't? Ianni and his Coast Guard will go searching for them."

"I don't know," Sabina said, lost in thought. "They wanted a new life, but somehow, it was too late. How things would look to them in those moments when they can see the windmills, the monastery, that new world so close and then—"

"Sabina!" Lyddie protested. She was thinking now of the boy, Bilimet, who not only was an orphan but who also had been blamed for what had happened.

"No, Lyddie, 'tis an interesting story. Every story has an ending." Sabina seemed to need to come to terms with the worst that could happen. To know whether her confidence would sustain her to the end.

"What's happening, Sabina?" Lyddie asked.

"I will finish telling if you will allow me."

"To you! What is happening?" Lyddie exclaimed.

Sabina seemed not to hear. "How must the others look to her

the last time before she goes under, knowing that from shore she is terribly small and unimportant. Does she hate them at that moment?"

Lyddie stood and crossed the room to open the shutter, letting the night air in. It was cool and smelled of the sea. "Don't hate me, Sabina," Lyddie said. "Please. I want you not to hate me." Sabina seemed to be coming apart and maybe Lyddie was part of the reason. It was as if she were standing on dry ground, watching Sabina go down.

"I don't," Sabina said.

There followed a long silence, during which Lyddie thought Sabina had fallen asleep.

"What do you want, Lyddie?" Sabina asked. "I mean really want." Her voice travelled the dark between them. "Is it Axel? To be with him?"

Lyddie had lived so long with her own conflicting desires that she found it hard to answer that question. She said, "When I feel the earth's pull on this island—that gravity—in some places it's so strong I almost know who I am. But everyone I've ever cared about—nearly everyone—has wanted me not to tell what was happening inside. Even you, Sabina. Even you seem to ask for something other than the truth."

"I do?"

"Yes. You do."

"The truth is not easy," Sabina said. "But I'm sorry. Truly, I am." They heard the rustle of sheets as Ulla turned in her bed. "You felt it at the monastery? The gravity?" Sabina said.

"Yes."

"I also."

"When you were looking out to the sea?" Lyddie said.

"Yes," Sabina said dreamily.

11

TWO DAYS LATER, SABINA WOKE early to meet Lothar at the
ferry from Piraeus. He would help her care for Siegfried and,
when Siegfried was ready, Lothar would take him back to Berlin.
Lothar and Sabina arrived back at the garden of Rooms Fani Vevis
bursting with news. They were talking excitedly with Lyddie when
Axel showed up. He leaned against the wall and listened.

"Axel, have you heard?" Sabina, said. "Thirty-five thousand
East Germans have crossed over to the West German embassy
in Prague. It's mass hysteria."

"Look," Siegfried said in German, holding up a newspaper Lothar had brought. "Lothar says they are climbing over
the walls and shitting in the courtyard." He obviously found
these particulars fascinating. Fani Vevis, who had apparently
been waiting for Siegfried to leave his room, came around with
a mop and bucket, asking if she could clean.

"Siegfried," said Lothar. "How are you?"

"Good," said Siegfried, somewhat warily. He looked at his

arm, the bandage having been removed just that morning, and then around at Fani Vevis, Lothar, Sabina and Lyddie as if some kind of conspiracy might be afoot.

"How did so many get across?" Lyddie asked Lothar. Neither she nor Sabina had been reading the news, and Ralph and the other Germans, their usual source, had gone back to Munich.

"Still they pretend to go for pleasure trips. They take just one suitcase," Lothar said.

"It's incredible!" Lyddie exclaimed. "Are the East Germans trying to stop them?"

"The Stasi, they are at the West German embassy with the Czech police, trying to beat them away, but they are climbing over the walls and onto the roof," Lothar said.

Sabina said in disbelief, "It is like you set down the novel you are reading and you go for a swim. You return to find that someone has rearranged the plot entirely."

Axel shook his head. He looked as though he might be calculating the distance between Prague and Greece. "The hordes," he said, "are shifting across the continent in search of some great paradigm of happiness. But they themselves are the unhappiness that becomes their condition wherever they go—the condition that works its unhappiness on others."

"Ah!" Sabina said. "The voice of experience!"

Lothar sat with Lyddie and Ulla at the table in the garden, while Sabina disappeared inside to bring out some clothes, which she began to scrub at the sink. Lothar helped Ulla sort the stones and bits of polished glass she had collected at the beach the day before. "Axel," Lothar said, "How is it with your grandfather? What he is doing?"

"The same as always, "Axel said. "He is busy with the café." All of them present knew about the refugee village and what had happened with Siegfried. Sabina had surely explained to

Lothar. But hardly a word of it had been spoken openly among them—even between Axel and Lyddie, each knowing the other was directly involved with the Kurds.

Axel looked at Lyddie, still apparently baffled by her sudden departure from his grandmother's house two days before and by her failure to flag down the bus when it had passed. She was quiet, having pulled a plastic chair over into the shade of the apricot tree. So Axel sat down at the table with Lothar, who was listening to Sabina tell about an incident at the swimming rocks the day before. Sabina looked over her shoulder at Lothar and laughed as she scrubbed. They were almost abnormally civil to one another. They talked about Siegfried, who had gone back to his room to read comic books. His wounds were healing well and he was calmer now that Sabina mostly stayed close by.

"When will we go to Berlin with Siegfried?" Ulla asked in German.

Sabina said, "In a few days, Ulla. Lothar has come to help us."

"We don't need help, do we?" Ulla said.

"Maybe we do, Ulla,"

"And Siegfried will cut himself at home too. He will not be careful. Will Lothar make sure he doesn't cut himself?"

It crossed Lyddie's mind that—as much as they resisted the idea—Lothar and Sabina and Ulla were like a family. Axel, too, seemed to observe the clothes hung neatly on a line near the prickly pear where Sabina had obviously put them that morning—her black cotton skirts and underwear, Lothar's sec-ond-hand trousers, Ulla's bright leggings. Ulla was blonde, like Lothar. Unlike Axel. There was, in fact, nothing about Ulla that was like Axel. Lothar was happy to father Axel's child. The child Axel had been told was his.

Axel pulled a prickly pear from the huge cactus growing in the corner of the courtyard and dragged a chair from the table, positioning it next to Lyddie. He took the knife out of his pocket and peeled the fruit, then cut a piece and explained to Lyddie how to eat it without chewing, how to work it with her tongue, swallowing the fleshy pulp along with the stones as his cousin had taught him. "Try some, Sabina," Axel said, in a voice that overcompensated for the bitterness Lyddie could tell he felt. For whatever reason, he wanted her to eat that very difficult fruit.

"I don't like it," Sabina said.

"But how would you know?" he said. "Have you tasted? Look, Lyddie is willing to try." He watched Lyddie work a mouthful with her tongue. It was like swallowing her own teeth. She ended up spitting it into the flowerbed. When Sabina turned around, drying her hands on her shorts, her face was wet with tears. She excused herself, taking Ulla in to nap.

Axel left then and headed in the direction of Dimitri's place.

"I think we should give her some room," Lyddie said to Lothar, looking at the doorway through which Sabina had disappeared.

"Walk with me," Lothar said. So he and Lyddie followed the stone-paved path through the white maze of houses and shops to the place where, at the edge of town, it dwindled as it rounded the mountain and led out toward the archaeological site. "What's the problem for Sabina?" Lothar said as they walked.

"She needs your help, Lothar," Lyddie said.

"Perhaps. But let me see… She cries in the garden because she is very happy to see me again? Come, Lyddie."

"You'll have to ask her, Lothar. It's not for me to say. Whenever I think I understand Sabina, everything changes."

Within a few minutes, they came to the ruin of the Minoan settlement. Pink laurel billowed around a spring above the few remaining Cyclopean blocks of the city wall. They stopped at the Roman cistern near the base of the tower, and Lyddie scuffed at the dirt with her sandal. "You know, Dimitri says that somewhere on this site a Cycladic idol was discovered last spring." She said this hoping they could talk about something else. "Right here in the dirt where it had been for five thousand years. Nobody noticed it until a French kid tripped over it on a school holiday."

"Maybe no one was looking," Lothar said, smiling. Not to be put off, he said, "So, what has changed this time? It is something about Axel?"

"Lothar, since you insist," Lyddie said, "I don't think it was the prickly pear she was crying about. But you need to talk to her, not me." Lyddie rose and Lothar followed as she mounted the three steps into the enclosure that had been the later Hellenistic temple. The decapitated body of a statue stood in the middle of the open area, surrounded by flat slabs outlining the foundation. The stones radiated the unremitting heat of the day.

"She told me that you were sleeping with him," he said.

"Axel? I don't think he sleeps much," Lyddie said.

"Ah! Now we arrive at something. So!" he exclaimed. He rolled his shirtsleeve with great efficiency and pleasure as a way of demonstrating the precision he felt he had achieved.

"Lothar," Lyddie protested.

"Let's talk about you and Axel."

"Just Axel," Lyddie said, touching the top of the stone tunic, out of which the neck would once have risen, and not wanting to say "Sabina and Axel." The tunic was smooth, as if it had grown comfortable with its loss. The sky was a blue uninterested in nuance. "I think there is no me and Axel. Tell me the truth Lothar. What do you think about Axel?"

"For you, Lyddie? To be honest, I am a bit jealous," he said, grinning. And then, more serious, "As, I think, Phelps may be. Sabina told me that you called him."

Lyddie looked away from Lothar and her gaze fell on her

hand, which had come to rest on the pitted folds of the statue's garment. Lothar looked at it too. She knew he must be thinking, as she was, that her ring looked like a bit of hammered gold from the Mycenaean Age. A relic of a time long ago and far away. Or that's how it had looked to her until she had spoken with Phelps. Only since then had she thought of taking it off. "Axel alone," she said. "By himself. As I think he may always be. Just Axel. Lothar, do you trust him?" She didn't see any point in telling Lothar about Sabina's claim on Axel, or in exposing Sabina's hurt and jealousy over the time Lyddie had spent with him. And she didn't want to talk about Phelps.

"Ah, Lyddie. Axel is difficult, there is no question. But he has always been harmless. Surely you know that." Lothar's lips were redder than usual from the Greek sun. His face looked sweet, and, despite what he was saying, a little forlorn. "And Trust? What is it?" Lothar said, serious still. "An agreement that invites injury and implies control. I will try to control no one, and I will allow no one to injure me."

This sounded to Lyddie like a rationalization Lothar had worked hard at. Maybe he had already been injured, which was why he protected himself with such ardent philosophies. "I know he's your oldest friend," Lyddie said. "He just confuses me, that's all. He sends mixed messages."

"Lyddie," he said, "Axel is no simple person. I agree with you." He glanced at the sky, where now a few gauzy clouds floated, not disturbing the very sane blue. "Are you jealous because Sabina loves him?" he asked calmly.

It wasn't at all clear to her which part was the question. Still, that Lothar knew about Sabina's feelings for Axel caught Lyddie off guard.

"Surely," Lothar continued, "it has not taken you so long to figure what any schoolboy can see," he said.

Lyddie wondered if Sabina's love would matter to Axel. As much as a person might change, certain things remained constant, belonging to some stubbornly essential part of who one was. "If she loves Axel, then why are you going back to her? What does that mean to you?" Lyddie said.

Lothar thought for a moment. "It means she sometimes washes my trousers and I keep her feet on the ground."

Lyddie shook her head, uncomprehending. She looked at the epically reduced ancient city wall, its stones stacked only two high most of the way around. She followed Lothar out of the temple.

"What Sabina and I do—" Lothar said, "it is a way of loving, Lyddie." He paused at the cistern on the way out and sat down again. He worked the dry dirt at his feet with a stone. "There are many ways. And though you may not think you love Axel, there will remain a level of artifacts, somewhere in your foundation, from the settlement called 'days with Axel.' It is part of your story."

OVER THE NEXT FEW DAYS, Sabina, Lothar and Lyddie followed the news with fascination as the East Germans continued to swell the refugee camp that the West German embassy in Prague had become. Lothar was caught up in the atmosphere of ferment as it grew to resemble revolt. Any resentment he had felt toward his countrymen gave way to anticipation as they defied the authorities boldly. His phone calls to Kristof yielded first-hand accounts of the excitement in Berlin when the foreign ministers of East Germany, West Germany and the U.S.S.R. agreed to send the refugees by train to West Germany, thereby releasing them to freedom. As a bogus demonstration that the Communists remained in control, the trains would take a long detour through East Germany. Kristof said many were afraid that this was a trick—that the East Germans were merely

being sent back home. When the trains actually set out and were
mobbed in Dresden by the Ossies left behind, word had it the
only thing keeping Egon Krenz's government from opening fire
after the model of the Chinese at Tiananmen Square was the
threat of bad publicity leading up to East Germany's fortieth
anniversary celebration.

ON THE AFTERNOON OF OCTOBER first, Lothar and Axel
and Lyddie were sitting with Dimitri inside the café watching TV
when the news came on. The report was in Greek, so only Axel
and Dimitri could understand, but soon it went to actual footage
in West Germany. "About the East Germans," Dimitri said.

Axel watched with fascination. He said, "It's at Hof. The
border. Where my car broke down on the way to Greece. I had
to take the train." Hof was a mob scene. Hundreds of people
blocked the streets, shouting and cheering. "*Die Züge!*" an old
woman was saying, her face a study in joy. "The trains! More
trains have arrived!"

"Arrived from where?" Lyddie said.

"Prague," Axel said. "From the West German embassy.
They sent them across the border."

The old woman said, "*Endlich frei!*" She said, "These are our
people, free at last!"

The camera panned the streets, and as it did, Axel pointed
out the Trabi, sitting where he had left it when the alternator
went, at the curb in front of an old hotel not far from the train
station. A pair of passing teenagers, seeing that the car was unlocked, opened the door and gave a couple of celebratory blasts
on the horn.

"If you'd been there, Axel," Lothar said, "they would have
thumped you on the back and given you chocolates and oranges."

Axel looked truly horrified.

Closer to the station, mounds of clothing and toys and baby carriages grew as the West Germans emptied their own houses to outfit the newcomers. And there, at the center, were the Ossies, looking exhausted and stunned, some of them holding D-Marks they had been handed by people on the street. Hundreds, maybe thousands of them pressed in, carrying bundles and suitcases.

A man pissed on the train tracks. A young woman cried on the shoulder of a man who seemed not to know what to do with her, let alone himself, as they stood beneath the West German sky—as sullen and impenetrable, Axel noted, as the sky they had left behind in the East. "She had waited so long," the woman kept sobbing. "How could we have left without her?"

"And how can you watch this?" Axel said. He got up and walked to the doorway. Then he turned around again, pulling his shirt open as if he were about to suffocate. "Why is she saying these things in public? No one will have his own life any more!"

The cameraman shoved his way through the thickening crowd back toward the car, which appeared well before he reached it. The iconic East German vehicle seemed to have levitated above the throng of celebrants, like a blimp or the host in a mass. As the camera closed in on it, it became apparent that a group of teenagers—maybe the same ones who had honked the horn—had together lifted the white Trabi as high as their shoulders, and people around them were chanting, "*Triumph der Trabant!*" Triumph of the Trabant!

"What are you afraid of?" Lothar said to Axel. "Why does that bother you so much?"

Lyddie, feeling awkwardly in the way, slipped out into the night air. She ran almost headlong into a man she had not seen standing just outside on the terrace. Lothar and Axel, hearing her gasp, came to the doorway.

For a long moment, no one moved. Lyddie backed away,

taking in the long, unwashed hair pulled back with a leather lace and the soiled clothing that conspired to make its wearer look like a prophet of doom. Were they all as guilty as their shock seemed to suggest?

Lothar stepped forward from behind Lyddie, offering his hand, and said, in an uncertain but annunciatory voice, "Phelps?"

Phelps shook Lothar's hand and said wearily, "Am I interrupting something? Will someone be kind enough to tell me if I should go?"

Lyddie, standing now off to the side, reached out and touched his elbow, his shoulder, verifying that he was not merely the Phelps she'd so often invented in order to argue with him. The British commentator on TV was interviewing East German Liberal Democratic leader Manfred Gerlach, who openly criticized the official newspaper accounts of the East Germans' exodus, which he said had "little to do with reality." Lyddie said, belatedly, "I can't believe that you're here!"

"You heard me say I would come, didn't you?" he said. Axel and Lothar turned quite deliberately back toward the TV, and Lyddie, reluctant to be alone with Phelps, walked past him to the terrace where a few others were drinking. She sat on the stucco bench along the wall near the steps. Her legs were shaking. Phelps joined her there.

"No," she said. "The connection was bad."

"I have so much to tell you."

"I'm sorry," she said, "I'm just…. I don't know how to act." How awkward a meeting this was—not like those she'd seen of the Germans from the East joyfully reunited with their families in the West, but as she imagined them two or three days or months later—neither having any idea what to do with the other, time having rendered them strangers.

"You shouldn't have to act," he said.

"Where have you been, Phelps? Were you a hostage?"

"Iraq. In the mountains and in Kirkuk. No, Lyddie. The things I saw, though. You can't imagine."

"Do you know what I have imagined?" Lyddie said. "Every night, awake and asleep, I saw you shot and buried with hundreds of others in the villages. Every night, taking round after round in the chest and trying to tell me something. Trying to speak to me, I thought." Her voice caught in her throat and she brushed away the tears. "Instead, you were alive and well. And keeping your mouth shut."

"Would you rather I were dead?"

"But why didn't you come home?" she pleaded.

Phelps shook his head and looked aggrieved. "I'm sorry."

She said, "You argue just the way I remember." She touched his face then put her arms around his neck and shoulders, breathing in the smell of him. There had been nights she had lain in bed aching for him. Too long ago.

"I was working with activists," he said, "on behalf of the Peshmerga. The Kurdish resistance."

Lyddie had heard that from the Kurds in Smardakito. Maybe Phelps was the man they had seen. The air was damp, the sirocco up from the Sahara, making everything just slightly uncomfortable. She said, "I don't know what to say to that." He reached up and covered her hand with his. They sat for a few moments before she pulled away and drew her sweater around her. She stood and went inside. Axel had come to the doorway and he looked down at her from close range as she pushed past him. On her way back out, he offered his pocketknife, seeing that she had forgotten to open the two Amstels she held. He opened them for her and they frothed onto her sun-browned hands. She crossed the terrace and set the bottles on the table. Then she pulled a chair around to sit opposite Phelps.

He said, "I was a dead man as far as anyone knew. They thought I'd been killed along with the rest of the village. I could do things others couldn't do. See, the Iraqis kept records on all of their own atrocities during the Anfal campaign and what came after." He glanced over at Axel's figure in the doorway. "Oddly enough, it was the East Germans who taught them such precise documentation of the horrors they perpetrated," he continued. "I was helping a human rights organization obtain some of those records."

"That's truly admirable," Lyddie said. "I mean it." She wanted to tell him about the Kurds at Smardakito, but she'd learned how much damage she could do with even her trust.

"But you think I abandoned you," he said.

"I, too, needed you. Had you come home, our baby would not—I wouldn't have left and she would not…"

"I didn't know about the baby," he said. "Why didn't you tell me?"

"I was waiting—" she said. "For you to—I wanted to feel the happiness I knew I would eventually feel. That's the way you and I did things."

"What happened?" he said.

"There I was with the baby you wanted, amid a jungle of plants eager for my downfall, proving daily how useless I was, and your brother insisting that I wait for you—"

"But you didn't. You couldn't wait. Tell me what happened."

"I was hiking in the heat," she said. "Here in Greece. I was a little bit lost."

"No. With Axel. You've been with Axel, haven't you?"

"That's not the way it was."

"But it is now," he said. "Isn't it?"

Lyddie stood up and walked away from him, into the square where the bus was turning around to go back down to the harbor.

Phelps went after her and she spun to face him. "You want me to tell you so much," she said. "But you would tell me nothing."

"What is it you want to know?" he shouted.

The bus completed its turn and sat with its doors agape.

But Lyddie knew all she needed to know. She'd found out on her own. They both glanced up at Axel's figure in the doorway of the cafe, his face in semi-profile lit by the bluish flicker of images from the TV screen. The bus driver was calling, in their direction, the name of the harbor.

Frustrated by her silence, Phelps climbed aboard the bus, pleading at once with the driver to wait for Lyddie and then pleading with her. But she couldn't climb the steps. The steps seemed a monumental impediment to progress toward him. The bus driver shook his head in frustration or helplessness and the doors closed; Phelps slumped into a seat halfway back and looked out at her angrily through the dusty, sealed window.

That night, Lyddie walked back by moonlight on the track to Smardakito but passed the village, retracing her steps in time, as if to unwind her karma. She followed the donkey path through the terrible quiet of the fields, past the threshing circles and the stone goat sheds, the Hermit Rock Beds where she and Sabina had found Siegfried. She walked quickly, with intention. It surprised her that she had not returned before. She trusted her instinct to guide her. But once she left the donkey path, she found herself disoriented. There were more olive trees than babies. More possible ways to go, and go wrong, than any one person could replicate. In the end, she threw herself down beneath a tree in resignation, wondering what it was she had thought to do if she had found the right one. Would she stuff the baby back? That the baby had not lived didn't mean she couldn't have a life with Phelps. But thinking of a life with him felt like trying to repatriate a fetus dead three weeks to the country of the womb.

Which was America. Which was not anymore a place she wanted to be. Or with him. What did she owe him? An olive branch? A peace offering? Overhead, the olive leaves shirred the night air. A rag? She picked up a stone and poked at a piece of white cloth that lay bleached in the dirt, catching the moonlight. She stopped suddenly and stood up. There, in the crotch of the tree, lay two of the stones she had put there. No baby. No bones. The crotch picked clean. Underwear on the ground. Carrion having been carried away. Part of a vulture hovering on a thermal now.

MACARIOS ONCE VISITED A SICK monk, and when he asked the monk if he wanted anything to eat, the brother replied, "Yes, I want some honeycakes." Thereupon Macarios set out for Alexandria, which was one hundred kilometers distant, and he brought back the sweetmeats and gave them to the monk. That was the first story Axel had told Lyddie about the Desert Fathers.

In another story, a certain brother had had a woman in his cell, and the monks wished to bring the matter home to him. But Bishop Ammon knew of this, and going into the cell he made the woman hide under a large earthenware jar, and then took his seat upon it. At his order the monks searched the cell and did not find the woman.

What were the themes, Lyddie had wondered aloud. Hunger? Indiscretions of the Fathers?

No, she thought now. Humility.

AFTER THE NIGHT OF PHELPS'S arrival, Axel disappeared from the island. He had told Lyddie before that he'd intended to go to Athos. Lyddie felt a kind of respite from the conundrum of the days of which he was a part. Phelps remained on the island but kept his distance. Lothar had moved down to the harbor to stay with him. Lothar and Phelps took Siegfried to the rocks in the harbor to swim. Lothar himself didn't know how, but Siegfried loved the water and Lothar and Phelps thought the exercise would do him good.

Ever since Siegfried had attacked Sarya, Sabina seemed to have insulated herself from the impact of all that had happened—not only with Siegfried, but with Axel and Lyddie too, as if she were wrapped in wind and standing quietly at the eye of the turbulence. In her own confusion, Lyddie had stood by, amazed and perplexed by the virulent sanity that persisted in Sabina, a stubborn strain of self-control almost as impervious to sympathy as it was to attack.

After her own swim at Aghia Margarita one morning, Lyddie stopped at the bakery and bought four pieces of baklava. She returned to the room at noon to find Sabina in bed, fully dressed.

"What has happened?" Lyddie exclaimed.

Ulla, sitting on the floor near the sink and cupboard, had poured a bag of white beans into an empty pot and was stirring them wildly. "*Mama schnitt mir ins Ohr*," she called out eagerly. Sabina was silent, but her eyes were puffy. Blonde curls lay in paisley patterns on the tile floor.

"You cut her hair?" Lyddie asked. "It's short, but it doesn't look bad," she said, uncomprehending.

"No," Sabina replied. "I cut her ear." Obscured partially by the silky wisps of Ulla's hair, a small bandage floated on the child's earlobe. "She wasn't even moving when I cut it. I could not feel it, the scissors were so sharp. And then I heard her scream and saw the flesh as I was finishing to close them." Sabina had begun to cry again. "She didn't want me to cut it because she was playing, but I would not listen to her. I could not see what I was doing."

"But Sabina," said Lyddie, sitting down beside her on the bed, "you didn't mean to do it. She seems fine. How bad is it?"

"I didn't cut her ear just. I cut part of it away. It looked like a tiny pork cutlet."

"Is it so awful?" Lyddie asked.

"It's just... graphic," Sabina answered, her voice oddly level, having lost its song. Her sobbing resumed. Lyddie lay down with her on the bed, and Sabina's sobs shook both their bodies.

Lyddie rose when at last Sabina grew quiet. She said, "Come on, Sabina. It's all right. Look at her." Sabina sat up on the bed, pulling at her shirt, which had slipped off her shoulder, exposing the expanse of scar tissue Lyddie had seen before. "What happened?" Lyddie asked, in almost a whisper, touching her own shoulder and chest at the place where the scarring was visible on Sabina's. "Here."

"Breast cancer when I was twenty. The doctor saved my breast but took half the muscle in my chest and upper arm. I sued the goddamn bastard."

"You were twenty?" Lyddie said. She swallowed hard for fear that if she spoke she wouldn't stop pressing in the places where it hurt. Again, she'd caught a glimpse of the valor she'd first seen in Sabina. And maybe just a little of the flawed logic that was part of its bravado. "I'm sorry," Lyddie said. "For everything." She could offer only the simplest of consolations, out of all proportion to the levels of pain she seemed somehow to excavate in Sabina's life.

In the days that followed, the air warm like a memory of summer, the little scrap of ear haunted Sabina. She relived, in conversation with Lyddie, the white angle that appeared in the smooth curve of the ear before the blood began to flow, the belated sensation of having had the child's flesh between the blades she was closing with such confidence. It seemed to her she had been unconscionably reckless. It was something Ulla would have to explain, even as a grown woman, just as Sabina had explained her own scars. Perhaps someone would hear the story and kiss the ear, as she herself kissed it daily, apologizing.

As Sabina did and said these things, it became apparent to Lyddie that the other woman no longer apologized simply for the minor calamity that had befallen her and Ulla a few days before with the scissors, but for the burden of the irreparable that she carried, for the triumph and bravado with which she had announced the terms that would become the broken lives of others. Sabina and Lothar would take Siegfried home as soon as Sabina was ready, but she didn't know what to do with him there, since her mother had already found him too difficult. Siegfried seemed happiest when he had Sabina to himself. As Lyddie tried to get to the bottom of Sabina's despair over the little scrap of ear, she was haunted by the image of Siegfried lying in the hollow of the hermit rock beds—like a Desert Father consumed with jealousy. *You burnt up all of your lovers, Sabina. You are so very selfish.*

Then one day Sabina said, "He was so desperate…" She glanced across the *plateia* to where Siegfried was crouched to Ulla's height, holding his hand out to receive the stones she gathered. "Lyddie, you won't hate me, will you? I only thought that he deserved what other men enjoyed." She stopped and lowered her eyes. "But giving him that only made everything worse."

Lyddie absorbed the shock of knowing what she had chastised herself for suspecting even momentarily after they'd found Siegfried up near Smardakito. Where would it end? She couldn't bring herself to ask if Siegfried were Ulla's father, but she thought she knew the answer.

PHELPS CAME BACK UP to the village to talk to Lyddie. He told her about the months in Iraq, said that when she understood everything, she would forgive him. And he could forgive her too. He explained, again, that it was important for him to "go missing" in order to be more or less invisible. Somehow, when he had arrived, a contingent of foreigners had found him and recruited him to help them get the records out. All he knew was that a man they called Gerdot had suspected he might be able to help—and that he might have reason to want to.

"Gerdot?" Lyddie said, a Greek coffee arrested mid-air between the table and her lips.

"Probably not his real name," Phelps said. "He was a German. I still don't know how he knew about me, but there was a sort of network, I guess. And I was significantly not a part of it. I was connected to Dow, a company thought of as having an interest in discretion. That's why I had to lie low—to stay more or less invisible while I waited to come into possession of the documents. I'm sorry, Lyddie. Truly I am. I never wanted to cause you pain."

Gerdot? Was Phelps's involvement Axel's doing? "That doesn't explain why you didn't tell me the truth before you left," she said. "Did you go to do your research believing it was funded by a company that was helping the Iraqis exterminate their own people? I know you knew that when you left. Axel had told you."

"Look," Phelps said. "I didn't know what I was going to do. I only knew I couldn't stay there and work for them, for Dow, and do nothing." Phelps's face was absolutely earnest. "I honestly had no idea what I would do when I got there. I just really needed to go." He reached over and touched the dents in her chin. "I had acted on a tip from a person I still have little respect for. He may have been right, but I have to question his motives, Lyddie, since he did manage to sleep with my wife while I was away."

"No, Phelps," she said. "Your wife, who thought she was a widow, went to him. Of her own free will. She left home—in much the same wreckless state that you did—and found him and slept with him because she remembered a life she'd left behind—a life that risked something—and a time when she had felt alive and connected to things that mattered. I'm not defending him, or myself, but that's the way it happened," she said.

Phelps studied her face. "You're different," he said.

"I know now that the world is full of violations and betrayals. And it is full of sadness and uncertainty."

When Phelps returned the next day and found Lyddie in the courtyard at Rooms Fani Vevis, hanging her towel after an early swim, he said, "I'm not leaving you."

"No," she said. "I'm the one who has left." Because though she admired him—admired the way he took care of people and things, and admired what he had done for the Kurdish people—admiration was no more love than mistrust or doubt was its opposite.

12

THE UPHEAVALS FOLLOWING Phelps's arrival on the island meant that Lyddie hadn't been to the village of the refugees in three days—not since the morning of the day they'd all seen Axel's Trabi levitated in the chaos at Hof. Lyddie had agreed to meet Lothar and Phelps at the feast of Saint Thomas the Apostle, which was to be held at the tiny church on the mountain called Profitis Ilias. Lothar and Phelps planned to hike up later in the day. On her way up that morning, Lyddie made a detour to Smardakito.

The whole way out, the path had been obscured in mist. Now the three cypresses all but disappeared into the fog, and the village was strangely quiet. A feral cat mewed at Lyddie from behind a rusted blue kerosene canister. Something was different, though Lyddie couldn't say what. It was always quiet in the morning, most of the refugees usually asleep when she arrived. Sometimes, when she had walked the entire way alone, she would find Dimitri's donkey already moored at the

top of the steps down into the *plateia*. But today the donkey's
station beneath the fig tree was unoccupied. Lyddie felt the
abandonment of the place in a way she had not felt it before.

When at last she entered the house that served as the can-
tina, it was empty. There were no bodies curled beneath the
table or stretched out along the walls. Just the dishpan, still on
the floor where the muscular one, Abdul, had used it as a pillow.
The Kurds, she was certain, were gone.

The authorities must have come in the night. Lyddie ran
back through the village, up the steps, and along the path toward Hora. Did Dimitri know? Her chest was pounding and she
wanted to scream. Back at the three cypresses, she ran almost
head-on into Coast Guard Ianni and the chief of police coming
the other direction. She stopped.

"You knew about this place?" Ianni said.

"I'm looking for the feast," she said, "but I'm lost. Everyone
seems to be gone from this village."

"That way," Ianni said. "You passed the turn. Look for a red
mark on the stone and go to your left, up the mountain."

Lyddie thanked him. How had they discovered the village? She and Sabina and Lothar had kept Siegfried under
close surveillance. Still, Axel knew. Had she been wrong not
to warn Dimitri about Axel's past when she knew the old man
had enlisted his help? She herself found it hard to believe that
Axel could be so malicious as to leak word to the authorities.
Hadn't he, like the rest of them, come to the island for a second
chance? But she remembered how he had thrilled at the explosion of the dynamite. And in the garden the other day, feeding
her and Sabina the prickly pear. Even then she had loved him,
the part of him that was truest—the Desert Father, the boy
who dreamed of staying all night in the mind of God—though
she had stepped aside, keeping to her policy of letting things

happen. That Axel, too, had disappeared made her doubt all the good of which she had thought him capable.

As she ran, the donkey thistle and the nettle clawed at her feet and ankles. Where was the antidote for this mess, she wondered, feeling the sting of the welts rising on her legs. Nature certainly had given a "prick." What would Dimitri find to make all of this better? He was like Phelps with his natural remedies, his easy attitude in the face of disaster. Dimitri had told her not to judge. Well, now he might agree she had good reason. Or maybe this was her fault. Maybe the authorities had somehow followed Siegfried's trail. Or Axel, sensing her mistrust, had decided to live up to it. She had not responded when he'd said he wanted her to think well of him. He was acting like the person he knew she thought he was. And how was it he could always deflect the blame? Even now, in his absence, he was managing to do that. Why had she not listened to Phelps and simply stayed away?

Before long, she grew tired and had to walk. About a third of the way back, she began to encounter men and women and priests and donkeys headed up the mountain. Dimitri, she realized, would most likely already be up at the little church on Profitis Ilias, since he would help slaughter the goat and prepare the giant stew they called patatato. So Lyddie fell in with the others. The mist grew denser as they climbed. Some of the feast-goers stopped at a tiny house where a man was offering coffee and honeycomb, but Lyddie pressed on. After another half hour the path emerged from a tortuous, rocky rise onto the level. At the right, the mountain jutted up, its side as steep and unvegetated as a pyramid. The path became nothing more than a dent. To the north, the earth fell away abruptly, and there was only fog. As Lyddie walked, tentative, she heard the sound of other feet skidding in the fine shingle.

When she had begun to feel shaky with vertigo and fatigue, there appeared, suddenly, other faces in the mist, and voices, people with dripping hair though there was no rain. They emerged like exiles or gods, or like the refugees, full-bodied in a mysterious other world she had supposed was uninhabited. To her left, barely visible, stood a small church with a barrel-vaulted roof. Careful, they told her. The sea is straight down. Beautiful on a clear day.

She followed the others to a stone shed built into the side of the mountain. Peering in, she expected the warm animal smell of donkeys, the sight of baskets and jugs slung over their backs. In her surprise, her breath caught sharply, and someone gave her a nudge of encouragement from behind. Inside were people—younger Greeks with heavy black mustaches and old men with soiled shirts, sprigs of basil tucked behind their ears. They pressed in together on two long benches facing one another, their breath steaming in the damp interior. The black headgear of a priest stood erect at the top of his settling body, and women in borrowed men's jackets were wedged in between the men, older and younger. The light of candles and the soft, embered glow of cigarettes in the cave-like space drew Lyddie to the low table, shaped of stone and plaster, where she sat among them, huddled against the chilling damp.

Pushing her wet hair behind her ears, Lyddie asked a young man for a cigarette and accepted the cup of retsina someone else put in front of her. The man lit the cigarette for her and she inhaled deeply. She got up again, taking the resinous wine and the cigarette and following the clatter to a cave-like room at the back, where Dimitri was one of three men wrestling a pot full of browning goat away from the fire, trying with ladles and spoons to transfer the meat and bones to another bubbling vessel. The feast required engineering on the part of these men, who had slaughtered the goat and who shouted to one another now as they lifted the hemispheric pot and heaved its contents out.

Knowing she would have to wait to talk to Dimitri, Lyddie stepped back outside, where the wind blew the mist in thicker coils through its general opacity. She walked in a careful, straight line toward the barrel-vaulted church and found its door open.

In front of her, the interior flickered in the light of tapers, brickle-colored and smelling of raw honey. She dropped a coin into the box and picked up a candle. Discarding a short stub, she lit the taper and mounted it in the tall, iron candelabra near the back of the church. She stood in silence, praying as cosmically as she knew how, to no one in particular, for no one in particular, and then for the dead baby and for Phelps and little Bilimet, the Kurdish boy, when a large hand and forearm in a sleeve too short extended from behind her, as if in response to her prayer, and snuffed the flame of the candle she had lit. She turned abruptly to find herself face to face, in the glow of the remaining candles, with Axel.

"I asked only that you believe I am capable of good."

"And are you, Axel?" she said. "I have tried to believe that."

"I know that you know what I've done," he said.

Lyddie was confused. She had just come from the village and had told no one. "I found the pen," he said. "My jacket still smelled like your hair."

"Oh!" she said, in a gasp that bore only a small remnant of her voice.

"Everywhere, Lyddie, you are watching. Making judgments."

"I won't accept the blame from you, Axel. Not now, and not ever," she said. "Not after what you have done, which I may have been willing to forgive, though I wasn't wronged by it. But if your betrayals aren't a thing of the past— Do you know the refugees are gone?"

"Yes," he said.

"Of course you do," she said.

He scrutinized her face in a way that had always gone to the bottom of her. His eyes looked tired, hollowed underneath, the way she had seen them after a night without sleep.

"I gave you everything I had to give, Axel—and every chance to make a case for yourself. Lothar has done the same, though he didn't know what you and I know. And from the beginning, you have been intent on demonstrating that no one else has any integrity."

"Lothar has not done the same."

"What do you mean?"

"Lothar despises me. I told him, and he despises me."

"You told him?" Lyddie said, astonished.

"Had you not come to Berlin," Axel said, more quietly, "I may have found it possible to live with myself. I would never have needed you. You have a way to make people need you, so perhaps it is a good thing that you have ended it this way. Because I don't need you now. I don't need you or any of them."

"I've tried to be faithful to the best in you," Lyddie said.

"I think you must agree with me, Lyddie, that many allegiances are, in the end, equal to none at all."

"Allegiances," Lyddie said, feeling threatened now and wanting to back up, but realizing that her hair flirted with the flames behind her. "It is always strange to hear you say that word."

"The word is English, but the catastrophe, I believe, is universal." Axel was as distant as the first time she'd met him. As if they had never known one another any further than that.

Her life of late had been full of precise and conflicting allegiances. To herself and to Phelps, to Phelps and Axel, to Axel and Sabina, even to Sabina and Dimitri. Still she knew, hearing Axel say these things, that he was wrong. If he were victim

and perpetrator, it wasn't because he was made of Nazi and
Jew. "No," she said. "I don't think so. Anymore. Maybe I never
did. Tragic things happen, Axel, to people you love, but not because you love people. You do your best by each of them. And
by yourself." She thought of Axel at the Jewish Cemetery, first
climbing the tree he knew had been climbed some hours earlier with unthinkable intention and then working out a way of
getting his father down. He told her once that when he had cut
the rope, the body had landed with a humpph in the dirt below,
barely avoiding the standing grave marker he knew would have
broken it. To avoid damaging the delicate skin, he had had to
use the knife again to gnaw gently at the rope that was tight
around the neck.

Now the part of Axel she had known and loved lay evacuat-
ed at the center, like the bombed out heart of a city she couldn't
return to.

Moving her aside with a forearm, Axel snuffed the remaining
candle flames one by one. The sibilance of fires dying between
his finger and thumb left behind a quiet tinged with smoke. She
could no longer see him, but she knew he was there, so close they
might again have been lovers. Then she felt him moving away.

"Axel!" she cried. But he was already gone, and her voice
sounded reedy and uncertain in the emptiness of the church.
She went to the door and shouted his name into the mist until
her throat hurt. Her words roiled up over her head and were
swept on by the wind. But he had begun to descend the mountain. She heard the skidding of hurried footsteps on the shingle
path, and she did not see him again.

Needing desperately to re-enter the human chain, to be im-
plicated in the spirit that brought the others high up and out to
the edge, she returned to the cave of feasting, alive with conversation and the wet warmth of bodies. People dipped thick chunks of

bread into bowls of goat *patatato*. She found a place among them, though Lothar and Phelps had not come. And the interference of elbows and the earthy human smell of drinking and of rest following labor helped ease the violence of her shaking.

13

THE MIST WAS THICK and isolating on the gravel track back from Profitis Ilias. It gave Dimitri a sense of safety he was willing to rely on until a tear in it afforded a glimpse of the actual sea, churning far below as if through the lens of a kaleidoscope. Dimitri heard someone coming along behind him, rapid footsteps skidding in the gravel. Whoever it was was walking much too fast for the conditions. Soon Dimitri was overtaken. "Hey!" he shouted. "Hey!" recognizing the tall, rambling shape that passed him. "Axel! Wait up!"

Axel slowed and Dimitri caught up with him. Dimitri had left the donkey at the top to help carry what was left of the supplies back down. Maroula had wanted to stay with the others from the village until the feast was over. "What's the hurry?" Dimitri said.

"Mold and beeswax!" Axel exclaimed. Dimitri heard him spit. "It makes me nauseous."

Axel picked up the pace again, his foot skidding dangerously.

Dimitri cried out, "Holy Mother of God!" He knew they must be nearing The Bridegroom's Plunge, where the path was a minute depression in the mountainside. "This is no place for recklessness," Dimitri warned.

"My experience of churches has not been one of transcendence," Axel said, either not hearing him or ignoring his warning.

"That doesn't surprise me," Dimitri called out. "But slowly! Slowly!"

Axel slowed so that Dimitri could talk without having to shout. "I've been up there before, haven't I?" he said.

"You were a child," Dimitri answered.

"I remember the smell," Axel said.

"We went together and we lit a candle for your father. It was just after we had heard the news of his death." Dimitri remembered that day, doing what he was doing for the boy's sake more than his own, and wondering if the boy sensed his anger.

"I doubt that it did him any good," Axel said, glancing back over his shoulder at Dimitri, a few meters behind. He seemed to know that Dimitri shared his skepticism.

"Did you go to church in Germany with your mother?" Dimitri asked.

Axel said, "The Communists confiscated the building. They turned it into a garage. A car repair. My trabi was there for months." Axel stopped walking as he spoke. "But still, Pappou," he said, "I experienced a conversion in that church."

"What sort?" Dimitri said, glad for the chance to catch his breath.

Axel began walking again, more slowly. He said, "I went in to ask when my Trabi would be repaired. 'Three weeks? Three years?' the mechanic said. 'What can you bring me?' 'Poems,' I told him. "Ach. Poems,' the mechanic said. 'Bring something perishable. Cabbages or yams. No one wants the eternal anymore.'"

As they continued their traverse of the mountain, Axel told Dimitri how the mechanic had laughed, then stood rubbing his hands with care. There was a wooden crucifix high up on the wall that someone had neglected to take down. Axel said he looked up and saw its teeth in the black rift of the mouth, under the eerie gleam of a utility light. He said he knew then how easily he could defect from the human family.

"The teeth revealed this to you?" Dimitri said.

"Like notes taped to the cupboard in a dark kitchen. I am leaving you."

"No, Axel," Dimitri said. "You are human, and you cannot defect."

"But I did, Pappou. I did."

Dimitri, like a confessor on the other side of the curtain of fog, listened hard. "How did you?"

"It doesn't matter now," Axel said. "At all." Axel walked faster again. A few seconds later, Dimitri heard the long skid of a footstep and then a cry. He lunged blindly at the ground in front of him and caught Axel's forearm as the rest of him disappeared over the edge, sliding down the scree of the mountainside at a forty-five degree angle. Dimitri strained to hold Axel and not be pulled over by his grandson's weight. His arm felt as though it would be jerked free from his shoulder socket. He grabbed Axel's arm with his other hand and used all of his strength to roll backward onto his side, shifting his weight away from the edge. "Let go!" Axel cried, his voice disappearing into the abyss.

"Climb back up here and God damn you if you don't," Dimitri shouted through clenched teeth. Dimitri heard Axel's boots trying to get a purchase on the crumbling slope. He released his hold on one arm and grabbed a handful of Axel's shirt along with a clump of his hair and pulled with all of his might. Axel's shoulders lurched forward, and he swung a knee back up onto the path, then pulled himself up and threw his body against the crumbling slate that rose steeply on the upside. Dimitri rolled over and sat up beside him, his heart pounding. Axel shook his head, trying to get the blood back into it.

"Who taught you," Dimitri gasped, "to think so little of yourself?"

Axel threw his head back, his chest heaving. "Well," he said, stopping to catch his breath. "My Greek father taught me the power of absences." He paused and examined his blood-ied arms. "My stepfather taught me that allegiances were best avoided. My Nazi grandfather taught me guilt, of which I have plenty." His measured thoughts seemed to discipline his breath-ing, which became more regular. "The Desert Fathers taught me deprivation as a way to deal with guilt. I have deprived myself of pleasure at every opportunity. And still there is much to think little of."

"Mother of God," Dimitri said. They stood again and be-gan to walk. "Slowly, slowly," he said.

The path metamorphosed into a dirt and stone cobble as it crossed the saddle between the mountains. Then it dropped gradually out of the mist, into a valley of fig and olive trees. They passed two or three abandoned houses, a cistern sealed over with algae, and a shed full of fresh goat droppings. The old Greek with the sweets must have seen them coming, because by the time they arrived at the last house, the man was waiting for them at the step to the terrace with a plastic cup of Greek coffee and a dripping slab of honeycomb.

Dimitri had bypassed this way station on the journey up, but he had seen a company of others talking as they rested and took refreshment. "*Oriste*! Welcome," the man said, handing Axel and Dimitri each a cup and, with a finger and a thumb, a piece of the raw honeycomb. Dimitri stuck the honeycomb into his mouth whole and began chewing. A sprig of basil tucked behind his ear, their host stood watching to see how Axel would manage.

There was nothing for Axel to do but to plunge the dripping wax—as much of it as he could—into his mouth. Honey ran down the three-day growth on his chin. The portion of the generous cut he still held in his hand leaked more profusely now that he had bitten into it. He could stop the flow down his wrist and into his shirt-sleeve only by putting this piece, too, into his mouth, though the smell and the sticky sweetness seemed already to be consuming him, a nausea he'd begun to experience in the chapel returning. As his tongue worked the wax, the bulk of it gagged him, sending him off to the nearest fig tree, under which he retched violently.

Afterward, Dimitri watched him tear two big leaves from the tree and try to wipe the honey off his hands but succeed only in spreading it around. Axel ran back to the old cistern to rinse his hands and splashed stagnant water on his face and neck. Wanting neither to drink the standing water nor to return to the house for the coffee he'd left on the terrace wall, he found a small patch of oregano and pulled off a few dried leaves. He crumbled them and chewed them before spitting them out onto the ground.

"In all the months, in all the years of my deprivation," Axel said, as he and Dimitri continued toward the village, "I had forgotten what it was to feel something completely. Even just looking into her face, seeing what she felt, gave me that shock."

"Lyddie," Dimitri said.

"Being with her was like dynamite exploding in a cove. It brought everything to the surface."

Dimitri listened intently. "Axel," he said. "Has anyone taught you about forgiveness?"

"I don't deserve it."

"I don't know what you've done," Dimitri said, "but that's the thing, Axel. Nobody deserves it. Still, you have to ask."

14

AFTER THE FEAST on Profitis Ilias, Lyddie found Dimitri sitting alone inside the café, asleep at a table by the unplugged glass refrigerator case, his head on his arms. "Dimitri!" she said, softly but urgently, shaking his shoulder to rouse him. "Dimitri!" The old man lifted his head slowly and looked around to see where he was. "Dimitri, they're gone," she said.

"Yes," he said, in a weary voice. "*Katzeh*. Sit down. I know."

"But what happened? Were you there when the authorities came?"

"*Katzeh, katzeh*," he said, trying to calm her with the lilt of his hand and his head. "Did not come the authorities."

Lyddie's eyes widened.

"No," he confirmed. "Did not come."

"But where are the refugees?"

"They go safe. Dimitri have a plan. They no can live long time in Smardakito. This island too small they stay here, Leda. When the crazy German boy know, is not so good. And so much people nearby for the feast."

"You had a plan? The whole time?" she said.

"Some time," he answered. "I'm sorry you don't know it. Better I not tell nobody. You understand? If I tell, I make trouble for friends who help, and for Axel."

"Axel?" she said.

"Yes, Amerikanida. I ask him to come to the island. He go with them by boat then by truck as far as Athos. From there, the monks Nikos know will help them. Ins'Allah, as the Kurds say. God wishing. But what is it?" Dimitri said, seeing her distress.

"Axel is not happy with me," she said.

"Why?" Dimitri said.

"He thinks that I have judged him unfairly."

"And you have judged, or no?"

"I suppose I have," she said. "But I have tried not to."

"Axel," Dimitri replied, "must find his own happiness or he is happy with nobody. He is like Frosso, his mama. You know, the husband to Frosso—my Theo—and the mama to Frosso die the same year. She believe then that no one here take care for her. She say she always will be the outsider here. She is born on this island, into the hands of the sister to my own mother. Why she say such stuff?" Dimitri took off his beret and mopped his head with a napkin.

"What will happen to the Kurdish boy?" Lyddie said.

Dimitri ignored two tourists in hiking shoes and shorts who sat down at a table, probably hoping for a nightcap. He was studying Lyddie instead, with a thoughtful expression. "The boy is OK," he said at last. "Bilimet. For now, he is OK."

"I hope you're right," Lyddie said.

Lyddie remembered the words Nuray had spoken to her the last time she'd seen her. "Dimitri, what does it mean—*Ona iyi bak?*" It's Kurdish—or Turkish maybe. Something Nuray said to me. Do you know?"

Dimitri's mouth puckered downwards in a shrug. Then he gave a slight jerk of the head back, which Lyddie had learned meant *no*. Lyddie could tell he was lying. "So what's the plan now?" she said.

"I sleep some more, then I make coffee," he said.

BACK AT ROOMS FANI VEVIS, Lyddie sat on the bed and opened the drawer of the nightstand. She removed the scraps of paper Siegfried had given her weeks before and, placing a book in her lap, laid out the bits of the note on top of it, writing side up. The pieces were fairly small. Something about the note must have made Siegfried angry. She had seen his handwriting when they'd been to the pharmacist a few days before, and it had not matched the hand this note was written in. She thought for a long moment. Then she took her money pouch from the stand and rummaged through it for the paper on which was written, in similarly bold strokes, 27 Griefenhagener Strasse—Axel's mother's address in East Berlin. She did not continue to assemble the message. She didn't need to look for a signature, and the note had not been meant for her eyes. She felt sick and sad as she put it back in the drawer.

It was 9:10. The bus would leave for its last run down to the harbor in five minutes. Lyddie made up her mind and ran all the way to Dimitri's place where the bus had already made its turn and was leaving the *plateia*. She ran after it, shouting, and the driver stopped for her. She believed now, more than ever, that Axel was trying to start a new life and that she had been unfair in assuming he was the same person who had acted badly ten years before. She should not have concluded that he had betrayed the refugees. That he had helped them and had not told her in his own defense made it clear that he was hurt by her assumptions. The truth didn't matter so much to him as her perceptions did. He had wanted her to believe in him and she had not been able.

When she got off the bus in the harbor, she saw a few people at Politimos's place, eating on the pavement protected from the wind by a plastic awning. Among them was Phelps, whom she had not seen at the feast at Profitis Ilias. Phelps stood up and called to her, but she waved him off as she hurried out along the ruined beach the hotel developer had turned into a causeway and then around the north side of the harbor, past the cafés where the owners drank with their friends and listened to American music now that the tourists were mostly gone. Axel's place was out along the little dirt road that passed the graveyard and ended at the point with the chapel, just beyond the harbor. She knocked and, after a minute or two, he came to the door. "What do you want?" he said.

"Will you go for a walk with me?" she said. "I want to talk to you."

"I'm sorry," he said. "I cannot." Lyddie thought he looked terrible, translucent purple wells beneath his eyes. He looked like a man who had given up.

"You cannot?" Lyddie said, fighting back tears.

"Come in," he said. She went inside and he indicated the little table near the back of the living area. Lyddie pulled out a chair and sat down.

Axel lit a small ceramic oil lamp on the table and, in its wavering light, he watched Lyddie. It seemed he had been sitting in the dark inside—perhaps had not realized that it had grown dark. The flame sizzled and sputtered and then rose in a steady tongue. At that moment there was a pounding on the door, and, startled, they both sat perfectly still. Lyddie imagined the scene that would ensue: an acrimonious confrontation with Phelps. Again, an angry pounding, and just as Axel stood to answer it the door burst inward and Lothar appeared.

"So all those years," Lothar said, "all those years that I was forgiving your strangeness, your coldness, your intolerance, you knew this thing you had done. And you felt no remorse." Lyddie had never seen Lothar look so wild. So angry. "All the years of my protecting you from yourself, because I thought I was your friend, and thought you were mine. And you had sold me off. For what, Axel? What did they give you?"

Axel stood just a couple of feet from Lothar, and Lothar shoved him in the chest so that he stumbled backwards. "I want to know. What were we not worth to you?"

Axel didn't reply, and Lothar grabbed him by the shirt and pushed him again so that he was dangerously near the table where Lyddie was sitting. Lyddie stood up and backed into the small room adjoining. "Lothar, please!" she said.

As Lothar pressed in on him, Axel ran up against the table, and he kicked Lothar in the shins. "Leave me!" he said. "I sold you for nothing! That makes it worse, doesn't it?" He stepped forward, threatening Lothar.

"You shit pig!" Lothar shouted. "You ass-fucking son of a bitch!" He flung a fist at Axel, and Lyddie heard it make contact with bone. Axel staggered, but did not return the blow. Lyddie sat down on the bed in the back room, shaking. She had the terrible feeling that whatever was happening must happen. If one of them were going to kill the other, she would have to find some way to accommodate that fact and all of its consequences. She wiped her tears and, listening to them argue, leaned back onto the bed when she felt something move. She jumped and then saw, in the soft light from the other room, a form beneath the covers. "Who's there?" she said, standing abruptly. Looking more closely in the dark, Lyddie reached out to touch whoever it was in the bed. Her hand came in contact with a very small arm. A pair of eyes gleamed, looking up at her. "Bilimet?" she said, astonished.

"I've known nothing but remorse," Axel shouted in the other room. "I've spent my life trying to outgrow it, but I can't. The day I went to your house, Lothar, and found your exhibition gone, your parents preparing quietly for bed when the Stasi had taken you away, I wanted to kill myself."

"So why didn't you?"

"I couldn't do that to my mother," Axel said. "Instead, I deprived myself of every pleasure I could think of. That, of course, was not enough—"

"You should have killed yourself," Lothar said, his voice wavering and wounded. Lyddie grabbed Bilimet and held him, knowing that though he couldn't understand what was being said, he was frightened by what was happening. It was quiet then in the other room, and she heard the creak of the wooden door opening. Bilimet in her arms, she walked back into the light. Axel had gone, and Lothar remained, his face tearstained.

Lothar looked over at her standing there with the child. "Why stop forgiving him now?" Lyddie said.

"He isn't sorry."

"Yes, he is," Lyddie said.

"Who is that?" he said.

"One of the refugees," she said. "Lothar, don't let him go. He will kill himself if he thinks that's what you require."

Lothar walked to the door, hesitated, looking out into the night, and then set out walking toward the harbor. Lyddie followed with Bilimet. After a few steps, Lothar began to run. Lyddie could hear the gruff burble of a motor starting down near the water, and she arrived in time to see Axel untying a wooden skiff. As Axel began to pull away from the edge of the harbor, Lothar leapt from the harbor wall into the boat. "What are you doing?" Axel shouted above the motor, which left the air smelling of gasoline. Axel was fastening something around his waist. It looked to Lyddie like a belt weighted for diving. "What the fuck do you care?"

"Motherfucking dirtbag," Lothar said, and they began to struggle over the belt, the boat rocking precariously as it puttered deeper into the harbor, unguided. Lyddie heard the two men exchanging insults, and then there was a splash. One of them had gone overboard, but Lyddie couldn't see which. The motor stopped, and it was Axel who was shouting. "Lothar! Where are you?"

"Oh my God," Lyddie said, holding Bilimet close, disbelieving what she was witnessing, and wondering, for a moment, if the boy really were some sort of curse. Lothar couldn't swim. She knew that from the excursions he and Phelps had made with Siegfried to the harbor rocks. She heard another splash and everything was quiet—for ten seconds, twenty, thirty, fifty. Lyddie stopped counting. She stood on the pavement in the light beneath the utility pole and closed her eyes to her horror. She was almost certain that Axel had never stayed under so long. Had he taken the weighted belt off? If he had not, then he and Lothar had probably both drowned. Even without the belt, she knew how such rescue missions usually ended.

The water lapped at the concrete of the harbor wall, oblivious to the terrors that were unfolding. A horrible moaning wail came up from Lyddie's belly and into the night, a wail full of the losses she had known in the past few months. A moment later, as if in response, something burst the water's surface, and there was heaving and gasping out near the boat, whether of one man or two she couldn't tell. Someone coughed and gagged. She heard more struggle and heaving and a thump. Lyddie was afraid to call out. To call the wrong name. To hope two were alive. Her own chest heaved. "Hello?" she shouted. There was no response but that of the boat beginning its journey back. As it came into sight, she saw a single figure at the rear, steering it in toward the harbor wall. Unable to tell who it was, Lyddie turned away, finding what she half knew unbearable. She set Bilimet down on the stone tree well. Then she turned back. It was Axel. He did not get out of the boat. Instead, he knelt in the hull, and she heard him sobbing, and saying Lothar's name, over and over again. With a terrible sobriety, she told Bilimet to stay where she had put him and walked back to the boat to see Lothar in the bottom, his arms closing loosely around the neck of his friend.

Lyddie went to the tree well and swept the boy up in her arms, wetting his face and his hair with her tears. Carrying him, she began walking away from Axel and Lothar toward town when she saw Phelps about twenty yards down the harbor. He appeared to have seen everything. He had a backpack and he kept his distance but gazed steadily at her as she approached. "They are alive," she said. "Both." Her voice broke on the last word. He nodded and said nothing. He remained intent on her and the child. She realized he must be wondering, and she might have tried to explain, but she couldn't answer the obvious question: whose?

Phelps turned, slinging his bag over his shoulder as the ferry appeared at the mouth of the harbor, its lone string of lights like a carnival of solitudes.

15

THE LANDSCAPE WAS BRILLIANT with the smell of thyme, as if the senses had been allowed to awaken one by one, olfactory first. Dimitri and Maroula prepared the equipment for Dimitri's descent to the watery underworld. On the beach, Lyddie and Sabina waited for the sun to come up and warm them enough for a swim. Dimitri had closed the café for a day of rest—and to celebrate his discovery that he'd somehow transposed the numbers in 1989 when he had figured his age on the calculator a few months before. That meant he was 81, not 90. His own math was still superior to that of the machine.

Dimitri had invited Lyddie and Sabina and the others to the cove to see the painting operation, from which he'd been away for more than three weeks, since the appearance of the body. Lothar had carried Ulla down the long path from Hora on his shoulders, and now she splashed at the water's edge under the watchful eye of Siegfried, who had been allowed to come out for a last swim before they took him back to Berlin that afternoon.

While Lothar watched Dimitri on the boat, Lyddie was talking to Sabina about what she had witnessed two nights before, when Lothar and Axel had almost drowned. "I never thought Lothar had that kind of fury in him," she said.

"You knew about Axel, too," Sabina said. "What he revealed did not surprise you. He had told you?"

"No. But I knew. When did he tell you?" Lyddie said.

"The day we went to the demonstration with you, when I was just back from Rio, and he followed us home. The only time I ever slept with him. But he was so wrong. About the freedom he wanted." She looked out over the water, as if what she meant to say were fathomless and she were afraid she wouldn't get it right. "He thought it would come from not caring about anyone enough that he could be hurt. Did you appreciate the way he tried to feed us fruit full of stones? To have you and I eating out of one hand and the other? Fruit that will break our teeth? He has always hated me," she said, "for knowing what he told me."

"And what did you tell Phelps? Did Phelps know?"

"I told him Axel was dangerous."

"To keep me away from him?"

"You had no idea, Lyddie, who he really was."

Carrying a snorkel and fins, Lothar came over to where they sat. "Anyone want to use these?" he asked. "I would do it but, as you know, I don't swim."

"Maybe you should learn," Lyddie said, hoping Lothar hadn't lost his sense of humor.

Hearing Dimitri grumble at Maroula on the boat, Lothar went back over to see what the commotion was about. Lyddie and Sabina followed. Politimos had puttered into the cove and Dimitri suspected that their swim and his work were about to be spoiled by a blast. Dimitri muttered in Greek, watching Politimos make his preparations. He warned Lothar to stay away, though it was too late for Dimitri himself and Maroula to come ashore. First light beginning to break, the fishing caique was not a hundred yards off.

Maroula gazed out into the gray air and shouted, "Politimos!" Her voice boomed across the water, but there was no reply. She shouted something more in Greek. Again, silence. Miraculously, after a few seconds, the little motor of the caique started again and the boat turned tail, heading away around the point.

"Who needs Coast Guard Ianni?" Dimitri said with a smile.

Dimitri's new sub-marine paintings were beginning to sell locally. People were asking for them, so Stelios had agreed to show the Maroula icons as well, and even they were selling. Not seen as desecrations, they were bringing Maroula a certain celebrity. People who had not grown up in the village were inclined to see her slowness as reticence, her reticence as mystery, particularly because the icons, no longer in production, were limited editions. It was now more difficult than ever to get a cup of coffee out of Maroula.

Sabina looked embarrassed at the mention of Coast Guard Ianni. She had stopped seeing him when Axel had arrived on the island, but she knew what the others thought of him. "What did Maroula say?" Lothar asked.

Sabina answered, "The Virgin is watching you.'"

The others looked puzzled, so Dimitri explained. "Now Maroula please to think she is The Virgin." Maroula beamed, hearing her name. "Maybe Politimos believe it too," Dimitri said. The traditional icons, they are not working. Politimos, he buy Saint Nicholas, painted who knows where. He ask protection from the wrong saint!"

Dimitri, still smiling, returned to his preparation of the compressor and the breathing tube. The blast, when it came a minute later from the next cove over, caused him to jerk the tube so hard he nearly ripped the valve from the reservoir. "Son of a bitch," he said in English. Maroula's face fell.

Lyddie and Sabina walked in silence back to the tamarisk tree on the beach, unsure whether or not they dared swim. But the sun, coming up over the water, warmed the air, coaxing them in. As Sabina slipped her dress over her head, Lyddie said, "Even knowing what you knew, you loved Axel, didn't you? Don't you? It wasn't just about Ulla."

Not as an answer, but as the lack of one, Sabina shook her head.

Lyddie said, "I think Axel tried to let you know he had come to the island. He thought you knew he was here. There was a note, but Siegfried tore it up." Lyddie waited for this information to register. She expected that it might send Sabina into a tailspin. Meanwhile, she was searching her own conscience for some explanation as to why she hadn't given the damaged note to Sabina, but it became clear that Sabina wasn't thinking about what the note might have said or how it could have changed things.

"You see, Siegfried, he was jealous," Sabina said. "Of Axel, especially." She hesitated and looked down at the sand. "Maybe Axel only reminded me of the sort of person I would love. Someone who violates others because he wants so much to be loved. Everything is different now."

"Now that…?" Lyddie encouraged her.

Sabina looked out to the sea again. "Siegfried has such troubles." Lyddie wondered how she could blame Sabina for making a mess of things by trying so hard to set them right, for herself and for others. "But Lyddie, I know that you, too, loved Axel. And maybe not a little," Sabina said. She folded her clothes into a neat pile and added, rather suddenly, "Lothar has asked me and Ulla to live with him."

Lyddie brightened. "And you will?" she exclaimed.

"It has never mattered to him who her father was." Sabina smiled. "You know, he cares for us. We will find help for Siegfried. It might be best for him to be away from me." Ulla ran up and threw herself into Sabina's arms. Sabina wrapped her in a towel and rubbed her back. "What will you do, Lyddie? Will you go back to the States?"

"Dimitri says I can help at the café for a while."

"Ulla!" Sabina called. "Come, take off your shorts so you can swim."

"Sabina, what is it like to be a mother?" Lyddie asked.

Sabina's chin dipped and she raised an eyebrow, no doubt wondering from what depths Lyddie's question had come, and whether it was colored by sadness or hope. "It is," she said, "like being God without knowing everything. With a bad memory, perhaps. Giving out names and instructions, calling the bright part day and the dark part night. Making lives from thin air. And then forgetting what it was that made you do it in such a way in the first, though it matters immensely that you did. But Lyddie, you are not—"

"No," Lyddie said. "But Ulla is a beautiful child. You know that, don't you?"

"It bothers me," Sabina said, not really hearing her. "I don't know if I am a real mother. Bad things have happened because of the way I have loved."

"But the love for a child, it is simple?"

"The love, Lyddie, you cannot begin to imagine."

They heard Dimitri slip over the side of the boat and into the water in his gear. Sabina helped Ulla take off her clothes to swim. Lothar had followed the path out onto the rocks and was sitting up high where he could watch the others. Lyddie climbed to the place where the rock fell away abruptly, the water oily smooth and inviting three feet below. She made a clean, arced dive and swam under the surface. There was a strange static, as if the sea were carbonated or carried a slight charge. It fizzed and crackled at her ears. Lyddie surfaced and let out a great whoop. From the water, she saw Sabina sit down and splat forward, coming up and wiping her eyes. Her distance vision was especially bad; she couldn't see far without contacts or glasses. Sabina turned back to the rock, treading water, and called, "Come, Ulla!" lifting a hand in the wrong direction.

"I will get her," Siegfried shouted. He came running and did a cannonball off the highest part of the rock, and then waited in the water for Ulla, who was wearing the life vest Lothar had bought for her, to jump in.

The water was at its warmest in September, and calm. Lyddie took a turn with the snorkel and mask. She could see quite clearly Dimitri's figure standing on the sandy floor of the sea, wavering in sunlight as he channeled submarine wonders. She came up exclaiming to the others that he was as strange and wonderful as a man on the moon. Meanwhile, Ulla cried out, "*Hallo, Axel!*" They looked to see Axel walking down from the rocky path onto the beach.

"Is the boy with him?" Sabina said, pulling herself out onto the rocks.

Lyddie treaded water, watching Axel and Bilimet, who hesitated at the far side of the cove. Lothar bounded ashore to greet them. He and Axel walked together along the beach toward the others, Bilimet howling when Axel got too close to the water. Axel crouched next to him and spoke to him. He was afraid, but Axel took him in his arms and waded in, talking to the boy all the while. Lyddie heard him say, in German, "Trust me. You must. You must." The boy was quiet, clinging to Axel's neck.

Lyddie swam in and kissed Bilimet, who put his arms out

to go to her. She took him. "How did this happen?" she said, indicating the boy.

Axel's jaw was badly bruised from the blow Lothar had dealt him. It made Lyddie cringe to see it, but Axel seemed at ease. "When it was time for Nikos's friend to take the refugees at Athos, he began to howl. I took him in my arms and they left."

"How could they do that?" she said.

"I don't know," Axel said. "But I like him very much."

"They believe he has the evil eye. Don't you believe in the evil eye?" Lyddie said, squinting at Axel against the rising sun.

"If I could be certain which one it was, perhaps I would believe," Axel said. "But look. Each has a story to tell."

In front of them the water was oily smooth. Axel took off his shirt and grabbed the mask and fins Lyddie had left on the sand. Lyddie sat with Bilimet to watch Axel as he put them on and swam out to where Dimitri was. Ulla, fascinated by the newcomer, approached Bilimet and showed him a scratch she'd gotten from climbing out of the water. She chattered to him in German about sea urchins. In the weight of his little body, Lyddie felt something of the gravity she had longed for. With his blue eye and his brown eye, he seemed at that moment like the offspring of two loves—that of the man who had loved her and wanted her to have a child, and that of the man she had loved at the time when the child had appeared. Since she now had neither of those men, it was fitting that the child was also not hers. She had never felt so much in possession of her losses.

In the early sunlight, the water was dimpled like the skin of a lemon. It seemed comfortable with its cargo of spirits and bones—the minute displacements where bodies entered it, the imperceptible sinking of the surface when the lucky ones climbed back out onto the rocks.

Dimitri had surfaced and was stashing his gear on the

boat. Axel swam ashore, laid out his towel, and sat down beside Bilimet. He looked over at Lyddie, who tucked her hair behind her ear and dug in the sand. "Dimitri says I must learn to say the things I have kept silent," he said. After a moment, he reached over and traced the shape of her ear with his finger. "I want to say that I thought always you treat your ear like a fixture for your hair, but now I wonder if you push the hair back in service of the ear. It is crimped slightly near the top—as if it were pricked up, awaiting signals."

Surprised and puzzled by him, Lyddie said, "I'm sorry, Axel, for the things I said to you. I wanted to tell you the other night but I didn't have a chance before all of the drowning began. I was afraid I would never have a chance." Her voice caught.

"What I mean is that so much has happened because of you," he said. "I don't wish for any of it not to have happened."

She shook her head, uncomprehending. "Because of me?"

"You made me tell you my life like a parable. You listened and because you were listening, the things I said—they changed."

Lyddie had learned that at the endings of parables—stories that began, "A certain brother went to buy some linen from a widow," or "Three men went to Macarius and one said, 'Father, make me a net'"—goods shifted hands unexpectedly and failings turned out to be strengths. Still, she'd always found it hard to work out what the stories meant. And she wasn't at all sure now what Axel was saying.

Dimitri, who was walking toward them from the rocks, appeared to be chuckling to himself beneath his big mustache as he approached. "*Ona iyi bak,*" he said. "I remember now. It means *Take care of him.*"

"Is that what Nuray said? To me?" Lyddie said.

Dimitri nodded then walked off and busied himself with his gear.

Lyddie asked Axel, "Did they plan to leave him behind? Is that what they meant to do from the start?"

Axel said, "I don't know, Lyddie. But here he is." His big hand rested on the boy's small shoulder. "He and I know of a village not so far from Hora. Fully furnished. The rent is next to nothing, and there are many vacancies." He watched Lyddie's face. "Only vacancies, in fact," he added.

Lyddie saw Dimitri look up from the wet suit he was rinsing and give Axel an almost imperceptible nod. Axel, embarrassed, looked away again, past Dimitri and up the mountain, past the ruined goat shed, as if he were trying to see what lay beyond. "What do you think?" he said.

Sensing in Axel's nervousness that this was a proposition involving her, and adjusting slowly to that turn, Lyddie said, "Will we live on prickly pear, like ascetics? Or will we be allowed to love?"

"We will have no other luxury," he said, "than loving and being loved."

EPILOGUE

IT IS SPRING, THE FIRST evening warm enough for dark to fall at open windows. The tenants who share among themselves the rent and upkeep of the old mansion have come to Potsdam to escape Berlin for the weekend. From what used to be the Eastern sectors of the city and from the West, they have arrived, some still carrying briefcases along with bags of groceries and comfortable shoes.

In its shabby grace, the house seems not to have forgotten its past—neither the baroque vision of the architect, expressed in sculpted ceilings and high oval windows, nor the bomb that lay for safe keeping in the massive staircase before it killed nearly everyone in the Wolf's Lair but Hitler, for whom it was intended. "Count Berthold von Stauffenberg," Sabina says as she and Lyddie mount the stairs the evening of Lyddie's arrival. "They hanged him with piano wire. Come. There are towels on the bed." As always, Sabina says such things with decorum, as if in the service of hospitality. Her composure is unwavering.

The house has not forgotten the Communist years, when portraits must have filled the pale rectangles their absence has left on the walls. It remembers a time when the crystal chandeliers and ornamental ceilings were merely tolerated. But among the new tenants, the old urgencies, it seems, are gone. The housemates are, as introduced to Lyddie, Fritz, a young architect from Prenzlauer Berg; David and Arnost, lawyers from Charlottenburg; and Katya, a homeopath from Friedrichshain. Together with Sabina, who works in the nearby film studios, and Lothar, now her husband and still an artist—they keep a garden; they clean the gutters and trim the grass. Hyacinths nose through the earth, and the lavender dusk grows in sympathy with the lilacs.

Outside, Lothar is using the last hours of daylight to prime the trim around the big windows in the back. He looks much as he did the day Lyddie met him years ago, though then his hands and shirt were covered with oil pigments rather than house paint, and he wore tall black boots, not Nikes. Lyddie hasn't seen Sabina and Lothar in well over a decade. They never really have known Billy, and he is a teenager now. Lyddie called Sabina on a whim when she and Billy came to Berlin to look at schools.

Seeing Sabina and Lothar again feels to Lyddie like being at a reunion of people who have shared a lifeboat. In another place and time, they wanted the same food, listened for the endings of the same stories, were thirsty together. Perhaps, in their own minds, she and Sabina have never fully put away the suspicion that, had they not made it to safety when they did, they might have turned on one another.

Now Lyddie and Sabina sit in armchairs looking out the tall windows into the yard. Though the sun went down a while ago, Billy still swats at a badminton birdie with Ulla and Lothar, who has come down from his ladder to join them. It is strange to Lyddie that the middle-aged bohemians of this household are fond of newly mown grass and badminton—that this is what their children know. It is nearly as strange as she found almost everything about Sabina and Lothar and Axel when she first arrived in West Berlin from the States so many years ago, when this mansion lay on the other side of the Wall.

Lyddie remembers high-ceilinged rooms on the wide avenues of Kreuzberg. It was before the trees had been replanted from the war, and the starkness of that landscape and of Lothar's manic art made Berlin feel like a city still in shock. She remembers poetry recited under bare bulbs, cigarette smoke, history breathing down their necks. Badminton she does not remember. When Lothar's bad arm sends the birdie flying into the lilac bush, Lyddie wonders if he remembers prison in the East. He doesn't call this house "bourgeois" or the weekend outside the city "romantic," as if these were diseases of the fainthearted. Lyddie smiles to think of how he used to say such things—perhaps just as a way of provoking her. He fetches the birdie now with good humor and lobs it over the net to Ulla with his good arm.

In the kitchen the others are working together at an extravagant couscous and the hum of their voices ushers in the dark. Lyddie's visit will be short; most of it so far has been spent arranging things in the kitchen and preparing food. It has been difficult to find a way back to Sabina—the part of her that isn't a hostess on a house tour.

"You are happy with Lothar?" Lyddie says, quite suddenly.

Sabina looks at her with a frankness of expression Lyddie does not remember having seen except in the days when things had begun to come apart for her. "He gave to me two chances," she says. "As you know, one was not enough." Between them on a marble-topped table lie the gifts Lyddie has brought from the island—figs and almonds, a small Aladdin-shaped lamp that burns olive oil, an icon that Dimitri painted with no saints—just sea grass. "That I am happy for," Sabina says, striking a match to light the lamp. The flame shudders on account of the open window but then burns steadily.

"You were always being given another chance, Sabina. You were like a cat, falling from the highest places and landing on your feet. If not, then you simply rearranged the world around you to make it appear upright." Lyddie smiled as she spoke.

"I do not any longer think this was a virtue," Sabina says. She rises momentarily in Lyddie's esteem for admitting that. And yet, Lyddie has always seen in Sabina's defiance if not virtue, then a kind of dignity. Outside, Ulla swipes at the air only to have the birdie sail down and land on her upturned face. She is seventeen and has a rancor of blond curls and an upturned nose like Lothar's. But there is some intensity in her that is distinctly not Lothar. Nor is it Sabina. Fascinated, Lyddie watches her collapse on the lawn in laughter, throwing her arms out to the sides as if in total surrender. Billy, olive-skinned and beautiful in a manly way though he is a year or two younger than Ulla, walks over and, standing tall, offers a hand to pull her back up. When he pulls with more strength than is needed and finds himself face to face with her, he does not step back, and for a moment it is as though he might kiss her. Lyddie nearly rises from the mohair cushion of the chair in protest. Someone she was long ago wants to cry out, "Anyone but Ulla!" But it is Lothar's voice that interrupts them, saying something about dinner. Billy drops Ulla's hand, and Lothar passes the window carrying a stepladder and a bucket of tools.

Needing to affirm the present, Lyddie says, "She looks so like him. Like Lothar."

Sabina smiles, appreciating the irony, but apparently pleased all the same by the observation. "Yes. Of course she does."

Lyddie falls silent again. Yes, of course. All of this time she has thought of Sabina and the others she knew in Berlin as a force of resistance. Putting aside whatever hurt there was, she has admired their courage and stubborn idealism. She has pictured them reading Celan and listening to Schoenberg, imprisoned for their art, marching against the World Bank. How long have they been playing badminton?

But of course. They have married, even. Ulla has one father, and he is in the yard doing what fathers do. How many other misperceptions has Lyddie allowed to change her life? And yet this—these moments of family and spring, the net disappearing into darkness—it is not a life to be dismissed. Perhaps it is one to envy. Lyddie feels a twinge of sadness over the life she gave up long ago. What might have been different had she and Sabina never met. She and Axel.

The door slams and Ulla bursts into the room, her cheeks radiant, a cloak of cool air following her like a fragrance. "Lyddie," she cries, "We're having a lovely time. Everyone is here now. You must stay!" Then, embarrassed at her own boldness, she runs up the great staircase, sliding a cut lilac along the banister where long ago a plot to save the world failed.

The others are beginning to make trips into the dining room from the kitchen, carrying steaming dishes of couscous and trays with stemware and bottles of wine. The two women fall silent, reluctant to move. Maybe both are thinking about what Ulla said. *Everyone is here.* It isn't true, exactly. Ulla probably does not remember, but not everyone is there. Lyddie wonders what she has been told.

"We never talked after what happened to him," Lyddie says.

It has been seven years since Axel went back to Berlin for his mother's funeral. Alone. And Lyddie will never know if it was with or without intent that the Trabi met the Linden tree on the road out at the edge of the city—not more than a kilometer past the amusement park. What she does know is that just before, Axel would have seen the abandoned park, the swan boats stranded and weirdly fixed with their otherworldly grace, the ferris wheel and its rusted buckets. Afterwards, Lyddie had driven out there herself, to the place where he had died in flames. That park was the one where Axel's stepfather had taken him. Where Axel had wondered that any happiness could come to him except as the result of a mistake. So many years it had taken her to unravel the meaning of one night spent with him in the stacks of the library. In the two and a half years she had lived with him, Axel had loved her and Billy, loved them well, but he had never really learned to be loved.

"No. It was his way, to—" Sabina pauses, running her finger around the rim of her wine glass. "Keep people apart. For me, that was another life. I have nearly forgotten."

Lyddie felt the cool air from the open windows brush past her. Maybe she would find a moment to talk with Lothar after dinner. Because Lothar would agree that Axel was anything but forgettable. It was not her presence but Axel's that had, somehow, made them all who they were that year when the ferment and confusion of their own lives had given way to the more general turbulence the Germans called The Change. He was the edge in every encounter, the question in every answer, and the longing behind every breach of friendship, every failure to love. Without him, they would all have been quite ordinary.

ACKNOWLEDGMENTS

For my thinking about the Bauhaus and the International Style of architecture, I am indebted to Tom Wolfe's *From Bauhaus to Our House,* among other sources. The poem Lothar attempts to translate beginning on p. 19 is *"Freigegeben auch dieser,"* from Paul Celan's *Lichtzwang.* The lines quoted on pp. 110-11 are from *"Magnetische Bläue im Mund,"* also from Celan's *Lichtzwang,* as translated by Katharine Washburn and Margret Guillemin. I owe Axel's stories of the Desert Fathers to *The Paradise or Garden of the Holy Fathers* by Athanasius et al. in the translation of E. A. Wallis Budge, from which some tellings have been taken nearly verbatim. Lyddie's mental patter about the psychological effects of color on pp. 146-7 are from Walter Gropius's articulation in *Scope of Total Architecture* of Howard Ketchum's ideas about color engineering as presented in a March 8, 1932 *New Yorker* article. The captions Lyddie reads to Ulla on p. 170 are quoted from a book on the architecture of cathedrals, the title and author of which are, unfortunately, lost to me now.

I acknowledge with gratitude the East and West Germans and the Greeks whose lives and stories inspired this story, the University of Pittsburgh for supporting my research in Berlin early on with a grant, and *The Southern Review,* where an excerpt of this novel first appeared as "The Sea Grass Icons."

My sincere gratitude goes also to those who have read the novel since its inception, offering encouragement, commiseration, and literary wisdom: Conrad Buck, Shirley Closson, Carys Evans-Corrales, Charlene Finn, Katie Hays, Kimi Cunningham Grant,

Anna Ryan, Joe Scapellato, Mary Suttles, David Swerdlow, Robert Taylor, Phil Terman, and John Van Kirk. To the tireless (or exhausted though dedicated) readers who kept on reading and saying what they thought, so giving me the courage to persist—Jim Buck, Shara McCallum, Robert Rosenberg, and Martha Vaccarella—I am even more deeply indebted. And inexpressible thanks to Marc Estrin and Donna Bister of Fomite, without whom this book would not now find its other readers.

Fomite

A fomite is a medium capable of transmitting infectious organisms from one individual to another.

"The activity of art is based on the capacity of people to be infected by the feelings of others." Tolstoy, *What Is Art?*

Writing a review on Amazon, Good Reads, Shelfari, Library Thing or other social media sites for readers will help the progress of independent publishing. To submit a review, go to the book page on any of the sites and follow the links for reviews. Books from independent presses rely on reader to reader communications.

For more information or to order any of our books, visit http://www.fomitepress.com/FOMITE/Our_Books.html

The Moment Before an Injury
Joshua Amses

Nothing Beside Remains
Jaysinh Birjépatil

The Way None of This Happened
Mike Breiner

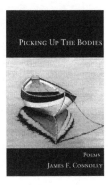

Victor Rand
David Brizer

Cycling in Plato's Cave
David Cavanagh

Picking Up the Bodies
James F. Connolly

Fomite

*Unfinished Stories
of Girls*
Catherine Zobal Dent

Drawing on Life
Mason Drukman

*Foreign Tales of
Exemplum and Woe*
J. C. Ellefson

Free Fall / Caída libre
Tina Escaja

Sinfonia Bulgarica
Zdravka Evtimova

*Derail This
Train Wreck*
Daniel Forbes

*Where There Are
Two or More*
Elizabeth Genovise

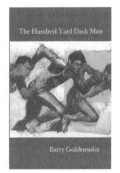

*The Hundred Yard
Dash Man*
Barry Goldensohn

*When You Remember
Deir Yassin*
R. L. Green

Fomite

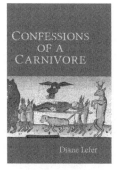

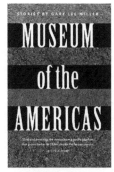

A Guide to the
Western Slopes
Roger Lebovitz

Confessions
of a Carnivore
Diane Lefer

Museum
of the Americas
Gary Lee Miller

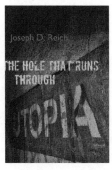

My Father's Keeper
Andrew Potok

The Hole That Runs
Through Utopia
Joseph D. Reich

Companion Plants
Kathryn Roberts

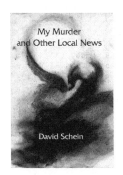

Rafi's World
Fred Russell

My Murder and
Other Local News
David Schein

Bread & Sentences
Peter Schumann

Fomite

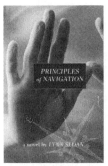

*Principles
of Navigation*
Lynn Sloan

Among Angelic Orders
Susan Thoma

*Everyone
Lives Here*
Sharon Webster

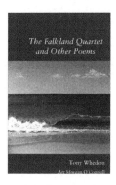

The Falkland Quartet
Tony Whedon

*The Return of
Jason Green*
Suzi Wizowaty

*The Inconveniece
of the Wings*
Silas Dent Zobal

Fomite

More Titles from Fomite...

Fomite

Charles Rafferty — *Saturday Night at Magellan's*

Joseph D. Reich — *The Derivation of Cowboys & Indian*s

Joseph D. Reich — *The Housing Market*

Fred Russell — *Rafi's World*

Peter Schumann — *Planet Kasper, Volume 1*

L. E. Smith — *The Consequence of Gesture*

L. E. Smith — *Travers' Inferno*

L. E. Smith — *Views Cost Extra*

Susan Thomas — *The Empty Notebook Interrogates Itself*

Tom Walker — *Signed Confessions*

Susan V. Weiss — *My God, What Have We Done?*

Peter Mathiessen Wheelwright — *As It Is On Earth*

29760129R00219

Made in the USA
San Bernardino, CA
29 January 2016